Mosaic

"If you have ever wondered how you might have felt and reacted had you lived in Palestine and heard tales about a wonderful 'Teacher' performing miracles down in Galilee, you will definitely enjoy this book."

Farifteh V. Robb, author of *In the Shadow of the Shahs: Finding Unexpected Grace*

Previous Books by Author
A Carpet Ride to Khiva (Icon Books)
Alabaster (Lion Fiction)
Manacle (Lion Fiction)

Chris Aslan spent his childhood in Turkey and Lebanon, and much of his adult life in Central Asia. He is a writer, a lecturer on art and textiles, and a leader of tours to Central Asia. You can connect with Chris via Facebook.

Mosaic

Chris Aslan

LION FICTION

Published by
Lion Hudson Limited
Wilkinson House, Jordan Hill Business Park
Banbury Road, Oxford OX2 8DR, England
www.lionhudson.com

ISBN 978 1 78264 338 8
e-ISBN 978 1 78264 341 8

Acknowledgments
Scripture reference marked NIV taken from The Holy Bible New International
Version®, NIV® Copyright © 1973, 1978, 1984, 2011 by Biblica, Inc.® Used
by permission. All rights reserved worldwide.

First edition 2021

A catalogue record for this book is available from the British Library

Printed and bound in the United Kingdom, January 2021, LH26

To my uncles and aunts, and also to Hatice and Aydin, Pam, and Julyan for fulfilling that role even though we're not related.
And, in loving memory of Ryan, Lora, and Caleb.

Chapter One

How can everything change so fast? I'm spreading handfuls of dried lentils onto grubby linen, squatting in the afternoon sun as I pick out stones. I'm seething at how unfair life is. I look up occasionally to crick my neck and to glower at my mother, who studiously ignores me as she weeds her patch of onions and leeks.

I wish you were dead, Amma, I think to myself, narrowing my eyes as I gaze at her.

She turns sharply on me. "Don't think you're too old for me to take a stick to you," she says testily.

I hold her gaze, determined that she'll turn away first, but then we both turn, because there are cries and shouts from further down the path to the main village square. One moment I'm spreading lentils, and the next I'm suddenly wishing life could go back to being that boring.

We glance at each other, resentments forgotten, wondering what's happened. Brushing our hands on our tunics and adjusting our headscarves, we head out through the gate and onto the rocky path down to the prayer house, bumping into neighbours, occupied until just now with their own similarly mundane chores. Together we flow down the mountainside toward the prayer house and the market.

As we get closer there's a particularly violent shriek and Amma's face turns pale.

"That was Shelamzion, I know it was," she whispers.

We both begin to run. We hear my aunt scream again, but this time it's drawn out, as if shock is giving way to grief. Then there's that long silence, like you get when a baby or a small child has hurt itself really badly and is drawing in enough breath to howl properly. And then it starts.

"No," Amma pants. She doesn't know what's happened, but whatever has, we both wish it hadn't.

We arrive at the market square. That's when we see the boys carrying the bodies, and I feel winded and breathless.

"Please, no, please no," I whisper as my mother's fingernails dig into my wrist and she surges forward, tugging me in her wake. Then she lets go of me and stumbles over to her sister, screeching and tearing her tunic in grief. And at this moment I would give anything, anything at all, to go back to sorting stones from lentils. Instead, the loss punches me right in the gut, leaving me doubled over and struggling to breathe.

We'd been talking about death just this morning, and the subject earned me a sharp slap. It started with me and Phanuel stepping around bulging bags of walnuts, rummaging in the storeroom, trying to find extra cloth sacks.

"We'll need rope as well," said Phanuel, handing me several coils. "Put them in the saddlebags."

My older brother has always been good at issuing orders. He's never been the tallest, the strongest, or the cleverest, but he has such confidence his demands will be met that they usually are.

"This must be the third, no, the fourth walnut harvest since my babies were taken from me," Amma said wistfully, watching us load up the donkey. She stroked her swollen belly and brushed away a stray tear. "At least this one is keeping me company." She patted her belly again.

Phanuel and I traded looks, hoping this was just a passing comment. Neither of us said anything that would encourage her further on the subject.

"Poor Helkiah and Azariah," she went on obliviously. "Taken before their skin had even felt the sun, or their mouths tasted my milk."

Amma likes to change their names. They were born dead, so the twins were never officially named. She'll stick with the same two names for a while, but then she'll experiment again with a different pairing. This was the first time we'd had a Helkiah or an Azariah. I was surprised she wasn't saving potential names for the new baby, although she might be cursed with another girl.

"Ah," she said with a faraway look, as if she were seeing them again, then patted her belly and the space next to her on the old walnut trunk that our grandfather had carved into a rough bench after it came down in a storm.

Perhaps it's surprising that we don't talk about death more often, given our empty household with just the four of us left. Grandfather died two years ago, which – although Amma wailed and threw dust on her head – came as a relief to her as much as to anyone else. He was old, impossible to please, and very demanding. Maybe that's where Phanuel gets it from. But what really pains Amma is the death of her children.

"Tabita." My mother tapped the walnut trunk more insistently.

"Amma, I haven't got time," I said, sighing and stuffing the rope into the donkey's saddlebag.

"No time for your own Amma?" she said reproachfully, getting herself into one of her fighting moods, where anything said is taken the wrong way.

I looked to Phanuel for help. She never listens to me but she will listen to him. He ignored my plea, as he didn't really want me in the forest anyway. I had become competition.

"Maryam would never have been like this," Amma went on. "She had a mother's heart."

"At thirteen?" I muttered under my breath, ignoring the warning raised eyebrows from Phanuel.

"But so much more grown up," Amma retorted. "It's hard to believe you're her age now."

"Yes, Amma," I said, unable to keep the insincerity from my voice.

I knew what was coming. Amma loves nothing more than comparing my dead older sister's virtues – which are numerous – with my failings, which are even more considerable.

"She would have given me a grandchild by now," Amma went on. "Just think, our babies would play together as brothers, even though mine would be his uncle." So, Amma had already determined this new baby would be a boy. "Death," she sighed. "Such a curse."

"Especially when it leaves me with all the work," I muttered under my breath.

That's when I got the sharp slap.

"Is that how you speak of your departed sister?" Amma glowered. "You want to know about hard work? What would you know about it? When did I become so lax, letting you and Sholum wander off into the forest with the Hand, coming home with a sack or two of nuts and calling that a full day's work?"

I drew a breath, about to remind her that the spring hail had ruined most of this year's walnut harvest before it could even ripen, but she continued.

"You're old enough now that tongues will start wagging if they aren't already. Who knows what mischief the Hand gets up to in the forest? I think it's about time you learned to work at home."

I glanced at Phanuel, who avoided my gaze. I was on my own.

Chris Aslan

"Yes, I've made up my mind. Phanuel, off you go. Tabita, you will be working with me today."

I started to protest, but Amma raised her slapping hand threateningly. Phanuel hurried out of the gate with the donkey before she could include him in her edict.

"Why does he get to go?" I complained.

"Because the walnuts won't collect themselves," said Amma.

"So let me help him, then," I wailed.

"Maryam would have been happy to keep her Amma company. How was it that she died and you lived? Where is the justice in that?"

"Please, Amma. Sholum will be waiting for me."

"Aha," said Amma triumphantly. "That's what this is really about, isn't it?" She folded her arms and scrutinized me. "When will you stop being your cousin's shadow?" Then she softened slightly with something almost akin to kindness. "You spend far too much time with that little princess and it's beginning to show. I don't like the influence she has on you, and don't you dare go repeating that to your aunt." She paused for a moment. "No, I've made up my mind. It's time I paid closer attention to you."

When Amma makes up her mind, neither logic nor pleading has any bearing on it. She's more stubborn than a donkey. So I stayed behind and sorted through the lentils.

At least I could punish Amma with silence, refusing to engage in any attempts at friendly conversation. But I was worried. What if this wasn't an isolated incident and Amma really did expect me to stay at home the whole time? The only one who really cares about me is Sholum. Is it any wonder I want to be her shadow? I know she's more interested in the Hand than in me, but still, she's closer to me than Maryam ever was, even if we're just cousins, and the possibility of us being separated was enough to cause silent tears to dot the piles of dried lentils as I sorted them.

I should probably explain about the Hand. In our village there were six boys all roughly my brother's age, but one of them died.

I can't remember his name. So that left five boys. Five: the Hand;
four fingers and a thumb. There's Menahem the wrestler and his
younger brother Yair – who has longer eyelashes than Sholum and
is just as pretty as a girl. Then there's Sabba who is the tallest and
bravest, and the only one who knows how to gather wild honey.
He's also the best slingshot. Ananias is finger number four. He's
the strongest swimmer and can carry the largest haystack. Then
there's Phanuel, my brother, who is referred to with affection by
the others as "the Thumb", not because he's short (although he is)
but because he makes the other four fingers into something useful
and powerful. I don't remember who first referred to this gang of
five as "the Hand" – whether it was one of the adults or someone
within the Hand itself – but that's what they've been called by
everyone ever since I can remember.

We live in the far north of our holy land, near the border,
and most of the rolling foothills below us are populated by
foreign occupiers with their enormous vineyards, expensive villas,
and drunken and idolatrous ways. I don't really know what this
means, but it's what everyone says about them. Our village is very
different: we're the highest of the villages clustered on the side
of the Many Peaked Mountain. The dawning sun hits the peaks,
which are always snow-covered – even in summer – and turns
them into flaming shades of orange. Even though I see this sight
every clear morning I never grow tired of it, and sometimes I'll
clamber up the stone staircase against the wall of our house and
just stand on the flat roof amid drying apricot halves or apple
slices, watching the colours of the mountain change.

It's up there, below the snowline, where the mountain grass is
long and lush, that my father spends much of the summer. He's
a shepherd, which suits him well, as he doesn't really like talking
and, like the rest of us, handles Amma best in small quantities. The
mountain range is wild, with eagles wheeling above it and bears,
leopards, wolves, and even mountain lions that live up beyond
the reach of most shepherds but occasionally come down to the

world of men. They're all a threat to Ubba's flock, even the eagles, which have been known to attack newborn lambs and kids. His Ubba, who died before I was born, once killed a mountain lioness with his sling and we used the skin as a rug, until one spring it got mouldy and eventually had to be thrown out. Ubba sewed together the skins of the wolves he'd killed using their own gut for thread, and he sleeps on them in the little mud-brick hut he lives in up on the snowline, away from Amma's constant chatter. He has a bearskin rug on the floor. He killed her, too. She had a cub with her, who nuzzled against her corpse and cried like a baby. Ubba didn't have the heart to kill the cub as well, so he brought it back down to the village.

Despite Amma's protests, the cub lived with us. Maryam was responsible for feeding him, Phanuel would wrestle with him, and I would curl up with him at night, letting his wet nose nestle into my neck. He would follow me around the house, and sometimes Sholum came and we dressed him up as our baby. Shemayah, our holy man, said it was against our laws to have a bear living with us, but then we're not very good at following all the laws we're supposed to, and even Shemayah couldn't help but chuckle when he saw Phanuel and the cub wrestle together.

That cub is the only thing I've ever loved as much as Sholum, and I called him Little Bear. He was the only one who ever really loved me, and not just when there was no one else to play with. Then, one day during the apple harvest, we returned home and Amma presented each of us with a date cake and a shifty expression. We knew something bad had happened and, sure enough, she had sold the cub to one of the apple merchants who knew someone with a dancing bear who was likely to pay good money for a growing cub. It was one of the few times we saw Ubba completely lose his temper with Amma, although she protested that the bear was getting too big and pointed at the claw marks raked over Phanuel's arms and shoulders. She was probably right, and the bear couldn't have lived with us forever, but that didn't stop me sobbing hot tears of rage

as I lay on my sleeping mat, cold and alone, feeling an ache deep inside me, with no wet nose nuzzling beside me.

While Ubba is killing wolves and finding bear cubs, Phanuel spends the summer months scything the meadows above the forest, spreading out the fragrant herbs and grasses to dry. Scything is the easy part, although Sholum always gets away with doing very little and usually spends her time making flower crowns for both of us to wear. Meanwhile, I'll help the Hand layer up the tangled masses of scythed meadow onto a long wooden spike with a leather base. The stronger boys can pile this fragrant hay high enough to form an impressive stack. One of them will crouch down as another loads the hay up and then fastens the leather thongs around the waist and over the shoulders. Standing up is the hardest bit, but then they trudge down to the village carrying the equivalent weight of a large sheep on their backs, looking like mini walking haystacks. I tried it once but was jeered as I tottered down with barely half the usual amount of meadow on my back.

I often join Amma on her weekly trips up to the shepherd camp, taking sacks of flour for my father and dried fish, olives, and firewood. Ubba does most of his cooking up there using blocks of dried cow dung for fuel. Amma always insists on walnut wood for heating the large vat of milk to make cheese because it's hard and burns for longer. She likes me going because I'm good at milking cows, sheep, and goats, which is possibly the one thing I do better than Maryam did. But when it comes to starting a fire, cooking almost any dish, all aspects of cheese-making, and baking flatbread on heated rocks in the embers so they puff up just right and don't burn, well, it's impossible to compete with a perfect dead sister.

After the hay harvesting comes the apple harvest and our villages' apples are considered some of the best in the country. It's the cold winters that make a good apple, or so Grandfather used to say – not that he had teeth to eat them with as far as I can

14

remember. With Ubba still up at the shepherd camp and Amma looking after her vegetable patch at home, it's me and Phanuel who harvest the orchard, each working our way along a terraced row of trees to see who can finish first. We separate out the good apples for sale and the bruised ones are brought home for Amma to boil up. She spreads the pulp on waxed cloths and they dry up on the roof and become apple leather. Before the first frosts, Ubba takes a whole donkey train laden with sacks of our apples down to the lowland towns and cities, and comes back with sacks of olives, dried fish, wheat, spelt, barley, and lentils.

But before winter there is the walnut harvest, which happens just as the leaves start to turn. I love our forest. In the summer, while we're mainly up in the meadows harvesting hay, it gets taken over by visiting occupiers who leave a detritus of empty wineskins and animal bones – they even eat pigs – behind them. They come up to escape the heat of the lowlands. I can't imagine what it must be like to live down there beneath the shimmering haze. Maybe it's what hell feels like. You can't even see the lowlands in the summer as they're hidden by the dust, and we only know they exist because caravans of horses and camels arrive bearing these rich idolaters who treat the forest as if it belongs to them.

We share the lake with the village below us. They've realized that these rich idolaters pay good coin to rent the pavilions and tents they set up around it. When I was young, Amma used to send me down to the lake – which I've always thought was huge, but apparently it's just a puddle compared to the Great Lake – with fresh cheeses wrapped in vine leaves. The adults are like small children, spending each day doing nothing but playing. The women don't even cook or anything; they have servants for that. Worse, even the women swim, or at least splash about in the lake, just as naked as the men, with no shame at all. When I asked Amma why they do this she stopped sending me down there.

This hasn't prevented the Hand from claiming the far side of the lake for themselves. There's a tangle of vegetation to get to the cliff, but there is a path if you know where to look. The occupiers don't, which keeps them at their end. The path leads to a narrow strip of sand. The Hand have adopted it and even fought the boys from the next village to ensure it remains exclusively theirs. They go down there in the early evenings after harvesting hay to swim and cool off.

I love the forest during harvest time. The giant cedars, which have been alive since the time of the Great Kings, stay green, towering over us with their spreading branches. However, the walnuts, poplars, and oaks all turn different shades of gold and bronze, and if we arrive really early, the dawning sun against their leaves sets them ablaze with colour. By walnut harvest time the occupiers have all returned to the lowlands and we reclaim the forest for ourselves.

Occasionally wild boar interrupt our foraging and the boys pull out their slings. The only one who's any good with the sling is Sabba, and one time last year he managed to stun a large boar with a direct hit. The boys discussed killing it and dragging the carcass down to the nearest idolater settlement further down the mountain, as we won't eat meat from pigs. Anyway, they were too busy devising a plan to notice the boar rouse itself and careen unsteadily away.

After the walnut harvest we scavenge for pine cones, which we collect and heap up around the fire during winter until they open and we can extract the pine nuts, before burning the cones, which splutter and crackle in the flames. Then I have to help Amma prepare her vegetable plot for winter, and then, after the first snows, Ubba returns from the shepherd camp, looking wild and smelling bad, and winter begins. This is what defines our village: winter. I've heard that in the south near the sea – which is even bigger than the Great Lake and full of sea monsters – they don't have winter. It never snows, and the weather in winter is even warmer than our spring. I don't know if it's true.

Winter is long and it's hard. Winter is when people usually

die. Sometimes there are avalanches, and we regularly see the paw prints of leopards or lions in the fresh snow, not to mention the wolves that come as near to our village and our slings as they dare. Packs of them come down from the mountains and Ubba sleeps beside the door with one ear cocked for the sound of alarmed bleating, ready to leap out with his sling. If I'm honest, I'm sometimes secretly glad when a sheep has been killed by a wolf or is so badly wounded that Ubba has to kill it. If Ubba gets to the carcass quickly it means we'll have meat that night. We don't often eat mutton, as most of our spare sheep and goats are sold to lowlanders in the autumn when they're nice and fat on summer meadow grass. We're not supposed to eat meat with the blood still in it, and the carcass is always hung to drain in an effort to keep to the Law, but who can afford to be that picky when a sheep dies in winter?

If the wolves have come down from the mountains, Amma doesn't mind me peeing into a bowl at night rather than stumbling through the snow to the unclean place. One of our neighbours once got caught in their unclean place by two wolves prowling outside it, with just a ragged curtain between her and them. Luckily, her screams brought out her son. Although he couldn't see much in the dark, he let fly enough stones with his sling that at least one of them found its mark and the wolves were scared off.

The worst part of winter is how our village closes in on itself. We visit each other, but we're not all working together in the fields or the forest. Families stay inside. Each house is made of stone with a flat roof for drying fruit on in summer, and one room to sleep in, cook in, and bicker in throughout winter. I've heard that some wealthy lowlanders have four or five inner rooms, but it was probably Phanuel just making it up. What would you do with five rooms?

Some families opt for warmth over light, keeping their door shut during the day and spinning or carving in just lamplight. I prefer cold air and sunlight, with our inner room door wide open.

Even then I hate being stuck in a room with my mother for days on end. I can tell Ubba does, too, and by spring he paces the inner room, getting in everyone's way, desperate to get back to roaming the mountain. I wish I could equalize my parents out, like two piles of lentils on hanging scales: taking a little from this pile and adding it over there. Amma talks too much and says things she would regret if she ever admitted mistakes. Ubba hardly talks at all. Amma gets too involved in controlling our lives, while Ubba doesn't seem bothered what we do.

Much of winter is spent digging snow. Sometimes it piles higher than me. We have to keep the roof from getting too much snow on it. A little is good, as it insulates the house better, but too much and the weight could cause the whole roof to collapse. We also have to dig paths to the woodpile, the unclean place, the haystack, the cowshed, and the sheep pen. Then there's the unspoken but agreed rule that you keep the section of path outside your house passable for everyone.

My main winter task is spinning wool. I used to get unfavourably compared to Maryam and her beautiful, even yarn, but over the last few years I think I've improved enough for Amma to simply say nothing. I usually work hard to get all my other chores done and then find some excuse to take my wool and drop spindle over to Auntie Shelamzion's so I can spin with Sholum. It's not far, but far enough that by the time I get there my leather boots are seeping wet and Sholum has to rub my feet to warm them up. Sholum's father, my Uncle Hanan, once presented me with a beautiful drop spindle he had carved with patterns all over the four spokes of cedar wood that give the spindle its weight. I cried. No one usually gives me anything. I don't know why Amma seemed cross that I'd been given something nice. It didn't cost her anything.

For Phanuel, when he's not digging snow the winter is spent pruning the orchards, collecting firewood from the forest if our woodpile gets low, and helping Ubba keep the livestock fed and watered. Sometimes we have winter wrestling matches down beside the prayer house. Menahem is the best. He's short and stocky and even beats some of the grown men. Amma tells me that Ubba used to be good, but he says he doesn't wrestle any more; he just sits watching with the other older men as they drink steaming bowls of mint tea.

Clothes don't dry in winter and hang rigid and frozen on the line for days. It's hard to wash ourselves, too. Amma still believes Maryam caught her fatal chill from having wet hair. So nothing gets washed much. Amma does her best to comb through our hair for lice, but then there are fleas as well and it feels like she's fighting a losing battle. Phanuel told me once that lowlanders have a big room that everybody uses for washing and it's even bigger than our prayer house. It's full of hot water and you can pay to go there and bathe in it, and the water is hot even in winter because they heat it underneath. He's always trying to make me believe things like that and then laughs when I do.

The worst part of winter is toward the end. We watch the haystack dwindle in size until it's just a pile, hoping it will last until the snow melts and new grass grows. Any remaining coins from the sale of apples and walnuts have also dwindled by this point. If it's been a bad harvest we might not have apple fruit leather or dried apricots to relieve the monotony of bread and lentils.

So, a recipe of one dark, smelly room with too many people in it, getting in each other's way, cooped up for too long, worried about wolves and whether our stocks will last us until spring, and added to this, my Amma in the midst of it all, and that's why I hate winter. It's also why we welcome the spring, even if it means a damp cold that seeps into your bones – which feels worse than the dry cold of winter – and mud everywhere: all over us, and both inside and outside the house, even if we leave our boots at the doorway. As well as melting snow there are the spring rains, and sometimes mudslides like the one that destroyed half of our neighbouring village three years ago.

But then the rain stops and everything becomes soft with mist, and the apple orchards blossom and the mountainside is dotted with crocuses, and then there's the feast where we sacrifice sheep to remember that we have always been delivered eventually, and then life returns to being a hard but enjoyable bustle of activity.

I suppose what I'm trying to explain is that life is beautiful in our village, but it's also tough. Most mothers have more children buried than running around their yard. Even though our holy man tells us not to, most mothers pin amulets to the tunics of their children to ward off the evil eye, and we spit after complimenting someone so the eye won't strike. Most of us can't read – what would be the point? We do have a prayer house, and we make sure we circumcise our sons and pray for good harvests, but we don't have time to be really religious. During harvest season we don't strictly observe our rest days, but we joke that we make up for them in winter. Life is about work, and if you don't work, you don't eat. Except Sholum, who does very little but seems to be able to charm everyone around her.

So, because life is tough and the survival rate to adulthood isn't very high, there aren't as many young people around as there probably are in other places. And we don't have that much to do with the other villages. The Hand view the boys in the next village as potential rivals, not potential friends. I think they feel threatened, as other boys being around would mean that they're not special. As it is, they're generally loved, or at least tolerated.

"The Hand has been up to mischief again," a neighbour will say with an affectionate sigh. Or, "Don't trouble yourself filling all those sacks alone, Mara. I'll get my son and the rest of the Hand to do it for you."

Obviously, I've always been jealous of the Hand. Even in our village – and I know this because Grandfather said it once while he was still alive – it's rare to see five boys so devoted to one another. They do everything together, and most people have given up trying to get, say, Menahem and Yair to help their father build a dry stone wall around their enlarged sheep pen when the

Hand has already promised to help Ananias and my uncle that day felling one of the cedars in the forest for their chest-making workshop. But when Yair and Menahem do help their father with the stone wall, you can be sure Phanuel, Ananias, and Sabba will be there to work, too.

They can be really helpful like that, but if they get up to mischief they'd rather all be punished than let one of them take the blame for anything. They call it honour. I think it's stupid. Last summer, all five of them got a beating from Shemayah, our holy man, for fighting down by the lake with the boys in the next village. Sabba used his sling and hit the gang leader of the other village just above his left eye, knocking him unconscious. The big cry from the boy's father when he came marching up to our village to confront Shemayah was that he could have taken the boy's eye out.

"If I wanted to take out his eye he'd be blind now," Sabba muttered under his breath.

Still, even though everyone knew it must have been Sabba who slung the stone, it was the whole Hand that considered itself culpable, and when Sabba offered to own up and take his punishment there were howls of affronted honour from the others, along with threats of all manner of horror thrown at me and Sholum if we ever ratted on them.

Even if there had been five girls my age in the village, I don't think we'd have been nearly as close as the Hand. For a start, we wouldn't have been able to spend as much time together. I'm forever being called in to help Amma with some chore or other, but boys get to roam. I think they're trying to prepare us girls for always being tied to our houses by babies. We might as well get used to it now.

Maybe there's also something about shared danger that brings the boys closer. There was the time when the Hand tried to scale a steep, almost cliff-like section of the mountain, determined to find an eagle's nest and capture a chick so they could train it to

hunt marmots and foxes. Yair slipped and, from what Phanuel said, if Ananias hadn't leaped and grabbed him – risking his own life in the process – Yair would have fallen and undoubtedly died. They didn't even find a nest.

But there aren't many other girls of my age. When I was little, some of the older girls enjoyed dressing me up and pretending I was their baby, but now they all have babies of their own, except for barren Yulia, and no one sees much of her, as she's probably too ashamed to show her face in public. I don't know why her husband hasn't divorced her yet.

So that's why it's just Sholum and me, and why, even though we're only cousins, we're even closer than sisters, and if someone forgets my name, which happens quite often, they just call me "Sholum's shadow" and I don't mind at all. No one forgets Sholum. She's fairer-skinned than most women in the village, even after a summer in the sun, and her hair has a beautiful reddish tint to it. Sometimes she lets me brush it, and it crackles as if it's made of fire. And she's beautiful. Her lips are full and her eyes are large and the colour of dark honey. She has the swell of breasts ripening beneath her tunic, while I'm still as flat as a boy, even though I'm only half a year younger. Sometimes I think about her when she's not there, and I feel something a bit like fire burning in my chest.

Sholum never gets into trouble. She has no brothers and sisters, which I thought would mean she'd have no one else to blame, but she doesn't need to blame anyone else because her parents are so devoted to her. I've heard Amma talk about the bloody parcels she's had to clean up, which her sister dropped before the babies had come to term. Amma constantly reminds her sister that she's spoiling Sholum, but it makes no difference. Uncle Hanan is no better. He's an excellent chest maker and uses the cedar, oak, and walnut from the forest to produce beautifully carved chests, which lowlanders planning weddings will pay really good money for. He's a kind man. Amma calls him indulgent. He certainly is with

Sholum. She just has to smile winningly and her father will forgive whatever it is she's done or hasn't done.

Because Auntie Shelamzion also lacks a robust slapping hand, Sholum is more competitive, argumentative, confident, and headstrong than most boys. She always tries to turn everything into a competition. Her favourite phrase is "Let's make this a game", leaving it understood that it's a game she intends to win. She's given up with me because I don't mind losing to her. I see how happy winning makes her and that makes me happy, too. Lacking someone to beat, Sholum has always resorted to goading and often beating the Hand.

The Hand are competitive about everything too, quick to jeer at each other's failures but just as quick to defend each other's honour to the death if the same slur is spoken by outsiders. When Sholum grew taller than Menahem and Phanuel she was quick to taunt them, and I thought Menahem was about to punch her in the face.

"Well, Sholum, when you've outgrown me you can come and crow like a hen pretending to be a cock," Sabba said scornfully, thus keeping the Hand's honour intact.

This left Sholum scowling, particularly because Sabba is so much better at using a sling than she is, even though she can beat Yair and Ananias in knocking a dried old sheep skull off a wall from twenty paces away.

Last winter Sholum came forward during one of the wrestling matches, wanting to challenge Menahem. She wasn't allowed to wrestle, of course. Whoever heard of a girl wrestling? And there's no doubt she would have been beaten. Still, she would have unleashed her fury on him and made sure he ended up with a bleeding lip or something. That girl isn't afraid of anything, except swimming. Girls aren't allowed to swim anyway, but that's not usually something that would stop her.

This past summer I thought she kept dragging me along to the lake to spy on the Hand because she wanted to secretly observe them and teach herself how to swim. I was right, except for the swimming part. One time she convinced my mother to let me off my cooking duties, begging for my help at Aunt Shelamzion's. Instead, we headed down to the lake in the slanting sun of late afternoon. We avoided the main bay and the waterfall – occupied by the occupiers – and picked our way around the rim of the lake until we could see the cliff where the Hand had climbed down and watched them splashing and racing each other. Although Ananias always won, it never stopped the others from trying.

"Let's get closer," Sholum whispered to me.

"Why? We can see them perfectly well from here," I hissed back, but already she'd started working her way nearer to them.

I was too busy keeping branches out of my face to pay much attention to where we were, but Sholum had brought us close to the sandbar. It was out of the reach of the surrounding trees' shadows and the boys would wade onto it once they'd got chilled or needed a break and then lie on their fronts, sunning themselves like lizards.

We crouched down behind some foliage.

"Why have you brought us so close?" I whispered. "They'll see us."

Sholum just put a finger to her lips, silently shushing me, and smiled.

"I'll race you to the sandbar," said Yair, then dived toward us before waiting for a reply.

Ananias still caught up with him, and they waded naked out of the water as Sholum peered eagerly.

"Which one's more handsome?" she whispered to me.

I looked at both of them, baffled. "Yair's prettier, but everyone knows that," I whispered back.

"Yes, but look at Ananias's strong arms. And he's bigger. You know, down below."

I narrowed my eyes, craning forward, but I really couldn't see much difference or why it would even matter. And it didn't feel right, spying on them like that. I felt as if we were stealing something from them without them even knowing. Then Phanuel, Sabba, and Menahem splashed onto the sandbar and Sholum dug her fingernails into my wrist, grinning and straining to see everything. Sabba is the tallest, but Menahem has the most hair over his body. I looked away, feeling uncomfortable. By now the boys were lying on their fronts in a rough circle, enjoying the sun.

"Seriously, we could make good money and it wouldn't be that hard," Phanuel was saying to them. "If we shovel enough snow right into the back of the cave, then brick it in with rocks and mud, it'll stay frozen until summer, and then we just take a little date syrup or honey, mix it with the snow, and sell it to the occupiers."

Yair raised the issue of bears and lions and other wild animals that probably used the cave in winter, and pointed out that the cave was halfway to the shepherd camp and that any snow would have melted by the time they'd carried it down to the lake.

"Then we cut ice from the lake," said Phanuel, unperturbed. "We carry big chunks of ice up to the cave in winter, or we get a donkey or Ananias to drag it up there. It would take much longer to melt and we could shave bits off with a knife and blend them with syrup."

Yair was about to object again, but my brother wasn't finished.

"Think of all those beautiful women, walking out of the water showing everything! They'd be so grateful for a cooling bowl of iced honey. It's not just money we'd be getting. Think of the *gratitude*."

This had the Hand sniggering and making lewd comments. A cloud passed over the setting sun and the air felt chill.

"Come on, we should head back," said Phanuel, getting up.

"I'll catch up with you," said Menahem, remaining put.

"Why? Has all that talk of naked idolaters had an effect on you?" said Yair.

When Menahem blushed, his brother pushed him, rolling him onto his side.

Sholum gasped as she caught sight of Menahem's arousal. "I knew this was a good spot," she hissed to me in delight.

I just gazed at the ground, feeling ashamed and knowing the Hand would be furious with us if they knew we were here.

"Seen all you want to see now?" Menahem was saying. "You're just jealous of a decent-sized wife-maker, *little* brother."

"I don't think you'll be winning any competitions," Yair retorted.

Sholum looked at me, eyes bulging and hand over her mouth to stop herself laughing. The next thing we knew, they'd decided to see who had the largest wife-maker and were kneeling in a circle inspecting one another. I kept my eyes on the ground, but Sholum was leaning out so far that she remained undiscovered only because the boys were all so preoccupied with each other.

I could hear them voting Sabba the definite winner, and they were arguing over who was joint second when the branch jutting out into the water, that Sholum had been leaning on too heavily, snapped. She fell in, and the boys, startled, jumped into the water for cover.

When they realized Sholum had been spying on them, and now of all moments, well, I won't repeat the words they used against her.

Sholum didn't seem bothered at all and simply laughed.

Phanuel, who was up to his waist in water, started wading threateningly toward her. "I'm telling your mother," he said. "This time you've gone too far."

Sholum backed out of the water, smiling innocently. "Tell her what? That you were fighting to come joint second?" she asked. Then, climbing out of the lake, she ran off laughing.

She'd forgotten about me, but for once I was grateful, remaining hidden as the boys cursed her, except for Sabba, who said she was welcome to tell whomever she liked. I waited until they were busy putting on their tunics before creeping away, managing to get home and chop leeks before Phanuel returned, sulking.

"What happens if there aren't enough girls in our village for the boys to have a wife each?" he asked Amma as he sat down on one of the grubby seating mattresses.

"Why, are you planning on settling down?" Amma replied with a smirk. "You've got a couple of years left before you need to start worrying about that."

It was then that I understood. Until now, we had been the girls who could be excluded from adventures and derided if we tried to form our own gang of two. The most scathing of insults was something like, "Even Tabita could do better." Now, though, everything was changing. The boys were becoming men and Sholum was becoming a woman. There were five of them and there was just one Sholum as their prize. I don't count myself, as I was still nothing but a child to them.

This shift in power was something I noticed the next morning when Sabba grinned at Sholum as he took off his tunic around mid-morning, scything in just his waistcloth. Before you knew it, three of the others were stripping off their tunics, eager for Sholum's approval.

Phanuel just shook his head in disgust and turned his back to her, using his scythe to lop the flower heads off a bank of poppies. I think he realized then that, of all the dangers the Hand had faced, Sholum was probably the greatest.

It was every boy for himself. Yair surprised them all by persuading Sholum to sit with him in the shade the following day when we broke for midday meal. He'd brought his lyre with him and began plucking it, batting his long eyelashes as he sang a sad love song. He was rewarded with applause and a kiss on the cheek.

"Sholum, could you help me with these straps?" Ananias tried after we'd eaten.

He had piled his haystack to a record height, yet managed to heave himself up with a manly grunt once she'd tightened the lashes and not totter too much as he made his way back to the village, turning once to wave at Sholum, who happily waved back.

"Sholum, what do you think of the occupiers? Their men shave the beards from their faces. I'm beginning to wonder if it's something I should try," said Menahem, sidling up to Sholum before Ananias was even out of view. "I mean, the others don't have a choice," he added, laughing unconvincingly, "but I've always wanted to know whether women prefer men with beards or not."

Sholum simpered. She loved being called a woman. Any previous attempt at romance by the Hand would have been met with a barbed responses, but now Sholum seemed to realize this was the best of all competitions because as the only prize she couldn't possibly lose.

The main loser in this new game was me. I felt as if she'd gone through a door I couldn't enter and had left me behind. None of these worthless boys would ever love her the way I loved her. They didn't know her. They hadn't faithfully followed her into all manner of mischief. They didn't see that she was far more than just a prize.

I burned with envy, and it meant that when Sholum turned to me for advice over which boy displayed the best attributes I was sulky and taciturn, and she ended up rolling her eyes and leaving me to my heartbroken jealousy. The other loser, for the moment, was my brother. Phanuel had always maintained complete command and control of the Hand, but no more. Now, each boy attempted to outdo the others. But Phanuel wasn't about to lose this competition. He might not have been tallest or have had the largest wife-maker, for which there was no remedy, but he wasn't about to lose a battle of wits against Sholum. So he did the very thing that was guaranteed to win her heart. He ignored her.

My brother understands how people work, and I've learned more from observing him than he probably realizes. He didn't scorn or compete against the blundering attempts of the other boys to impress Sholum; he simply shrugged or laughed good-humouredly. Nothing could have vexed Sholum more. As the apple harvest began, she offered to help in our orchard on the pretext of showing solidarity with me. This was a strategic blunder, as everyone had apple trees to harvest and it was the one time the Hand didn't work together. So, there were no other suitors she could pit Phanuel against. And still he showed indifference. One time she dropped her basket of apples and stormed off. I followed her, of course, trying to console her, and glanced back to see that my brother wasn't indifferent at all. He had a savage smile of triumph on his face.

Once the walnut harvest began the Hand worked together again, joined by me, Sholum, and a handful of the younger children. The girls and smaller children were supposed to wait under the larger trees, dashing for cover when the boys up in the canopy started beating the branches, causing a pattering rain of nuts. The nuts, mostly still in their husks, could be quite painful if they hit you on the head, which was usually the boys' intent. Yair, the lightest of the boys, could climb the highest and was often difficult to spot. Climbing to such heights is the one thing they do that really impresses me.

I'm terrified of heights. One time I managed to shimmy up to the first branches of a large walnut tree and then had to be coaxed down, with Phanuel alternately berating and reassuring me that I wasn't going to fall to my death. For the boys up in the tree canopy a fall would probably be fatal. The last boy to die this way was Sabba's uncle before any of us were born. Luckily, the Hand climb like squirrels and Uncle Hanan says they're the best harvesters our village has ever produced.

Not so Sholum, who did little but squeal and run for cover when the walnuts came raining down. She made brief forays to collect nuts in her wooden pail before dumping the contents beside me and the younger children who were responsible for de-husking the nuts. Sholum refused to de-husk them, pretending to search for more nuts on the forest floor instead. I've always known why. The sap from the husks stains skin brown and eventually black, turning our fingernails orange. Sholum is too vain to let that happen.

Unlike my brother, I couldn't pretend indifference regarding the romantic attempts of the Hand toward my Sholum. My anguish at the thought of losing her to them made me constantly moody.

"Why can't you do your fair share of the work like everyone else?" I snapped one day as she poured out her pail of nuts beside me. "The sap won't kill you, you know."

"Don't be like that, Tabi," she pouted, rubbing a knot in her back. "I'm doing the hard bit, scrabbling in the dirt for all these jewels. It's really hurting my back. Here, could you rub this knot for me?"

It wasn't really a question, and of course I was happy to massage the knot in her back as she piled up her hair, exposing her long, graceful neck and glancing up at the boys in the branches above us, making sure they had noticed too.

By dusk, the boys had climbed back down to earth. They helped us load the donkeys – who were growing fat on a steady diet of green walnut husks all day – then left us for a brisk swim, making the most of the last days before it was too cold.

"You're right, Tabi," said Sholum, linking her arm through mine as we led the donkeys back to the village, followed by the little ones. "I should work harder."

I glanced up in genuine surprise.

"Don't be like that," she pouted, then graced me with a smile. "I don't want to spend the whole day scrabbling around like a chicken on the forest floor. Not when I could be flying like a bird." She saw my puzzled expression. "I'm going to climb with the Hand tomorrow. Why should they have all the fun trying to pelt everyone below?"

I rolled my eyes. "You know they're not going to like that."

Sholum just slid her eyes in my direction and smiled conspiratorially.

Chris Aslan

That was yesterday.

Today I was supposed to go to the forest with everyone else. I would have been monitoring the little ones, making sure they de-husked the walnuts, wiping noses that dripped, and separating squabblers. I'd also have been the main gatherer given that Sholum would be climbing up the largest branches, determined to get higher than even Yair would dare climb, and possibly allowing the boys below a flash of her legs.

Instead, I've been cooped up with my mother all day, sorting lentils. Now, amid the wailing and screaming and people jostling and shouting for someone to fetch Shemayah, our holy man, I can barely see the faces of the two bodies as Auntie Shelamzion and my mother sprawl over them both, weeping hysterically. Somehow Sholum still manages to look beautiful, even though her body is broken, with her arms and legs bent in the wrong places. Her tunic oozes a spreading red stain. I fall beside my aunt and shake Sholum's body gently.

"Please, Sholum, come back to us," I whisper, stroking her hair. Her beautiful, beautiful hair. "Don't leave me," I cry.

It's my last moment of sanity before I, too, am gripped with the fever of grief and start ripping my tunic, grabbing handfuls of dust and throwing them over my head, slapping my face far harder than Amma did this morning, and wailing and screaming until my lungs burn.

I barely notice when someone drags Amma off the other corpse until I realize the corpse is my brother, Phanuel. Amma tries to claw them away but they hold her back and tell her to give him air, and then everyone's looking and they see that my brother has opened his eyes.

"What's happened?" he croaks.

Then my mother falls unconscious and Shemayah arrives, and some people start praising God and calling it a miracle, and I stop paying attention to all of them. All I know is that Sholum won't roll her eyes and get up, laughing as if it's all been a prank, because

31

her face is already turning grey, like the dead. Someone puts their arms around me and I swear at them using language I didn't even know I knew.

"Come back to me," I wail as men arrive with a pallet and lift her body gently onto it, leaving a reddish brown smear behind in the dust. I try to go with them, but someone holds me back. So instead I just weep and moan, and wish that I, too, were dead.

Chapter Two

I hold her hand in mine. I don't ever want to let go, and I can tell that she feels the same because her hand has set around mine. It feels cold, but maybe I can warm it up. Maybe something of my living and breathing can go into her. I'd give her all my breath if I could.

Old Mara's voice quavers as she sings a lament in our holy language, which I don't understand. A few women sigh or tut their tongues, but our grief has taken on a dull numbness and with so many women crammed into Shelamzion's inner room to stay with Sholum until dawn, and with all those lamps flickering in every alcove, everyone is drowsy. There's even a steady snore from some of the women. I'm worn out as well, but I won't sleep and I won't let go of her hand. In the flickering lamplight, her face seems almost animated and loses the grey tinge it had before.

Aunt Shelamzion holds Sholum's other hand, stroking it and humming a tuneless lullaby under her breath.

Yohannah comes forward and places a hand on Shelamzion's

shoulder, leaning down and kissing her head gently. "It's time," she says softly. "The salt has arrived. Why don't we choose an outfit for her to wear?"

Yohannah is the stout wife of our holy man, Shemayah. She's a wise woman and knows how to deal with people. In fact, if she were a man she would probably be our holy man. She knows, for example, that Sholum has more than one outfit, and not just a spare one to wear while the other one is being washed, either. Sholum has several tunics, including a heavy woollen one dyed red in madder root, which she wears in winter, and a beautiful soft linen tunic of faded indigo, which Uncle Hanan brought back from the lowlands last year after he'd sold several wedding chests. I know this is the tunic Aunt Shelamzion will pick, even though it's a summer one and too cold to wear now.

Shelamzion pulls her hand from Sholum's grasp, gently placing it on the mat, and opens one of two beautiful waist-high cedar chests against the wall furthest from the door. Yohannah brings a lamp over and holds it aloft to give her light. Shelamzion draws out the tunic, holding it up in the lamplight and looking at it for a moment. Then she slowly crumples into a kneeling position, completely silently, clutching the tunic to her chest. Her shoulders go up and down, which is the only indication she's crying. Finally, she draws a ragged breath and then sobs loudly, burying her face in Yohannah's shoulder. Yohannah cradles her like a child, smoothing her hair and kissing her head.

There is only one man in this crowded room of women, and that's Uncle Hanan. He sits glassy-eyed on a sheepskin, leaning back against one of the chests he made. There's a bruise above his right temple where he punched himself, his cheeks are raked with nail marks down to his beard, and his fingernails are still brown with dried blood. Yohannah glances over at him and then at me and Sholum. She waits until Shelamzion has exhausted herself weeping and then she speaks, addressing my uncle.

"Hanan, it's time for us to wash the body. Would you take

your wife outside for some air? She'll need a blanket around her shoulders. It's a cold night."

Hanan doesn't stir but Shelamzion looks up with swollen eyes. "What? No. No, I'm not going anywhere. I have to be with my daughter."

Yohannah puts her arm around her. "Please," she says, stroking Shelamzion's hair. "Let me do this for her and for you. Let me wash away the things you don't need to see. Let me make Sholum look beautiful again. Let that be your last memory of your precious girl."

Shelamzion just looks at her blankly. I don't know if she's really aware of what's happening. I feel a bit that way myself: numb and detached, as if all this is happening somewhere else and not to us, not to Sholum.

"Hanan, please," Yohannah says, directing her gaze back toward him. "Let us spare you this. This isn't how you want to remember her."

He still just looks ahead, as if he were asleep with his eyes open.

"Hanan!" Yohannah raises her voice a little and it rouses him.

He blinks, shakes himself, then nods, picks up a blanket made with the wool Sholum and I spun together two winters ago, and drapes it over Shelamzion's shoulders.

"Come," he says quietly, helping his wife to her feet and leading her as they pick their way among the seated forms of our village's women.

Then Yohannah remembers me. "You, too, Tabita. This is not how you want to remember your cousin."

"No," I say quietly but with absolutely no intention of compromise. "I stay with her."

Yohannah holds my gaze. I don't flinch or look away. Finally she glances down at Sholum and I know that I have her permission. She directs some of the other women to bring over the sack of salt on which the body must be laid, the indigo tunic, and a clay bowl of hyssop water with a sponge soaking in it. Usually people use a simple bowl for washing the body, as it will have to be broken afterwards, but Shelamzion has set out a large clay bowl with a floral pattern. This is what it means to be rich.

"If you stay, then you don't get in the way," says Yohannah to me. "Now, let go of her hand," she adds, drawing out a sharp knife. I have to lift each of Sholum's fingers to pull my hand from them. I want to protest as Yohannah begins to cut down Sholum's tunic from the neck, but it's blood-drenched and there can be no saving it. It must be burned. She draws the tunic open, revealing the swell of Sholum's new breasts and an angry bruise that covers the whole of her right side in different shades of blue and purple. Yohannah has to tug at the robe on the left side where it clings with dried blood against Sholum's body. She uses a little of the warm hyssop water to loosen it. It steams in the lamplight. As she tugs it away, I can see that bits of Sholum have spilled out from inside her. My eyes blur with tears, but I won't weep and give them cause to send me away. I swallow the bile in my throat and help lift one of Sholum's shoulders as Yohannah attempts to pull the arm out of the tunic sleeve. It's already too stiff, so she simply cuts the sleeve down the length of the arm and peels the tunic away. I can't help but gasp when I see that one of her arms has the broken splinter of a bone poking out of it.

Once the tunic is removed, Yohannah unties Sholum's waistcloth. It doesn't feel right to have Sholum exposed like this, but she must be washed properly before burial. Once the waistcloth is removed, Yohannah scrutinizes Sholum's shameful place and then gently probes a finger around it. I look away in embarrassment.

Once satisfied, she addresses us all. "Sholum is still a girl. There has been no damage done to her honour or to the honour of the Hand."

A woman starts weeping and I realize it's Ananias's mother. Her tunic is threadbare and patched. They're one of the poorest families in the village. Menahem and Yair's mother comes over to comfort her and they sit together, weeping with relief. It takes a moment for me to fully grasp the implications of what Yohannah just said. I remember the time Amma sat me down and explained about the shameful place and how no man but your husband must ever see or touch it, and that it would be better to die than to ever allow a man who isn't your husband to "do his bidding", which is what Ubba does sometimes in the night with Amma when he thinks we're asleep.

It's the first time I wonder what happened out there in the forest. What did happen out there? What did the women think might have happened? I realize Yohannah was not only concerned with sparing the parents' grief at seeing the full extent of their daughter's injuries; she was also checking to ensure that no harm had befallen Sholum's honour. The thought that anyone in the Hand would even be capable of doing such a thing – that anyone would defile or dishonour someone from our own village – leaves me shaking. Suddenly the air closes in around me and I know I have to get out. I stumble outside, just making it past all the sandals cluttering up the doorway before I vomit.

I return, smearing my face with my sleeve, and watch Yohannah singing the holy song we sing when we wash the dead while two of the eldest women in our village sponge Sholum down, wringing brown, old-blood water into the bowl, methodically working from her head to her toes. When they've finished, more women come forward to help lift Sholum's rigid body and pull the tunic over it, holding her up so that salt can be spread out beneath her. I watch all this from the doorway and then have an idea. I head back outside, and there's enough moonlight to let me climb the slope above Sholum's house to collect several bunches of violet daisies: the last flowers of the year. I return shivering, grateful for the crowded inner room and its warmth, and pick my way around the women back to Sholum's side. They've laid her on the bed of salt now, and the old women are busy preparing spices and strips of linen. There's the fresh, astringent smell of dried pine sap, but under that the sweet, musky tones of myrrh. Few people could afford such a costly resin in our village.

"I picked these for her," I say to Yohannah, passing her the flowers.

She nods, and places them in Sholum's hand. I tuck one gently behind Sholum's ear and she looks so beautiful that I'm angry with myself when tears blur my vision. Yohannah puts her arm around me and strokes my hair, letting me weep and weep. Eventually, she pulls away.

"I'll find Shelamzion on my way out and let her know her daughter is ready," she says to the older women. "It's time I visited Phanuel to see how he's doing."

The women part for her, while I lie down beside Sholum and twine some of her hair in my fingers. I don't remember falling asleep.

I wake up. I've been moved. Someone has laid me down on a sheepskin and draped a blanket over me. The room is full of shrouded lumps of slumbering women littering the sleeping mattresses and the felt rugs Shelamzion made herself. Barren Yulia lies inert by my feet. I can see from the cracks around the door that it's almost dawn.

The door opens and Uncle Hanan comes in, treading quietly. There's enough light to see that where Sholum was lying before, looking almost as if she were merely asleep, there's now just a body, wrapped in linen strips and ready for burial. It could be anyone small. I glance down and see a generous lock of Sholum's beautiful autumn-coloured hair, with all its curls, still clutched in my fist. It's been cut cleanly with a knife. I don't know who did this, but I'm so grateful to have this keepsake of hers. I'll fold this lock of hair into one of the pieces of linen that my mother keeps at the bottom of her wedding chest and treasure it forever.

Hanan leaves the door open, reluctant to wake the women, but outside I can hear the hushed whispers of the men waiting. The grave must be dug already. Soon the light, the noise, and the chill early morning air cause everyone to stir. When the first women realize the hour has come, they start wailing and ululating. This swiftly works its way through the room until everyone is keening and crying. The men will take the body to bury it. It's not for women to be there.

"No!" screams Aunt Shelamzion, taking the shrouded thing and cradling it in her arms as if it were still Sholum. "No, don't take her. You can't have her!"

This is the way of women. No one wants to relinquish the body of a loved one to the mountain.

"I won't let you take her!" Shelamzion screeches, eliciting a murmur of sympathy from the men outside.

Her neighbours and closest cousins gather around her, protecting the body, even though they all know it must be buried.

Shemayah comes with his wife, Yohannah, and their male neighbours, all removing their sandals at the doorstep. Yohannah steps aside. This is a battle for the men alone. They work their way through the grieving women, who beat and punch them, shrieking abuse. It gets worse as they near the body itself. The men take the punches and scratches. It's the one time in our village when it's the women who beat the men. Shelamzion is the most savage. She rakes her nails down Shemayah's face. He flinches and mumbles his apologies, then begins tugging at the wrapped corpse.

More men come in and help him, battered ineffectually by the women. By the time they've stumbled to the doorway, all of them are bleeding from scratches but they carry the body with them, laid on the pallet with the bed of salt. Someone's even remembered to take the washing bowl, which will be broken over the grave to mark it. Even in her grief-stricken frenzy, Aunt Shelamzion knows not to go beyond the lintel, and simply screeches and wails as the corpse is taken by the men. I'm not a woman yet, so I duck out of the door behind them. I can't go to the grave with the men, of course, but I can still watch the procession leave.

I feel numb as I climb the stone stairs up to the flat roof. I see Sabba, his face ashen with circles under his eyes. Then I spot Yair and Menahem, whose eyes are red with weeping. I look for Ananias but can't see him anywhere. I don't know why I'm not crying right now. Maybe I don't have anything left. Below me the women shriek and wail. I just feel hollowed out, like an apple the wasps have eaten from the inside. I watch the procession leave and still just stand there, staring, for a long time afterwards. The women eventually dribble out of the courtyard and back to their own homes. Only Yohannah and our close neighbours and relatives will stay with Shelamzion.

It suddenly occurs to me that Amma should be here. How could she miss this? When Shelamzion has recovered a little she will remember the absence too. I wonder if she'll be able to forgive her sister. I know I should probably go home and see what's happened with Phanuel, but right now I just don't care. I curl up on an old, ratty sheepskin beside slices of drying apple and hold the lock of hair right under my nose so I can inhale the smell of her.

I'm so still that a mouse nudges its way from under an old burlap sack and sniffs the air cautiously before beginning a series of furtive moves toward the dried apple slices, picking a slice up, and nibbling at it hurriedly. It doesn't even notice me. I'm good at that – not being noticed. The mouse drags the apple slice back under the sack. I should probably try to stamp on it or something, but why shouldn't the mouse eat, too?

Thinking about food makes me hungry and this is what eventually prompts me to wander down from the roof. Aunt Shelamzion sits inside the inner room with her closest neighbours. She looks up with bleary eyes as I come in.

"I thought you'd gone home," she says.

"I think I should," I say, and the neighbours nod in a way that makes me think they know more than I do.

As soon as I walk through our door, I wish I hadn't. It smells of urine. Amma is bent over Phanuel and she's wringing a rag into a bowl. She looks up and sees me, and immediately her face is filled with absolute rage.

"Oh, so now you show up?" she hisses.

"I've been at Aunt Shelamzion's to be with Sholum," I say. "Everyone was there except you."

For a moment my mother is speechless, which is a rarity. "You are not my daughter!" She somehow manages to make a hissed whisper sound like a shout. "Curse the day I brought you into this world! Why have I missed my own niece's wake? Uh? Tell me, why? Because you just left without any care or concern about your brother, your only brother. I've had to tend him all night alone. You animal! If only Maryam had lived and you had died."

I think she says more but I stop listening. I can't be here right now. I turn to leave and Amma dispenses with any pretence of whispering and starts shouting at me. She can't leave Phanuel, so she doesn't rush after me. Outside, the chickens cluster reproachfully around me, hemming me in. They've clearly not been fed all day, so I go into the storage room and take a handful of grain to toss to them. I'm about to leave when Ubba comes through the main gate of our compound.

"How is he?" he says, his brow knotted with concern. "Ananias came up to the camp and told me what happened. He's staying with the sheep." This is a long speech for my Ubba.

I shrug. "He's inside with Amma," I say, and then I walk out.

I'm not sure where to go. At first I assume I'll go back to my aunt's house. I'd really like some food, as I haven't eaten anything since yesterday afternoon. Instead, I find myself walking along toward Menahem and Yair's house, which is near the top of the village. A few women nod sympathetically at me as I pass, and one or two talk to each other behind their hands. I'm not used to being noticed.

At Menahem and Yair's place, they're eating lunch outside spread on a faded food cloth and making the most of the midday sun.

"Tabita, come join us," says their mother as I knock on the gatepost. "Boys, make some room."

The family, including the boys' grandparents who live with them, are gathered around a common dish of beans.

"They just got back from…" she trails off.

We're an unusual village. Other people down in the lowlands would never dream of putting their dead under the ground. They have special caves for the dead and clay pots for placing their bones in. I know because Grandfather told me. If we did that, it wouldn't matter how well you sealed the cave with rocks, some mountain animal would find its way in and eat the body. That's why we have to put them under the soil. We give them back to the earth.

"Do you think I could plant some flowers or something beside her broken bowl?" I ask.

"Of course you could," says their mother, smiling sympathetically. "Now come and sit down."

She tears off some flatbread and hands it to me and I use it to scoop up some beans. I have to restrain myself from wolfing the whole lot down. I'm really hungry.

"So," says their mother in a way that sounds as if she's encouraging us all to talk about something. But we just eat silently.

The grandmother wants to know whose daughter I am, and this requires yelling a response because she's deaf. It means the mother does at least get some conversation. Once the food is all gone, Yair and Menahem get up to take the dish and a small bowl of date pits up to the spring to wash. It's women's work but their only sister is two.

"I'll come with you," I say.

At first their mother fusses and says I'm a guest, but then she lets me go.

"So, tell me what happened," I say as we squat beside a spring that gurgles out from the roots of an old tree. "I want to know everything."

The boys give each other a look.

"No," I say. "You're not going to give me your official version. I want to know the truth."

"There's nothing to say," says Menahem. "It was an accident. We already told everyone, it was an accident."

"What was an accident?" I ask him. "What actually happened?"

Menahem sighs in frustration. "You know what happened, Tabita. They both fell from the tree. It was an accident."

"How? One person falling from a tree is an accident, but two at the same time? Menahem, just tell me everything."

He looks surprised at how forceful I am. I'm a bit surprised, too. I sigh in exasperation and turn my attention to Yair.

"Who fell first? Were they up the same tree?"

"I was right at the top of one of the taller trees," says Yair flatly. "I didn't see what happened. I just heard something falling and then I heard the shouts and I climbed down as fast as I could."

"And you?" I ask Menahem. "Where were you when it happened?"

I don't get an answer because we hear their mother calling us to come down from the spring. Shemayah has come to visit.

"Wait," I say before they head down, and I grab Menahem's left thumb and check it and then do the same with Yair's. They both have small nicks in them, made with the sharp end of a knife. "You swore a blood oath over this, didn't you?" I whisper as we walk down to join Shemayah. "I don't care about your oaths. I will find out," I mutter.

"Thank you, I've eaten already," Shemayah is explaining as we arrive outside the house. "Some mint and sage tea would be nice, though."

Yair's mother sends her husband to pick some leaves from beside the spring. She senses that Shemayah is here to speak to the boys.

"Welcome, Uncle," says Yair.

"We're just on our way to the forest," Menahem adds.

"Actually, you're the reason I've come," says Shemayah. "I want to know exactly what happened in the forest yesterday."

Shemayah nods at me. He looks as if he might be about to ask me to leave, so I turn my back to help Menahem's mother with tea preparation. I feed a few sticks to the fire, squatting beside the pot, ears pricked.

"How is Phanuel?" Menahem asks.

"It's still too early to say," says Shemayah. "He made it through the night, but he can't feel anything below the neck. This might just be temporary, but until we can get a lowlander doctor to come and visit him…"

"Tell him he's in our prayers," says Menahem.

"Why don't you tell him yourselves?" says Shemayah. "I'm sure he'll be eager for visitors soon. Now, let me hear your account of what happened yesterday."

I listen, frustrated that neither of the brothers says anything new. They both claim to have been up trees when the fall happened, and then go into detail about how they made sleds afterwards to bring the bodies back to the village.

I know there's something they're not saying, but I also know that they won't tell Shemayah or me or anyone else. The Hand can be stubborn like that.

"You mentioned that you were heading into the forest," says Shemayah. "I'd like to join you. I want you to show me where it happened."

I bring the tea, ladling it into bowls, and once we've finished I thank the boys' mother for her hospitality and prepare to follow Shemayah.

"Shouldn't you be helping your mother with Phanuel?" he asks.

"I want to see where it happened. Where she died."

He gives me a searching look, then shrugs, and we trudge toward the forest in silence.

"Why weren't you helping with the harvest yesterday?" Shemayah asks me as we follow the rocky path that leads into the forest.

"I was needed at home," I reply.

We pass oaks and cedars, arriving at the part of the forest where the walnut trees grow. I look up at the tallest boughs and imagine someone falling. Would they just drop straight to the ground, or would they hit some of the lower branches on their way down?

"Here," says Yair. "This was the tree they fell from."

We stop. There are still some half-filled sacks of walnuts strewn around. There was no time to think about them yesterday. I look up and notice that one of the larger branches is broken, although not snapped in two.

"This is where they landed," says Menahem, pointing to a depression in the dry leaves and earth. There's a gnarled root there that protrudes from the forest floor. It seems to be coated in dried blood.

Shemayah looks up sharply. "So they both landed on the same spot," he says. "Did one land on the other?"

Yair flashes his brother a look.

"I don't know," Menahem adds quickly. "This is just where we found them once we'd climbed down."

"Did either of them move, or groan, or something? Did you know if they were dead or alive?"

"We didn't think about it," says Yair. "We just knew we had to get them back to the village as quickly as we could. There was no time to think."

"What was Sholum doing up a tree in the first place? She knows that's the boys' job."

Menahem and Yair glance at each other and just shrug.

I spot a rag doll dumped beside one of the sacks. "And the little ones, were they with you, too?" I add.

"They couldn't help with carrying the bodies but they came back with us," says Menahem.

I pick up the doll. "This belongs to Heras," I say. "I'll make sure she gets it back."

We return to the village together. I say goodbye to the others and head for Heras's house.

She's squatting beside a flat stone with a hammer she uses to crack open walnuts. She may only be six or seven years old, but she's already an expert in tapping the shell just right so the nut inside isn't damaged and comes out whole. Whole nuts sell for more down in the lowlands.

"Where's your mother?" I ask her, letting myself in through the gate.

"She's sleeping," says Heras.

I remember seeing her mother at Shelamzion's house last night.

"I found your doll," I say, passing it to her.

Heras smiles and takes the doll, hugging it gently to herself. "I thought I'd lost you," she whispers to it.

"It was with the walnut sacks in the forest," I say, trying to pick my words carefully. "You must have forgotten about it when you saw Sholum and Phan fall."

She stares at me solemnly.

"It must have been horrible," I say, hoping to draw her out. "Can you tell me about it?"

She shakes her head. "Sabba told me not to," she states.

"Yes, he told you not to tell the grown-ups," I improvise, "but you can tell me. I was meant to be there, remember? What happened?"

She shrugs. "I was collecting underneath Sabba's tree. Then I heard something crashing and it was really loud, and it was Sholum and then Phan landed on top of her." She stares hard at me.

"Thank you," I say, letting myself out through the gate.

I walk back toward home, toward my brother who came crashing down on Sholum. Maybe she was still alive until he landed on her. I know what a walnut feels like being dropped from that height. Who could survive the weight of a human body? I think he killed her. What I want to know is what made her fall in the first place. Was she pushed?

I don't want to go home, but where else can I go? I feel dread as I push the gate open, leave my sandals at the door, and enter our room. Ubba is sitting beside Phanuel, who has his eyes closed. Amma is asleep, even though the sun is only just beginning to set. I suppose she was up most of the night. I breathe a sigh of relief. I'm not sure I could handle my mother right now.

"How is he?" I whisper to Ubba.

Ubba just shrugs.

"Was he awake before?"

Ubba shakes his head.

"Does that mean—"

"We don't know, Tabi. He has a pulse and Amma spooned some broth down him. Shemayah has sent for a lowland doctor."

"When will the doctor—"

"Enough," says Ubba.

I sigh and look around our inner room. It's a mess. I don't want to clear up in case I wake Amma. I go outside, light a fire, and put water on to boil while I pull some carrots and leeks and wash them in the channel above our house. I throw in a handful of barley, some powdered walnuts to thicken the stew, some herbs, and a little salt, which has got wet and clumps together. We won't be using our outdoor kitchen for much longer this year. As the sun sets behind the mountains, a chill breeze picks up, rustling the golden leaves and causing a few to drift down around me.

I squat by the pot, stirring absently and feeding the fire with extra sticks every now and then. It's almost over: my first day without Sholum. How many more will there be? How am I supposed to carry on without her?

The moon is beginning to rise and I'm shivering by the time I carry a large wooden bowl of stew back to the house. I manage to open the door with a foot but it's completely dark inside. Placing the bowl down, I return to our summer kitchen, find a lamp, and light it from the embers, screening the flickering light with my hand. Ubba is asleep now as well. I wonder about waking my parents, but the lamplight does that for me. My mother gives me a baleful look but she's exhausted and doesn't have any fight left in her right now. We sit, eating in silence.

"Should I try to give some of the broth to Phan?" I ask. "I saved some, it's still in the pot."

Amma nods. "Here's what you do," she says, cradling her son's head. "Make sure you lift his head up and only try very small amounts." I take my brother's head in my lap, as if he were a baby, and gently mimic how my mother fed him. She sighs. "What a cursed day," she mutters, then lays out the beautiful bridal felt rug Shelamzion gave her on her wedding day, puts a sleeping mat atop it and some blankets, and turns her back toward us.

I expect the soft purr of her snores to follow, but they don't. Even though she's exhausted, sleep won't come. It's the same for me. I clear everything up and blow out the lamp and lie there in the darkness as sadness drifts down, like dew, covering every part of me.

I don't know when I fell asleep, but I'm roused by Phanuel. "I didn't mean to," he murmurs over and over again feverishly.

Amma is already up and sponges his forehead with a damp rag, making shushing sounds.

"It's all right," she says. "It wasn't your fault."

Except that it was. Why else would the Hand swear a blood oath? I should probably be happy he's conscious, but I'm not. Why should he live and Sholum die? I keep my eyes closed and eventually drift back to sleep.

The next day, Ubba tells me to go to the forest and fetch our walnut sacks. I'm to go to Ananias's house and give them to his parents to thank them. After all, it was Ananias who went back and found our donkey wandering unattended in the forest. It was also Ananias who got up before dawn and climbed up to the shepherd's camp to alert Ubba, and who is still up there now taking care of our sheep.

"He's a good boy," said Ubba, which for him is a huge compliment.

I'm grateful to be out of the house. Phanuel is still sleeping when I lead our donkey away. Amma has already gone out. She's finally gone to sit with her sister and mourn. I'm greeted outside Ananias's house by ragged toddlers. One of his sisters-in-law sees me and calls Ananias's mother. There's barely a path to their house because the whole of their compound is planted with vegetables. Their problem is too many sons and not enough land. I dread to think what their inner room is like in winter, and feel sorry for whoever marries Ananias and has to fight for space among the four sisters-in-law already living there.

I return home and lead the donkey into the empty sheep pen. The doorway leading to our inner room is open and covered in sandals. Shemayah and Yohannah are there, along with the Hand, our neighbours, and even barren Yulia. Lamps are lit everywhere – an unusual extravagance – and then I notice the lowlander and I know why. He looks intently into Phanuel's eyes, asking him to say if he feels any pain. Meanwhile, out of Phanuel's line of vision, he holds a needle in his hand. He pricks his leg first, then works his way up until Phanuel flinches when the needle jabs his neck.

The doctor nods as if this means something important. He then asks for help in stripping Phanuel for a full examination. The women look at each other and leave, with just me and Amma remaining. I'm called forward and I help to ease Phanuel's tunic off until he's just in his waistcloth. It's the first time I've seen him properly awake. The whole of one side of him is purple with bruising, and despite hating him for what I suspect he did to Sholum, I'm shocked at how ravaged his body looks and can't help feeling pity. The doctor gives us a salve and prods the bruises. I keep expecting Phanuel to yell and kick him, but he just lies there. I'm glad he can't see how bad it is.

Then the doctor removes Phanuel's waistcloth and continues to prod the bruising around it. I feel ashamed for my brother being exposed like this, even if it's only men present. Then something worse happens. As the doctor presses near Phanuel's wife-maker, it begins to leak a slow, steady stream of urine. I grab his waistcloth and try to mop up as much as I can. It takes a moment before Phanuel sniffs the air and sees our expressions and then, in quiet horror, he asks, "Was that me?"

"Is this the first movement?" the doctor asks Amma.

She looks blank.

"Is this the first time he's passed water since the accident?"

"No, it happened yesterday evening as well."

"Well, that's a good sign. And bowels?"

She shakes her head. "When will he get better?" she asks, trying to keep the tremor from her voice.

"Can you roll your shoulder for me?" the doctor asks Phanuel, ignoring her question.

Phanuel scrunches up his face, which must mean he's trying, but nothing moves, not even a bit.

"Focus on movement through the shoulders," the doctor persists, but still nothing happens. "And now let's see you lift your head," says the doctor.

Phanuel breaks out in a sweat from the exertion but manages to raise his head a little. He puts it back down and tries to smile.

"I can still move my neck," he says with relief. "When will I be able to move the rest of me?"

"Well, that is in the hands of God," says the doctor. He turns to Amma. "You'll need to make pads, like you would for a newborn. Old tunics will do. He won't have any control over his bowel movements, so you'll need to change them regularly."

"But when will he get better?" Ubba asks. He asks it in a way that makes it clear that he is no woman to be fobbed off but a man in his own home who will be given an honest answer.

The doctor shrugs. "Perhaps he will regain control of his muscles, but it's also possible that he won't. It's important not to give up hope, but you should be prepared that this might be the full extent of his recovery."

"Recovery?" says my father, wondering how this word could possibly describe Phanuel's condition.

I turn to Phanuel, expecting him to protest and at least lift his shoulders up to prove this lowlander wrong and show him what we mountain people can do when we put our minds to it. Phanuel does the only thing he can do. He closes his eyes and turns his head to face the wall. My big brother, leader of the Hand, lies exposed before us, covered in just a urine-soaked cloth and imprisoned in a body that doesn't work any more. Whatever he's done, I wouldn't wish this on anyone.

My mother begins to keen and wail, beating her chest, as if Phanuel were already dead. One of the men restrains her, because although Phanuel has turned his head to the wall we can still hear him sobbing quietly. No one says anything.

What would words do, anyway?

Chapter Three

After the men have left with Ubba and the doctor, Amma sets about sponging Phanuel clean while I wring out and clean his waistcloth. Amma digs out her supply of padded linen from one of the chests and shows me how to fold one the right way between Phanuel's legs so it will absorb as much as possible. I look away as his wife-maker flops around and I try not to touch it.

"Can't you do this?" I plead.

Phanuel is silent but reddens too, and I see that he is as embarrassed as I am.

"You dog!" Amma starts. "Who do you think kept you clean all those years when you would soil yourself the moment my back was turned? Eh?"

And so we become used to this uncomfortable intimacy. It's an impossible job keeping Phanuel clean. The next morning we discover that the felt he has been lying on is saturated with urine and we have to call Ubba to help us roll him so we can ease it out from under him. I take it down to the stream and leave it submerged, pinioned with rocks, just grateful to be out of the house. By the time I return, Phanuel has managed his first bowel movement. We try to celebrate this as progress, but the smell lingers, even with the door left open.

"We might as well get used to the house always smelling of his filth," I mutter to myself as I hang up the washed padded linen that is still stained and brown.

"Aren't you at all grateful he's alive?" Amma snaps.

I say nothing. Phanuel, to his credit, never mentions the stench, although he must suffer more than the rest of us. At least I can escape outside. It's really dawning on me just how awful his situation is. I'm dreading winter.

I go back inside, where Phanuel now lies on a sheepskin, which should be easier to move from under him when it gets stained and needs washing. Sweat beads on his forehead as he practises raising his head up and down. Then his face clenches again, but that's all, and I realize he's trying to move an arm or a leg or something. He goes back to lifting his neck, then we both turn our heads as the light from the open door is blocked and we hear applause.

"Look at you!" says Menahem, as if Phanuel had just shifted the huge boulder the Hand used to optimistically take turns trying to budge up near Cousin Yusef's orchard.

"You'd better watch out, Menahem," says Sabba. "Phan'll be wrestling you to the ground in no time."

The rest of the Hand laugh heartily as if this was really funny, and Menahem nods enthusiastically as if nothing would please him better.

"Phan, we heard you can move your neck and that the doctor says soon you should be able to move the rest of you," says Yair, coming over to sit beside Phanuel and managing not to wrinkle his nose at the smell.

"We need you back on your feet, brother," says Ananias.

Phanuel glances at me quickly. No one else notices. I may not be able to read words on a scroll but I can read my brother pretty well. He's nervous that he'll lose his place among them, but he can't have them see that.

"I'll be back on my feet in no time," he says, trying to make his voice sound light-hearted. "Can't have Menahem winning all the wrestling matches."

We all laugh dutifully and Phanuel smiles.

"So," he says, "what's been going on with all of you?"

The boys try to answer but it's not a question that really works with us. Of course, when Amma's brother came to visit us from the lowlands, Amma spent hours telling him about who had married whom, or had died or had children, long after my uncle regretted ever asking. But day to day, well, we just do what we did the day before. Once the boys had finished explaining that they were still busy finishing the walnut harvest and that they missed Phanuel's help, there wasn't much else to say. After an awkward pause, I offered to boil water for tea and then everyone spoke at once, saying that there was no need and that they should probably head back out to the forest but they would be back the next day.

So, we get used to seeing the Hand each morning. Phanuel often seems agitated and snappy before they arrive and then withdrawn afterwards, but while they visit he tries to crack jokes or remind them of a time when one of them did something stupid or dangerous or funny. The past is safe and familiar territory for all of them. There's one time when Phanuel has a bowel movement while the Hand are visiting. They really impress me, with no one saying anything or mentioning the stench. It almost makes me forgive them for not telling me what really happened in the forest.

The first thing one of them always asks when they arrive is, "How's the lifting?"

"I lifted my head off the pillow fifty times in a row without stopping," says Phanuel, or something similar, as they ruffle his hair or pat his shoulders in congratulation.

The reality is that he still can't move anything else.

"How about your wife-maker? I hope that's still moving," says

Sabba one day. His grin fades quickly when he sees Phanuel's face and realizes what a stupid thing it was to say. Menahem thumps Sabba hard on the shoulder. It's not a friendly thump.

"Hey," says Phanuel, trying really hard to master his emotion. "Do you remember that time when we tried to catch an eagle chick?"

With relief they all listen to him as he retells the story, occasionally butting in but not like they would have done before, and giving him the chance to tell the best bits.

After that, no one asks about Phanuel's progress when they visit. Instead, each boy tries to find at least one interesting thing they can mention about their previous day.

"Ubba says we'll have three days of rain this week," says Yair. "He can tell from the way his bones ache."

Ananias mentions an old apple tree he helped his neighbour chop down, and how he wants to use some of the wood to carve into wooden spoons. See? Not that interesting. Still, it's better than Phanuel lying alone in a cold room all day with no one but me and Amma for company. Ubba has to return to his flocks, and seems relieved to escape, even though he wants regular reports on Phanuel's progress.

I'm expected to look after Phanuel, do all my old chores, including weekly visits up to the shepherd camp, and take on the tasks Phanuel would have been doing. Surprisingly, I'm pretty happy with this arrangement. Keeping busy means less time to notice the aching absence of Sholum, and it means I'm not stuck in that one room all the time with Phanuel. His silences are louder than words. He just lies there, smelling of filth, and everything shouts misery and despair. He might as well be dead. I miss my brother, but the old one who was alive, not this one, who won't tell me what happened to Sholum; who fluctuates between fury and despair. It's only when the Hand visit that he forces himself to be like the old Phanuel.

The few times I try to engage him in hissed conversation,

mindful of potential intrusions from Amma, it's to find out what happened to Sholum. He just closes his eyes and says nothing. I wait for market day when Amma is out buying provisions. It's a few weeks after the accident.

"Phan, there's nobody else here. Now will you tell me what happened between you and Sholum? How did you fall?"

He says nothing for a while, then whispers, "What does it matter now?"

"It matters because it matters! She was my best friend. I want to know what happened."

Phanuel just turns his face to the wall.

"Tell me," I say, coming over and shaking him.

"You can hit me if you like," he says. "You know I can't hit back. It's what I deserve."

"I don't know what you deserve because you won't tell me. I have a right to know. She was my best friend."

He wins with silence and I hate him.

The day Shemayah arrives with the lowland doctor, we hear Amma greeting them outside.

Phanuel hisses, "But I'm not ready. Why didn't someone say the doctor was coming now?"

I light some lamps and boil water for mint tea.

Amma, who was feeding the chickens, comes inside with a pinched look on her face. At least the room isn't full of people like last time. The doctor waves away the tea, saying he'll drink it afterwards. He inspects Phanuel and asks if he's been eating enough. Now that he mentions it, Phanuel does seem skinnier, but that might also be because he's losing muscle. The doctor talks to Phanuel, maintaining eye contact so Phanuel doesn't notice as he pricks Phanuel's skin.

"I've been practising my neck moves," says Phanuel, desperate for any sign of hope from the doctor. Then he starts to lift his head up and down.

"And the shoulders and arms?" asks the doctor.

"I can do up to a hundred neck moves without stopping," says Phanuel.

You can hear the desperation in his voice.

When the doctor gives us his verdict and the last shreds of hope are torn away, I expect him to rage or wail, but he doesn't. That comes later. He just turns his head to the wall and stays silent. Amma and I walk the doctor and Shemayah out through the gate and down the rocky path toward the centre of the village. We both just want to escape that room full of despair.

"Oh," says Amma, as we get to where the doctor's horse is grazing, "I forgot to bring payment. Just wait here."

"No, Drusilla," says Shemayah. "It has been done."

Amma protests but Shemayah insists.

Then Amma pauses and says, "But what are we to do?"

She crumples slowly and I have to support her. That's how the doctor leaves us, with Amma clinging to me and sobbing, and Shemayah looking on awkwardly.

"Should I go up to the shepherd camp and tell Ubba?" I ask as we walk back to the house, Amma still leaning heavily on me.

"No," she says, wiping her nose on the muddy hem of her tunic. "Let him have a few more days of hope." She lets out a long sigh and then clutches her swollen belly. "If this baby isn't a boy, what are we to do?"

"I'm still here," I say.

"A daughter is for the present but a son is for the future," says Amma, quoting a proverb. "We'll have to give you away soon and then who will take care of us?"

We walk in silence. I haven't really thought about marriage, but I suppose it will happen in a few years' time. And what of Phanuel? He worked as hard as any other village boy, but now, not only will he never work again but he will need someone to feed him, to wash him, and to clean his soiled bedding and linen, and that's time spent not scything hay or harvesting apples and walnuts. Mother will soon be busy with this new baby. It's not going to be easy.

"I'm still here, and I can work hard," I say, squeezing my mother's hand and attempting a smile.

The next morning, the Hand arrive as usual but Phanuel turns his face to the wall.

"Tell them I'm too tired," he says.

"What do you mean?" says Amma, trying to sound light-hearted. "They won't stay for long and you can sleep afterwards."

"I don't want to see them," Phanuel says through gritted teeth.

"But Phanuel—" Amma starts.

She is cut off as Phanuel lets loose a barrage of foul language at her. The door is open and the Hand can hear everything. He says things that no boy should ever say to his mother.

"Stop it," says Amma, and I'm not sure if she plans to give him a good hard slap or start crying. She's as shocked as I am.

But it's Phanuel who starts crying first. "Who would want to be friends with a living corpse?" he shouts. "I'm nothing. I'm just this *thing* that uses up air and food and spreads filth everywhere."

"Come on, son," says Amma with surprising tenderness, but all he does is start swearing again.

We both get up and leave him to it.

"You know he doesn't mean it," says Sabba outside, placing a hand on her shoulder.

The boys all look shaken.

"My son has never said anything he doesn't mean," she replies, shrugging his hand away and brushing angrily at a tear that has spilled down her cheek. She sighs. "Thank you for coming," she says, trying to smile. "Don't give up on him. If we give up on him he'll give up on himself."

"Perhaps we should give him some time to get used to the news," says Ananias, and the others nod with relief.

They must find these visits as hard as Phanuel does.

Phanuel is angry for the next two days. I look for any excuse to stay out of the house, and I notice Amma seems more preoccupied with preparing her vegetable garden for winter than normal. When I change his soiled linen he glowers at me. When I try to lift his head to feed him or let him sip a bowl of tea, he glowers. Nothing I do is right.

"You know it's not easy for us either," I say, finally giving him the fight he's been looking for.

"Not easy?" he sneers. "Then walk away. Go on. You've got legs that work. You can just run out of here. Me? I'm stuck in this sack of skin in this room. It's like I'm dead already but still alive. I might as well be in hell."

Amma comes in and glances over at us nervously.

Then Phanuel lifts his voice and yells: "I curse God. I curse the Most High."

I rush to shut the door, even though we've no lamps lit.

"Phanuel!" says Amma in a voice that would usually silence anyone. "You could be stoned for that."

"Why do you think I said it?" he replies, then starts again. "I curse God. I, Phanuel, son of –"

He doesn't finish because Amma rushes over and slaps him hard, and a hard slap from my mother is a *hard* slap.

"Hitting your own crippled son, Amma?" he mocks triumphantly, running his tongue over a split lip.

"Son? No son of mine would say things like that," Amma shoots back at him.

He's stung into silence for a moment and then, in the dark, we hear his voice become querulous like a small boy's. "You have no idea what it's like. None of you do." He begins to sob. "Please, just take me outside. Let them hear me curse God and be done with me. What future do I have? This room, this body, it's just a prison. Just let me break out."

Amma sighs and goes outside. What could she say in response? It's what she's thinking as well. It would have been a mercy if he had died with Sholum, his honour intact. Then we could have mourned him properly.

"Go and tell your Ubba," she says to me. "It's time he knew."

I'm so relieved to have a whole day away from the house and away from Phanuel that I almost smile. And anyway, why should we have to carry the burden of Phanuel alone? Ubba should do more.

Ubba leaves me in charge of the flock while he heads back, telling me he'll be back tomorrow. He doesn't want to get stuck with Phanuel either. It seems almost normal that he's asked me to look after the flock. This would never have happened before, but who else is there? Does this make me an honorary boy?

Up here it already feels like winter, although there's still no snow. That evening, once the livestock are penned up for the night and I've finished a solitary meal, I light a few lamps and try to tidy up the hut. I lie in my father's bed, keeping one lamp lit as the wind whistles through cracks in the door, and I draw the blankets and skins up around my chin, realizing this is the first time I've ever slept alone. I've enjoyed it so far, just being able to breathe in a way that I can't at home, not when Phanuel is a constant lingering presence. But then I start to think about Sholum and I miss her, and I blow out the lamp and lie in the dark feeling the sorrow I've tried to keep at bay.

The next day Ubba comes and finds me with the livestock around midday. "You can go now," he says, by way of greeting and dismissal.

"Do I have to?"

He nods and he sighs, but sits down beside me on a flat rock, picking a dried stalk of grass and chewing on it thoughtfully.

"What does this mean for us?" I ask.

He shrugs. "Perhaps God is punishing us for something," he says. "I pray for a boy who can inherit my name and my flock, and take care of us and Phanuel."

"Do you think Phan will live that long?" I ask.

He just shrugs.

I head back down the mountain, taking my time, desperate for any excuse not to return home. The sun is setting by the time I walk through the gate. Amma is squatting before the fire, stirring a pot of stew.

"What did Ubba say?" I ask, squatting down beside her and keeping my voice low.

"What does that man ever say?" Amma mutters. She can't squat very well any more with her swollen belly.

Phanuel, on the other hand, continues to diminish; not just emotionally, but physically as well. I don't notice it so much because I see him every day, but the Hand, who have taken to visiting once a week now, are more observant. Phanuel says very little during their visits, and the boys spend most of the time trying to remember funny moments from the past or talking about what they've been doing. Once or twice they actually have something interesting to say, and they forget their performance and just talk. That's when I notice Phanuel really listening. I listen in too; anything to relieve the monotony of our life in this one room.

"Shemayah says one of the reasons young men are joining these hard-line groups is that they don't know their religion properly," Sabba explains. "He says he's neglected our religious education and that he wants to start lessons over the winter."

They talk about incidents in some of the nearby villages where young men have left to join the radicals. Two of them got themselves caught by the idolaters and ended up nailed. I've never seen a nailing or even a stoning. We're all too busy just surviving to worry about things like that in our village, and I don't really know why the boys are so interested in what happens in other villages or in the lowlands. Maybe they're just trying to make conversation.

I always walk the Hand to the gate after their visits, and this is when I hear what they really think. "His skin has gone grey," Sabba whispers at the gate, casting an eye back at the open door to our inner room.

"Did you see his arms?" says Menahem. "There's nothing left but skin and bone."

"Are you feeding him enough?" Ananias asks me directly. "If you need help…"

"What? Do you think we're starving him?" I snap, with more anger than I'd intended.

"No, that's not –"

"Yes it is, that's exactly what you meant, Ananias. In between cleaning up all his filth, and then making sure I do all the jobs around here that he's supposed to be doing, as well as my own, I also try to make him eat, one spoonful at a time, which takes forever because he can't swallow much, and because he refuses food most days and has to be coaxed to eat something so he doesn't die."

"Sorry, I –" Ananias starts, but I interrupt him.

"You know, it's your fault this happened in the first place," I say quietly, aware that I'm going down a road I can't return from. "I may not know everything, but I know that if there was no Hand then Sholum would still be alive and my brother would be up and working."

"Come on, Tabi," says Yair. "That's not fair. You know it was an accident."

"Do I? I know you swore a blood oath together. I know you keep lying."

"Tabi," Menahem starts.

"Just leave," I say flatly, and I don't say another word.

"She really is turning into her mother," I hear Yair whisper on the other side of our wall after they've left, and I want to chase after him and prove him right with a good hard slap.

After they've gone I feel bad about my outburst, mainly because Ananias took the brunt of it and I haven't forgotten his kindness to us. Then I reason that I'm the one paying the price for their mistakes, and I don't feel so bad any more.

I'm first to spot the sores. I point them out to Amma and she says they're common among bedridden old people, particularly if they're skinny. His bones are grinding down against his skin from inside him and making sores where his body constantly lies in the same position.

"What does it matter?" says Phanuel. "It's not like I can feel them."

Yohannah is consulted and comes to examine Phanuel, who glowers at the indignity of being exposed to a woman outside the family.

"You'll need to roll him regularly," says Yohannah, directing her instruction toward me. "He can lie on his front during the morning and then his left side until the sun hits three fingers higher than the mountain, and his right side after that, then back on his front before you sleep. Keep this up until the sores have healed."

I want to shout: *Why? When did he become my problem? Why is it me who has to do everything for him? I get nothing back; no gratitude or appreciation. Do you think I enjoy mopping and cleaning everything that dribbles out of him, day in and day out? How am I meant to keep him clean as the weather gets colder and it takes longer and longer for anything hung on the tree branches to dry? If the sores don't hurt him, then just leave them be. If they worsen, maybe that will be a mercy. Maybe he can just slip away. He's right. Why are we keeping him alive, imprisoned in this body that seems to be slowly falling apart?*

"Tabi, answer the elder!" my mother snaps, bringing me back to reality.

"I'm sorry," I say. "I'm just tired."

"And how do you think your brother feels?" Amma adds.

I want to hit my mother so badly. I've had enough hard wallops from her to have learned a thing or two, and Amma isn't as agile now, with her swollen belly and ankles. I want to hit her hard across the face, hard enough to send her sprawling. I think Yohannah reads something of this in my face.

"You're working very hard," she says to me gently, and I want to tell her to stop being kind because it will make me cry or maybe just start screaming. "Why don't you go and get some fresh air? I'll sit with Phanuel for the rest of the day."

I mumble my gratitude and leave before Amma can interfere. I climb up behind our house where our terraced orchards make steps into the mountainside. The apples and leaves are all gone now. I keep going, past our neighbours and then up the mountainside, where stubby dry grass is all that's left of the mountain pastures. I climb up to the Looking Rocks, as we call them. There's one that juts out and gives a great view, and as long as I'm not too close to the edge, I can enjoy the whole village spread before me. Directly below is the meadow I scythed while Sholum made flower chains. It wasn't that long ago that Sholum was alive and my brother was properly alive, too. I feel a rage welling up inside me.

"I curse you, too," I whisper to the sky. I don't say it for anyone else to hear. Just God. "I curse you for ruining my life," I say louder, making sure he can hear. If he wants to send a bear to eat me as punishment, which is probably what Amma would say will happen, then he's welcome to. I don't know why I'm alive.

I draw my knees up and observe the village stretched out below me. There are several women on one of the rooftops shelling walnuts. I'm not close enough to see the nuts themselves, but they'll be dividing them into two piles, with the whole ones to be sold and the broken ones for home use. Most of the activity is from women in their vegetable patches, pulling out the last leeks and carrots before the snow comes and storing them in bags on hooks to keep them away from rats. There are three men working on a terrace stone wall. I peer closer and realize one of them is Ananias. From here he looks like a man.

I'm high up enough not to hear the village sounds. If there are cries of anguish or misery, or even laughter, they're all just silence to me. I wonder if this is what it's like to be God. I look around but there's still no bear or mountain lion coming to punish me. Maybe looking after Phanuel is punishment enough.

It's cold and I don't have a shawl with me, but it's sunny as well, and I don't want to go back, so I just sit here, huddled, not doing anything, just breathing in air that doesn't smell of soiled linen. At first it feels good, but then, with nothing to do, I find my thoughts turning to Sholum, and when the tears come I don't try to hold them back. No one is here to reprimand me. I weep because life is bad. It wasn't wonderful before, but now it is bad and that seems worth crying about. I only start for home when the sun dips behind the mountain and the breeze picks up, rustling through the empty boughs of the forest stretched beyond the village, but too far away for me to hear.

I stop off at Auntie Shelamzion's house on my way home. I hear hammering from the workshop and put my head around the wall to greet Uncle Hanan. His workshop consists of three stone walls and a roof, so it's really cold in winter but always light. He stops hammering when he sees me.

"Sorry, Uncle," I say, "I didn't mean to disturb you."

He comes over and takes me in his arms. He's never done this before, and nor has Ubba. Even though I thought I'd leaked all my tears on the mountain, this undoes me again. He begins to cry as well.

"Oh, Tabi, how we miss her," he whispers to me, stroking my mousy brown hair with all the tenderness with which he used to stroke hers. Eventually Uncle Hanan breathes in, as if drawing himself back together, and holds me by my shoulders, appraising me. "You're getting skinny, Tabita," he says, trying to smile. "Come and eat with us. It will do your aunt good."

Inside, there are far more lamps lit than necessary. My mother would call it an extravagance. Shelamzion sits on a felt rug against one of their chests, holding her embroidery up to the lamplight.

"Tabita," she says when she sees me, her eyes brimming with tears.

"She's come to join us for supper," says Uncle Hanan.

Aunt Shelamzion smiles, which makes the tears spill over.

"We need to feed you up," she says. She's already using their winter kitchen, which is an alcove by the chimney. I can smell chicken cooking. My aunt stirs the stew and blows on a wooden ladle of it before taking a sip. "She's always laid well, but I won't get another spring out of her, so…" She shrugs and starts ladling the chicken broth into a common bowl.

We almost never eat chicken unless we have guests. The bowl is decorated with flowers and I realize it's the same as the one used to wash Sholum's body. The other one must lie broken on top of Sholum's grave. I still can't bring myself to go there.

"How is your brother?" Uncle Hanan asks.

"The same," I say, "except now he has bedsores."

"Poor Drusilla," he says.

"At least she still has him," says my aunt testily.

"And how are you both?" I ask quickly. "I'm sorry I haven't been to visit much."

"You can whitewash a tomb, but it's still a tomb," she says, quoting a proverb, and then gestures at all the lamps. "There will never be enough light to take away our darkness."

"Come now," says Hanan gently, stooping down and kissing the top of his wife's head where her hair meets her headscarf.

"I never know what it will be," says Shelamzion, brushing a tear away, "but every day there's something that reminds me of her. She still feels so fresh. I can't believe she isn't going to come walking through the door right now. When I see you, it seems… unimaginable that Sholum wouldn't be right there beside you."

"Oh, Auntie," I say, and I hold her and she holds me back and we both cry.

Uncle Hanan lays out the food cloth and the common bowl,

even though this is women's work, and props three decorated wooden spoons he made himself against the bowl rim, and when everything is ready, he coughs gently.

I don't expect to have an appetite after all this weeping, but it's chicken, which is a luxury, and I'm soon wolfing down as much as I can.

"Anyone would think you're about to flee from Egypt," says Hanan, smiling.

"I'm sorry," I reply, using a piece of flatbread to wipe an oily dribble from my chin. "I've always had to keep up with Phan." I smile. Chicken stew can make anyone smile.

"It's nice to have someone else to cook for," says Shelamzion, smiling. She almost laughs when Hanan makes a comical face that says: *Don't I count?*

"I love your spoons," I say as we finish up. "Ananias told Phan he's going to try to carve some this winter."

"He's turning into a fine young man," says Shelamzion, looking pointedly at me.

I blush. "I was just thinking, he seems to enjoy working with wood and if you wanted an apprentice or something, he works really hard."

Hanan nods. "Well, it's something to consider."

After supper, my aunt trims the lamp wicks and then opens one of her bridal chests. She draws out the madder-red woollen tunic Sholum used to wear, and smooths it gently as if it were a person and not a piece of clothing.

"Here, I want you to have this," she says. "It's what Sholum would have wanted."

"No, it's too much," I say. I also know that Sholum would have been livid if she'd caught her mother giving away her favourite winter tunic.

"Why keep it in a chest?" she says. "Am I going to have another daughter?"

"If God wills it. Just look at my mother," I say, then wish I hadn't as I see bitterness flicker over my aunt's face. Her sister still has a daughter and a son and another child on the way.

"Take it," she says, a little more roughly than I think she means.

I run my hands over the weaving and marvel at how fine the two-ply yarn is. "I wish I could spin like this," I say, distracted by its beauty for a moment. I look up and see Shelamzion appraising me as if she's never really seen me before.

"You have the eye of a weaver," she says. "If you could see some of the clothes those lowlanders wear, why, the colours!"

"How come we can't spin yarn like this? Everyone says mountain wool is the best."

This comment would have earned me a reprimand from Amma, who would have taken it personally, but Shelamzion just cocks her head in thought. How can these two women be sisters?

"My lion," she says to Hanan, "could you leave us for a moment? Tabita is going to try on the tunic."

Hanan excuses himself and Shelamzion makes me stand up and drop my tunic. Then she helps me put my head through the neck of Sholum's tunic and guides my arms into the sleeves as if I was a little girl, then she smooths it around me. It fits well. "She probably would have outgrown it this winter anyway," Shelamzion says.

Then she sits me down, takes a comb, and begins to comb my hair, humming tunelessly as she does. I lean back into her and let my eyes slip shut and give myself to the rhythm of the comb working through the tangles. I can't remember feeling this relaxed with the sound of her humming and the comfort of being touched. Occasionally I feel fingernails scurry hurriedly across my scalp and then hear a satisfying crunch, and I smile because I know that she's caught a louse.

I'm not sure how long this takes, but I'm roused from this wonderful stupor by Hanan, who tells me he'll walk me home because it's too late for me to be returning home alone. We walk in amiable silence and he leaves me at our gate. Inside our house it's dark and cold, and it smells. I know my way around, though, so I lay out my bedding and crawl silently under the blankets without any lamplight. I wish we could keep our house lit like they do. This is what the burial caves in the lowlands must be like: all these people trapped together in the dark. I'm still wearing the tunic, and even though it's wool it's not scratchy at all. I put the hem of the sleeve up to my nose and it still smells a little of Sholum. I breathe her in and feel sad, but for the first time since the accident I feel something else. It's not quite hope, but perhaps it's the softening of despair.

Chapter Four

Over the next few days Amma makes continual barbed comments about my new tunic, resenting her sister's generosity. She complains even more about her swollen belly and her need for constant trips to the unclean place, never failing to add that this is something her sister couldn't understand. I wish Shelamzion was my mother.

Phanuel is sullen and silent, and has locked himself away somewhere deep inside. I'm more unsettled by this than by his outbursts of anger, and I try unsuccessfully to cheer him up.

Then I feel that something isn't quite right inside me and down below. When I go to the unclean place, I notice blood spotting my waistcloth. I tell Amma and she makes me show her my waistcloth – as if I would lie about something like this. She tells me I'm now a woman, and that I must pray that I'm no fruitless tree like barren Yulia. She gives me a charm to wear to protect me from the evil eye, even though I know it's against our religion to worry about such things.

I wonder if I'll be punished with barrenness for having cursed

God, even though nobody heard. It doesn't seem like such a bad punishment anyway, seeing the heartache Sholum and Phanuel have both caused their parents. That evening Amma notes the shape of the moon. "Next time there's a waxing harvest moon you'll have to be ready. I'll teach you how to wear padding to absorb the blood," she says.

The idea of having to wash anything more than I already have to makes me want to weep.

"And don't go talking about this with the other girls or start boasting that you're a woman now. We've got enough to worry about without the eye striking because you were boastful."

I nod, feeling tired and grumpy, and wonder whom I'd tell anyway. Sholum was the only one, and now she's dead. Becoming a woman doesn't feel much different from being a girl, just messier.

The next morning I wake up, and for a moment I'm not sure what's changed. I listen to the muffled sounds outside and see just how bright the light seeping in around the doorframe is. I open the door and, sure enough, snow is falling and has already covered our sandals out on the doorstep.

"Look, Phan, it's snowing," I say. I want to try to enjoy this first fall while it's still fresh and new. The children on our street will all rush outside to make snow towers, but I no longer count myself among them. I bleed. I'm a woman now.

"And?" Phanuel sneers. "Do you want me to make a snow tower with you?"

I ignore this. "Ubba will be bringing the livestock back today. I should get the pen shovelled."

I open one of the chests and find my leather boots, wrap woollen strips around my feet, and put on my woollen shawl and woollen headscarf. Icy melted snow will still seep through these simple leather boots that don't have much of a sole, but if I keep moving my feet shouldn't feel too cold.

In fact, it's not long before I'm sweating. I shovel snow from our flat roof and from the animal pen, and I manage to dig a path from the pen to the gate and another path from the unclean place to the summer kitchen, and then to the house. I only stop when Amma calls me inside for the midday meal.

"I've already fed him," she says, glancing over at Phanuel.

It's usually my job, but this is my mother's way of acknowledging that I'm being helpful.

"Honestly, it's like trying to coax a fussy baby to eat," she says. "No wonder he's just skin and bones."

Phanuel stares at us balefully but says nothing. I've just done the work my brother would usually do. I enjoyed being outside in the snow, even though the hem of my tunic is now sodden and steams gently as I huddle nearer the fire, where I peel off the strips of sodden foot wrappings and hang them beside the cooking pot so they can dry. It felt good to be outside and do heavy work. Now it's Phanuel who is stuck inside with our mother. How things have changed.

Later in the afternoon I hear the clank of bells and go out to help Ubba bring in the livestock. He notices the paths I've shovelled, although they're quickly filling up with new snow.

"You did this?" he says and I nod, trying not to look too pleased with myself. "Mmm," he grunts, which means I've done a good job.

I help him corral the sheep and goats into one side of the pen and the cows into the other. Once the gates are shut, we fork hay from the stack beside the pen and fill the stone manger while the animals bleat and low and jostle around it.

I realized something today: a girl is a useful thing. She doesn't eat as much as a boy but she can work almost as hard, or harder if she really tries. She doesn't expect as much as a boy does. She's easier to control, and you can make her do all the jobs no one else wants to do. So why is it that if your firstborn is a girl, the neighbours try to console you for not having a son? The consolation is that a firstborn girl will be able to help look after the boys when they come along.

That afternoon Amma goes over to the chicken coop, which is just a sheltered wall with some sticks stuck into it at intervals so the chickens can hop up and roost out of the reach of foxes or wolves. She comes back with an older hen under her arm and it runs around in the snow after she has put an axe to its neck, spurting blood everywhere. She hangs it up to drain the blood. This treat is Amma's way of welcoming Ubba back home. I'm set to boil water to scald the carcass and then pluck it.

The nights are getting longer and it's dark by the time the broth is ready. I feed Phanuel before the rest of us eat, and even he won't refuse chicken stew, however stringy. Then we sit together and Ubba prays for the meal and breaks the flatbread, and we almost feel happy. Later, after the lamps have been out for a while and they think we might be asleep, I hear Amma giggle in the dark and whisper: "You can't get on top of me – not with the baby due so soon. Try on your side." And then they make parent noises.

The joy of being together wears off as quickly as the novelty of snow. I seem to spend my whole time shovelling paths through the snow with Ubba, although we're both grateful for hard work and silence because the three of us cooped up in that room with Phanuel and all his misery is just awful. Ubba suddenly becomes more sociable, but not with us. He looks for reasons to escape the house, helping neighbours or visiting one of his brothers who, like him, are content to work in silence.

Finally there's a clear sunny day, so I get out my drop spindle and examine the warp and weft of the sleeve of my tunic from Sholum, wondering if I can mimic the fine spinning. I root around in the storeroom for the sack of lambswool left from the spring shearing, scattered with dried herbs to keep moths at bay. I sit on the fallen walnut log, my back against the south-facing wall of our house, and try to spin yarn much finer than any I've seen in our village. The thread keeps snapping, though. I finally give up but still manage to spin thinner thread than I usually do. When I've finished two balls I ply them together, spinning the spindle in the opposite direction this time.

I'm pleased with the results, and after the midday meal I ask Amma if I can visit Aunt Shelamzion to show her.

Amma puts both her hands against the small of her back, sighs, and says: "Off you go, then. Abandon your poor mother when her waters might break at any moment."

I smile at her and then leave. When I get to Aunt Shelamzion's I hear voices from Uncle Hanan's workshop. I find Hanan and Ananias together, discussing which kind of spoon to make from a small log.

"Oh, so you found an apprentice, then," I say, smiling as they both look up.

Hanan nods and turns to Ananias. "Actually, it was thanks to Tabita that I thought I'd trial you," he says.

"Thank you," Ananias says to me. "This is just my fourth day but I've already learned so much."

"And he has a real talent for it," says Hanan, putting a hand on Ananias's broad shoulder.

"Well, I'm here to see Auntie," I say, and smile again before leaving them.

Maybe Ananias will forgive me for my former outburst.

Aunt Shelamzion brings my bulging drop spindle outside so she can inspect the yarn in sunlight. "Not bad. Not bad at all," she murmurs, as we sit down on their wooden bench that catches the winter sun. "Let's see what it's like off the spindle." She puts out her arms, and I start unravelling the yarn and winding it around them. Once I'm finished, she gives the skein a quick shake and then feels the texture of the yarn and tries tugging it in places to test its strength, before looking up with a grin.

"Perhaps my husband isn't the only one who should be seeking out an apprentice," she says.

She doesn't get a chance to say more because we hear Ubba calling my name. He's by the gate and out of breath. "It's started," he says. "I'll go and call Yohannah. You go back to the house and stay with her."

"I'll catch you up," Shelamzion says to me. "Let me just tell Hanan what's happening."

I grin as I hurry as fast as it's possible to hurry through thick snow. Shelamzion was impressed with my spinning. What would it mean to be my aunt's apprentice, doing something I actually enjoy? I hope Amma is all right. As I run, I offer up a quick prayer for a safe birth and for this new baby to be a boy. I'm sure God doesn't listen to a blasphemer, but I pray anyway.

At home, Amma leans forward with both hands on the door lintel, breathing hard. "They'd better come quick," she pants. "This baby doesn't want to wait."

I glance through the door and see Phanuel looking gaunt and anxious.

"Here, hold my hand," I say to Amma, "and take deep breaths."

"Deep breaths, my girl?" Amma blusters. "I know more about deep breaths than –" She cuts herself off with a cry and a grunt.

"Don't let it out yet," I say. "We don't have the birthing stool or the strap ready or anything."

"There'll be no time for that," Amma wheezes and then cries out again, digging her fingers painfully into my arm.

"You're doing really well," I say, but Amma can only reply with a dismissive toss of her head and then a couple of groans.

I look around in panic and see our neighbour Elisheba hurrying over, having heard the commotion. She takes Amma's other arm and tells her to pant, not push. Amma ignores her advice and Elisheba tugs up Amma's tunic and says: "I can see the head!"

She hurries inside and comes out with a sheepskin, which she puts on the ground between Amma's legs. Amma pants and then grunts and then howls, and a slippery, bloody package comes out. Elisheba lays it on the sheepskin and Amma is still catching her breath when she asks: "What is it, what is it?"

Then Elisheba says, "It's a boy," and Amma begins to weep tired tears of joy.

Shelamzion arrives and starts ululating, and behind her come Ubba and Yohannah, just as Elisheba cuts the cord and slaps the baby to make him cry.

"Come on, let's get you inside, out of this cold," says Yohannah, scooping the baby up and placing it in Amma's arms.

"I brought salt and the swaddling bands; that's why I was late," Shelamzion adds.

"It's a boy," Amma manages to croak to Ubba as she's led inside.

As I lift the bloodied sheepskin to take down to the stream to wash, I glance back through the open doorway and see Phanuel. He looks devastated; he's just been replaced.

Soon the house fills with the women of our village. I was worried that they might stay away, fearing the misfortune that has fallen on our house in recent times, but Amma has been blessed with a boy, and it's winter and no one has much else to do, so they come. They bring small gifts of food or old swaddling. Shelamzion even presents her new nephew with a rattle made by Hanan. It's not until they arrive that I realize how few guests we've had since the accident, apart from the Hand. On the eighth day Shemayah comes with his knife and holds the circumcision ceremony. Our little brother is officially named Helkias, and he bellows as he's cut. It's the one part of the day that I'm inside, as I spend the rest of my time working in the outside kitchen with Elisheba and a few other neighbours, preparing food for the guests.

Ubba has chosen to sacrifice one of his prize male lambs as a thanksgiving offering, even though two doves would do. "We don't want to take any chances now, do we?" he mutters, as he leads the half-year-old lamb out for Shemayah to bless before the slaughter.

I'm washing out the lamb entrails when barren Yulia shows up.

"Tabita, is that you?" she asks, peering closer and squinting with her poor eyesight.

The rest of us exchange a look. It's not good to have a barren woman at an event like this; she could put the evil eye on my baby brother, even unintentionally. She should know better than to show up.

"What are you doing here?" I ask, with more hostility in my tone than I'd intended.

"Oh, don't worry, I won't go inside," she says. "I don't want your mother concerned about the evil eye. I just thought you could maybe do with some help."

My cheeks immediately colour at my rudeness, and I thank her, offering a knife and handing her a slab of meat and a cutting board as we squat in the muddy snow together.

The Hand arrive. Ananias presents me with a carved wooden spoon, which provokes jeers that only get worse when I blush.

"It's to say thank you for my apprenticeship," he says hurriedly. "That's all."

I tell him I'm sure he's earned it and usher them inside.

"How can he sleep through all this?" Menahem asks, pointing at Phanuel.

I smile and shrug, knowing full well that Phanuel is just pretending to sleep so he won't have to talk to anyone or see their pitying glances. He's barely said a word since Helkias was born, and just keeps his face turned to the wall for the most part. The Hand depart as quickly as they arrived.

A steady stream of guests come and go, and all the while Yulia helps, cleaning bowls and plates, even though she must be cold squatting in the snow.

"Here, I've made you up a platter of some of the best food," I say, returning to her from the inner room after Elisheba and the others have already gone inside. "There's a generous dollop of Sabba's honey," I add.

Sabba never says how he obtains the honey, although swarms often form in the tree branches of the forest. Every summer he returns to the village, swollen from bee stings but triumphant, with honey oozing and trickling from large combs wrapped in burlap. It's probably the only thing he does without the rest of the Hand.

Yulia dips her finger into the honey and then sucks it, her eyes closing in pleasure.

"Is it hard for you being here?" I ask. The words are out of my mouth before I have time to consider them.

Yulia shrugs. "It's just hard being a fruitless tree," she says, "but I don't begrudge anyone else for having their fifth or sixth when I just want one. I'm happy for them. I just want to be happy for me as well."

"You shouldn't call yourself a fruitless tree," I say.

"Why not? Everyone else does." We're silent for a moment and then she adds: "If I was your mother, I wouldn't be as worried about the jealousy of a barren woman as the jealousy of a crippled son."

She's right, of course. Not that Phanuel could ever harm Helkias. At least, I don't think men can put the evil eye on others.

She eats in silence, and when she's finished she brushes the crumbs from her tunic. "I should probably go," she says. "You don't want to be stuck outside talking to me."

"No," I say, "I like talking with you." And I realize when I say it that it's true. "You can be sure that I'll come and help out when we celebrate the birth of your son."

She smiles sadly, and then turns to leave.

Now our nights are punctuated by the cries of Helkias. Added to the washing created by Phanuel is everything Helkias manages to soil as well. There seems to be more to do than ever, and any hope I had of being my aunt's apprentice is swiftly quashed. "How can I put this around my baby? It's still damp," Amma complains as I hand her the driest of the swaddling hung outside.

"I'll put it by the fire for a little while," I state.

"So he has to wear something that reeks of smoke?" she complains.

I don't know what else she expects me to do.

"And don't forget to feed Phanuel," she says as if he were a bear cub or some other animal we were raising. Then she turns her attention to Helkias, offering him her breast. "You have your mouth to feed and I have mine," she adds.

I realize then that there will be no more help from her in caring for Phanuel. He really has been replaced. Phanuel seems to recognize this, and starts refusing to eat. He's clever. He doesn't refuse a meal outright, but he takes a couple of spoonfuls of broth, then says he's full. Amma wouldn't stand for this and, although Phanuel feels nothing below the neck, he's not immune to one of her hard slaps or a savage pinch. After a few days he gets even skinnier than he was before, his cheeks sunken and grey. He catches a cold, his eyes become red, and his nose constantly drips.

"You might think Amma is too busy to see what's happening, but I'm going to tell Ubba," I hiss at him, trying to force the wooden spoon past his clenched teeth.

"Ubba?" he hisses back, eyes blazing. "You mean the man who will never look at me; the one who walks around me as if I'm not here? Ha! Didn't you see him when Helkias was born? He almost wept with relief because now he finally has a son – a proper son with a working wife-maker who can give him grandchildren. Go ahead and tell Ubba. He'll thank me."

I think he's going to say more, but I make the most of his open mouth and shove the spoon in it. The annoying thing is that he's right. After another two meals of battling with Phanuel, I enlist Amma's help.

"He's trying to starve himself," I say. "He won't listen to me and he won't eat more than a few mouthfuls of stew."

"You can't force him to eat if he's not hungry," says Amma, jigging Helkias on her hip.

"I can't, but you can," I reply. "Can't you see what he's trying to do?"

Amma sighs and gets up, and I wonder which of us is in for

a hard slap. "I told you, Tabita, I can't feed two babies," she says. "I'm going out."

I watch, open-mouthed, as she wraps a shawl around herself and nestles the swaddled Helkias under it, then leaves to visit one of the other women on our street who has also just given birth. Outside there's no sign of Ubba either. They've both given up on Phanuel, neither wanting the responsibility of looking after him. Nor do I, yet here I am.

"Are you happy now?" I ask, wheeling on him and glaring.

He's smiling, but it's a twisted, angry, hateful smile. "Why are you so slow to see what all the rest of us see?" he says. "There's no point in me. There's no future for me. I'm like a sheep tick sucking everyone dry, and you'd all be better off without me."

I want to give him a clever answer, but I can't think of one.

"Stop fighting me and stop feeding me," he says softly. "Just let me die like I was supposed to."

"Don't tempt me," I reply.

He's thoughtful and quiet, as if I've just said something important. I watch him cautiously for a moment and then remember to feed the chickens. I collect grain. I usually feed the chickens at the door so Phanuel has something to watch, and as I stand in the doorway, he says: "Tabi, I don't expect you to help me. Why should you? You don't owe me anything. But what if I give you something in return, like a reward for helping me?"

I don't really understand what he means, but I'm interested. "Like what?"

"You know they made a blood oath after what happened in the forest." I realize he's talking about the Hand. "They swore never to speak of what happened, and you know what they're like; they'll never break that oath." I put the sack of grain down and step back inside. "But I didn't make any blood oath," he continues. "I've never promised to keep it a secret, and I was there. I know more than anyone else about what really happened."

I fling one last handful of grain as far as I can and the chickens

Chris Aslan

scatter after it. Then I come inside and kneel beside him. "Please, tell me," I whisper, almost holding my breath for fear that he might change his mind.

Phanuel smiles. He knows he has me. "I'll tell you everything," he says, "I promise. But first you have to help me. There's something I need. Something you have to give me." He pauses, trying to find the right words. "We both know that I'm dying slowly; too slowly. I have sores, my muscles have disappeared, my arms and legs are useless, even my wife-maker..." His voice starts to wobble, so he pauses to steady it. "I'm a living corpse, but with no peace, no rest. And yes, I've stopped eating so the end comes quicker. But it will still take too long. So I just need you to do this one thing for me, and then I can tell you everything you need to know."

I nod, and then he tells me what I must do.

I know this will work out better if I don't think about it and just do it. Pausing to think will be as useful as pausing before a series of rocks across a fast-flowing stream. That moment when you start trying to calculate the best route over and then start to think about what will happen if you slip. No; better to just run at it and trust my feet to be nimble.

So I leave Phanuel unattended, making the most of my parents' absence. Wearing my boots and shawl, I trudge through the snow down to the main square. I don't let myself think about what I'm about to do, only how I'm to do it. I curse under my breath when I see Sabba, who is helping one of his neighbours chop firewood.

He waves and calls, "What are you doing out?"

"You mean why am I not still chained to my brother?" I say, and his grin fades.

"No, that's not —"

"Amma has me running an errand for Shemayah," I lie, "so I probably shouldn't keep her waiting."

He smiles nervously, relieved to see me go. I head toward Shemayah's house. What I'm about to do is made more difficult

81

by the presence of snow and the tracks I might leave. I enter through the gate, looking purposeful so as not to arouse Sabba's suspicion or anyone else's in the square who might be watching. Then I turn toward their inner room but make it look as if I've just remembered that I need to use their unclean place, and I follow the path cut into the snow that leads there. I glance around and no one is watching, so I wade through the snowdrifts behind the house to where Yohannah has her medicinal storeroom. I'm leaving a trail, having to hitch my tunic up, with the snow unpleasantly cold against my legs, but that can't be helped.

The door is wedged shut with snow, so there's nothing for it but to shovel it aside with my hands, trying to ignore the biting cold. Finally, there's enough space for me to squeeze my way inside. I haven't been in here before and, once my eyes have adjusted to the gloom, I take a look around. Sacks hang on hooks from the walls, and there are shelves full of clay jars, bulging pouches, and bowls of various powders. Hanging from the ceiling are all manner of dried bundles of mountain herbs. Although my breath fogs the air, the room smells of summer, and I close my eyes for a moment and inhale. Then I try to think where Yohannah would put what I'm looking for.

I scan the shelves but then I notice a few sacks and smaller pouches in the corner on the ground. Why would they be left there and not hung up away from rats and mice like everything else? I undo a couple of sacks and then try the smaller pouches, and I find what I've been looking for. In the forest where they grow, they gleam, dark and inviting, and every child is shown them and reminded of what happened to the first man and woman when they ate what they shouldn't. The berries are shrivelled and dusty now, but still just as potent – just as deadly.

I know about these berries because I was with Sholum spinning wool when Shelamzion began to moan in pain three winters ago and then started to bleed. Sholum was terrified and left me to stay with her mother while she ran off to call Yohannah. I remember

Chris Aslan

Shelamzion clutching my hand as she became feverish and the bleeding wouldn't stop.

"Has someone put the eye on me?" she wailed. "Who would do this to a woman with just one child and a daughter at that?"

She became delirious and shouted accusations at the empty room that someone had put these berries in her tea. It's true. I'd heard from Yohannah that one berry boiled in a large pot, from which a few sips might be taken by a woman when her baby wouldn't come, could bring on labour, but any more than that would lead to miscarriage, and a handful of berries boiled would create a potent and deadly poison.

It's a handful I grab, and I place them in the pocket of my tunic. A tea made from these would probably be enough to kill our whole family. I return the way I've come, wondering if I should cover my tracks, but the sky is overcast and more snow seems likely. I'm just emerging from beside the unclean place when I almost collide with Shemayah. He looks at me, puzzled.

"I was just about to use your..." I gesture at the unclean place, not wanting to say its name to our holy man. "But I can wait," I add.

"So can I," he says, looking a little amused. "That still doesn't explain what you're doing here."

"Oh yes, I'm sorry, I should explain why I'm here," I stammer, trying desperately to think of something. "I heard from the Hand that you wanted to teach them more about religion now that winter has come."

"Yes."

"Well, I thought that maybe you could do the lessons in our house instead of here or in the prayer house. That way Phanuel can be there as well. It would give him something to do."

Shemayah thinks for a moment. "Yes," he nods his head. "That would be good for him." He looks up and smiles, then flourishes his hand toward the unclean place. "Now, after you."

"No, I... I'll just wait until I get home," I say. "Can I tell Phanuel about the plan?"

He nods and I thank him and leave. Although it's cold, I can feel sweat spreading under my arms and I realize how fast my heart is beating from the encounter. But I'm pretty good at lying, as long as it's not to my mother. I nod briefly at Sabba as I pass him and then hurry home. I don't know how much time we'll have.

"Let me see them," says Phanuel once I'm back and have tended the fire and hung my sodden foot wrappings up to steam beside it. I show him the berries and he nods in satisfaction. "Put them to boil and while we're waiting I'll tell you everything you want to know," he says.

So I do.

"I can answer your specific questions," he continues, while I squat beside the fire, "or I can just start from the beginning and tell you what happened that way."

"Just start from the beginning."

He pauses, collecting his thoughts. "You know what was going on between us in the Hand when it came to Sholum. Everyone wanted her, like we've never wanted anything else. We knew it and she knew it. I think she was glad Amma wouldn't let you come to the forest that day. She didn't want any competition from you."

"From me?" I ask, bewildered.

Phanuel just shrugs. He can't move his shoulders, obviously, but somehow he conveys a shrug with just his eyebrows.

"So, all eyes were on Sholum. She said she was going to join us boys climbing trees. Normally we wouldn't have let her, and would have told her it was too dangerous, but instead we all offered to give her a hand. Ananias, Menahem, and Yair all offered to help her up one of the easier trees to climb. So I just laughed and said she'd never be able to climb like a boy. Of course, that was when she insisted that we climb the tallest tree together."

As he speaks I can see it in my mind's eye: Sholum wearing her least favourite tunic because it would inevitably get stained by walnut husks. Her hands are on her hips, eyes flashing with my brother's challenge.

"Go on," I say quietly.

"She was a better climber than I'd expected and once we'd got to the first branch, it got easier to find higher branches to pull ourselves up on. At one point I thought she would overtake me. But then I saw her look down and there was real fear in her eyes. 'You can always go back down,' I said to her, but of course she couldn't; she had to be better than us. We carried on climbing right to the top of the canopy where you get a really good view of the mountain. She loved it up there and seemed to forget where she was, stretching on tiptoe to see everything. 'Just don't look down,' I said, which was stupid, because that's exactly what she did, and then she got scared. 'It's all right, I've got you,' I said, and I put my arm around her waist."

He swallows and glances at me, and I can see he doesn't want to go on. I say nothing and the silence hangs there until he breaks it.

"I thought it was such a beautiful view, especially if you've never seen it before, and I didn't think she'd mind me having my hand around her waist. You know how she liked to flirt. I know I shouldn't have, but I pressed into her. It was nothing more than that, but she just turned on me. But you can't do that when you're up a tree. She yanked my arm away and was about to shout at me or something."

I realize I'm holding my breath, not wanting to interrupt him.

"And then she lost her balance and she screamed and I grabbed her." Phanuel looks straight up at the ceiling now, avoiding all eye contact, and I hear his voice catch. "But she thought I was grabbing her, you know, in a different way. But I wasn't, was I? I was just trying to save her. If she'd just let me, I think I could have." Sweat beads his brow, even though the room is cold. "She tried to bat my hand away, but as she toppled I managed to grab the back of her tunic. Her feet were still on the branch, but her hands were just flailing in the air. I tried to pull her back, even though I could hear that her tunic was choking her, and then she tried to turn around and her arm reached for me, but at the same time her feet slipped, and it all happened so suddenly, and I wasn't ready, and when she fell she yanked me off balance as well, even though I'd been holding onto the overhead branch. She wasn't even that heavy, it just caught me off guard. So, then I was dangling with one fist holding the branch and the other trying to pull her back, but she wouldn't stop thrashing around and I couldn't hold on to the branch any more, but I couldn't let go of her, could I? So we fell together. I managed to grab one of the branches on the way down but it just broke off in my hand. I could hear her scream and then it stopped when she hit one of the larger branches and all I remember is thinking I was going to die. And then I did, or I thought I had, but then I woke up when Menahem dragged me off Sholum's body, and he was crying and so were the others, but I just didn't feel anything and then everything went dark and the next thing I knew I was waking up in here."

Tears dampen my cheeks, but I'm not sobbing. I'm just trying to make sense of what happened. "So, all this happened because you just wanted to tell the Hand what it felt like to hold her. Do you realize what you've done?"

He sobs. "I don't know what to do." His voice is tremulous. "I think maybe all this is God punishing me for what I did. I never meant for this to happen. But it's all that happens, all the time, every day. All I do is lie here and watch over and over as she falls and I don't save her. What do I do?"

I say nothing. I don't know what to think or even how I feel, except that the ache I have for Sholum is almost physical.

"I think I'm ready for that tea now," he adds quietly. "I can't live like this. We need to do it before Amma gets back."

I'm trying to get rid of the sound in my mind of Sholum's scream being cut short as she hits that first branch, and the heavy sound she makes when she thuds to the ground, and then the thud, or maybe even crunch, when Phanuel lands on top of her.

"You know it's painful, don't you?" I say, my voice husky with emotion. "I mean, I know the poison's quick, but it's not *that* quick."

"It's not as slow as this: stuck in a living corpse. And it's what I deserve."

I have to agree that it probably would be a mercy. And then, when I think about it, I'm not so sure it is what he deserves. It seems too quick, too easy. And that's when I make up my mind. I get up and pour some of the poisoned tea into a small bowl. Just a few sips and he will begin to die. "It'll need to cool a bit before you drink it," I say, "and I don't want anyone else drinking the rest by mistake," I add, picking up the pot and taking it outside and then pouring the steaming contents into the snow. I then take the empty pot to the stream, breaking the ice forming at the sides, and submerge the pot so that all traces of poison are washed away.

"Tabi?" I hear Phanuel call out plaintively. He doesn't usually call out to me, even when he's just soiled himself. "Please, come back inside. Let's just finish this."

I return to him and carry the steaming bowl of berry poison over.

"I'm sorry I had to involve you," he says, "but what you're doing is a kindness. They won't know it was poison. They'll just think the fall finally killed me. They'll probably be too relieved to do much thinking. You're not breaking any commandments; it's just what Ubba would do if a sheep broke its leg or something."

"Are you sure about this?" I ask.

"Just give it to me," he snaps. "Of course I'm sure. How could anything be worse than living like this?"

"Yes," I say gently, "I think you're right," and then I take the bowl and I raise his head so he can see what I'm doing, and I place it carefully in his right hand.

He looks at me in confusion.

"There you go," I say evenly. "Ready, whenever you want it."

"I don't understand," he says.

"I've done what you asked. I've given you the berry tea, now the rest is up to you." I can hear the steel in my own voice.

"Stop playing around, Tabi. Just spoon it into my mouth," he growls.

"Would you stop fighting," we hear from outside.

It's Amma – she's back.

"Quick!" Phanuel hisses. "Just give it to me."

"You said it yourself, it's your fault," I hiss back. "*You* killed her. Why should you get the easy way out, eh? Living is going to be your punishment."

"I'm warning you," he threatens.

"Or you'll do what? Get up and hit me?"

Then I knock the tea over. It's probably scalded Phanuel's hand but he can't feel it. He starts screaming at me with impotent rage. I just smile back at him and take the bowl out of his limp hand.

"Can't I leave you two for a few hours without you fighting?" says Amma, silhouetted against the doorway. "What's going on?"

"I'm sorry," I say. "I just knocked over Phan's tea and now he's upset about it. I can be so clumsy sometimes."

Phanuel swears at me again, using disgusting language. Amma, quick on her feet, gives him a hard slap mid-sentence and glowers over him.

"All this fuss over some spilled tea? She's not the only one around here who keeps spilling things, but she's still the one who has to clean it all up! You cause enough trouble around here without using such foul language! You should be ashamed of yourself, you good-for-nothing, useless boy."

She says more, but I've already slipped my sodden boots on again and gone to wash the bowl and bring back the pot from the stream. I permit myself a tight smile of satisfaction; not just because Amma is actually defending me, which has to be a first, but because Phanuel is getting punished. Now each new day

Chris Aslan

will be his punishment for what he did. Each long and lonely day.

I'm not sure if it's the feeling of justice or of revenge, but I haven't felt this good in ages.

Chapter Five

"Good," I say gently, but I'm not being gentle. I force the soup spoon between his clenched teeth, clamping his head between my knees so he can't toss from side to side. His gums are bleeding from where the spoon rammed into them a moment ago.

"Come on, Phanuel, don't be difficult," says Amma from the other side of the room, where she's cradling Helkias in her arms. She barely looks up, smiling down at her baby.

"Good," I say again, as if talking to a baby, and he looks up at me with such utter hatred that I almost start laughing.

Something has changed in me since that moment last week when I almost killed my brother and then realized his punishment must be to live. I've realized that if he lives it will cost me. I still have to clean up after him and nothing dries properly, even on sunny days. The constant dampness around Phanuel's waist has made his skin grey and wrinkled, as if he's spent all day in the lake. Not that he'll be doing that again. I can handle the cost, but I'm not going to stop living just because he has.

"He's finished," I say to Amma, letting his head fall back onto the pillow with a thud. "I'm going to Auntie Shelamzion's."

Amma purses her lips and just grunts. "I want you cooking supper, though," she calls after me as I leave.

This is also new. The day after the poison incident, I force-fed Phanuel at midday, ate, then prepared to go out.

"And where do you think you're going?" Amma demanded.

"I'm going to Auntie's house to continue my spinning," I replied. There was no threat to my voice, but there was a certainty that none of us were used to.

"Are you, now? And what about me? Am I supposed to look after both of them alone?"

"That's up to you," I said. "Phan isn't a baby. He doesn't need constant supervision. I'll be back in time to feed and change him this evening."

Amma was at a loss for a moment. "You can't just leave him here," she said finally.

"He was the one who fell out of the tree. I'm not paying for his mistakes any more," I replied.

Amma seemed to know better than to push me on this. She watched as I picked up my drop spindle, put on my boots at the threshold, and waded through the snow to our storeroom behind the house to collect more lambswool.

For the past week, I've kept Phanuel relatively clean and fed, but rushed through my chores so I can spend the afternoons with my auntie, particularly as Hanan was away until last night, selling chests in the lowlands.

"Let me show you what he brought back for me," says Shelamzion as we greet at the gate with a kiss. She takes off her new shawl and lifts it into the air, letting it waft slowly around my shoulders.

I breathe out in wonder.

"I know," she says, eyes shining. "It's so light and airy, yet it still feels so warm."

"What's it made from?" I ask, running my fingers through the delicate lacy pattern.

"Mohair. No different from the mohair you comb from your own goats."

"But how can they get enough strength in the yarn? This shawl is so fine."

"I don't know how they do it, but it's clearly possible."

"Auntie, who's 'they'?"

"Hanan bought this in Blood City, but the shawl actually comes from a village less than a day from us, further along the mountain range. How much do you think it cost?"

I shrug. I only know the price of lentils and beans. She tells me and my jaw drops. "For this?" I hold up the shawl. "But isn't that more than you charge for a whole wedding-felt rug?"

"I know," she says. "I have a very kind husband. Think about it, Tabita. People will pay good coin for something they value. Take our village. We're known for our apples down in the lowlands, and people spend extra on them because they're so crisp and full of juice. And now we're getting known for our wooden chests, too. Hanan sold four to just one family and came back with orders for more."

"Four?" I say sceptically. "Who could afford four chests?"

"I don't think you realize just how wealthy those lowlanders are, Tabi. They have servants to do everything for them. They have fountains! Do you even know what a fountain is? And their baths! Rooms filled with hot water to wallow in and never feel dirty again."

"I thought Phan was lying about them," I mutter to myself.

"They'll buy the best of whatever is available," she goes on. "If we could start making shawls like this, well, we could have fountains and slaves as well!"

"Really?"

"Well, maybe not fountains and slaves, but I think we would have a chance of making good coin."

I notice how she says "we", and I instinctively try to fight back the sense of hope and excitement that starts bubbling up in me, because I don't want to be disappointed. "Would you stop making your bridal felts?"

"Of course I would," she says. "Just think how much wool I use for one felt rug, plus all the plants I have to harvest for the dyes, and the other dyes, like indigo, I have to order from the lowlands. Or, we can learn how to make one of these." She takes the shawl and lifts it up in the air and it almost seems to float. The yarn on my spindle looks so coarse by comparison.

I take the shawl and run my fingers lightly over it and then hold up one of the gauzy threads to check that it's two-ply.

"If I spin it this thin the yarn will just snap. The spindle is too heavy for it," I say.

"Yes, I was thinking about that." Then, with a girlish grin on her face, she says, "If only I knew someone good with wood who could make us a lighter one."

Uncle Hanan works on a smaller, more delicate prototype, still rough around the edges. It looks like a child's toy, not a real tool. While he's doing that, Shelamzion raids her stores for soft mohair, combed from yearling kids in the spring before they started moulting. We card it with our fingers, picking out stray bits of twig or grass.

Uncle Hanan and Ananias find us and present me with the prototype spinner. I twist some lambswool until I have enough to wrap around the spindle, then I make a twist around the cleft at the top and give the spindle a decent spin, feeding out newly wound yarn as the spindle rotates and drops. I nod my head at my uncle, impressed that this little spindle spins true with a good centre.

"It's not finished yet," says Ananias, who has been watching my progress with Hanan. He takes the spindle and smooths down the wood so the yarn won't get snagged on it.

"I can smooth it down better and decorate it if you can wait until tomorrow," he says shyly.

"Thanks," I say, "but it's good enough as it is. And anyway, I don't want to wait until tomorrow."

The men leave us, and while Shelamzion focuses on cleaning and carding the mohair, I sit outside and spin. The light is golden as the sun dips. I know I'm supposed to be at home cooking but I'm determined to produce a small ball of yarn before I go. At first I spin the yarn much thicker than I'd like, twirling the spindle as I feed and twist. I start feeding less wool through my fingers and the yarn is soon much thinner. It snaps but I reattach it and try again. I get several more snaps, but I've gauged the maximum fineness this spindle can produce and focus on keeping my yarn to the same uniform thinness. I'm frowning in concentration and glance up to see Shelamzion grinning.

"Do you want to try?" I ask. "This spindle's really good."

"I think I'll leave the spinning to you," she says. "You have such nimble fingers. I'll be responsible for the dyeing. Also, this shawl isn't knitted. They use a hook for making it. I need to find out how."

"Could you visit the village that makes them?" I ask. "You said it's only a day's travel."

"Not without Hanan, and he's too busy with the Blood City order. Anyway, no village is going to give away their craft secrets."

"So what are we going to do?"

"Well, you're going to go home before you get into trouble with that sister of mine. Let me worry about the rest."

I leave the spindle with her and promise to come back tomorrow. As I walk home I examine my fingers. *Nimble is what she called them*, I think to myself and smile. When I get through the gate I'm surprised to see so many pairs of boots on the threshold. The door is closed, and inside Amma or someone has lit several lamps – certainly more than we usually use. The Hand are all there, including Ananias, who is seated beside Phanuel. They're all listening to Elder Shemayah, who is holding a scroll and is in the middle of explaining something. Even Ubba is home, and he always seems to find some reason to be tending the sheep or to simply be elsewhere.

I catch Amma's eye and she manages to convey with just one look that I need to get a move on and start preparing supper. I realize I'll make too much noise if I use our inside kitchen so I put a knife, some lentils, and vegetables into a pot and head outside to the kitchen there. While the vegetables boil, I scoop some spelt and barley out of hanging sacks and feed handfuls into the millstone and grind them. Last winter I could only manage the millstone using both hands and with great effort. Now, it doesn't seem so difficult. As I squat there by the millstone, I'm also aware that when my knees press against my chest, they're more cushioned than they used to be. I pause and feel my breasts and then smooth my tunic down over them. I'm not nearly as flat as I used to be. I really am becoming a woman. I wish Sholum were here so I could show her. It occurs to me, for the first time, that perhaps Sholum wouldn't be as happy about this as I'd like to think. In fact, I can imagine her belittling me, wanting to keep me firmly in her shadow and seeing me no longer as a beloved friend but as a potential competitor. I shake my head angrily, as if to dislodge such a disloyal thought.

I make a second fire, and when the water's boiled I add dried mountain herbs and bring in a large common tea bowl for the Hand to share, and a smaller one for our holy man.

"Thank you, Tabi," he says, cupping the bowl gratefully. "I think we're finished for today. You all know what I want you to memorize by next week."

They nod, even Phanuel. Although he's lying down and the others sit cross-legged on a warm bridal felt, he doesn't look that different from them. I haven't seen him this engaged in anything since the accident.

"How was the spindle?" Ananias asks me as I ladle out a bowl of tea for him.

"Really good, actually," I say. "Thanks for your help with it."

"What's this?" Amma enquires from her spot on the other side of the room, where she is rocking Helkias.

"I'm just trying out a new spindle," I explain. "We're trying to spin a thinner yarn for these shawls we want to make –"

I stop because Helkias makes a squalling sound, even though he's still half asleep, and Amma is distracted, shushing him and rocking him back to sleep again. I go outside to stir the stew and make flatbread with the milled flour, on a rock I've left in the embers to heat up.

The guests finish their tea and are keen to return home before it gets much darker. I expect to have my nightly battle to feed Phanuel, but he doesn't put up a fight at all.

"Has my cooking suddenly improved?" I ask under my breath as he lets me ladle the stew down.

Once I've finished, he announces: "The problem with our village is that we've neglected our religion. We're all too busy with work to think about God."

"Yes, I can see how that's a problem for you," I say sarcastically, as my brother gives himself airs after just one lesson with our holy man.

He ignores me and continues. "We need to know the Law. It shouldn't just be written on scrolls; it should be written on our hearts."

"Well, I'm glad it's given you something to do," says Amma. "Shemayah tells me it was Tabi's suggestion to host the lessons at our house so you could join in."

Phanuel looks at me in surprise and I just shrug.

Before we sleep, Phanuel soils himself, so I rekindle the fire to boil water and realize I'll have to rinse the filthy padded cloth in the stream at night, which always leaves me spooked at every creak or rustle, which in my mind must be wolves.

"Could you wash this out, too?" Amma asks, changing Helkias into clean swaddling.

By the time I come back in, I'm shivering and my hands are

clawed from the icy stream-water. I rub them and feel hot needles all over as they get used to the relative warmth of our inner room: a room that smells of Phanuel's leakages, unwashed bodies, Amma's milk, and lentil stew.

"Good night, Tabi," Phanuel whispers as I lie down near him. I don't say anything; I just blow out the lamp.

We fall into a rhythm. Amma spends her mornings with Sholum. Not my Sholum, obviously, but the woman further down our street who has a newborn girl. She usually naps with Helkias in the afternoons at home with Phanuel. Ubba is barely around. He's taken to playing dice with the other old men in the square, although Amma has forbidden him to gamble. I've noticed how uncomfortable Ubba is around Phanuel now. They barely communicate, and when Phanuel asks him a question Ubba can never bring himself to look Phanuel in the eye.

Our holy man visits with the Hand every week, and they discuss the Law and memorize scrolls. Phanuel is the best at memorization – with Sabba's help in holding the scroll – but that's probably because he has nothing else to do. I only understand a few words in our holy language, although I've memorized some of the prayers we're all supposed to know. Phanuel asks Shemayah if he'll come more often to teach him more of the holy tongue. Shemayah says he will, but only until the spring rains come, and then he'll have to work on his land.

I ask Amma to buy more padded linen as I can't keep up with Phanuel's bowel movements and there's never enough time for the pads to dry out before they need to be reused. I don't even bother washing our own clothes, which probably smell, but who'd notice when Helkias and Phanuel between them ensure that whenever anyone visits they sit as close to the open door as possible, no matter how cold it is outside?

My hands crack and bleed from the time they spend submerged in icy water. Unbidden, Amma visits Yohannah for a balm of spiced olive oil and beeswax. She must appreciate just how hard I'm working. I start using Yohannah's balm on Phanuel, too, because his skin is getting really bad from being constantly cold and damp. After the first time, I scold myself for taking care of him, reminding myself that he should suffer, but in the end I decide he's already suffering enough without his skin needing to fester.

I manage to visit Aunt Shelamzion briefly each afternoon. I've now spun several skeins of soft two-ply yarn and they're almost as fine as the spun mohair that makes Shelamzion's shawl so light and warm. Pleased with my progress, Aunt Shelamzion takes out her heavy mortar and pestle one day and we take turns pounding madder root and pomegranate rind to powder, and then she soaks the skeins in a bath of spice stone so they'll take the dye. We submerge the whitest skeins in a warm bath of pomegranate rind, and when they emerge, dripping, the skeins are a deep golden colour. We hang the skeins to dry and the drips sink through the snow, colouring it yellow just like wolf urine.

"I talked with the traders last market day." Shelamzion pours me a bowl of tea as we sit outside in the afternoon sun. "And I'm one step closer to learning how to actually make the shawls. I've found out the name of the village they're from. There's a street in Blood City where some of them live. So, when Hanan completes his order and takes the chests there, I'm going to join him and Ananias to see if I can pay someone there to teach me how to use the hook."

"I thought you said the villagers would never reveal their secrets."

"Well, not in the village itself, but people change when they move to the city. For the right price, I'll find someone."

I'm struck by this. I don't know why, but it never occurred to me that people could move and live somewhere other than where they were born – like when you dig up a sapling with its roots and move it to a new place to grow. I know several women who were married into our village from one of the neighbouring villages, but I don't know of anyone who has left the mountainside and gone down to the lowlands. Where would you go, and who would look after you if you didn't know anyone? If I was in need of a meal or a bed for the night there isn't a single house in our village that would turn me away. We're like a family of families. We don't always get on, but that's families for you.

"When will you go?" I ask my aunt.

"With Ananias helping now, Hanan thinks one moon will be enough."

"Can I come?" I blurt the question out without even thinking.

"I'm not sure your mother can spare you," she says. "And also I have a request. Would you be willing to stay here to feed the chickens and make sure we don't return to a room full of wolves and robbers?"

"On my own? I don't think Amma will let me."

"I'll talk to her," says Shelamzion.

I make sure I'm out of the house and at the stream washing Phanuel's soiled linen when Shelamzion comes to visit the next day. I hear Amma objecting, stating that I'm needed here, and Shelamzion countering each of her excuses. I deliberately loiter, not wanting to get caught up in the argument, but eventually the linen is hanging on tree branches where it will become less damp, if not dry.

I come nearer the house to listen for the sound of argument, but when I step over the threshold Amma and Shelamzion are drinking tea amicably together. I'm confused for a moment until I see the triumphant look in Amma's eye and note the new shawl she's wearing: a shawl that would have cost more than the large felt bridal rug they are both sitting on. They gossip together for a while and then I walk Aunt Shelamzion to our gate.

"The shawl?" is all I say.

Shelamzion shrugs. "Let her have something nice. That

husband of hers will never give her anything more than sons and sheep. Besides, it'll do you good to have a break from all this and let your hands heal. I'd rather she had the shawl than return to find it taken by a thieving neighbour."

But I know she is doing this for me. "I'll make sure everything is cleaner than spring," I say.

Then I hug her, which I wasn't expecting to do, and she wasn't ready for it, and it makes her eyes brim with tears. She turns abruptly to go home, reminding me in an unsteady voice to come at first light tomorrow.

I don't visit my aunt that afternoon, so I'm at home when the Hand arrive for their weekly lesson. Although the snow is still heavy on the ground, it's melted from the tree branches. I suggest that they lift Phanuel and carry him outside.

"No," he protests. "I don't want people to see me."

"What people?" Amma asks. "There's no one around apart from the same people who see you here now."

"And this room could do with a good clean," I add, a truth no one can argue with.

Phanuel squints against the sunlight as two boys lift him at one end and two lift him at the other. His padded linen slips off and they all look away in embarrassment.

"Really? How many times have you gone swimming together?" I mutter, dragging a couple of sheepskins behind them and trying to lay them out under my brother, then covering him with the padded linen and some blankets. He looks deathly pale in the sunlight and is still painfully thin.

"Can you help me roll him onto his side?" I ask Menahem. "If he just lies on his back he gets bedsores."

"Are we ready now?" Shemayah asks impatiently. Then he begins his recitation.

Amma joins them outside, nursing Helkias, while I start dragging everything out of the inner room and then attack the floor with a broom.

Chris Aslan

By the time the Hand are ready to leave, I'm more or less done, and they help carry our chests back inside and then Phanuel. He's lighter than the chests.

"I'll see you tomorrow," says Sabba as he leaves.

Although the Hand still come for the weekly lesson, the others are too busy or disinterested to memorize scrolls or to try to learn our holy language. But Sabba has really taken to it and it's become something he and Phanuel do together. Sabba comes a couple of times a week before supper and lies beside Phanuel, holding a lamp aloft with one hand and tracing his finger along each line of the scroll with the other.

I see the Hand to our gate and wish Ananias a safe trip. I'd noticed he hadn't talked about the trip much, even though none of the boys have ever left this mountain. I think he was worried Phanuel might be jealous.

"I wish I could come to Blood City, too," I say. "You'll have to tell me all about it."

"I will," he says, and then he reddens and turns to catch up with the others. I go to collect wood from the pile, wondering why I'm smiling.

Inside, Amma is chopping carrots for the evening meal. "I'm still not sure about you being away for a whole week. How am I meant to cope with both boys?"

"Well, I can let Aunt Shelamzion know tomorrow morning when I return your shawl," I say, which silences her for a while.

"The house won't feel the same without you," she says quietly as she squats beside the pot, stirring it.

I come and squat beside her, picking up a carrot and knife and helping her chop. "I'll still come in the mornings to change Phan and wash his linen," I say, and she looks up and smiles at me, and I realize she doesn't smile very often and it makes her look beautiful.

The next morning Ubba comes with me to Uncle Hanan's house, leading our donkey, which they're borrowing for the trip.

Mosaic

Ananias and Hanan are already loading chests onto donkeys and strapping them securely and Ubba goes to help them. The whole journey will take two days there and two days back, with at least one night in Blood City itself. "If we could get camels up here I could build the larger-sized wedding chests, which are what people really want," Hanan explains to Ubba as they work.

Ubba comments to me that he thinks the hardest part will be the start of the journey and getting through the snowdrifts.

"None of the Hand have ever been this far away before," I say to Ananias.

He smiles nervously at me. "I'm excited, but I don't really know what to expect."

"I'm sure Phan will love to hear all about it when you're back."

Shelamzion comes out of the house carrying a cloth bundle, which she fits into one of the donkey saddlebags. She smiles when she sees me. "I think that's everything," she says. "I've left a chicken hanging in the kitchen to drain. She'll still need plucking."

"What, a whole chicken just for me?"

"We'll be gone for almost a week. You can make it last."

Shemayah arrives just as the caravan is ready to go. He gives Hanan a pouch of coins and an order for more scrolls, then he prays a blessing for the trip and leaves with them, saying he'll walk them out of the village. I watch from the doorway. After they're gone the house feels oddly quiet. I love it. I breathe in and, apart from the tang of chicken blood in the air, the house smells so clean and fresh. I take out my spindle, sit myself down, and lose myself in spinning. There'll be plenty of time for plucking the chicken later.

When later comes, and after the chicken is plucked and cut up and frying in the butter my aunt has generously left me, and after I've fed the other chickens, and done some cleaning of the house, I find myself in an unusual state of boredom. Of course, I could do some more spinning, and now the afternoon sun is

Chris Aslan

perfectly angled to set myself outside on the bench. But it would be more enjoyable to spin with someone else and have someone to talk to. I feel a pang of sadness as I imagine how much fun we'd be having together if Sholum were here. I shouldn't have let myself think about her because now I can't stop, and then I'm torn between visiting her grave for the first time – if I can even find it in all this snow – or rooting through Shelamzion's wedding chests to see what else she's kept of Sholum's.

I remember how this time last year Sholum and I spun together, chattering away or working in companionable silence. It strikes me how permanent her absence is. She'll never be there to spin or laugh with again. She'll still be dead tomorrow and next year and when Phanuel dies, which might even be before then. She'll be dead when I get married and when I'm old and when one winter I finally don't wake up. This is what I think about, and I feel sad and I cry. And then, as I think about how permanent this is and that the problem with dead people is that they stay dead, I realize what I have to do: I have to keep on living.

So I wrap my shawl around me and head out of the house. I trudge through the snow, which is soft and wet in the afternoon sun. It's not long before I'm outside Yulia's house, where she and her mother-in-law are also making the most of the setting sun, sitting outside, muffled in robes and tunics, mending. Yulia holds the needle close to her face as they sit together, and her mother-in-law says something that makes Yulia laugh. This fruitless tree, which can't see properly and yet laughs so readily; I want her to be my friend. She glances up and sees that someone is there. As she squints, her mother-in-law says, "It's Drusilla's daughter," and a smile breaks over Yulia's face again. She gets up to greet me and I feel awkward and happy, and as if I want to cry, all at the same time.

"I brought my spindle with me," I explain. "I'm looking after my aunt's house while they're away and, well, I'm the only one there, so I thought –"

"Of course you don't want to be on your own," says Yulia,

taking my hand and sitting me down beside her mother-in-law. "I'll make some tea," she says. Then she collects some water from a channel that runs beside their house and sets it to boil.

And so I spend an enjoyable late afternoon in the company of these two women. They want to hear all about the trip to Blood City, and both speak highly of Ananias. His family is poor, even by our standards, and he has two older brothers, so he won't inherit much, and they agree that it's a good thing for him to learn a trade and make something of himself.

"Hanan will train him well, and you can be sure that young man will be looking for a wife for himself soon enough," says the mother-in-law, looking at me pointedly.

"What?" I laugh in embarrassment, which makes her cackle.

I'm sure this woman, whose name I forget but am too embarrassed to ask, must long for grandchildren, but she doesn't seem to blame or shame Yulia. I remember the times I've simply nodded when a neighbour or some other village gossip has made fun of Yulia or speculated as to what sin must have led to her punishment of barrenness. I promise myself I'll never let a comment like that pass again.

Looking up at the slanting sun, I realize I've got chickens to feed as well as one to eat. "I should be getting back. My aunt's convinced that wolves and robbers are just waiting for their moment to strike."

"Well, don't let us keep you," says the mother-in-law.

"I hope we'll see you again," adds Yulia.

I've said goodbye and am out of the gate before it occurs to me, and I turn back. "Auntie Shelamzion left me a whole chicken, which I can't possibly eat by myself. Would you like to come for midday meal tomorrow?"

They confer briefly and then agree.

The inner room feels so large that first night, especially with only me in it. I light more lamps than Amma would approve of, but still probably fewer than Shelamzion usually does. I scare myself remembering all the stories I've heard about unclean spirits lurking in the dark or prowling outside like wolves, looking for a place they can make a home inside the soul of someone. Then I scold myself for not enjoying the smell of cedar wood and chicken broth, as well as the peace, with no snoring from Ubba or complaining from Amma, or crying from Helkias, or stuff I'm going to have to clean up from Phanuel, or my parents bickering or making parent noises when they think we're asleep. I wonder how the journey is going for the others, and whether Aunt Shelamzion will discover the secret of the hook. I dream of shawls.

The next morning after my chores, I visit home. Amma is in a foul mood and complains about everything. Her payment of the shawl has been completely forgotten and she now considers her indulgence in letting me sit around her sister's house all day as the height of folly. I ignore her, clean up Phanuel, and carry the dirty linen outside to wash. Sabba comes by and I hear them both reciting the Law together. They've learned several chapters off by heart and are slowly and painfully trying to read a fourth.

"Why can't you learn some of the songs or stories in our own language?" I ask as I come inside.

Phanuel looks at Sabba and rolls his eyes. "That's just the kind of thing uneducated people say," he states scornfully.

This actually makes me smile, because for a moment he sounds like the old Phanuel.

Sabba notices too and says in a simpering voice, "Yes, Phan, read us a story," and they both laugh.

I just tug Phanuel's blankets back to put the almost-dry clean linen in place between his legs. "Would you like to help?" I ask Sabba, who decides hurriedly that it's time he went and helped his father with the new wall they're building for one of the terraces in their orchard.

Once I'm done I go outside to wash my hands again, then head off without saying goodbye in case Amma tries to find a reason to keep me back. Back at Shelamzion's I knead some spelt and barley and bake flat loaves to eat with the chicken broth, which I heat up, filling the inner room with a wonderful smell.

Yulia and her mother-in-law arrive and the mother-in-law says my name in greeting. Then I blush and confess that I can't remember hers, and we laugh as I welcome Auntie Rohul into the house. We break bread together. Perhaps it's the chicken that puts us all in a good mood, but we seem to laugh far too much as we gossip about which women in the village have good relationships with their mothers-in-law and which relationships are particularly strained.

After we've finished, Rohul belches her appreciation and then asks if it would be all right if she took a quick nap. I take my spindle and mohair outside with Yulia.

"I can card the mohair for you, if you like," says Yulia as I take a clump of carded mohair in my hands and begin feeding it to my spindle. Then she asks shyly, "Would you mind if I try your new spindle? I've never seen yarn so fine."

"Of course," I say, and offer her a few tips. At first, the yarn keeps snapping, sending the spindle spinning into the snow. But she eventually gets the hang of it.

"Almost, but yours is still finer," Yulia points out.

I pretend to disagree, but feel undeniably pleased with myself. "When Uncle Hanan gets back, I'm sure he could make you a spindle like this, and then you could join us," I say.

I should have checked with my aunt before making such rash invitations, but as soon as I say it, I long for it to be true.

She spins and I card, and I tell her all about the shawl.

The week passes quickly, mainly because Yulia and Auntie Rohul come to visit each afternoon. I go home every morning to look after Phanuel. He's almost memorized a whole scroll and is eager to recite it as I mop him up, letting the words wash over me, as I do Amma's constant complaints. It snows in the middle of the week, which gives me extra work at Shelamzion's, cutting paths from the gate to the house and then to the workshop, the woodpile, and the unclean place. The snow is wet, though, and the next morning in the sun you can hear meltwater gurgling beneath the snow. Looking at the colourful bases of the trees I can see that the sap is rising. Spring is almost upon us.

On the day of their planned return I sweep the house and take all the felts and sheepskins outside to beat the dust out of them, then rub them with snow to clean them. I bake bread with Shelamzion's best wheat flour, which she buys ready milled – a luxury undreamed of in our household – and make a large pot of lentil stew, nipping out every now and then to see if they're coming up the path toward the gate.

It gets dark, so I light lamps and place one in a niche outside, where it flickers but doesn't gutter, hoping it will light their way home. I finally give in to my growling stomach and eat alone. By the time I've finished, it's completely dark outside and there's still no sign of them. I start to worry about robbers and wolves. There are probably other dangers down in the lowlands that I don't even know about.

I lie on my mat, lamps still lit, blanket around my neck, worrying but gradually growing drowsy. I can't have been asleep long when I feel a gust of cold air, which makes the lamplight dance. I sit bolt upright and see Uncle Hanan smiling, with Auntie Shelamzion behind him.

"We thought we'd be back by nightfall but the roads are so muddy with all the rains," says my uncle.

"No, no, go back to sleep," my aunt protests as I leap up to rekindle the kitchen fire.

"Sleep?" I say. "How could I sleep without hearing all your adventures?"

"Have you had any adventures here? No bandits or wolves?" she asks, laughter in her voice.

"The most exciting news from here is that Phan can now recite a whole scroll," I say. "But anyway, tell me everything." I catch Shelamzion's eye. "Were you successful?"

She says nothing and just smiles playfully, reaching into her tunic pocket and drawing out two knitting needles. I look crestfallen until she flourishes them and I realize they're shorter than needles and each one has a hook at the end. "I think we may be in business," she says.

I can't help it; I shriek, and then hug her.

"We've had a long day of travel, so I might leave some of the details until tomorrow," says Shelamzion, yawning, which sets her husband to yawning as well. I prepare the food and some mint tea, while she explains how she left the men on the street where wooden items are sold, and made her way to the street selling prayer shawls and from there found a few stalls selling women's shawls.

"If we'd left it another few weeks, there'd have been no winter shawls for sale, as spring has started down there and they're already selling bowls of fresh clover on every street corner. I just told the woman who I was, where I'd come from, and that if she could find someone to teach me the technique they use for those shawls I'd pay her, and sell her the ones we make for less than she currently pays to the other village. She dispatched her daughter to find someone and I spent the next day hook-knitting with an old woman who left her village as a young bride but can still remember how to do it."

"Hook-knitting," I echo, trying out the word for the first time.

"I showed her your yarn and we hook-knitted a shawl together from start to finish."

"Can I see it?" I ask.

"I let her keep it as part-payment for teaching me. She made no complaint about your yarn."

"Didn't she mind sharing her secrets?"

"No, she was actually happy to teach me. She said that women in the city are too busy to spin and knit, and she was just happy to meet someone who valued these skills."

"Hook-knitting," I say again. I can't help it.

"I didn't take any of the dyed yarn, so we can start with that tomorrow. I need to teach you while it's still fresh in my mind."

"Could you teach Yulia, too?" I ask.

"What, barren Yulia?" she says.

"She's just Yulia," I reply, "and she picked up spinning with the lighter spindle really quickly."

Shelamzion nods thoughtfully. "Yes, we'll need more women working with us," she says. "We can start with Yulia."

"I did plenty of spinning while you were away," I say, "but now you're back I might not be able to come over as much. Amma really wasn't happy with me neglecting Phan."

"Well," says Shelamzion, "we might have a solution for that as well."

Hanan catches her eye and adds, "We can only pass on what we've heard. We're not making any promises or anything."

"What?" I say. "What have you heard?"

"There's a holy man," Hanan explains. "He's one of us. Even as far off as Blood City he's all people are talking about. He's from the South, and right now he's travelling around the Great Lake."

I don't understand what this has to do with Phanuel.

"They say he can do things that no doctor can do, and that he teaches in a way no teacher can teach," says Shelamzion. "There was a man in the bazaar. We couldn't hear everything because there were too many people jostling and we couldn't get close, but he took his tunic off and kept showing his back to the crowd. He was saying the holy man had cured him of a hunched back."

"But you can't be cured of a hunchback," I say. "Remember Meir, the hunchback boy from the next village?"

"Exactly," says Hanan. "And there are so many tricksters in the city trying to sell potions that can cure anything, so I told Shelamzion and Ananias to ignore the man. But Ananias had got talking with someone else who swore that he lived on the same street as the hunchback, and that they used to laugh and make fun of him if he ever left his house."

"So we listened more, and the man speaking wasn't trying to sell anything. He just couldn't keep quiet," says Shelamzion, her eyes shining. "And then, before we knew it, we'd lost Ananias. It's impossible to find someone once they're lost in the bazaar. You can't imagine how many people there are all in one place. Just one street might have more people living on it than our whole village. Anyway, we finally spotted him. He was elbowing his way closer to the man, then he called out to the former hunchback and asked him if this holy man could cure someone who couldn't move. The man just shrugged and said that he cured anyone who came to him and didn't charge a single coin."

"That's why Ananias isn't here now. He went straight to your house to tell Phanuel," says Hanan.

"Imagine if he could cure Phanuel," says Shelamzion, clutching my hand. "Imagine!"

Chapter Six

Of course, I don't sleep after that. I just lie awake trying to think about everything I've heard. How can someone be cured of a hunchback? I remember Sholum once dared us to creep up on Meir, the hunchback boy, when we were by the lake. All the boys from their village were stripped and swimming. He sat on his own watching them. It wasn't as if he simply had a lump on his back; his whole body was strangely shaped and disproportioned as a result of it, and he rasped when he breathed. How can you cure something like that? Maybe they have better medicines down in the lowlands. We just have Yohannah's herbs. I think Meir died, although I can't remember when.

I don't just think about hunchbacks. I think about shawls, too. I never thought I'd be anything more than a girl, and maybe a wife. Is it possible that something I made could be sought after by people living in a big city far away? I try to imagine what it must be like to live far away. My problem is that I don't know what to believe, as Phanuel and the others were always telling me tales of the big city – not that they'd been – and laughed when I believed that there really were giant sea monsters, and then got upset if I didn't believe that most lowland houses of holy men had a ritual pool with running water to purify themselves before prayers. My mind keeps moving, but at some point I fall asleep.

The next morning we rise early. I'm about to head home, but Shelamzion is determined that we make a start on hooking our first shawl while she still remembers her lesson.

"What about Amma? She'll know you're back by now. She'll expect me to look after Phan."

Shelamzion arches an eyebrow. "It was a *very* expensive shawl," is all she says.

We sit in the morning sun, which already has heat in it. Around us the snow is retreating, leaving dripping, icy shapes behind. I soon lose myself in the intricacies of the hooking method. At first I'm a little clumsy, but once I understand the principles, it makes sense. The shawl feels as if it will unravel, as it doesn't have the tight density of something knitted, but I see how this enables the shawl to be so light and yet feel so warm.

"And if we slip a stitch here and do that with every other stitch, I think we can create a sort of border," I say.

"Who's teaching whom?" says my aunt with a wry smile. "I was about to explain that to you."

I don't even notice Amma's arrival until I hear her wheezing. Helkias is wrapped in an old shawl and being carried on her back. I brace myself as she marches over to us, expecting a barrage of abuse for not coming home, but instead she shunts me over without even greeting us so she can sit beside her sister. She hands me Helkias, then says, "Tell me everything about this hunchback."

They're still discussing it when Yulia and Rohul arrive at the gate. "May we come in?" they ask, and I reluctantly put down the hook and make tea. I wish my mother wasn't here so we could include Yulia in this first lesson. I'm sure Ananias could easily make a wooden hook for her, although I'm also wondering if a metal one wouldn't be stronger.

But they, too, are uninterested in the shawl. "We heard from Yair," says Rohul, sitting beside Amma, "and we wanted to hear from you, too. Is it true that this holy man can cure anyone and doesn't even charge for it?"

"Would he be able to –" Yulia starts, but then her voice catches and she stops.

"Can he cure barrenness?" says Rohul for her. "And eyes… is he able to cure bad eyes?"

"I don't know," says Shelamzion. "We only know what the hunchback told us."

"But you believed him?" says my mother.

"Why would he lie? He wasn't trying to sell anything."

"Yair said this holy man is a wanderer but that right now he's down by the Great Lake," says Rohul. "Do we know how much longer he'll be there? Or if he'll come to the North?"

"I'm sorry, I don't know anything more," says Shelamzion, getting up to pour the tea and escape.

"We have to get you to him soon," says Rohul. Then she turns to Amma. "Let Yulia go with Tabita and the Hand. She can't travel alone and Azariah must finish a new terrace wall before the spring rains come."

Amma just looks confused. "Tabita isn't going anywhere."

"But Yair told us, the Hand have decided. They're taking Phanuel to this holy man."

"You can't just make decisions without consulting me first," snaps Amma to Phanuel once we're back home. "Who do you children think you are? I am still your mother."

"But Amma, you heard Ananias. What if it's true? If there's even a tiny chance the holy man can cure me, then what is there to discuss?" Phanuel's eyes are shining. I haven't seen him this animated for a long time.

"And what am I supposed to do with Helkias? Don't you care that I'll be alone in the house?" she demands.

"You won't be alone. Ubba is still around," I point out.

She dismisses the thought of Ubba with a wave of her hand. "I don't see why Tabita needs to go."

"Yulia's husband won't let her travel alone with the Hand," I say. "You know how people talk. And I know the Hand. None of them will clean up Phan's messes. I have to go."

And I do. I've hardly had a chance to get used to the idea, but I already feel the thrill of adventure. I've never been off this mountain, and even if this holy man is just a hoax, I might never get the chance to travel to the Great Lake again.

"What do we even know about this holy man?" says Amma. "What if you're getting your hopes up for nothing?"

"You're right," says Phanuel, swallowing. "We know almost nothing. Maybe we'll have to pay him something. Ananias says he'll bring his share of the coins Uncle got from the wedding chests. And maybe the holy man can't help me." He looks up at us pitifully. "But Amma, we've got to try. What if he can? What if I could be cured?"

Amma stands with her hands on her hips, silent for a moment. Then she sighs, reaches up, and with a wince unclasps her nose ring. "Here," she says, putting it into my hand. "You'd better not lose it."

I just stare at her dumbly.

"What?" she says. "You don't really think this man will cure your brother for free? He's a man. They always want something."

"But this was your wedding gift," I stammer. It's the only thing of value my mother owns.

Amma shrugs. "Phanuel can work hard to buy me a new one when he's better," she says gruffly. "We'll have to ask your uncle if he can make some kind of pallet to carry you on," she adds. "And he'll have to be quick. Who knows when this holy man will move on or come to his senses and start charging a fortune?"

There are no secrets in our village. Soon everyone is talking about our plan. I head for Shelamzion's house, ready to ask my uncle to make a pallet and hoping to work on the new shawl while I'm there. On my way, one of our neighbours carrying a cloth bundle of steaming flatbreads stops and hands them to me. "For the journey," she says.

"Thank you, Auntie, but we still don't know when we'll be leaving."

"You leave tomorrow morning," she says. "Everyone knows."

I hurry on and discover Ananias and Hanan already at work on a pallet. There really are no secrets.

"I've also made a start on this," says Hanan, and pulls out a strong, slender cedar branch. It's been beautifully whittled and would already make a perfectly serviceable walking staff. "I want to make it special. I'll spend tonight carving it. You're to give it to the holy man. That's if he agrees to cure Phanuel, of course."

I find Shelamzion working on the shawl, sitting in the sun. The snow around her bench has completely melted now, exposing mud and dead grass.

"I've just heard we'll be leaving tomorrow," I explain, sitting down beside her. "I really want to work on this new shawl, but it'll have to wait."

My aunt looks up. "This could be good for us, Tabi. It's probably too hot down at the Great Lake to find anyone selling woollen shawls by now, but you can ask around for prices. I'll also give you some coins to buy dyes."

"I'm not sure we'll be able to bring them back. We're taking two donkeys, but with bedding and clothing and food, we'll all still be walking and the Hand will be carrying Phan."

"If this holy man can cure Phan, the boys can carry their own bags back and you can use a donkey to bring back the dyes," she says. "How can Phan argue with you after the way you've tended him all this time?"

The memory of me refusing Phanuel the poisoned tea pops

115

into my mind, but I try not to think about it and to focus on what my aunt is telling me.

She draws out a pouch from her tunic pocket and hands it to me. "There's enough in here for what we'll need but also for you to buy a new tunic for yourself and one for Phan. Make sure you look presentable when you meet the holy man. Don't let him look down on you because you're from the mountains."

"But Auntie, this is too much," I start.

"This isn't charity," she says. "Consider it your first wages for all the wool you've spun. Now, let me explain the ways of the lowlanders. First of all, we need to teach you to haggle."

After my lesson, I head to Yulia's. Several older women kneel on a felt rug they've dragged outside, facing south toward our Holy City. Their arms are raised as they pray for God to open Yulia's womb and sharpen her eyes. They may well be the same women who gossip about her, but perhaps their prayers will count for something. We arrange for her to bring her loaded donkey to our house before sunrise, then we'll all leave from there.

"Don't forget to take extra water-skins with you," says Rohul. "There are springs while you're on the mountain but after that you'll have to use wells, and it will already feel like summer down in the plains. Better to wear sandals. The snow won't be around for much longer."

We confer about food and what to wear, deciding on summer tunics, but with shawls for night-time and while we're still on the mountain. Back home I have a similar conversation with Amma and we load up the saddlebags with several changes of padded linen for Phanuel. I hope there'll be places to wash them along the way, and as for drying, if it truly is hot already down in the lowlands, the linen can be tied to the saddlebags to dry as we move.

That evening Hanan and Ananias come around with the pallet and we practise lifting Phanuel onto it. With four of us holding a handle each, Phanuel doesn't feel that heavy but the journey is going to take us three days, and I'm sure the Hand will be exhausted by the time we arrive at the Great Lake.

I'm tired, but I lie awake, full of excitement and worry for Yulia. Then my thoughts drift to Phanuel. I haven't really let myself think about how I feel toward my brother. I think back to what he told me about the accident. That's what it was: an accident. Phanuel was stupid, trying to impress the others, but he never meant for Sholum to get hurt. And she'd been stupid as well.

What if we're simply following a rumour that comes to nothing? I've been so concerned with what I've lost since the accident: my freedom and my best friend. But what would it be like to be Phanuel? I wonder if I should tell him that if this whole trip is a waste of time I'll make him that tea and grant him release from his torment.

I hear Phanuel whispering prayers under his breath. I wonder how he feels, suddenly granted hope but also terrified that this will all come to nothing. Then I wonder how I feel. A part of me has felt detached or just absent since Sholum died. I remember how I used to laugh and cry, but that feels as if it happened to someone else. Whenever I think of Sholum, my heart hardens again and I feel bitterness and rage toward Phanuel, even if it wasn't all his fault. So, I'm full of bitterness, but also pity. I want him to be cured, but I also wonder if he's been punished enough. I miss him, but I also hate him. If these were ingredients in a stew, all I know is that no one would want to eat it.

Almost the whole village turns up before sunrise to see us off. We're handed pouches of shelled walnuts, dates, raisins, boiled eggs, butter-dough flatbread, and more. There's debate over whether old Chuza should also join our group as he has a club foot. In the end he decides he'll slow us down and that he's too old and has lived all his life with it. Why make a long journey like this when he only has a few more winters in him?

Then Shemayah and Yohannah take turns to pray, as do the

117

old men from the village. They finish just as the sun begins to rise, turning the remaining snow orange.

"We should get going," says Sabba.

The rest of the Hand nod, eager to depart.

"Here, this is for you – just something extra," says Amma, pressing a coin brusquely into my hand and waving away any attempt at gratitude. "We'll be praying."

"Thank you, Amma," I say and kiss her on the cheek. I suddenly feel quite emotional. I don't know why as we won't be gone long, but still, to travel three days away from everything I know…

"Don't speak to anyone or believe anything they say. Those lowlanders are all conniving robbers," Amma states emphatically, despite having never left this mountain herself. "Look after your brother. And boys," she addresses the Hand, "look after my son." She's about to say more, but starts to sob.

Ubba puts an arm around her and looks uncomfortable.

Phanuel's face is tired and drawn. I don't think he slept much last night. He catches my eye and tries to smile. I'm caught off guard, as Phanuel seems to consider me an ally now.

I never realized how terrifying hope is. What if nothing comes of this?

The boys each take one of the handles and lift the pallet. I take the rope for our donkey and Yulia takes the rope for hers, then we're about to leave when a voice calls to us.

"Wait!" I recognize my uncle's voice. "Here," he says, breathless from running. "Here is the staff you're to give him. You can use it now to help you when the path is steep."

I take it from him and marvel at the vine and pomegranate motifs that wind and spiral up it. It's exquisite.

We're finally ready and set off, with the children and some of the adults following us down to our lake and the village limits. My feet are freezing in sandals, and the summer tunic doesn't feel warm enough. I consider running back to get my winter one, but there's a limit to what the donkeys can carry, so instead I draw my shawl closer around me and hope we'll warm up as we walk. We pass the next village and some of the people there stop what they're doing to stare at us. A woman dispatches her daughter to hand us a pouch of shelled walnut pieces and raisins. They've heard about our trip as well.

The path is stony and uneven. It's not a problem for the donkeys, which are used to navigating much worse. Yulia and I are fine, too, but it's harder for the Hand, and at one point Menahem trips and Phanuel almost comes sliding off the pallet, caught by Ananias at the last moment.

We walk in silence. I think we all need more time to think. Then Yair calls, "Tabita, I think you need to do something."

They lower the pallet and there is a spreading stain and smell. The others find reasons to busy themselves with the donkeys or look for a tree or rock to do their own business behind. I mop up, using snow to wash Phanuel as best I can, and as I'm putting clean linen on him, Phanuel says, "Yulia" – more as a warning than a greeting.

"Don't worry," says Yulia, coming up behind me. "You're just a blur. Here, give me the dirty linen. There's a stream over there."

I'm not used to having help. We drape the washed linen over her donkey, hoping it will dry, and then continue past a village where Amma's younger cousin got married a few years ago. It's the furthest away I've ever been. From now on everything is new for me. Then we pass another couple of villages where the Hand have been for weddings or circumcisions of distant relatives. We also pass the fork where Ananias turned off for Blood City. So, from now on the road is new to all of us. It's heading steadily downhill, and shaded by mature trees, which, even though they're not in leaf, shelters the path and means the snow hasn't melted much yet. It also means that our feet are still cold and wet, but at least it's less treacherous underfoot than spring mud.

We stop regularly for the boys to swap positions around the pallet and to eat handfuls of nuts and raisins. At midday we pause to eat the flatbread given me and goat's cheese made by Menahem and Yair's mother. We eat in a clearing, where there's only snow left in the shady crevices. Crocuses dot the ground, along with the first shoots of new grass. After we've eaten I pass around the bowl of Yohannah's salve. The boys gratefully smear it on their blistered hands. Yulia offers to carry a corner of the pallet for a while, but this affront to the Hand's honour is swiftly rebuffed.

We pass other people on the path and each time they want us to explain which village we're from and why we are carrying my brother on a pallet. Several villagers ask us to stop by on our way back because they have a neighbour or relative who needs curing, and they want to hear if the holy man is genuine. I'm also given several offers of money for the walking staff, but I explain that it's a gift for the holy man, and they know better than to ask twice.

When it's time for me to clean up Phanuel again, the Hand are glad of the break. Once it's done, Yulia again offers to carry a corner for a while. "With my poor eyesight and this unfamiliar road, it would actually be easier for me to carry one of the corners at the back," she says.

"Well, in that case…" says Yair, gratefully offering her his end.

We continue, with me taking over from Yulia after a while, then Yair swapping with Menahem. Honour is maintained.

"I'm sorry I'm so heavy," says Phanuel quietly.

We all pretend we didn't hear him.

Although Phanuel is getting bounced around, he can turn his head and see quite a bit. I wonder how I'd feel if I'd seen practically nothing but our ceiling since last autumn.

"Even if things don't work out, I'm glad we're trying," Phanuel whispers to me the next time I have to change him. I'm so used to him being angry, bitter, or sullen, but now he just seems frightened and vulnerable. He is so utterly dependent on us. If we wanted to, we could just put him down and leave him, and there would be nothing he could do. I try to think of something encouraging to say, but nothing springs to mind, so I give him a smile.

Chris Aslan

The snow peters out and we have to negotiate mud. A few times one of the Hand slips over, but each time they make sure Phanuel isn't dropped, even if it means extra bruises for themselves. We all look wild and mud-spattered.

I needn't have worried about the cold. Already by late afternoon the air feels warmer and those of us carrying the pallet are sweating. Eventually the sun passes behind the mountain and stirs a breeze through the tree branches. It starts to get cooler again and we stop at the next village. Sabba has brought a jar of his wild honey, which we plan on offering to the village elder or holy man in return for a place to sleep, donkey fodder, and maybe an evening meal. When they see the pallet and hear what we're doing, the elder refuses payment of any sort but he doesn't stop Sabba from placing the honey jar on the food cloth as we eat, served by his daughter-in-law. Of course, they want to know about our journey and we feel a little foolish for making such a long trip without knowing much about the holy man himself. The elder's wife lays out sleeping mats for me and Yulia beside her, and the boys sleep on the other side of the room with the elder, near the door.

The next morning I have to clean up Phanuel's night messes and notice that his sores have got worse from lying in the same position all day, and being bumped around on the pallet. There's nothing to be done about it. Maybe the holy man can cure those as well.

"Did you get much sleep?" Phanuel asks.

I nod. I barely remember lying down.

"Maybe I will tonight," he says, glancing at me anxiously with sunken, dark eyes.

I smooth a few curls out of his eyes. All these months of tending to him, but that's the first time I've actually felt tender.

We're sent off with prayer and dried apricots. Although we're still going downhill, the path is less steep now. I look back at where we've come from and see our mountain. It's hazy this far away but for the first time I see its higher peaks which aren't visible from our village, and I try to find Ubba's shepherd hut, but it's too far away. Our mountain is even higher than I realized.

The fruit trees down here are already in blossom, and everything feels so wide open. I'm not used to how flat things are. We try to identify some of the unfamiliar trees, asking passers-by who point out squat, bush-like pomegranate trees and the persimmon trees with their waxy leaves. Then we pass our first villa. It's like a house, but much, much bigger and more beautiful. We stop and crane our heads from the road, trying to see more.

"How do they sleep in summer?" I ask.

"What do you mean?" says Sabba.

"Well, look how their roofs slope. Don't they roll off?"

Ananias laughs. "They don't sleep on their roofs, Tabi. Do you know how many rooms they have inside? This is just a small villa. Some of them even have two storeys."

"But why make sloping roofs?"

"It's so the rain washes straight off, and so does the snow. And they look nice," Ananias explains. We all defer to him as he's been to Blood City and knows about these things. We ask him what they look like inside, and how they make the red roof things called tiles, which are like flat pottery.

As we walk we pass another, grander villa with rows of trees that look like spears leading up to it. We ask a passer-by what they're called. They're cypress trees. I ask what fruit they give, but they're not useful for fruits or nuts. "They just plant them to look nice," says the young man, and I marvel at this extravagance. We barely notice the distance we cover or how hot and tired we are because there's always something new to see as we learn more about lowlander life.

We run out of water and the donkeys have had nothing to drink for a while. Up in the mountains there are springs, streams, and channels everywhere. You're never far from the sound of rushing water. Here in the undulating valleys they do have a system of irrigation channels, but apparently this water isn't safe to drink, so we have to wait until we reach a well.

Ananias explains how to lower the bucket and draw water. We each take a turn to peer down into the darkness and see a broken circle of reflected sky way down at the bottom. Sabba throws a stone in. There's a wooden trough beside us, which we fill for the donkeys. They're happy with all the spring grass sprouting everywhere. I can't believe the difference a day's journey has made. We're walking through seasons.

We arrive at a huge lake. I'm confused because I thought we had another day of travel, but the boys explain this isn't the Great Lake, which is even bigger. Although the air feels warm, the water is far too cold to swim in. Still, we all need a wash, so Yulia and I thread our way along the bank to a tall cluster of reeds, crouching down to wash ourselves as best we can.

"I'm going to wash my tunic as well," says Yulia. "It really stinks and it's so muddy from yesterday. I know Rohul wouldn't approve of us walking in damp clothes, but if we get sick the holy man can always cure us."

We decide to also wash our hair while we're at it. I can't remember the last time I washed mine. We emerge from the reeds, combing out tangles with our fingers as the boys yell at us to hurry up. They've washed Phanuel, which is good.

After the lake, the path leads onto a long, straight road. I've never seen a proper road before. They're so wide and flat and straight, which means horses and chariots can travel along them at a really fast rate. I've never seen a chariot before. Then one approaches. It's not going as fast as I imagined, but still a lot faster than we are managing by foot.

"Is this a chariot?" I blurt out as the rider comes to a halt beside us.

He laughs, and says, "I won't be winning any races in this old cart." He asks where we're going and why we're carrying Phanuel.

I'm surprised when it's Phanuel who answers. "We would love

to tell you everything," he explains, "but my friends are tired from carrying me. We seem to be going in the same direction. Could I rest for a while in the back of your wagon?"

So, it's definitely not a chariot.

The man agrees, and Yulia and I end up sitting either side of Phanuel in the back while the boys walk alongside us with the donkeys. It's such a strange feeling, because we're moving forward but we're also sitting still on planks of wood as if we were in our own inner room. I feel a bit sick from the movement, but I don't say anything.

The rider has heard of our holy man. There's a boy in his village who was deaf from birth but can now hear.

Phanuel smiles tightly, his jaw clenched. He's trying really hard not to hope in case he's disappointed. "Do you know how much he charged?" he asks.

The man shakes his head and says that no money was involved. He tells Sabba he'll take us to his village and that if we walk from there we can be at the next town by nightfall and should seek hospitality at the main prayer house. "There's no charge, but don't expect them to provide food for you. Although in your case," he gestures at Phanuel, "they might be more generous."

We continue downhill and the air feels hot and close. Even just sitting in the back of the wagon, we sweat. The grass seems taller here and the trees already have leaves. It almost feels like summer. I can't imagine how hot it must get when it actually is summer, or how people bear it.

We arrive at the man's village and thank him for his help, and then continue by foot. Phanuel has slept a bit in the back of the wagon, or at least his eyes were closed. Flies circle eagerly around him but no one has the energy to brush them away, and Phanuel has to wrinkle his face each time they attempt to land on it. We don't talk any more as we walk on, and no one argues about surrendering their corner for a girl to carry for a while. Everything is flat and hazy around us, and when I look behind I can only just see a faint outline of the mountain.

We come to a crossroads and at one corner are five large posts. They're spattered with brown stains and I'm trying to work out what they might be for when Ananias explains quietly how he saw posts like this outside Blood City. It's where the idolaters take their worst enemies and criminals, forcing them to carry a cross-beam. They're nailed to it and the cross-beam is raised up and then they nail the person's feet to the main pole and leave them there as a warning to anyone who passes by that our country is not our own. It usually takes several days to die, Ananias tells us, and it's the worst punishment the idolaters have. I shudder, and even though I'm holding one corner of the pallet and I'm tired, I don't object when we speed up, passing this horrible site as quickly as possible.

As the sun sets we see more people on the road, many of them carrying hoes, returning from the fields. I love watching the wagons pass us. One of them is piled high with enough hay to feed a small flock over winter. People talk to us along the way, wanting to know what's wrong with Phanuel. A woman asks if I have a spare cloth sack, which she fills with freshly harvested spring clover for us to cook with our evening meal. The people have different accents from ours and their clothes look nicer and cleaner. I'm glad we stopped at that lake, but I'm aware that we still look dirty and dishevelled.

Until now, the villages have been made up of simple villas, but as the road becomes a street and cuts straight through the town, we see double-storied villas, with archways and columns. We even see some buildings made from marble. The only marble I've seen before was a marble cup that Yohannah uses for mixing her salves. Here, they have enough marble for entire buildings. There are idolaters in this town and we pass one of their temples, hurrying past in fear, but also wanting to linger to catch a glimpse of what happens inside. Their women have their hair oiled and braided into elaborate designs, and drip with jewellery. I'm surprised they're not worried about being robbed. We're surrounded by a chattering gaggle of children speaking a language I don't know. There are so many people everywhere, it's overwhelming. Menahem asks a passer-by if today is their market day but it isn't.

We're cowed into silence by how big and how strange everything is. I ask Menahem, "Is it true that they have rooms of hot water where you can wash? I think we should get clean before we meet the holy man."

The others nod in agreement and we decide we'll go there first thing in the morning. Sabba asks for directions to the prayer house, which turns out to be on this same main street, just a little further down. We have to crane our necks to see the roof when we stand before it. I wonder how long it took to build and how many men worked on it.

The arched doorway leading into a courtyard is open, so we walk through and a man asks us why we've come. At first he seems sympathetic and promises us food as well as shelter, but once he hears about the holy man his attitude changes. "Who is he?" he raises his voice in a challenge. "Tell me whose feet he has sat at. Which school did he attend? He comes out of nowhere and everyone chases after him hoping for this and that, but what do we really know about him?"

We don't know anything, so we keep quiet as we're led to a covered porch with carpets on the floor and piles of bedding. There are lamps in the alcoves but none are lit yet because the open archways let in the last rays of evening sun. "We have this for the evening meal," I say to the man, showing him the bundle of wilting clover. He shows me where their outdoor kitchen is, and Yulia and I head over there.

"I wish I could see clearly," says Yulia. "Every step of this journey has brought new things for you all, but for me anything further than my hand is blurry, even if I squint."

"Perhaps tomorrow everything will change," I say, and then add, "What if you had to choose between seeing clearly or having a baby?"

Yulia pauses for a moment in thought. "If I had to choose, well, with a baby I could still hold him close and see every detail of his precious face," she says, which I think is a good answer.

We explain ourselves to the three women at the open kitchen and offer the clover, the remaining bread, and our service. We're soon set to washing clover, peeling onions, and fetching water from the well. It hasn't taken long to master the art of drawing water from the well, even though I'd never seen one until this morning. This is the third well I've drawn water from, and the first one I've seen inside a courtyard.

Yulia is explaining that we're from the mountain and the eldest of the women says she knows because they can hear it in our accents. "And everything else," she adds, casting a dismissive look at our general appearance. Whereas we smell of sweat, these women smell of scented oils and frying onions.

"We want to look more presentable when we meet the holy man tomorrow," I say. "I heard that there are places to wash with hot water…"

"You mean the public baths?" says the elder woman.

I nod, hoping that this is, in fact, what I mean.

"Just make sure you don't leave any valuables in the changing rooms."

"I think they'll be all right," says the third woman, catching the other woman's eye and suppressing a smile.

They continue to talk but we have been shamed into silence. We are despised, and maybe deservedly so. Maybe we don't know as much as people who live in towns or cities. As we carry food over to the boys, Yulia whispers, "That's how the mothers make me feel back home when they sit around talking about their babies."

"I hope they're barren," I hiss back.

Yulia stops me and makes me face her. "Be careful of your words, Tabi. May the evil eye not strike. I wouldn't wish that on any woman."

Stung by her rebuke, I kneel down and start to feed Phanuel. At first he turns his head away and says he's not hungry. He does look flushed, which I had assumed was sunburn. I feel his forehead and it's hot to the touch. I wonder if he's had enough to drink.

"Come on, you need to eat and drink something, and then what you really need is sleep," I tell him.

He tries to smile. I'm glad we're talking nicely to each other, even though I still don't really know how I feel toward him.

By the time Yulia and I have washed and returned the prayer house bowls it's dark, but the moonlight from the courtyard is enough to guide me. Yulia walks hesitantly beside me.

"Wait," she says. "You go to sleep. I'm going back to the main room. I want to pray for tomorrow."

The boys are already asleep, sprawled over mats on the floor, except for Phanuel who lies there silently, eyes open. I should probably be worried about him but I'm too tired from the travel and fall asleep almost immediately.

The next morning, the people at the prayer house offer us bread, olives, and cheese. We're grateful, even though I don't like the women. We fill our water-skins, collect the donkeys from around the back, where they've been grazing, and then continue on our journey. We've been told we should reach the Great Lake by noon. We decide not to bother with the public baths for now, as we'll only get sweaty and dusty again on the road.

We're not far out of the town when a dozen or so foreign soldiers march toward us in formation. I try not to stare but I can't help it. I've never seen soldiers before. They look lighter-skinned than us, and some have hair the colour of bronze. The soldiers all keep their faces directly forward, but I see eyes dart toward the pallet we carry. There's a soldier on horseback who must be their leader or something. He stops us and says something in a language we don't understand. When he sees our blank faces, he switches to speaking clumsily in our language. He wants to know who we are and where we're going. Sabba explains.

"I've seen this before when a soldier broke his neck falling off his horse," says the head soldier. "No doctor can cure that."

He gives us a last pitying glance and then they march past us.

"What does he know?" says Menahem once they're out of earshot, but that doesn't change our mood, which is quiet and apprehensive. We carry on, each lost in our own thoughts. Phanuel has his eyes closed but I can tell from the way he clenches his jaw that he's not asleep.

As the sun rises, we wilt. It's as warm as the hottest day of summer in our village. Cherries and apricots are already swelling and ripening on the tree branches, and we see our first pomegranate flowers. Fig trees have their musty-smelling leaves out and the first buds of fruit. There are rows of vines in the fields in such large quantities. We even pass some date palms. They're more common in the South, but they do grow here.

We put Phanuel down so we can feel the strange rough bark of their trunks and squint up at their palm branches. So that's where dates come from. We stop at every well and make sure we give the donkeys plenty of water. They still have their winter coats and are suffering in the heat.

As we crest a slight hill, Ananias halts abruptly. He shades his eyes and peers ahead. "Yes," he says, "look, down there. It's the Great Lake."

We lower Phanuel and take in the view. There's too much haze to see clearly, but then I realize the darker blue haze isn't haze, or sky; it's water. And it just seems to go on and on. Along the shore is a town. This is our destination.

Chapter Seven

We still don't know if the holy man is even in the town, or off travelling somewhere. The main road takes us down toward the town and the lake shore. Puffs of dust from our sandals and the donkeys' hooves settle on our sweaty tunics and leave muddy creases in the lines of our faces.

"Is it just me, or is it even hotter than yesterday?" I ask.

"I feel like I'm inside a cooking pot. The heat is so wet," Yair complains.

"How do people live here?" says Yulia, almost to herself.

The path is flanked by olive groves and vineyards. We see men stripped to the waist in the fields, tending their vines.

"Do you know if the holy man is in town?" Ananias shouts to one of the nearby labourers. The man shrugs and calls to another labourer further away, who nods.

"He's here. Thank God, he's here." Phanuel sighs, and for a moment his jaw unclenches. "Can we ask them how long he'll be around for? He's not planning on leaving today, is he?"

But the labourer has already turned his back to us and we

still don't really know the ways of lowlanders, so no one has the courage to call to him again.

As we get closer to the Great Lake, we can see waves. They're like the ripples the boys make when they splash around, but they're much bigger. I don't know what makes them. A few years ago I would have believed they were made by a giant sea monster out in the middle of the lake, beyond where we can see.

"Look at the boats," says Sabba. They still look tiny from where we are, but they can fit five or six men inside them, and the ones we can see are carrying large bales.

"They're transport boats," says Sabba with authority. "The fishing boats won't head out until evening." I don't know how he knows these things.

"What makes them move?" I ask. "They don't have any donkeys or horses to pull them along."

"It's the sails," says Sabba. "See those big sheets of material? They fill up with wind and the wind makes the boats move."

"Do you think we could go in one?" says Ananias.

We're all transfixed.

"Let's get to the town first and find the holy man," says Yulia. She doesn't usually speak out like that, but she's right to remind us why we've actually come. We lift up Phanuel and pick our way down a rocky, narrower section of the path as farmland gives way to scrub and boulders. We pass twin pines that have entwined with each other, then come to the outskirts of the town.

"Wait," says Menahem. "Put Phan down for a moment."

No one needs to be told twice. The boys flex their blistered hands.

"We need a plan," he continues.

"I think we should just find the holy man straight away," says Yulia firmly. "We can ask for directions to where he's staying. Who knows how long we've got before he leaves again? We don't want to miss our chance."

"I agree," says Phanuel, glancing at Yulia gratefully. "Let's not waste any more time."

"Let's go, then," says Ananias.

"Wait," says Menahem. "What do we actually know about him? How do we know he won't require payment, and what if he refuses to see us looking like this," he sniffs his tunic at the armpit, "and smelling worse?"

Yair and Sabba nod. "We never did find the public baths this morning," says Sabba. "We need to get cleaned up and make enquiries about the holy man. Let's find the town baths, and if we hear that he's about to leave we'll just go straight to where he's staying."

"What about our donkeys and all our stuff?" I ask. "The woman at the prayer house told us to watch out for thieves in the changing rooms."

"And I don't know if they'll let me go inside the baths," says Phanuel. "How are you going to carry me in, and what if I – you know – make a mess?"

"Look," says Ananias, pointing. "This path seems to go straight down to the lake. Why don't we wash down there and then look for the holy man?"

We all agree. I'm disappointed not to see what these rooms full of warm water look like, but then I imagine wading into the lake and feeling the waves as they race into the shore, and that seems pretty exciting, too.

The path is steep and much of it stepped. I leave the boys to carry Phanuel. When we finally emerge from the shade of scraggy pines onto the shore itself, we're blinded by the sun reflecting off the sand. I haven't seen sand before. It's like lots of tiny, tiny rocks. Yulia takes a pinch and holds it really close to her eye and comments on the different colours you can see, even though from far away it all looks the same.

We tether the donkeys as the boys, still fully clothed, carry Phanuel into the water. A wave washes over him, leaving him coughing and spluttering but grinning. It isn't long before the boys start splashing each other and tugging off their dirty tunics.

Sabba and Ananias manage to hold Phanuel in the water while Menahem and Yair start washing themselves. The donkeys graze on scrubby grass, and Yulia and I take a nub of soap and start looking for a reedy spot where we'll have some cover. We pass beached boats drawn up onto the shore. They look a bit like wagons, but nicer and sleeker, and I really want to sit in one and let its sail take me right to the middle of this lake until I'm just surrounded by water and waves and fishes and that's all. No one's around, probably because it's too hot and there's no shade. We pass a spit that juts out, and on the other side we have the whole beach to ourselves.

"I don't think we'll find anywhere better," I say and start taking off my sandals. "Maybe they don't have reeds here."

"But what if someone comes?" says Yulia.

"Well, we'll be in the water, and at least we don't know people here. Anyway, you'll be fine; you can't see them!"

"Not yet," she says and smiles shyly.

"I hope we find him," I say quietly.

We squeal as the first wave slaps against our knees as if it's alive. We wade up to our waists, both standing on tiptoes to keep the cold water from getting any higher.

"Tabi, come closer," says Yulia earnestly, and when I do she splashes me.

I shriek and splash her back, then we both drop under the surface and come back up breathless from the chilled water but laughing as well. We tug off our tunics and take turns to rub them with the dwindling nub of soap Amma gave me, then use the last of it on our hair and bodies. When we washed together before we were both squatting, but now as Yulia scoops up water in her hands and douses herself with it, I see just how beautiful she is with her womanly curves. It occurs to me that she doesn't know her own beauty if everything is always a blur.

"Come on," she says, grinning at me. "If we keep the boys waiting they'll send someone to look for us."

We scamper out of the lake, clutching our bundled tunics to cover ourselves, then squat behind a beached boat and wring out our tunics and comb the tangles from our hair with our fingers. We carry our sandals as we walk back so we can enjoy the feeling of sand between our toes. We round the spit to see Yair on Ananias's shoulders and Sabba on Menahem's, grappling each other while Phanuel shouts encouragement to both sides from the shore.

"Who's winning?" I call out.

With an embarrassed yelp, Yair and Sabba slither into the water and the others also submerge themselves.

"Don't worry, it's nothing I haven't seen before," I call out brazenly. "You think Sholum was alone that time by the lake?"

I turn to Yulia and giggle, ignoring their outrage, and we walk over to Phanuel, who is clean but unclothed.

"You can't bring her over here," he protests.

"She can't see anything," I say. Then I notice Phanuel has already soiled himself again.

"Boys, time to go," I shout across the beach as the boys put on their waistcloths and come over. "Ananias and Sabba, I'm going to need your help with Phan."

They come over, and together we drag the pallet back into the water. Ananias holds Phanuel by the shoulders while I use some linen to wash away the mess between his legs. Sabba heads back to join the others. Phanuel looks really upset.

"It's all right," I say. "Better to happen now by the water than later on when we meet the holy man. You probably won't need to go again for a while."

"What if he knows?" says Phanuel in a strangled whisper.

"What if who knows what?" I ask.

Phanuel sighs. "You can wash me clean, but I'm still full of filth. What if he knows?" I still don't understand what he's talking about. "The holy man, Tabi. What if he knows what I've done, that it was my fault... that I killed Sholum?"

A tear rolls down, or it might just be the lake water. I haven't really thought about it, but I suppose that if the holy man can cure people, he may also know their secrets.

"Phan, you can't think like that," says Ananias. "Come on, tell me honestly: did you want to kill Sholum?"

"What? Of course not," says Phanuel.

"Exactly. It was an accident. And anyway, how could the holy man know about it? Come on, let's get you dry and clothed."

I wonder what I'd do if I were the holy man and knew what Phanuel had done. There's no time for further speculation because we need to get going.

The boys carry Phanuel to the donkeys, and I fish around in the saddlebags for his old tunic. We lift him into a sitting position and push his arms and head through. The tunic is far too big for him now as he's lost so much weight, but seeing him in proper clothes makes him look more normal again.

"What do you want me to do with the padded linen?" I ask.

Phanuel reddens. "Just put some between my legs," he says. "Hopefully no one will notice. I can't afford a mess in front of the holy man."

Yulia hands around a pouch of nuts and raisins, and the last of the water from the skins. Then we set off in our damp clothes along the shore toward a large street that seems to run into the town centre. In the shade of some pines is a simple food stall, and Sabba goes to ask the woman there if she knows where the holy man would be.

"She says he sometimes stays in the houses of his followers, but that today there's a delegation of elders and holy men meeting him in the main prayer house," he says on his return. "It's further up this street and then left at the market."

We've already started when Yair says, "You forgot to ask how much he charges."

It doesn't matter because a young man with two donkeys loaded with bales comes toward us. "Are you looking for the Teacher?" he says, gesturing at Phanuel.

"Is that the holy man?" Sabba asks. "We're hoping he can help our friend."

"Holy man, Teacher, Doctor, he has lots of names," he says. "And he can help anyone. Look." The man pulls off his tunic and stands before us in just his waistcloth. He looks beautiful. "See," says the man with a chuckle, running a hand over his own torso, "it's completely clear. I'm clean. There's nothing left of the disease."

"What disease?" asks Phanuel.

"I had leprosy. I was a leper."

"What's a leper?" I whisper to Yulia.

He hears me. "Leprosy is a terrible affliction with no cure. It kills you slowly, but not before robbing you of everyone you love and leaving you cast out and alone. A leper is treated worse than a stray dog. That's what I was until a week ago."

"How can you be better if there's no cure?" says Menahem, taking a step back.

The man grins and puts his tunic back on. "Come, I'll take you to him. My name's Malchus. Where have you come from?"

We all speak at once, everyone excited, nervous, and wanting to know more.

Malchus tries to answer our questions as he manoeuvres his donkeys around, their original trip forgotten. "You're right; the Teacher refuses payment. Sometimes people force gifts on him anyway, but the next thing you know he's given them away to a beggar or a prostitute. He doesn't cure people for money. He cures them because they need curing. He says it's a sign to show that he's from God."

"Will he like this walking staff?" I ask. "Will it be enough?"

Malchus smiles. "I told you, he doesn't expect any payment."

"Will he be leaving soon?" asks Yulia anxiously.

"I don't know," says Malchus. "He's quite unpredictable."

"Could he help me with my eyesight and… other things?" asks Yulia. "Does he cure women as well?"

Malchus laughs. "He cures everyone who comes to him. I've

never seen anyone leave him who hasn't been cured. He cured me."

We look at each other with nervous excitement and pick up our pace. Phanuel is practically bouncing up and down on the pallet.

"Should we slow down?" I ask him, but he shakes his head and avoids making eye contact with me. Muscles twitch and pulse in his jaw.

"Tell me how it happened," Phanuel calls out.

"I was a leper," Malchus says, almost casually. "I was riddled with the disease and I was weakening. I came back up north having heard about the Teacher. Even if I couldn't find him, I wanted to see my family one last time. Of course, I would never show myself to them. How could they bear to see what I'd become? I found the Teacher and begged him to have pity on me. Others tried to shoo me away, and one or two pelted me with coins. The Teacher told me I would never have to beg for anything again, and then he touched me and I was well."

Phanuel opens his mouth to say something, but we're getting jostled as we enter the crowded marketplace, and his voice is lost in the hubbub. I can hear the sound of my blood pumping in my ears and struggle to keep my breath even. It's not just our hurried pace and all the new sights and sounds around me; if the Teacher can cure a leper – and one near death – there really is hope for my brother.

One of the stalls is selling beautiful tunics, and at any other time I would have stopped and stared, transfixed, but not today. I barely notice the people or the buildings, tugging the rope of my reluctant donkey as the road turns to the left and opens up in front of a large building that must be the prayer house. We stop and then even Malchus looks unsure of himself.

"I wish I still had my bell. That would clear them," he says to himself.

Ahead of us, spilling out from the prayer house and at least fifty people deep, is a huge crowd, jostling and pushing and trying to gain access. I don't think I've ever seen so many people in one place. None of us have, except maybe Ananias when he was in Blood City. We watch a man with a bandaged arm try to convince people to let him through. Even though I can't hear him from here, it's clear from his expression that he's pleading with them, but no one listens and he resigns himself to standing in the shade of a huge spreading oak, where other sick people have gathered. One family has set up a stall, frying fish over a small fire and wrapping them in strips of flatbread with fresh herbs.

There's a courtyard beyond the main archway, and then the main hall of the prayer house itself. There are people everywhere. A lot of the men wear long black shawls over their heads which look too hot for this weather.

"Who are they?" I point.

"The crows? They're the holy men who've studied our religious law," says Malchus.

I wonder how there can be so many of them when our village has just one.

"They've come from all over. Now they've heard about the Teacher, they want to see for themselves what he can do and hear whether his teaching is correct."

"There are so many of them," says Sabba.

"How are we supposed to get inside?" asks Yair.

"I'm sure we've come the furthest," says Menahem. "We just need to push our way in."

"I'm with Menahem," says Phanuel. "Who knows how long it will be before the Teacher comes out? Even then he'll be surrounded by all those people."

Ananias shakes his head, "You saw that man with the injured arm. Look how many people are already pushing forward. There's no way we could get Phan through all of that."

"I don't care if you drop me," says Phanuel, a note of desperation in his voice. He's slick with sweat, his eyes blazing almost feverishly

138

in that hollowed-out face. As I suspected yesterday, he isn't well. "Come on, you've got to get me to the Teacher. Please! We're so close!"

I notice he's started referring to the holy man the same way Malchus does, and already in my mind I find myself doing the same.

There are youths lining the courtyard walls, a few of them helping others clamber up. They're the only ones who have got any closer. They keep calling out to the men packed in the doorway to the inner chamber, asking them to repeat what the Teacher is saying. No one does; they're all straining to hear above the general noise of the crowd outside.

"Do you live here?" asks Yulia. Malchus nods. "Then maybe you know of another way into the prayer house?"

Malchus brightens. "Yes, there are the servants' quarters behind the prayer house. They have their own entrance. Come on."

We follow him down a side street that's almost deserted, past mud-brick walls high enough to ensure privacy, and then through a narrow alleyway until we've come to the back of the prayer house. I don't know why they call it a prayer house. It isn't just one room like ours; there are whole courtyards that connect to the main inner room, which is covered by a sloping tiled roof.

We come to a large wooden door, which is locked. Malchus raps on it but there's no response. "They're probably all inside listening to the Teacher," he says. He tries again, and eventually a small slat I hadn't noticed before slides open and we see someone's eyes.

"Yes?" comes the voice of a woman.

"We have a sick man here to see the Teacher," says Malchus, stepping back. "Look, he's paralysed."

The eyes flick down to the pallet and then back up again. "I'm under strict instruction. We can't let anyone in."

"Please, Auntie," says Phanuel, and he doesn't have to try to look pitiful. "Please, I'm begging you."

"I'm sorry," says the voice and the eyes shift away, unwilling to meet ours. "We already have people fainting inside because of the heat and the crowds pressing in."

The slat shuts and Phanuel swears. Sabba steps forward, and for a moment I think he's going to try to kick the door down, which would be stupid as it's far too strong for that. He contents himself with banging a fist against it and yelling after the woman.

Yulia wipes a hand against her cheek but doesn't say anything. We look to each other, wondering what to do.

Phanuel stares up at the sky. "I still remember, just before I passed out, seeing that map of branches, except the leaves were golden and falling," he whispers. I look up and realize we're in the shade of a huge walnut tree. I wonder how they decide whom the nuts belong to as the tree is out here on the path where the nuts must belong to anyone, but many of its branches hang over the flat roof of the servants' quarters.

Then I have an idea.

"It was climbing that stupid tree that got you into this mess in the first place," I say to Phanuel, but taking the others in my gaze in turn. "Maybe it can get you out of it as well."

"What do you mean?" says Ananias.

"We climb the tree and pull Phan up on the pallet, then we walk along that branch there and drop down onto the roof. There's probably a courtyard somewhere. That'll get us inside the servants' quarters."

A grin slowly spreads from Yair to Menahem.

"We can go one better," says Sabba, his eyes alight with possibility. "Look, the flat roof joins up to the main prayer house roof. It can't be that hard to take off the tiles. We could lower Phan down right in front of the holy man."

Ananias gives a little whoop of excitement.

"Will it be safe for Phan?" says Yulia. She's so concerned about him that it hasn't even occurred to her that the current plan doesn't include her meeting the Teacher.

"Just do it," says Phanuel. He looks nervous, but when he smiles I believe it's a real smile.

"We're going to need some ropes," says Ananias. "I have some coins with me. I could see where they sell them in the market."

"No need," says Malchus. "We have plenty at my home. Can you run?"

Ananias nods and Malchus hands the tether for his donkeys to me. The next thing we know, they're sprinting away down the path.

Sabba and Menahem start appraising the walnut tree. There are no low branches to climb onto, and even the lowest branch is higher than one of the boys standing on the shoulders of the other. It's a problem.

"Phan, can I borrow some of your linen?" says Sabba.

I find a thick strip that's relatively dry and clean. He tests it for strength and then passes it around the trunk so he's holding it in both hands. Then he braces himself against it and climbs a little. He whips the linen strip higher, bracing himself again before he can fall down, and levers himself further up the trunk. This must be how he gets at those wild beehives. It's ingenious but dangerous, and he's doing all this for Phanuel, and I suddenly realize how good these boys are. When he reaches the first large branch we all cheer, watching as he clambers onto it.

"Let me try," says Menahem, but he can't get the hang of it and ends up grazing himself against the trunk.

It's not long before Malchus and Ananias pound toward us, both carrying coils of rope and dripping with sweat.

"After the Teacher's cured you, we'll have to make another trip to the lake," says Ananias, winking at Phanuel and wiping his brow.

They throw up a coil to Sabba, and once he's secured it Yair and Menahem use it to clamber up the tree. As they climb higher to the third branch, the rest of us tie ropes to each corner of Phanuel's pallet and then throw them up to the boys. Ananias shimmies up one of the ropes and climbs onto the third branch. Seeing how high they are, I'm starting to wonder if this was such a good idea after all. They toss the rope ends over a higher branch to give them some leverage and take their positions.

"We're going to have to work together," says Sabba, taking command. "Down below, when you're ready, let us know and we'll start pulling slowly. If one of the corners is unbalanced, tell us and make sure you help steady the pallet. Phan, just yell 'Stop!' if you start to tip."

"Wait," says Malchus. Then he lifts his hands and prays that God will help us in our endeavour and keep Phanuel safe.

Sabba counts to three, then the boys start pulling. Phanuel is jerked to knee height and then to our waists.

"Don't worry, Tabi," he says when he sees my face. "This was such a good idea."

I'm about to reply, but then he's yanked to our head level and we're under the pallet trying to steady it. With the next pull Phanuel yells to stop and Malchus braces himself under one corner. Yair's rope is snagged on something.

"Boys, let's not rush this," Malchus calls up.

As Phanuel is tugged higher, Malchus gestures to us to back away so we're not under the pallet if it falls. I can't help thinking that it wouldn't be the first time Phanuel has landed on someone.

There's another wobble where Menahem has pulled harder than the others and the pallet swings. Phanuel says nothing, although it must be pretty terrifying and probably brings back memories of his fall. Once the pallet is at branch height, Sabba hands his rope to Ananias and then leaps off the branch onto the flat roof. He can just reach the head of Phanuel's pallet and pulls it over as the boys give a little on the rope until the pallet sits on the flat roof. As I watch I feel something like warm rain and realize it's sweat dripping from the boys, and duck out of the way.

"We did it," Yair shouts down.

The boys clamber over to the roof.

"Wait, Ananias," I call out. "You can't just leave us here. What about Yulia? She needs to see the Teacher as well."

Ananias unties one of the ropes from the pallet and drops one end.

"I'll stay here with the donkeys," says Malchus.

"Are you sure?" Yulia asks.

"Come, let's make a knot here," he says.

He creates a loop and tells Yulia to put her foot into it and then hold on. Yulia looks terrified.

"Wait, I'll go first," I say. "I'll be there for you on the branch and we can climb off together."

I lean the walking staff against the tree, and the rope noose is soon biting into my sandal as I hold on and Ananias heaves me up. With just one person pulling it's more work and the rope swings around. I'm terrified but keep the quaver out of my voice when I call down, "Yulia, it's fine."

Once I'm level with Ananias he grabs me and holds me close as I try to find my footing on the branch.

"Sorry about the sweat," he says.

His powerful arms glisten with it, and it's not just the journey up here that's making my heart beat too quickly. I smile, lean against the main trunk, and take my foot from the noose so Ananias can lower it for Yulia.

She's white and trembling by the time we help her onto the branch. I notice Ananias doesn't hold her the way he held me. It must be because she's a married woman. Yulia grabs on to me too tightly, and I realize how easy it must have been for Sholum to unbalance Phanuel that time. We edge along the main branch, holding on to smaller branches above our heads to keep ourselves steady, and then each leap onto the flat roof.

"My tunic is wet through," says Yulia weakly. "I don't think I've ever felt so frightened."

"It'll all be worth it soon," I tell her, taking her hand as we walk over to Phanuel, who lies in the shadow of the prayer house's roof eaves. Up on the pitched roof, halfway along it, Sabba, Menahem, and Yair have started pulling away the tiles. They've removed enough to peer down into the gloom below. Yair scrambles back over to us, looking concerned. I glance down at the drop beneath him and the angle of the pitched roof and wonder how this could possibly work.

"They're not happy down there," Yair says. "We need to be quick. We're going to have to tie Phan to the pallet so he doesn't slip off when we bring him over to the hole."

Ananias joins us carrying the ropes he's just untied from the tree branch. Yair uses one to wrap around Phanuel, making sure he's anchored in place. There's a splintering crash as one of the dislodged tiles slips down and breaks on the path below. It draws the attention of some of the crowd, who come over to watch us, shading their eyes as they look up. Now that the hole is bigger, we can hear an unhappy murmuring from inside. It reminds me of the sound the bees made when Sholum made us get too close to a wild beehive that had fallen from a tree and they became angry. We managed to run away with just a few bee-stings each. I don't know what will happen this time.

"Is he ready?" Sabba hisses over at us.

He looks really worried and we can hear people shouting at us from inside. I'm glad none of the tiles fell inside the prayer house. I nod and the boys slither across the sloping tiles back to the safety of the servants' flat roof.

"Oh God," Yulia whispers, and I realize she's praying.

"Are you sure about this?" Menahem says to Phanuel. I think what he really means is: *This is a really stupid, reckless thing we're doing here, but it's not too late to stop.*

"Quick," says Phanuel, "before any of us see sense."

The boys nod at each other and wipe their sweaty hands on their tunics, then each takes a corner of the pallet. Sabba and Menahem go first with Phanuel at their head. It's much harder not to slip with the pallet in one hand, clinging on to the tiles with the other. The boys squat low to the roof with Phanuel tipped sideways and sagging against the rope that binds him. His eyes are closed and his mouth is moving silently. I glance at Yulia, who is also still praying.

Ananias slips on one of the tiles, and as his foot scrabbles for purchase it dislodges another roof tile, which slides down and then over the edge of the roof and smashes a moment later, causing the growing crowd below to jump back. My wrist hurts, and then I realize it's because I'm digging my fingernails into it as I hold my breath.

Sabba makes it to the hole, where there's a roof beam he can hold on to. We both realize at the same time that they'll need the other ropes to lower the pallet through it.

"Don't worry," I call out. "I'll bring them."

Yulia grabs my arm and says, "Wait!"

But if I do I'll think about what I'm about to attempt and lose my courage. I shrug her off, putting the rope coils over my head and poking one arm through them. Women's tunics are longer than men's, which makes it harder to keep my legs wide and my balance strong. Ananias holds his corner of the pallet with one hand and reaches out to me with the other. I just keep my eyes on him and don't look down at the drop to my left, and then I'm there.

Once we've secured ropes to each corner, we face the trickiest part, which is manoeuvring Phanuel through the small hole while not toppling off the roof ourselves. Sabba and Menahem thread their ropes over the roof beam and start lowering Phanuel's head through. He starts to tip at an alarming rate and cries out, but now the pallet is through the hole, and Sabba and Menahem pull on their side and the pallet rights itself. I try to look down into the hole but it's too bright out here and I can't see anything, although I can feel the hot, stuffy air rising up from too many people crammed together down there.

"Enough," says Sabba quietly, holding up a hand to halt the

feeding out of the rope. He sighs with relief and exhaustion. "We got him there, and that's all we can do."

Menahem peers through and calls down, "Please, will you help our friend? We've travelled a long way and you're our only hope." He pauses, listening, then he turns to us. "They're telling us to come down," he says.

"What? Through the servants' entrance?" says Yair.

"No, down now, through the hole," says Menahem, tugging at his rope and finding that it's been untied. He knots his end around the roof beam and gives it an experimental pull. Then he shrugs and takes hold of it, lowering himself down.

I turn to Ananias. "We're not leaving Yulia up here. She needs to come down, too."

He nods and clambers back to fetch her.

"You're going to have to lower her down," I say to Sabba. "And me."

He nods, makes a loop in his rope, which I put around my foot, and then he checks below to see if Menahem has landed. "We need to be quick," he says.

So, without thinking and without looking, I sit myself on the edge of the hole and then cling to the rope, bracing myself with my one foothold as the darkness swallows me.

Chapter Eight

It takes a moment for my eyes to adjust to the gloom, but when I look around I see a sea of black shawls and the eyes of various holy men glaring up at me as I'm lowered down. I pass the balcony, which is packed and muttering, and I make sure my tunic doesn't billow or reveal anything to the men below.

I look down. There's a small space around Phanuel. Menahem reaches up to help me down the last bit. I've barely removed the rope before Yair is lowered down with Yulia. I'm not sure if women are allowed into this part of the prayer house, but that's probably the least of our offences right now.

An older man with the same uniform beard and shawl, and who seems to be in charge, sighs loudly. "How many more of you are there?" he demands as Yair and Yulia reach the ground.

"The other two are just coming, Uncle," says Menahem respectfully, keeping his eyes downcast.

"And who's going to pay for all this damage?" the old holy man asks.

"I have some money," I blurt out.

147

"I'm not speaking to you, girl," he states icily.

What if this is *our* holy man – the Teacher – the one we've come all this way to see? At least if we'd waited outside the prayer house, we would have had a chance to beg him for help. Now, thanks to my stupid plan and our general recklessness, we'll be lucky to leave without some kind of fine or punishment.

Yulia clings to me. "Which one is he?" she whispers, squinting around her.

"I'm not sure," I whisper back. They all look the same, all around us: the younger men squashed together on mats on the floor and the older ones on benches beside the pillars or on steps that rise up to create seats at the sides of this great hall. The air is hot and stale, and the muttering has petered out into expectant silence. It's obvious why we're here, and everyone wants to see what will happen to Phanuel.

We stand around my brother awkwardly, unsure where to look. Menahem calls up for the others to hurry, and Sabba and Ananias shimmy quickly down the ropes, dropping the last part in their haste and almost sprawling into the first row of holy men.

"Is that everyone?" the old holy man asks, and we nod. Then he turns to one of the other men and says, "And now?"

This man stands up. He's dressed the same as the rest, except he looks totally different because, instead of glaring at us, his eyes are full of mirth. "Where have you come from?" he asks.

And somehow I know this must be *him*.

"From the roof, Uncle," Yair blurts out, which makes the man laugh.

"And before that?"

Sabba steps forward and bows slightly, giving the name of our village and our mountain, and explaining that it's taken us three days to get here.

"And do you not have doors in your village?" the Teacher asks, trying not to smile.

Sabba reddens. "We're really sorry. We didn't come here to

damage your prayer house, and we can help fix the roof if you show us how, but our friend Phan… Phanuel… he can't move and we heard about you and, well, you're our only hope."

"Didn't you see all the sick outside?" the older holy man demands.

I remember what Malchus called them: crows. It's a good name.

"They manage to wait patiently. Why not you? And what makes you think you can repair the work of our finest roofers?"

The Teacher smiles at the old crow. "Nothing is beyond repair," he says with quiet authority, and then he turns back to us. "Was it impatience or simply persistence? It took a lot of faith to come here, especially through the roof."

He steps toward us and we part so that he can view Phanuel. He kneels down and asks him quietly, "What do you want me to do for you?"

"Teacher, you know what I need," Phanuel replies softly.

The Teacher looks up at us and says, "Because of your faith," then takes one of Phanuel's limp hands in his own and holds his gaze, and then says, "Son, your sins are forgiven."

There's no audible gasp, but there is an immediate change in the room: a stiffening or a holding of the breath. I only notice it for a moment, because then my attention turns to Phanuel, who begins to weep.

"Thank you, thank you," he sobs, even though the Teacher hasn't done anything yet and my brother is still stuck on that pallet.

The stuffy, crowded hall is silent except for the sound of Phanuel weeping. I don't know what I thought would happen, but it wasn't this. Then several scowling crows stand abruptly, shake out their robes, and start pushing through the crowd toward the main entrance in silent fury.

"You all came here to find out who I am," says the Teacher loudly, "and I know what you're thinking," he goes on. "Who but God has the right to forgive sins?"

The crows pushing their way out pause and turn to listen. It's a really good question. Even if the Teacher is the holiest holy man there is, he's not God. I look down at Phanuel, and he smiles at me through his tears. It's not one of those tight, forced smiles I'm used to. For the first time since the accident, he gives me an honest smile and I realize something has already happened inside him. Something has changed.

"So, I have a question for you," states the Teacher, looking around the hall and taking in everyone with his gaze. "Which is easier? To tell this boy his sins are forgiven or to tell him to get up and walk?"

It had never occurred to me before that you could have different kinds of silence. Before, the silence was hostile but now it's filled with expectation. No one dares break it except the Teacher.

"I want you to know this," he declares. "The Son of Man has the authority to forgive sin." He looks down at Phanuel and then tells him, "Phanuel, get up, take up this pallet and walk."

Phanuel gives him a look that says: *What?*

The Teacher nods and Phanuel closes his eyes for a moment with the intense concentration he used to show when he was trying to make his limbs work. Then his arms move and he lifts himself into a sitting position. Yulia, squinting to see properly, stumbles back into me and I wonder if she's about to faint. Phanuel lifts one leg off the pallet with his hands, then tries and finds that he can move the other leg all by itself. Now he's sitting sideways on the pallet. This is impossible. I know that boy's body better than he knows it himself and I know that this is impossible.

Ananias reaches out a trembling hand. Phanuel takes it and clambers to his feet. The padded linen that was wadded between his legs drops unceremoniously from beneath his tunic to the ground. It feels as if time has slowed down. I look at Phanuel and he stares back at me, and even though he's standing now and close enough for me to reach out and touch him, neither of us can believe that this is real and actually happening. Phanuel seems shocked. The boys stand with jaws dropped, with a sea of holy men behind them, all holding their breath, disbelieving.

Then Yair shouts, "Yes!" and flings himself at Phanuel, almost knocking him over, kissing his neck and his forehead.

Time resumes and the whole place erupts into chaos.

Some of the crows begin to clap, as if this were some kind of performance. Others raise hands to the heavens in prayer. Still others shake out their robes and leave. Phanuel is nowhere to be seen as the Hand mob him, hugging and kissing his face. We all start laughing and crying at the same time. Menahem lifts Phanuel up onto his shoulders.

"Wait, you've carried me enough," Phanuel laughs, wiping tears from his eyes. "Let me walk."

"No, they've got to see you!" Menahem shouts, eyes shining with tears. "Let them see what the Teacher can do!"

The younger holy men, ignoring the disapproval of their elders, get up and reach out to touch Phanuel, as if to catch some of the blessing for themselves.

News of what's happened ripples outside the entrance, and from there we hear a cheer and then the ululating of women. They're even more excited than the crows, and soon start chanting, "Bring him out! Bring him out!"

Phanuel looks down at the Hand, grinning, and they all shrug their shoulders in agreement and start carrying him toward the entrance. People squeeze back to let them through, reaching out to touch Phanuel as they pass, and everywhere people are shouting, "God is great!" and "God be praised!" The younger crows follow the Hand out and there's a deafening cheer as Phanuel disappears through the entrance and into the crowd outside.

I look down at the discarded padded linen and the pallet and the ropes – all things we won't need to take back with us. Then I glance up and see that the Teacher has come to stand next to me. He's almost been forgotten in all of this.

"Thank you for curing my brother," I say quietly.

He nods and smiles down at me.

But I'm bothered by something. "Teacher, how could you forgive Phanuel when you don't even know what he's done wrong? He killed my cousin, Sholum. He didn't mean to, but she's still dead. Shouldn't he pay for it?"

"Yes, he should," says the Teacher. "Forgiveness never says otherwise. Forgiveness is choosing to cancel that debt."

"That just seems too easy," I say.

"Not if you're the one forgiving," he replies. "Forgiveness always costs."

I'm struck by this truth, and for a moment I don't trust myself to speak. "Yes," I whisper, brushing a tear away. "It does." I look up at him. "I loved her. I loved my cousin so much. I miss her and it still aches here in my heart. I don't think I've forgiven Phanuel properly. I don't know how to. It's easier for you to forgive him. You didn't know her. It doesn't cost you anything."

"Oh, but it will," he says, and even though I don't understand what he means, and even though he's smiling, I see that his own eyes brim with tears.

I pause for a moment, forgetting the older crows still milling around and the servant woman who is now sweeping up the dust and bits of broken tile around Phanuel's pallet as Yulia carefully folds the discarded linen.

"Could you forgive me, Teacher? I was angry with God. I said things I should never have said. I really wish I hadn't."

"Come, my daughter, I forgive you," he says, and he takes me in his arms and I feel my tear-stained cheek against the scratchy coarseness of his woollen shawl. Something happens inside me, as if a hundred lamps have just been brought into a room that was dark and cold before, flooding it with warmth and light. For the first time since the accident, or maybe even the first time ever, I feel true peace.

Then someone pulls at me roughly.

"This is a house of prayer! What do you think you're doing?"

says the voice of the old holy man, pulling me away from the Teacher as he addresses him. "We've arranged a meal for you, but first you'll have to deal with the sick waiting outside or we'll get no peace and have no roofs left intact." He shoots a look my way. "Many of these learned men have come long distances to meet with you. It is a great privilege, particularly for one so unknown, you understand. A great privilege."

"Wait," I say, brushing away a tear. "Please, my friend Yulia came all this way with us to see you. She needs your help."

The old crow sighs in exasperation as the Teacher turns to Yulia. "Thank you for making this journey," he says. "What is it you want me to do for you?"

Yulia reddens and looks down at the ground. "I'm a fruitless tree," she says. "Something's wrong with me and I can't have children." Then she begins to weep. "And I can't see properly."

The Teacher looks at her with such kindness that it makes me cry again as well. "Come," he says, and cups her face in his hands, using his thumbs to wipe away her tears. "Is that better?" I hear the old crow behind me tut in disapproval at this physical intimacy.

Yulia looks up at him, puzzled. She wipes her eyes and shakes her head, then looks at him again. Her bottom lip begins to quiver and then she begins a fresh bout of sobbing. She keeps brushing the tears from her eyes and looking around. I watch with alarm as she drops to her knees and tries to kiss the Teacher's feet.

"Stop it, stop it," says the old crow, pulling the Teacher away. "Enough of this." He hurries the Teacher out of the hall.

I kneel beside Yulia, and tuck a strand of hair back beneath her headscarf. "Yulia, what is it?"

"Tabita, my beautiful Tabita." She looks up and cradles my face in her hands. "I can see you. I can see everything." She wipes her nose on her sleeve and grins. "I can see everything!" She stands up and ululates, attracting displeasure from the holy men who haven't left yet. "Tabi, he's cured me. I can see!"

I ululate too; I can't help myself.

153

Then Yulia cries out, "Blessings upon him! Blessings upon the Son of Man."

I'm caught up with her, and we're both crying and shouting, "Blessings upon the Son of Man."

I don't even know what this title means, but it's what the Teacher called himself, and I still feel the warmth from those hundreds of lamps lighting me up inside. A few men approach us with tight lips, about to tell us to be quiet, but I think they realize we will not be silenced and simply shake their heads and walk away.

We only stop when Malchus comes toward us, and we forget ourselves and our modesty and rush to embrace him, still calling out blessings and praises.

"This is a house of prayer," snaps another of the older men, and we let go of Malchus, step back, adjust our headscarves, and wipe our dust- and tear-stained faces.

"He did it," I tell him, pointing to the empty pallet.

"I know," says Malchus, beaming. "You should see outside. The crowd has taken over. Last I saw, Phanuel was being carried around the market catching coins thrown at him by the stallholders. The whole town is in uproar. The Teacher has really offended some of the holy men by what he said. But when they start curing people miraculously they can argue about whether or not he can forgive sins." Malchus looks at Yulia. "Did you see him?"

"Yes! And I can see you, and Tabi, and even those people right over there." She grins and then sobs again, and then laughs. "It's all too much," she sighs. "And if he cured me of this, I think my other problem must be dealt with as well."

"What's your other probl –"

"Who's watching the donkeys?" I quickly intercept.

Malchus shrugs, as if donkey theft could do little to dampen the events of today. He's probably right.

"Oh, and I forgot to give the Teacher the walking staff. We'll have to find him."

"Come on then," says Malchus. "Let's find the staff and donkeys."

"Yulia." I take her hand as we leave. Her head is craning to see the archways above. She can't stop looking at everything.

"It's all so clear," she whispers to herself.

"It'll take a bit of getting used to," Malchus says. "I still flinch sometimes when someone comes too close or accidentally brushes against me. I have to keep reminding myself that I'm clean, that the sickness isn't there any more."

"How does he have the power to do this?" I ask. "I've never heard of anything like it."

It's Yulia who answers. "You heard him, Tabi. He has authority from God. He has the authority to forgive sins."

Malchus nods, clearly impressed.

"He forgave Phan," I say quietly. "I think Phan needed that even more than he needed to walk again. And then he forgave me, too. I was so bitter, and it's like he sucked all the bitterness right out of me. Now I need to let my brother know that I forgive him for what happened. How can we find them?"

"Spotting him will be easy," says Malchus, "but you should see the size of the crowd. And it's only going to get bigger. I don't think you'll be talking to your brother for a while."

Yulia gasps and twirls as we step outside, taking in the blue sky with a few wisps of cloud, the dappled shade from the walnut trees, and all the people and bustle of this main square.

Malchus gives her shoulder an affectionate squeeze and then looks embarrassed. "I'm sorry. Like I said, I forget myself sometimes. At the leper colony all the usual rules changed. We weren't men or women, or young or old, or rich or poor. We were just lepers, and that was all that mattered. We became family to each other. I forget that when people see me with two women who aren't my relatives, they might start to talk."

"Let people talk," says Yulia, standing taller than she usually does. "They do anyway, although after what they've seen happen to Phan, I don't think we'll be the main topic of gossip."

I'm still dragging the wooden pallet, and Yulia has the folded linen strips in her hand. There's a woman boiling eggs over a fire and I stop to take the linen strips from Yulia and put them in the fire, watching them blacken, shrivel, and burn. I'll never have to wash them again. "Here," I say to the woman beside the fire, and hand her the pallet handle. "You can use this for fuel, but let me put the first piece in the fire."

"You're the ones who came with the boy," she says and I nod.

She brings her foot down hard, breaking one side and bending it back until it fully snaps, then she hands it to me. This feels like a ceremony, and maybe that's what it is. I place a piece in the fire and watch the flames lick around it.

"And me," says Yulia, and she takes another piece and feeds it to the flames.

We're distracted by commotion as the old crow appears from an alleyway, bustling the Teacher ahead of him, followed by the sick. It clearly isn't the quiet departure the old holy man had hoped for. He harries the Teacher along, but he pauses under the shade of a large plane tree and a woman is brought to him. She seems to writhe in the arms of the young people who carry her, and doesn't want to get near the Teacher. He raises his hand and says something quietly to her and then she shrieks, dropping to the ground and writhing.

The crowd move in around her, obstructing our view. There's another scream and then the two young people help her clamber to her feet, picking up the woman's headscarf and tying it back in place. We draw closer.

"Amma, it's me, Yaqim," says the boy, smoothing her hair back under her headscarf. "It's me, Yaqim."

The woman looks around her, dazed. "Yaqim?" she says. "What are we doing here? Where's your father?"

"Oh, Amma," he sobs, burying his head in her shoulder as the girl joins their embrace.

Yulia and I stare at each other, amazed. Then we recognize the man with the bandage around his arm. He finally gets his turn with the Teacher, and moments later we watch him unwinding the bandage and laughing in disbelief, flexing his arm up and down. After that, the holy men surround the Teacher and bundle him away.

"Will we get a chance to hear him speak?" asks Yulia.

"Not this afternoon," says Malchus as we walk back behind the prayer house, "but I can find out where he's staying tonight. You should hear him. He's not like these others. You don't even notice that hours have passed when you hear him talk."

"And I have the walking staff to give him," I add.

Behind the prayer house, the donkeys are still tethered where we left them. Seeing the saddlebags, I remember how I'm supposed to buy dyes for Aunt Shelamzion. I mention this to Malchus, who tells me the market is over on the other side of the main square. This is where we go. We keep losing Yulia, who is supposed to be in charge of the donkeys but instead caresses the heads of children, telling them how beautiful they are, and lifts up various vegetables, laughing at their colour and beauty. I'm sure they all think she's mad. We make our way to the textile quarter and find stalls selling spun yarn, mostly not as fine as mine, I'm gratified to discover. I enquire about shawls and the stallholder laughs and asks me if I'm cold. She rummages through a large burlap sack and finds one knitted shawl buried at the bottom. It's not nearly as fine or as light as the one we made, and is a non-descript grey. I'm shocked at how much money she wants for it. "It's made with mountain wool," she says. "Only the best."

I believed my aunt, but now I see for myself that we really could start our own business. I describe the shawl Shelamzion gave my mother and ask if they sell anything similar. She sucks her teeth and says that they do in winter but they're very expensive. I ask how much and then whether she'd be interested in buying shawls of similar quality but cheaper. Her eyes glint and I make sure to remember her name.

"I'm here six days a week," she assures me.

The dyes are sold alongside herbal remedies, and I discover that I'm quite good at haggling. I manage to buy two sacks of madder root, making sure the roots aren't too big or woody, a sack of oak gall, which Shelamzion will blend with the madder root to give a brighter, stronger red dye, and some blocks of pressed indigo leaves. These are really expensive, but I'd been warned by Shelamzion about this before we left. There are still plenty of coins left in my pouch at the end of these purchases, and we return to the tunic stall I saw when Phanuel was still on his pallet. It already seems a lifetime ago.

There's enough money to buy a nice new tunic for Phanuel and one for me. My eyes linger on a beautiful green tunic. "I've never seen anything the colour of forests," I say. "How do you dye it?"

The stallholder smiles and explains that they dye the cloth with dried and powdered pomegranate skin to make it yellow and then dip it into an indigo dye. It's too extravagant for me, but as Yulia wanders off, distracted, I haggle hard for three new tunics that are still much nicer than anything at home.

"Will it fit her?" I ask the stallholder, holding up the third tunic and pointing to Yulia. "Even if she's with child?"

After much bargaining, I finally agree to a price for the three tunics, demanding that two strings of river pearls are thrown in to complete the deal. The stallholder shakes his head and sucks his teeth, but eventually I walk away victorious. I'll give one string to Amma and one to Aunt Shelamzion. Amma's nose ring is still tied safely at the bottom of my pouch with the last remaining coins.

I pause for breath and realize I've done everything we were supposed to do here. Everything except find my brother and give the Teacher our gift.

"Malchus, you've helped us so much already," I say, "but could you also help us find Phan?"

"You and Yulia wait with the donkeys under that tree and I'll make some enquiries," says Malchus, wandering off.

The woman who is using the pallet for fuel comes over with a boiled egg for each of us and refuses payment. A woman passes, a flat basket on her head laden with herb-filled pastries. Yulia and

I glance at each other, and silently agree that today is a day for treats. We make a meal of the pastries and the eggs, saving some for Malchus. He soon returns and tells us that Phanuel and the other boys are down by the lakeshore.

"That's where I'll drop you off," he says. "I should have delivered these sacks of smoked fish and returned home for a second load by now."

We walk together down to the shore and stop in the shade of some pines planted around a well. Yulia shades her eyes with her hands and looks out toward the shore. "Yes, I can see them. They're swimming," she says.

It's me who has to squint this time.

We thank Malchus for his help and hug him. We don't care about gossip today. "You were sent to us by God, I'm sure of it," says Yulia, and I nod in agreement.

Malchus smiles and then leaves.

"I'll water the donkeys," I tell Yulia, pointing at the animal trough beside the well. "You go and call the boys over. We need to decide what we're going to do next."

I set about taking care of the donkeys and find a patch of grass for them to graze once I've unloaded their saddlebags and they've finished drinking. I'm just wondering whether to risk leaving the saddlebags for a little while and join Yulia when I see her returning, Phanuel and Ananias following behind in their waistcloths.

Phanuel still looks painfully thin, particularly compared with the muscular bulk of Ananias, but he also looks well. It's mainly his eyes; they're shining with joy. I don't wait for him to arrive but run toward him and grab him and hold him close, ignoring how wet he is.

"You've come back to us," I whisper, then kiss his forehead. Then I draw him back and feel the muscles in his arms tense, where earlier today these arms were floppy and useless. He is a walking miracle.

"I've come alive again, Tabi," he says. "It's like I've been in a prison, knowing I was going to die there, and then someone unlocked the door and suddenly I'm free."

Ananias and Yulia fuss over the donkeys, giving us a chance to talk.

"Phan, when the miracle happened, something happened to me as well. The Teacher forgave me, too. You know how much I've hated you all these months. Will you forgive me?"

"What? It's me who should be asking you for forgiveness. It was right that I paid for my mistake in the forest, but why should you have had to suffer as well? If it wasn't for you I wouldn't even be here." He smiles sadly. "You could have given me that tea. It's what I asked for. It was all I wanted."

"Wasn't I kind?" I say sarcastically. "But yes, you do owe me a lot of chores, which you can repay when we get home."

We laugh and he hugs me again. I don't remember us ever being this close or loving before the accident.

"Where are the others?" I ask, looking around for the rest of the Hand.

"Oh, we've just been swimming with some of the younger holy men," says Ananias. "They think they're cleverer than us, but I still beat them in the swimming races."

"Aren't they going to join us?"

Phanuel and Ananias look at each other.

"I don't think so. The holy men know so much. They offered to show us their scrolls, and this might be the only opportunity," says Phanuel.

"I've made all the purchases Auntie Shelamzion asked for, but we forgot to give the Teacher the walking staff. I think we should try to find him. Don't you want to hear him speak?"

Phanuel thinks for a moment. "Ananias, you go with the girls and find out where the Teacher is. I'll talk with the others and we'll come and find you."

He speaks with a calm authority, just like he used to. And just like we used to, we find ourselves doing exactly what he says.

"I don't understand why he doesn't just come with us now," I mutter as Ananias helps me reload the donkeys' saddlebags.

"Don't worry, he has his reasons," says Ananias in a way that suggests he knows what they are.

The three of us head back toward the town centre. Ananias shakes his head, chuckling to himself.

"What?" says Yulia.

"Nothing," says Ananias, grinning. "I just still can't believe it. I mean, I know that's why we came all this way, but it actually *worked*! Phan will be walking back like us on his own two feet tomorrow."

"Walking?" I say with a raised eyebrow. "He'll be carrying all our stuff while we ride on the donkeys. Isn't that right, Yulia?"

She laughs. "I love the muscles on your arms," she says, looking at Ananias, then immediately reddens. "I'm so sorry. Please forget I said anything. I seem to have lost control of my mouth."

Ananias looks puzzled.

"You don't know, do you?" I say. "The Teacher cured Yulia. She can see properly!"

Ananias grins and runs ahead of us, then turns. "How many fingers am I holding up?" he says.

"Two," says Yulia, adding, "Three if you're also including your thumb."

Ananias lets out a whoop of delight and almost hugs her before he remembers his manners. I don't know why, but this annoys me. "God's blessings on the Teacher," he says. "Come on, let's find him."

"Ananias, could you just stay with the donkeys for a little while?" I ask. "I want one more chance to wash and get clean before we see the Teacher again."

Yulia nods in agreement and we head away from the boys, spotting a reedy area. I know the Teacher has already seen us looking dishevelled and lowered on ropes, but I don't want the townspeople to think mountain-dwellers are dirty, even if it might be true.

Once screened by the reeds, we wade out up to our shoulders in the lake and Yulia scares me when she suddenly disappears beneath the water. I'm about to call for help when she emerges, spluttering. "I can even see underwater. I think I saw a couple of fish!"

Her wonder is infectious and we both duck under, watching each other as our hair blooms around our heads like plants, and seeing the bubbles come out of each other's noses.

"I wish we had time to visit one of those bathhouses you were talking about," says Yulia as we dress. "But finding the Teacher is more important."

This proves easier said than done. No one seems to know where he's staying, or if they do they're not telling us. In the end we realize our mistake. We've been asking holy men and other adults. Yulia takes a handful of dates from a pouch in one of the saddlebags and gives them to some of the boys playing on the street. "There will be more of these if you can take us to where the Teacher's staying," she says, and they run off to find out.

We wait in the shade, glad of some rest, and when they return they take us to a prosperous part of the town. I hear snatches of conversation on the street in the common tongue, which is what the idolaters who come up to our mountain lake speak. I only understand a few words. We stop outside a villa with rows of cypress trees planted outside. It's two storeys high and magnificent.

"Who lives here?" Yulia asks one of the boys, handing out dates.

We're told that it belongs to a wealthy government official responsible for tax. Clearly his profession pays well.

"What do we do about the donkeys and saddlebags?" I ask.

Yulia holds up the remaining pouch of dates. "We can take our valuables with us and have one of these boys watch over the donkeys."

She pays a boy in dates and, once that's done, I take the walking staff and we enter through open gates made of metal, not wood.

"We're here to see the Teacher," I explain when one of the servant girls questions us. "We're his friends," I add, which is perhaps not strictly true, "and we have a gift for him."

This seems to satisfy her and she lets us pass. We walk under stone archways into an inner courtyard with a small fountain in the centre. The Teacher is seated on a beautiful wooden chair beside it, surrounded by people sitting at his feet or standing crammed together around the pillars; everyone is listening in rapt silence.

We take off our sandals and the marble feels cool beneath our feet. The upper floor of the courtyard seems less populated, so we look for the stairs and find a spot where we can see him. I expect to hear the Teacher speaking in our holy language: the language of our religious scrolls. I'm surprised that he speaks just like anyone else. He's just finishing a story, and for a moment I worry that when it's done, the host will usher him away and we'll have missed everything.

A young girl escapes her mother's grasp and runs to the Teacher, tugging at his tunic and wanting to be taken up onto his lap. The mother mouths silent fury at the girl, who ignores her, but the Teacher just smiles and takes the girl on his lap, where she glances up at him impishly before settling down.

"What would you like me to talk to you about?" he asks, taking in the crowd around him.

"What about the foreign rulers?" shouts one of the young men provocatively.

"Is there anything else you'd like me to talk about?" says the Teacher with a smile and everyone laughs.

There's silence for a moment, and before I realize what I'm doing I've filled it. "What about forgiveness?" I cry out.

A few people look at me. Maybe they're puzzled by my accent or disapproving because I'm a young woman speaking out.

The Teacher looks up at the balcony, holds my gaze for a moment, and then begins to tell a story. I'm riveted and feel as if he's speaking just to me.

Everyone is quiet at the end of this story. No one needs an

explanation; it's clear what the Teacher is telling us. Although his gaze has taken in everyone in the courtyard, his eyes fall on me again as he finishes and I nod solemnly, hoping he understands my silent gratitude. Someone asks him another question but I don't hear any of it. I just see the face of Amma before me; Amma whom I love but would also happily murder. Then I see Sholum, who left me; who died because of her pride and stupidity, and who never really valued my friendship. I see Phanuel, his face puckered in rage as I force him to eat, or his head turned to the wall, ungrateful as I clean up his filth. *I forgive you,* I say in my mind to each of them. And I mean it. I do forgive them. I'm almost surprised when I also ask them in turn, *Will you forgive me?*

I think about the times I've hated my brother and my mother and cursed them in my heart; the times when I've been possessive of Sholum, unhelpful to my mother, and scorning of my brother's misery and pain. Hot tears slide down my cheeks, but I also feel as though I've just heard the sound of a key turning in a lock, and a door to a prison I didn't realize I'd built myself swings open.

"What have I missed?" says Phanuel from behind us, startling me. His brow furrows when he sees my tears. "What's the matter?" he whispers, attracting irritated glances from people around us.

"Not here," I whisper back.

We leave Ananias and Yulia and weave our way out to the gardens. The evening is warm and we sit behind a cypress tree.

"Phan, will you forgive me?" I ask.

"Tabi, we already talked about this," he says dismissively. "There's nothing more to say."

"There is. You said I've got nothing to ask forgiveness for, but we both know that's not true. I've resented you and having to take care of you. I used to wish it had been you who died instead of Sholum. I need to hear you say it, if you mean it. Do you forgive me?"

"Yes," he says hurriedly, then he looks at me properly and says, more slowly and convincingly, "Yes." He takes my hands in his. "And do you forgive me?"

"Yes," I say, "I do. I'm not saying it didn't matter or that I didn't pay a price, but I forgive you, completely."

Phanuel stretches a skinny arm around my shoulder and kisses my forehead. I lean my head against his shoulder.

"For all the joy today has brought, I've done a serious amount of crying," I sniff.

"Here," he says, and that's when I notice he's carrying something wrapped in burlap.

I gasp. The forest-green tunic looks even more alluring in moonlight. I let the thick, luxurious weave of the linen fall through my fingers.

"But we don't have enough coin for this."

"I do," he chuckles, "or I did. The crowd kept throwing me coins and the Hand kept collecting them up. There wasn't quite enough to buy this, but when the stallholder recognized me he said it would bring him blessing to sell it to me for the coins I had."

"I'll be too afraid to wear it in case it gets stained or caught on thorns or something," I say, stroking the material with my hand and wondering how something this stunning could actually be mine. "Thank you, Phan. Thank you."

One of the serving girls stops and stares at Phanuel. "You're that boy from today, aren't you? The one the Teacher cured?"

Phanuel nods and does a little jump as if to prove it.

"If you need somewhere for the night, I can find somewhere for you here in the stables, as long as you bless the house."

"There are four of us," says Phanuel. "Will that be all right?"

The girl laughs. "My master thinks nothing of accommodating forty guests."

"And two donkeys?"

"Bring them to the stable boy and say that Tabita sent you."

"That's my name, too," I say, and she nods briefly at me.

"Thank you," says Phanuel. "May God richly bless you for your hospitality, and bless this whole household."

This seems to satisfy Tabita and she goes on her way.

"You said 'four'. What about the others?" I ask.

"Oh, they're staying with the holy men," he explains. "They asked us to tell their families not to worry and that they'll be home within the next week or so."

"So they won't be returning with us?"

Phanuel shakes his head. "Come on. Let's get the donkeys stabled and then go and listen to the Teacher."

"And you can give him the walking staff," I say.

I feel bothered, lost in thought as we fetch the donkeys. The Hand have always done everything together, or at least they did until the accident. They came together again for this journey. But now it feels as if something is changing; there's a split and division that no one else seems to see. I scold myself for not being more grateful for everything today has brought, but I can't shake this feeling of disquiet.

Chapter Nine

We leave at first light but Yulia is so easily distracted by her new-found sight that we both soon lag behind the boys, who lead a donkey each. I'm lost in thought, interrupted periodically by Yulia pointing out a cloud or villa or tree she finds particularly interesting, or placing a roadside flower behind my ear.

On our way here, I worried so much about the future but never allowed myself to plan for the possibility of Phanuel being cured. Considering this question, I realize that, while Amma will no doubt happily leave most of the household chores to me, I'll have much more time to work on the shawls with my aunt. I can't wait to get back to shawl-making. I wonder if we can stop at the largest town in the foothills of the mountains to see if their markets still sell shawls and whether I can get some new ideas for patterns.

"What are you thinking about?" Yulia asks, and we discuss shawls and the business we want to start.

"Of course, you'll have to be involved, too," I say.

"Well, at the start," says Yulia, "but then it depends on whether the Teacher was able to heal me completely." She rubs her belly gently. "At the earliest, it would be summer before I was showing and winter before I'd give birth." She smiles shyly and a little nervously and adds, "If it's God's will."

We walk in silence for a while and then she says, "I can't wait to see Azariah. He's been without me for a week, which is the longest time we've gone without…" She trails off, blushing.

"What's it actually like?" I ask, relieved that we're walking and don't have to make eye contact. "You know, the married business couples do in the dark. Sometimes I hear my mother telling Ubba to leave her alone but usually I think she likes it. I've seen animals do it and it just looks horrible."

"Donkeys are the worst," Yulia laughs. "I probably know more about techniques than most. Every woman in our village has wanted to know if we're doing it properly, giving me suggestions for ways that they say will guarantee a boy child, although I'd be happy with any child. I know some women don't like it when their husbands bother them, especially if they've already got too many mouths to feed. And if a man is selfish and thinks only of himself, it's over quickly and becomes just another chore for a wife. But if he thinks about her, and if he's gentle, then it can feel really nice."

I glance at her, feeling flushed, but she doesn't notice.

"With Azariah I was scared the first time, and of course it feels embarrassing to be so close to someone you don't know very well, even if you're under the blankets. We were both clumsy, but gradually we learned how to make it work and then it was wonderful until it became something we had to do to plant his seed.

"When nothing grew in my womb, I found myself dreading the shape of the moon, because when it reaches mid-crescent, my moon blood always begins and I know that I've failed again and that one day it will become too late for me and that if I wasn't so selfish, I'd tell my husband to go and find another wife who can bear him children. Tabi, what if I haven't been cured? What if I'll always be a fruitless tree?"

"Yulia, how many fingers am I holding up?" I ask, and hold my arm away from her.

"Four," she says.

"And now?" I run ahead and hold up my hand.

"Two." She smiles a little.

"And now?" I sprint ahead.

"Three."

"So," I wheeze once she's caught up with me, "stop worrying. Did you see anyone yesterday leave the Teacher without being changed in some way?"

She nods and gives my hand a squeeze.

We walk on and I take in more of the countryside than I did when we were coming here. I walk backwards for a few paces, looking at the Great Lake stretched behind us.

"How many people from our village can say they've swum in that?" I ask, unable to keep the pride from my voice.

"I wish we could go in once more," says Yulia. "And we never did visit a bathhouse."

"Maybe we can make the trip again," I say. "Rohul can look after your children, and the donkey will be laden down with all those shawls we'll be selling, and we'll wear our new tunics and not mind that they get dusty along the way because we'll have plenty of money to buy new ones."

"I'd bring Azariah. I want him to see all of this. And you'd be with Ananias."

I look at her sharply.

"Sorry," she says, "I thought… Did I say something wrong?"

"No, it's just, I don't know why you think I'd be with Ananias."

"Well, wouldn't you like to be with him? I see the way you look at each other."

"What?" I protest.

She arches an eyebrow and smirks.

"Ananias!" she calls out and the boys turn around.

"Don't!" I hiss at her.

"Wait for us!" she calls, then turns to me. "Don't worry, I won't say anything."

We catch up with them and Yulia digs into a saddlebag and finds a bag of honeyed almonds, which she offers around.

"These are delicious," says Phanuel. "Where did you find them?"

"You two weren't the only ones making purchases in the market yesterday," she says with a wink. "Here." She offers Phanuel another handful. "We need to put some meat on those bones."

I suddenly feel awkward around Ananias, and what's worse, he seems just as ill at ease with me. We pass a skin of water around, sweat and dust turning to smears of dirt. Ananias's hand brushes against mine as he passes me the skin and we both blurt out hurried apologies.

I look up at the sun, which is still on the rise. "I have a suggestion," I state. "We're making really good progress home now that we don't have to carry Phan, and no one will expect us to arrive back for a couple more days at least. Why don't we stop at the next big town, and you boys can watch the donkeys while we ladies enjoy our first experience of the bathhouse."

Phanuel looks impressed by my leadership. "As long as you look after the donkeys after us so we can have our turn as well."

It's agreed.

"Do you mind if I talk with my brother?" I say when it's time to move on.

"I was hoping to hear about your experience with the Teacher, and how he cured your eyes," Ananias says to Yulia.

I'm grateful to escape Ananias. Phanuel and I walk on ahead.

"So," I say, "tell me in your own words what happened to you yesterday. I want to know everything."

He tells me about the hopes, fears, and worries of the journey, and how he'd contemplated begging the Hand to take him into the lake if he wasn't cured, to let him drown. "I felt so helpless and so indebted to you all. Every drip of sweat on my face from whoever bent over me to give me water, every time someone lost their footing and stumbled; it was all for me. I just don't deserve it.

"The worst bit was being lowered down in the pallet, all eyes on me. Eyes of judgment. I knew what they were thinking: *What has he done that God would curse him in such a way?* But the Teacher was different, even if he dressed the same as them. When he told me I was forgiven I felt as if he could see inside me, see how trapped I was; not just with a body that didn't work, but trapped with everything. It felt like… Well, I can't expect you to understand."

"Don't be so sure," I say quietly, then tell him about my own experiences with the Teacher.

"Yes," he exclaims as I get to the point where I tell the Teacher that my brother didn't deserve to be forgiven. "That's how I felt, too. At that moment, all I could do was weep. It was as if I was made of ice, and now he was pouring boiling water over me and all that was left was steam. I knew I didn't deserve this – that there was nothing I could offer back, no bargain I could strike – and that felt so wonderful and so terrible at the same time."

Then I tell him how the Teacher forgave me as well. "You can't see my change, not like with you, walking and moving and everything. But I'm different. I can feel it inside. I think I'm melted, too. I didn't fully understand what was happening. That's why I asked the Teacher, in that crowded courtyard last night, to explain more about forgiveness. He didn't give me an answer. He gave us a story. He asked us to imagine a great city that would make the town seem like a village. At first I couldn't picture anything bigger than this town, but then I thought about our lake and how it seems so tiny now that I've seen the Great Lake, and maybe seeing a city is like that. Anyway, there was a king in this city and one day he called in a servant who owed him a whole chest of gold coins."

"But why would the king lend such a great sum to his servant?"

"I don't know, but the king told his servant that if he didn't repay the money now, the servant and his family would be sold to pay off the debt. So the servant begged him for more time to make the repayment."

"But how could he ever repay so much with his own wages?"

"Exactly. Then the king did something even more incredible. He cancelled the debt."

"What? That's unheard of!"

"No, that's what happened. The king cancelled the whole debt and the servant walked out with a huge burden lifted off his shoulders, knowing that he and his family wouldn't be sold after all. On his way home, he bumped into another servant who owed him a few silver coins. 'I want my money back,' he said to this other servant, who begged for more time and promised to pay back the money soon. But the first servant wouldn't listen and had the second servant thrown into prison. The other servants couldn't believe this and went and told the king. When the king heard, he was furious and had the first servant brought before him. The king told him, 'Because you didn't show mercy, neither will I,' and had the bad servant thrown into the deepest, darkest dungeon."

"That's a horrible story," says Phanuel.

"And when he finished telling it, the Teacher looked around the courtyard and told us that this is how God will treat us if we don't forgive our brother or sister. He looked straight at me when he said it, and I realized how much I'd resented you and Amma and Sholum, and that I'd built myself my own dungeon, just like that servant, and that the key to getting out was to forgive. That's why I was crying when you found me."

Phanuel walks in thoughtful silence for a while. "I need more time to think about this, and who I still need to forgive or ask to forgive me."

"Speaking to the Teacher, I realized that forgiveness isn't free. It really costs the person who gives it. Which reminds me, what did the Teacher say when you gave him the walking staff?"

"I didn't get a chance to say much as he was being hurried up to a banquet. He just thanked me and told me that he has no home, so a staff will be really useful."

At midday we stop for lunch under spreading oak trees, where there's a well, some logs fashioned into rough benches, and a water trough.

"I'll draw water for the donkeys," says Ananias.

"No, it's all right, I can do it," Phanuel insists, picking up the bucket and rope beside the well.

Ananias spots an apricot tree, which is already studded with green, unripe fruit. "Some of the young holy men we met yesterday told us how you can eat them, stone and all, when they're like this. They're sour but good for you." He lopes off to pick some.

The donkeys guzzle at the trough, and once they're sated Ananias is about to lead them to a grassy spot nearby, but Phanuel grabs the ropes from him.

"It's okay, I'll do it," he says, tethering them to a bush with the longest ropes to give them room to graze.

I'm laying out flatbread, olives, cucumbers, and some boiled eggs, which were given to us by the servant girl, as Phanuel returns.

"Oh, I could have done that," he says. "What else can I do?"

We grin at each other. "You can sit and eat," says Ananias, rolling his eyes, his big hands full of green apricots. "You don't have to make up for anything."

Phanuel looks sheepish.

"Actually, you can feed me olives," I say, "and fan me while I eat to keep away the flies."

"It would be nice to have some music, please," says Yulia, joining in the gentle mockery, "and I think Ananias wanted his back rubbed."

Phanuel gets the point and sits down.

"How do your legs feel after a whole morning of walking?" asks Ananias.

He grins. "Sore. It's a wonderful feeling!"

Around mid-afternoon we reach another of the large towns: the last one we'll encounter.

"This is our final chance to experience a bathhouse," I say.

We ask for directions and find the public baths.

"I'm going to take one of my new tunics in with me to wear afterwards. I'll wash this one out tonight and wear it for travelling tomorrow."

Yulia does likewise. We feel a little self-conscious, aware of our scruffy appearance, and Yulia goes over to check the price so that we can take the exact amount of coins we'll need, wary of the thieves in the changing rooms we were told about.

"Let us speak with our finest voices," she says, affecting a town accent, and we giggle together as we enter through the large stone archway and then through a small side door into the women's section.

In the changing room we don't know where to look. The sight of naked women doesn't interest us; it's the floor and the walls, which are covered in pictures, that do.

"I've never seen anything like it," I whisper, pointing at a large sea creature spuming water from the waves, surrounded by creatures with lower bodies of fish and upper bodies of women.

Yulia bends down to touch the floor and look closer, ignoring a sniff of derision from one of the townswomen. "Look," she says, "they're just squares in different colours. When you look closely there's no picture. They just look like tiny paving stones, but then when you step back and see them all together, it's like some kind of trickery. The squares disappear and they become something else entirely."

"Is this your first time?" asks a plump woman, smiling. It's not a question. "It's called a mosaic. There are plenty more inside. Where are you from?"

"We're from the mountains," I explain, trying not to sound too much like a mountain girl.

We undress, but we can't keep our eyes from darting over the mosaics. We follow the other women, who all bend down to open a squat wooden door. As we close it behind us, we feel a hot, wet blast of steam. All is quiet except for the dripping of water from the walls and ceiling. We're soon dripping too, and sit down, jumping back up at the unexpected heat from the marble and trying not to slip over in the clumsy bath sandals we've been loaned.

"Look," whispers Yulia, "there are people dancing in this mosaic and over here. And over there. Oh no, don't look over there," she blushes.

I stare down at the floor and focus on the small squares that make up the bigger picture. "It's all of life but in pieces," I whisper as my eyes wander over scenes of grapes and drinking, framed by trees with pigeons in them.

Just as I'm beginning to feel light-headed, the plump woman ushers us into the next room, where there truly is a pool made from marble with a mosaic floor, filled with hot water. We slide into it and it comes up to our waists. There are steps all around the pool and we sit on them, submerged, luxuriating in the warmth, which eases our sore muscles and blistered feet.

By the time we exit, hair still drying and proud of our new tunics, the boys are snappy with impatience.

"The sun has almost set," they fume, but nothing can ruffle our tranquillity.

"See if you don't take your time, too," I state, "and don't forget to look at the floors. There are pictures made of tiny tiles called mosaics."

Feeling replete and happy, we sit beside the donkeys and watch town life pass by as the warm evening draws in. Sometimes Yulia points out an unusual-style tunic, robe, or toga, and once we spot a man darker than anyone we've ever seen before, and we try not to stare in fascination.

By the time the boys emerge, flushed, clean, and wearing their new tunics, lamps are being lit and placed on stalls selling fresh bread, vegetables, and dried fish. We decide to locate the town's prayer house and see if we can stay there. However, the main entrance is locked and we knock for a while but get no response.

"There always seems to be a back entrance," says Phanuel, and sure enough we find a back door that opens onto a courtyard. "I'll go," he says, assured of his new fame. The rest of us wait with the donkeys.

He returns a while later, fuming. "Come on," he says. "It's a warm evening. Let's leave this stupid town and find somewhere to sleep off the road." He marches off, taking the tether of one of the donkeys.

"What happened?" Yulia asks, trotting alongside him, trying to keep up.

"It doesn't matter."

"Come on, Phan, tell us," I insist.

"Well, I introduced myself to the woman inside and asked if we could stay the night. She just said, 'This isn't an inn, you know,' and was about to walk off when I explained that we had been to see the Teacher by the Great Lake and that he had healed me. So then she went and got their holy man, and I repeated it all to him. And then he told me that he'd heard about this trickster fooling the masses and obviously I'd been fooled as well. I told him I'd been healed, not fooled, and that he was the fool if he couldn't believe that, and then he chased me out."

"Beware of blind guides," Yulia says.

"What?"

"That's what the Teacher said last night when you two went outside. He said that we should put our trust in God and not in man, and to beware of blind guides who lead others into destruction. I think he was talking about the crows."

"Yesterday, when we were swimming with the young holy men and I kept winning each race, they just kept telling me how uneducated we must be living in the mountains," says Ananias. "Everything's a competition to them: who's memorized the most scrolls, who can recite the best, who keeps every tiny part of the Law. I can't understand why the others wanted to stay with them."

The moon is almost full and begins to rise. By its light we follow the main road until it passes over a small brook. We lead the donkeys away from the road and find a sheltered clearing. Yulia and I sleep on my cloak and use hers to wrap over us like a blanket. It's a little chilly just before dawn, but we're tired and sleep well.

The next day we drink water from the brook and eat stale bread and raisins before heading onward. The going is harder as the road really begins to incline upwards, although the air feels cooler as we gain height.

"Yulia, I still haven't heard how the Teacher cured you," says Phanuel, striding purposefully forward. "Come on, you can tell me more about it. I know Tabi and Ananias have heard it all already."

Yulia matches his pace and off they head with the donkeys.

"We should probably keep up with them," I say, frustrated as Ananias seems to be taking forever retying his sandals.

"Sorry, I should have done this before," he says, and points toward the larger rocks. I sigh as he goes off to relieve himself. Once he's washed his hands in the stream we finally set off.

We walk in awkward silence. I'm annoyed with Phanuel and Yulia for abandoning me with him.

"Tabita, I'm so happy for Phan and Yulia and everything that's happened to them. This has been such an amazing journey."

"Yes," I reply, wondering why he's stating the obvious.

"I don't think we could have done it without you and Yulia helping out. My hands are still covered in blisters from that pallet."

He looks at me as if I'm supposed to say something. "Well, I think we've all got blisters now," I state and walk on, keeping my eyes on the path ahead as the sun begins to gather height and heat.

I can hear him beside me but I refuse to look at him.

"Tabi, you looked really nice in that new tunic yesterday," he says.

This irritates me. Everything he says irritates me and I don't know why. "Thank you," I say curtly. "So did Yulia."

"Yes," he says and then, "Tabi." He comes to a halt, forcing me to stop and face him. "Would it really be so bad?"

"What?"

He grins apologetically. "Sorry, I keep having these conversations in my head and then I forget we haven't actually talked about it. Phan could explain it much better."

"Explain what?"

"Tabita, I want to ask you if… whether you'd consider… would you be my wife?"

His big brown eyes make him look boyish and I'm reminded of the bear cub I used to love. I look at those broad shoulders and big arms and imagine being folded into them, and I think it would feel nice. I know that Ananias is a good man. Then I shake myself.

"No," I reply firmly.

He seems to grow visibly smaller before me.

"Why are you even talking about marriage, anyway? I'm too young, and so are you. Sholum hasn't been dead for a year yet, and she's my close relative. You know our traditions. Also, how could I squeeze into that cramped house of yours with all your brothers and their wives and children? I don't even know what my father would say or if he'd give his permission. And that's without even mentioning my mother."

I walk on, but he catches up with me.

"You're right about all those things, but I thought we could find a way if you… if you liked me, or thought you could grow to like me, the way I think I like you."

"I like you, too," I say. "You're a good man. But I can't think about marriage now."

We walk in silence for a while.

"So, it's not that you don't like me. It's because of the housing situation and being too soon since Sholum died."

"And I'm too young. I'm not ready for marriage and babies and all of that. And you know how much I want to start this shawl business with my aunt."

"Yes, she thought you might react like this," he says quietly.

"What? You've been talking to my aunt about this?"

He waits for me to calm down.

"There's a reason," he explains. "Hanan asked me something before we left. He and Shelamzion asked if they could adopt me – if I could become their son. They don't want to take me away from my parents, and they don't expect me to take on their name, but they offered me land beside Hanan's workshop if I'll stay and take care of them in their old age. They know I'll never be able to afford my own house, and how cramped things are at home. They both said they'd be proud to have me as a son. Hanan says he'll help me build a new house and it was Shelamzion who suggested I speak to you if things worked out with Phan. She knew the answer would definitely be no if Phan wasn't cured, but she thought you'd enjoy escaping your house and living with them… and with me."

This is a lot to take in. My aunt is always two steps ahead of everyone else, and I'm peeved that she said nothing about this to me. I think about them: my uncle and aunt. They seem so capable and wealthy – at least by the standards of our village. I've never considered how heavily the future must weigh on them with no children of their own who will take care of them. One day Amma will find a hard-working daughter-in-law for Phanuel and then for Helkias, and she'll boss them both around in her old age. But what about Shelamzion? I've seen the love and pride in Hanan's eyes when he looks at Ananias. He's already like a son to him, and he'd be the pride of any father. I remember how Ananias took care of our flock when Sholum died so Ubba could come and be with us as we cared for Phanuel. Ananias is reliable, kind, hard-working, and caring. I imagine living with Ananias and working with my aunt each day, away from my mother's constant demands.

"Tabi?" he says anxiously, clearly still waiting for some kind of response.

"So, we'd live with my aunt and uncle but build a new house for us?"

Ananias comes to another halt. I wish he'd stop doing this. "What are you saying?"

"I don't know what I'm saying," I snap. "This is all new to me." I imagine all those lamps they light every evening winking and glowing as we eat around a common dish with Phanuel coming to visit for the evening, so different from the friction in my own home. "Is this what you and Phan were talking about yesterday?"

Ananias nods.

I sigh in exasperation. "I can understand why you'd talk to Hanan and Shelamzion first, and your own parents, but why are you discussing this with Phan? He's not an elder."

Ananias shrugs sheepishly. "He was just giving me courage."

"You have enough courage of your own," I state. "You're a good man and will make a good husband."

I try not to get annoyed when Ananias stops again.

"Does this mean that you accept me?"

Again, those big brown eyes look at me beseechingly, and my body responds without consulting me. "It means I'll give your proposal serious thought. You've already talked about it with practically everyone else. Can't I talk it over with my aunt first?"

"Of course," he stumbles, and we walk in agonizing silence for a few moments.

I'm wondering how to extricate myself when he says, "I'll just —"

"Yes, you should," I interrupt.

He runs ahead to find Phanuel and I breathe a sigh of relief. I need time to think.

How can I say that the rest of the journey is uneventful? This is only the second time in my life that I've journeyed along paved roads, experienced flat land, drawn water from wells, and seen villas and houses that are bigger than one room. We even pass a caravan of camels that loom over us as they pass, dwarfing the donkeys and carrying so much more on their backs.

Whenever we lift our eyes from the road, we see our many-peaked mountain ahead of us, growing larger. The peaks are still covered in snow. I'm told that when Ubba was young, he and some of the other boys from the village climbed for almost a week, and just when they thought they'd climbed the highest peak they discovered another in the distance. In the end they had to turn back because of the snow, and that was in the middle of summer.

As we walk I wonder if Ananias will try to talk to me again or if Phanuel will come to ask what my answer was. Thankfully neither of them does, although, as the boys walk ahead, I'm pretty sure I'm the main topic of conversation.

Yulia suggests that we buy fresh greens to take a taste of spring home for our families. It's hard to imagine we're returning to the end of winter when I just spent a night sleeping outside. I'm filled with an eagerness to return and see everyone's faces as Phanuel walks up to them. He's already looking stronger and healthier than he did that first day. The hard work of walking has been good for him. At the same time, I'm seeing so much of the world and enjoying so many new experiences. What if the village feels too small now?

Yulia is the most eager to return, but we keep getting delayed by Phanuel. True to his word, he makes sure that people hear about the Teacher and his miracles in each of the towns and villages we pass. Many people recognize us and walk with us, wanting to hear his story. Yulia tells them about her eyes as well, but doesn't mention the other thing.

The same thing happens in one of the large villages we pass at sunset, and the villagers insist that we stay in their prayer house. The holy man wants to hear everything. Phanuel tells him what happened, including how the Teacher forgave him his sins. The holy man looks troubled. "Who can forgive sins but God?" he says.

"But then who can heal so miraculously?" Phanuel asks right back at him.

The following day we don't talk much as we're now climbing steadily up and everyone is exhausted. I've put my old tunic back on, although it looks shabby compared to my new clothes. Our feet sting with cold as we trudge through mud and snow. Phanuel looks pensive. "Are you all right?" I ask, wondering if the pace is too much for him.

He nods curtly and I raise an eyebrow, waiting for honesty. Then he sighs. "It's probably nothing, and I don't want anything to detract from how special today will be."

"Just tell me what it is," I say, keeping my voice down, mindful of the other two who are ahead.

"I had a dream last night," Phanuel starts. "It was of a hand. A knife came down and severed the hand in half, with the thumb and a finger on one side and three fingers on the other."

"Maybe you were lying on top of your hand and it just got sore," I venture unconvincingly.

"It was about us, the Hand. I know it," he says. "Where are the other three now? It already feels as if we're pulling apart."

"They'll be back soon enough," I state, and then we stop talking because Ananias whoops, having arrived at our lake. It really does looks like a puddle now that I've seen the Great Lake. There's still ice encrusted around the edges, and it's hard to believe that a few days ago we were actually swimming in lake water.

The first cry of recognition comes from a young cousin of Yair and Menahem, and he runs up to us and starts whistling loudly. We have a special whistle in our village that we sometimes use in winter to alert everyone if we've seen a bear or lion, or if someone is in trouble.

Soon others come running and the whistles turn to ululations of joy as they see Phanuel trudging along in front of his donkey. Before we know it, we're surrounded, and Phanuel is lifted onto the shoulders of the village men and carried to our home. Ubba and Amma come rushing out at the sound of the commotion, and when they see Phanuel grinning down from the shoulders of our neighbours they both start weeping, even Ubba. I've never seen him cry before. Phanuel slithers down and rushes to them, and is lost in a fierce embrace. There's an indignant wail from inside the house as Helkias is abandoned, but no one pays him any attention.

People shout "God be praised!" and everyone seems to be laughing or crying or both. I've never seen anything like it in our village, but then who has ever seen someone healed like this?

Shemayah and Yohannah arrive, and I'm relieved to see how happy they are, hugging and kissing Phanuel as if he were their own son. Then I notice Sabba's father and Yair and Menahem's mother, as happy as everyone else, but craning their heads, looking for their sons.

Yulia's mother-in-law, Rohul, appears with Azariah. No one pays much attention to Yulia as they're all so focused on Phanuel. Azariah pushes toward Yulia, thinking that she won't be able to see him until he's really close, but she spots him and waves, and his eyes are suddenly bright with tears as he shoulders his way forward. Azariah grabs his wife around the waist, lifting her up and spinning her around, almost toppling them both into a bank of snow. He kisses her on the mouth, which is something you never see in public, but no one seems to mind today.

"I can finally see you, my handsome lion," she says to him, laughing.

People nearby hear her and start a fresh wave of ululating.

I spot my uncle and aunt and wave to them, but they're too far back to do anything more than wave and beam back at me.

Menahem's mother is trying to push through the crowd that's formed, no doubt wanting to know where her boys are. I'm wondering if I should step forward to say something, but it's Shemayah who raises his hands and calls for quiet. By now the tree branches around our house are filled with children, perched like overgrown roosting hens, all wanting good views. I look around and estimate that almost the entire village is here. Eventually the cheering and ululating die down and Phanuel steps forward.

"Come, let us all get a look at you, our son," says Shemayah.

Phanuel steps forward and then does a little jig, which makes everyone smile.

"Is it really you?" Yohannah asks in astonishment. "Truly this is a miracle from God."

"My boys," blurts out Menahem's mother, making the most of the silence, "where are they?"

"They're fine. They're with Sabba and send their greetings. They'll be back in a few days," says Ananias.

She slumps with relief.

"If it wasn't for them, if it wasn't for the Hand, I'd still be lying in that room," Phanuel announces in a voice that carries. "I owe them my life."

For a moment I think about his dream again, but then we're distracted by someone who calls out that we should all move to the prayer house, where it will be easier to hear what Phanuel has to say, but he's shushed by everyone else. Everyone is impatient to hear the story.

So, Phanuel starts to tell it, and he tells it well. I watch Shemayah's face when Phanuel gets to the part where the Teacher forgives him. He doesn't frown, but just seems as enthralled as everyone else.

Then, when Phanuel describes standing up and being lifted into the air, the whole village starts cheering and ululating again.

"Wait, there's more," he says, then looks over at Yulia expectantly.

Yulia sees everyone staring at her and removes Azariah's arm from around her waist. She clears her throat, collects her thoughts, then begins.

"While the crowds were chanting for Phanuel and carrying him around, I approached the Teacher. I told him that I was a fruitless tree and that my eyes were weak." She clears her throat again, fighting back the emotion. "The way he looked at me was with such compassion. He didn't seem to think that it was God's punishment on me for something I had done, which I know is how some of you think. He healed me. When I opened my tear-filled eyes, the first thing I saw was his smile. He didn't ask me if I deserved this. Who deserves this grace from God? None of us. All I know is that he cured me and he cured everyone who came to him, whatever their problem was. I give thanks to God for the Son of Man. I give praise and thanks to God!"

There's silence for a moment as the women in our village feel the sting of her rebuke, and so they should. Then the silence is broken by one lone woman ululating. It's Aunt Shelamzion. I love my aunt so much for this. I join in and soon everyone is cheering and praising God once more.

Ubba steps forward. "Halafqa, Yaqim, take the four largest rams from my flock and have Shemayah bless them for slaughter. Tonight we will all feast. My son has been given back to me!"

A cheer goes up from the crowd.

Yohannah steps forward and begins commandeering various women to bake bread and gather the last of the winter apples for the feast. She calls on the men to build a fire outside the prayer house ready for the roasted sheep, and Yaqim and Halafqa return from the sheep pen dragging a ram in each hand by the horns, while Ubba sharpens his slaughter knives.

"I'll see you tonight," says Yulia, adding with a whisper, "It's time I returned home with my husband. I'll ask my mother-in-law to stay here with Yohannah and help with preparations."

"Today you start your baby," I whisper back and give her hand a squeeze.

As she leaves I hear my name called. I turn and am almost knocked over by Shelamzion and Hanan. They hug and kiss me and welcome me home. We lead the donkeys up to their house and I unpack the river pearls for Shelamzion while Hanan starts unloading the bundles of dyes. I start to explain prices but Shelamzion puts a finger to her lips.

"There'll be plenty of time to tell me all about it, and I want to hear about *everything*." I sense that she's specifically referring to Ananias. "But not now. Now is a time for rejoicing!"

My aunt can play the tambour well and she sends one of her neighbour girls to fetch it for her. Soon, she is pounding out a rhythm and the women of our village dance as we proceed toward the prayer house.

Young men, older than Phanuel by several years, gather around him, eager to simply be in his company. Before, they would never have wasted their time on a youngster, but who doesn't want to be near the miracle boy now? I'm about to follow the procession but then feel a pat on my shoulder.

"Tabi! Won't you even greet your own mother?"

I try not to roll my eyes. I've barely returned. "Amma!" I cry, and turn to embrace her. "I brought you pearls," I tell her. "And don't worry, I still have your nose ring."

"God bless this Teacher, whoever he is. God's blessing be upon him!" she says, and wipes away a fresh bout of tears. "You have no idea how much we've worried these past few days. I've barely eaten a thing."

And suddenly life seems very normal, and yet very special and extraordinary at the same time.

"I brought you some fresh greens. I can fry them up now so you don't have to wait until the feast," I say, and I happily step inside, away from the crowd and scrutiny, into our poor, shabby, one-room house that still smells of Phanuel's filth.

Chapter Ten

"Absolutely not! I forbid it. Ubba forbids it as well, don't you, Ubba? How typical of my sister – with her own child dead, scheming ways to steal my only surviving, precious daughter."

I blow a strand of hair out of my face and look to Phanuel. He gives me a reassuring nod and takes over. "No one's stealing anyone," he says soothingly. "It's not like this is someone from a different village come to take Tabi away. What could be better than having her live with our own relatives, who we know will take care of her? And I owe Ananias my life. He's closer than a brother to me."

Amma simply purses her lips and tosses her head dismissively.

"Ubba?" I say. "You haven't said anything yet. What do you think?"

My father's solution to my mother's rants is usually to escape to the mountain or the sheep pen, depending on the time of year. He sighs. "You own a son but you borrow a daughter," he says, quoting one of our proverbs. "We always knew she would leave us one day to marry."

"Yes, but not while she's still a child! And speaking of children, who's going to look after the house with me taking care of Helkias?"

"Ah!" I crow. "So that's what this is really about!" My voice is raised. "You just want someone to scrub floors and cook meals. You don't really care about me."

"Tabi," Phanuel pleads for peace. "Let's all calm down. We don't have to make any decisions now."

"I am calm, and I'm not a child. And now I have work to do, because I'm not a child, I'm a woman of business."

And with that, somewhat haughtily, I march out.

Amma mutters, "That poor Ananias doesn't know what misery he's in for." This is my mother's way of warming to the idea.

I know she'll see sense eventually, just as I did. It's been four days since the feast and life has more or less returned to normal in the village, except that people keep visiting from other villages to hear about the miracles. Also, Sabba, Menahem, and Yair still haven't returned.

On the morning of my first day back, I went over to Aunt Shelamzion's. Ananias was there in the workshop talking with my uncle. As soon as they saw me they quickly busied themselves with work. That means Hanan knows. I told my aunt all about the trip. She didn't rush me and was particularly keen to hear about Yulia, wiping away tears as she heard about this overshadowed miracle. Finally, I told her about the conversation with Ananias.

"Have you decided what your answer will be?" she asked.

Her question struck me as so different from the sort of response I'd expect from my own mother. There were no demands, just respect. I imagined what it would be like living with her and Hanan, and this just confirmed what my answer would be.

"If Ananias is good enough to be your son, then he's good enough to be my husband," I told her.

She kissed me and we hugged and she wept. I think the tears were partly happiness for me and partly sorrow for Sholum.

"When will you tell him?" she asked, dabbing her eyes with a sleeve.

"When he asks again. If he dares!"

He waited another day before approaching me, and I suspected my aunt's hand in this.

"Am I interrupting?" he asked as I sat in the sun working on a new shawl. He looked so tentative and nervous that I realized my aunt had said nothing.

I put down my work and nodded at the space beside me.

"I'll stand, if that's all right," he said, shifting from one foot to another.

"Well, are you going to ask me?" I said with a raised eyebrow and a smile playing on my lips.

"Well, that depends," he said, smiling back. "Do you think I should?"

"Yes, I think you should," I said.

So, he asked and I answered. And I felt a warmth spread through me and couldn't keep myself from grinning, because I knew this was right. Then he stepped forward to embrace me, but it was all fumbled and embarrassing.

"We don't have to discuss the arrangements just yet," I explained, trying to recover my composure. "Let's wait until after I've told my parents. My mother will need to get used to the idea of losing her hardest-working servant!"

Then we went and told Shelamzion and Hanan, asking them to keep it a secret until I could talk with my parents. I told Phanuel as well, who whooped and spun me around. When Amma came rushing in at the commotion, still expecting misfortune to strike at any moment, Phanuel just said that he was happy to be well again, then distracted her by offering to help drag furniture outside ready for our spring clean.

Emptying the whole house and scrubbing it properly clean was a deeply satisfying experience, even if it took all day. Although nothing ever gets thrown away in our household, we all agreed that

Phanuel's stained old mattress could begin a new life as nesting material for the spring chicks Amma's hens were sitting on.

Ubba purchased some slaked lime, and he and Phanuel whitewashed the walls, leaving a sharp, clean smell that made a welcome change from the lingering scent of urine. I'd never seen Phanuel so helpful. He'd already shovelled the remaining snow into piles around the fruit trees for extra water, dug out the chicken coop – an unenviable task – and blended it with the earth in Amma's vegetable patch, which he has also worked over now that it's no longer frozen, and dug into furrows ready for planting.

"Don't overdo it, my boy," said Amma, surprising everyone.

Phanuel just grinned and wiped his brow. "I have many, many months to make up for and I don't want to spend one moment longer on my back than I have to."

Perhaps that was what prompted the discussion at breakfast this morning about what Phanuel would do now that he was well again. Ubba was suggesting that after Phanuel had helped him with the lambing, he could join him in the mountains for the summer, learning how to use a sling properly and taking care of our flock.

"I'd love that, but for now I think I should stay closer to home. I'd like to spend more time with Shemayah, reading his scrolls and discussing what the Teacher said. I could still come and visit you in the hut regularly, but I'd also like to help Amma around the house. I know Tabi wants to concentrate on her new business, and we might as well start getting used to fending for ourselves without her."

Amma looked sharply at me, and I decided that then was as good a time as any. So I told them about the proposal.

"What if she persuades Ubba to forbid the match?" I ask my aunt as she pounds some of our newly purchased dried madder root in a copper mortar.

"Here, you have a go," she says, passing me the heavy copper pestle. "It'll be good for your frustration."

I happily grind the spindly little roots into powder. "Auntie, you know what she's like. She won't let me go willingly; not with all the work I do around the house."

"I do know what she's like and, don't forget, I've known her for a lot longer than you." Her eyes narrow and a conspiratorial smile grows slowly. "Your mother has always envied me, ever since we were little girls. If I made myself a rag doll, she had to have it. If there was a boy I liked, she would flirt with him. You seem to have forgotten the bride price, Tabi, but let me assure you, your mother has not."

I hadn't even thought about that. "But what if she becomes unreasonable and starts demanding too much?"

"What if?" Shelamzion laughs. "Of course she'll demand too much! I expect nothing less. I'll haggle hard with her but reluctantly agree to most of her demands, and then she'll be able to impress all the women on her street with what a hard bargain she drives. By the time she's finished with me, your mother will be able to employ one of the women on your street to do your share of the cooking and cleaning."

"I don't understand."

"And nor does your mother," says Shelamzion cupping my face in her hands and kissing my forehead. "Tabi, think about everything you learned at that big town market. We have abundant supplies of the best mountain wool from sheep or goat, and we know how to grade it, only using the finest quality. We know how to dye wool evenly and spin it finely, and Hanan can produce those smaller, lighter spindles for us right here. And now we know the hooking technique to make shawls that are light yet incredibly warm and highly sought after. Think how many shawls one donkey could carry, never mind two? That keeps our transportation costs to a minimum. Every winter we have a village full of bored women who'd love to earn some extra income beyond shelling walnuts. You saw how easy it is to find market sellers in these big towns. We know there's a demand for these shawls and that we can undercut the competition. Tabi, I have, right here in my hands, a person who dreams designs and patterns and who knows how to innovate and won't cease until she's satisfied with each shawl. I don't think you realize how valuable you are, and your mother certainly doesn't. Anyone can cook and clean, but for our business, there's no one I'd rather have at my side than you."

We stare silently and happily at each other, her hands still cupping my face, as my tears make her face blur and wobble.

"Oh come now," she scolds gently. "There's no need to cry."

"I'm sorry," I say. "It's just that no one has ever believed in me like this before."

"That's not totally true," she answers. "I think you underestimate just how much Ananias admires you. I watch him watching you, and he's bolder in his compliments about you to others than anything he might say to your face. He was always commenting on how well you cared for your brother."

I feel a stab of shame as I remember stealing those berries from Yohannah's stores and how close I came to poisoning Phanuel. I decide to tell Yohannah and ask for her forgiveness.

My aunt could be a fortune teller, at least when it comes to my mother. Sure enough, when I return home that evening, Amma rounds on me.

"Well, I hope that sister of mine doesn't think that because we're sisters she can cheat me out of a decent bride price," she states, hands on hips.

"No, Amma, I'm sure she doesn't."

"And she knows you're my only daughter. I can't be expected to give you up easily."

And so it goes on. I keep quiet and appreciate the looks of sympathy I get from Phanuel. It's Ubba who eventually tires of Amma's endless scheming monologue.

"Enough, woman," he snaps. "Go and talk to her now or go tomorrow, but stop talking about this to us."

Even Ubba has his limits.

The steady stream of visitors to the village wanting to meet Phanuel or Yulia continues. At first the pilgrims were just the curious from the next village and some of the nearby holy men. Now, the sick, the crazy, and the barren turn up from all over the mountain range. They ask for prayers of blessing, which are dispensed clumsily as neither Yulia nor my brother has ever had to pray in public before. Some people think they can somehow open barren wombs or cause lame legs to walk again, but they simply explain, "Seek out the Teacher. He's the one who can help you. He helps everyone. He turns no one away. No one."

I thought Amma would be resentful about these uninvited guests who must be provided with bread, tea, and dried fruit, particularly as I'm not around to help much. Instead, she revels in the attention, rocking Helkias and interrupting with details Phanuel has forgotten each time he's obliged to recount his miracle.

One morning I arrive at Shelamzion's at the same time as Yulia and observe the way people on the street smile when they see her, even the ones who used to bad-mouth or shun her. Now she represents blessing: a walking reminder that God can change lives.

Spring begins wet, with two days of freezing rain that force me and Shelamzion to work on our shawls by lamplight indoors. There are even a few mudslides further up the mountain, with boulders raining down onto the upper orchard terraces and the meadows above, damaging several trees. This is followed by mild days of mist and blossom, everything grey and pink with the first shoots of grass emerging and then, finally, sun. I join Amma and the other women up on the mountainside collecting the first shoots of clover, which make a delicious spring filling for pastries. The mountainside is studded with orange and violet crocuses, and wild tulips and irises are also beginning to appear.

My mother regales the other women with her bridal price triumphs, tirelessly reeling off her inventory of loot. This isn't even my dowry, which I'll take with me, but the price Ananias must pay for me. It includes a fat ram, a small decorated cedar chest, new tunics, and several copper bangles. Amma even tried for a cow, which elicits whistles of admiration from some of the other women at such a brazen request, but my aunt also has her limits. Amma has made arrangements for us to visit a jeweller who lives two villages away to pierce my nose and fit my nose ring. Then it will be official; I will be betrothed.

My aunt takes me to visit Ananias's mother and her various daughters-in-law. I think Shelamzion is more nervous about the visit than I am, as she doesn't want to be seen as a son stealer. She needn't have worried; his mother is thrilled to have one less mouth to feed and Shelamzion has told Ananias that he should still give his family part of his wages each month, even after we're married. Thankfully the sunny weather means we can all sit outside, as there are so many of them stuck in that one, cramped room with at least one child crying at any time. I shudder as I imagine having to squeeze in there with Ananias. Shelamzion has brought gifts for each woman of the house and makes a great show of kissing and embracing them all. They want to hear me tell the story of the miracles, even though I'm sure they've already heard everything from Ananias.

I still feel a bit awkward around Ananias, but it's a nice, shy kind of awkwardness my aunt assures me will cease after we're married. We see each other most days as we now work in the same place. Yulia joins us making shawls whenever she isn't hosting pilgrims, and spins while I master the hook technique. Now that her eyesight is cured, Yulia spins yarn almost as fine as mine. She arrives one morning looking flushed. It was a clear, frosty night and she could see the moon clearly. It was the right shape for her moon-blood time, but it hasn't come. We're both reluctant to celebrate too soon, but I'm sure that she's with child.

Sabba, Menahem, and Yair eventually return, having stayed away twice as long as they said they would. They're all eagerly welcomed home and each has brought gifts for family members. Shemayah visits them all in turn and insists we're all to come to his house the following night for a special meal to welcome us back and to thank God for all that has happened.

Yulia and I arrive early to help Yohannah with food preparation, since Yohannah's daughters are all grown and married. As we roll out rich pastries made with eggs now that it's spring and the hens are laying, I confess that I stole some of her berries and tell her why, then ask for forgiveness.

Yohannah listens gravely, but finally says, "We all make mistakes. I'm glad you've recognized yours. And I'm glad you didn't give Phanuel that tea."

We fill the pastries with finely chopped mountain clover and goat's cheese. There's even a delicious, thick barley broth to go with it, which Yohannah flavours with mysterious pinches of various herbs and spices, refusing to divulge the recipe.

The Hand arrive together, laughing and joking. Watching them around the common bowl, arms draped over each other's shoulders and making quick work of the food, fills me with relief. I haven't forgotten Phanuel's dream about the hand with the severed fingers, and I was really worried that the others might change after spending all this time with the young crows. But they all seem to be as united as ever, just as comfortable in each other's presence as before. Nor do they exclude or ignore me and Yulia, as they would have done once. Something about the adversity of our shared journey together has created a bond between us all.

Or so I think, until Yulia and Phanuel are asked to retell what happened. That's when the trouble starts.

At first, we each interrupt and add detail as Yohannah and Shemayah hang on their every word. There's joking and laughter as we recount how we met Malchus and how he led us behind the prayer house, and then we decided the only way in was through the roof. It's when we get to the part where the Teacher said he forgave Phanuel's sins that everything begins to unravel.

"You could have heard a mouse squeak," says Phanuel, his eyes shining as he relives the moment. "No one said a word, although you could tell they were angry at him and thought he was blaspheming."

"They were right to be angry, though," Sabba adds. "After all, no one but God can forgive sin, and it must be through a blood sacrifice on the altar, and only with a male animal without blemish and by a priest of the right tribe."

At first I think Sabba is just presenting the holy men's view as part of the story, so I pick up the thread. "And that's why the Teacher told them he knew what thoughts they were harbouring in their hearts and then asked them all whether it was harder to forgive Phan his sins or to tell him to get up and walk."

"So then the Teacher looked at me and told me to stand up."

"And he did!" adds Ananias.

Yohannah and Shelamzion chuckle with happiness.

"Which meant that it was impossible for anyone to deny this Teacher's power," says Menahem, but in a tone that sounds as though he is doing just that. "After all, we saw with our own eyes all manner of wonders. But the question still remains: where does he get that power from?"

"His power comes from God, obviously. Where else could it come from?" says Yulia, looking puzzled.

"Well, if the Teacher really was from God, why didn't he heal Phanuel and then tell him to go to the city and make an animal sacrifice for his sins?" says Sabba. "He would have known that only God can forgive if he was a real holy man, properly educated after years of sitting at the feet of an older holy man to receive proper instruction."

"Is this you talking or all those young crows you were so

196

desperate to impress?" asks Phanuel, hoping this will be an end to it.

"We just want to know where this man came from and why he thinks he can ignore the Law and everything recorded in the scrolls," says Menahem hotly.

"You saw with your own eyes what happened to Phanuel, and you know what happened to me. How can you be asking these questions?" Yulia says, her voice rising. "And as for all those crows – no disrespect, Uncle Shemayah – why would you listen to them? Did they help anyone? Have you forgotten that they wouldn't even let us near the Teacher in the first place? How can you possibly defend them?"

"See," says Yair, "if the Teacher was truly from God, he wouldn't be in opposition to our religion or our holy men. How do we know his power doesn't come from some kind of evil spirit?"

"Are you saying I've been healed by a demon?" Phanuel demands, getting to his feet as Ananias tries to make him sit back down again.

"Let's all calm down and talk about this properly," says Shemayah, raising his hands in peace.

"Don't you see what this is?" says Yulia. I've never seen her angry like this before. "It's just typical boy behaviour, no different from the time a girl from the other village was better at the sling than my older brother and all his friends. Did they accept that she was better? No. They said she was a witch and that was how she could hit anything she liked with that sling of hers. These crows are no different. They're just jealous little boys."

"You can't say that!" Sabba shouts. "Have you no respect? What do you know about anything, anyway? You're just some blind, barren village girl."

"Would you like to say that when my husband is in the room?" Yulia snaps back.

I speak out. "For a start, Sabba, she's not barren any more, and nor is she blind, thanks to the Teacher. It was his power that healed her. And we saw him help a woman who was troubled by demons, didn't we, Yulia? So tell me this: how could the Teacher get his power from a demon and then work against himself? It makes no sense."

"There's no point trying to discuss our religion with village girls who can't even read," says Yair, getting to his feet.

"That's because you're losing this discussion," Ananias says, standing up and looming over Yair. "I think it's time you apologized for your insulting behaviour and for doubting the best thing that's ever happened to anyone in our village, and then we can all go home."

"Division and questioning," says Sabba, also scrambling to his feet. "How can that be from God? That's what happens to communities wherever that man goes."

And with that, he, Yair, and Menahem shake out their tunics in disgust and leave without thanking their hosts or saying goodbye to any of us.

"What kind of madness has got into them?" says Phanuel. He seems more hurt than angry.

"I'm so sorry," Ananias says to Yohannah.

"Why are you apologizing for them?" I demand. "Those stupid little boys think they're experts in religion after a couple of weeks with the crows! Phan, I'm telling you now that none of them are ever welcome in our house again. Not until they apologize for what they said, especially to Yulia."

"Let me talk with them," says Shemayah. "It's just youthful zeal."

"Come now," soothes Yohannah, "let me make some tea. We still want to hear the rest of your story."

"Well, I'll leave that to Phanuel," says Yulia, fighting back tears. "I think it's time I went home."

"Ananias, could you walk Yulia back?" I ask, knowing her house is just a short detour for him. "I think we should be heading home as well. I'm sure we can finish the story another time."

"I think we should tell Amma about this," I state as we trudge back home. "Sabba's mother is her cousin, and she should go and visit her and tell her what kind of boy her son is turning into."

"Tabi, please. Let's not make the situation any worse," says Phanuel. "It's started. This is what I saw in my dream."

He looks so stricken that I keep quiet and say nothing to my mother.

I arrange for Yohannah and Yulia to visit Shelamzion's home later the next day so Yohannah can hear the rest of the story. We don't hide from Shelamzion what happened last night.

"It was the best moment of my life, suddenly being able to see clearly," Yulia finishes. "So how can they think the Teacher's power has come from anyone but God?"

"I think you should speak to Sabba's mother and tell her what he said to Yulia," I say to Shelamzion. "She should make him apologize."

"As long as Azariah doesn't hear about it. He feels very protective of me, especially now," says Yulia, stroking her belly.

Word soon spreads about Yulia's pregnancy, then Azariah hears about the insults levelled at his wife. A day or so later he ends up fighting in the mud outside Sabba's house and breaks Sabba's nose.

"You should go back to the Teacher and ask him to heal it," I say, smiling spitefully as I pass him sulking outside his house.

He just spits on the ground in response.

Later, when I pass Menahem and Yair I give them a withering look and they ignore me.

I hear from Shelamzion via Hanan that Ananias is considering a visit to Menahem and Yair's house to try to patch things up.

"Did you hear the way they spoke to me, and to my brother and my best friend?" I snap at him over lunch. "If you're going round to their house then be the man you should be and break their noses too."

The whole village is aware that the Hand has fractured, and this division simply fuels the rumour that questions the Teacher's power. This could all have been so easily avoided if those stupid boys had just returned to the village when we did instead of staying behind and being poisoned by the crows. I'm furious with them for ruining the miracle.

The situation worsens when Amma hears of it and is soon shouting at her cousin about her son's disgraceful behaviour. Then I hear Menahem's married sister speculating on whether Yulia's pregnancy is a result of an evil spirit and whether the child will be born cursed.

"You should be ashamed of yourself and your poison tongue," I say to her loudly when we pass on the street. "The poison seems to run in your whole cursed family."

She gasps and turns to others to make sure they heard this slight as well. I know I'm not helping matters, but she deserves it.

As for Phanuel, he spends his time hauling dung from the sheep pen out to our orchard and spreading it around the tree roots, while at home he's planting and enlarging Amma's vegetable garden or helping Ubba whenever a new lamb is born. His industry means that my only chores at home are cooking the evening meal and keeping the house clean. Most evenings Phanuel goes to visit Shemayah, wanting to read scrolls from the prophets.

"There must be something written in them about the Teacher," he says. "Perhaps he's the chosen one who will save our people?"

Sometimes Phanuel visits Hanan's workshop and we hear animated discussions, although we're too far away to make out words.

I've taken to sitting up on the roof with my aunt now that we don't need the shelter of a wall. I love seeing the land come to life around us again. Everything is in blossom and the meadows turn greener daily as the snow retreats further up the mountainside.

Soon we see the first butterflies of spring and the wild bees from the forest come out collecting nectar. Ubba takes his flocks to graze along the snowline and says that the snow will have retreated past the shepherd hut within the month, and then he'll stay up there for summer grazing.

I finish my first shawl. It's taken me over two weeks to make, but that included unravelling bits and reworking them as I experimented with patterns and tried to get the hang of this hook technique. Shelamzion is convinced that, with practice, I'll be able to hook a shawl in half the time.

I compare my first shawl with Amma's. It's not quite as fine, nor have I got the design right, but for a first attempt it's not bad. I'm keen to make a few more before it's time for the first scything of meadow grass, as we'll all have to pitch in.

Ananias and I seem to communicate compliments about each other via Shelamzion and Hanan, both too shy to say much face to face just yet. We have a few moments that deepen our friendship. He feels me watching him carving beautiful curling patterns that look like forests of leaves and flowers onto a large cedar wedding chest.

"How do you know what to carve?" I ask in wonder.

He shows me how he marks up each side, measuring it out and drawing the pattern on with a nub of charcoal.

"You'd be amazed at how much more we can sell a wedding chest for if it's covered in wood carving. It looks more impressive and the groom's family always want to impress," he explains with enthusiasm, until he realizes he's talking about grooms and weddings and then stops.

"I need some kind of technique for planning the patterns of my shawls. At the moment I try to keep them all in my head but it doesn't always work."

He smiles and I think nothing more of my comment until later that day he climbs up the stone steps to the roof and presents me with a smooth wooden square of cedar, stained with slaked lime to bleach it, and a stick of charcoal.

"Here," he says. "Once you're finished with a design, you can just rub the charcoal off with a damp cloth."

"This is perfect," I cry out, and in my enthusiasm I peck him on the cheek.

He blushes and Yulia and Shelamzion trade a look. It's our first kiss.

Ananias hurries back down the steps, smiling to himself, and I ignore the women and concentrate on mapping out my shawl design. The map really helps and I make far fewer mistakes. I take my work home, squinting in the lamplight with Amma warning me that I'll end up with eyesight like Yulia's if I'm not careful. I remind her that Yulia has perfect eyesight now.

"You don't have to tell me," she states. "I won't stand for a bad word said about that Teacher of yours, whatever Sabba's mother thinks she knows. All I know is that my son was as good as dead and now he's come back to me, and I've never seen him more alive."

But the next week, Sabba, Yair, and Menahem are gone and the rift in the Hand is complete. We hear from our neighbours that they've returned to the Great Lake to see if they can study at the prayer house there. Despite everything, I'm hurt they didn't say goodbye to Phanuel or Ananias. But I'm also relieved they've left, because they've been like urine in a well, poisoning the whole village. Before they showed up, everyone in the village looked at Yulia and Phanuel as signs of God's blessing. Now, the same women who used to call Yulia a fruitless tree speculate about whether her swelling belly is really a gift from God or "the result of some terrible, devilish union" as I heard one of the worst gossips on our street whisper, lips pursed in silence when she noticed me.

"And I thought age brought wisdom," I retorted.

I made sure I told Amma about the exchange, knowing she would head out visiting and ensure that rumours about the old gossip herself were soon circulating.

So, not only is the Hand fractured, but so is the village. Whether someone nods at my brother or pretends they haven't seen him tells you which side they're on. The blessing has curdled, all because of those stupid boys.

The night after they leave there's more heavy rain, and I find myself hoping for a mudslide and a large rock to bound down the mountainside and flatten all three of them.

Chapter Eleven

"What's the matter?" I ask a boy who passes by, studiously avoiding any acknowledgment or greeting. "Didn't you see us, or do your eyes need healing by the Teacher as well?"

"Tabi," says Phanuel, "you don't have to be so aggressive. It's not helping matters."

"I'm sick of it, Phan. Give me one example anywhere when an evil spirit has done something good. All they do is make people crazy. They never make anyone better. How can these stupid people believe such lies?"

Phanuel sighs. "People fear what they don't understand," he says.

"*I* don't understand. *I* don't know who the Teacher is or why he has the power he has. All I know is what he does. He does good. It's obvious."

Phanuel smiles. "This time last year you were still Sholum's shadow. Who'd have thought you'd become even fierier than she was?"

"It's not about me being fiery; it's about them being wrong," I state, voice raised and, admittedly, a little fiery. We climb up the path to our orchard, which is now full of the swelling nubs that will become apples. It's been a month since the boys left, and Yulia has missed her second moon blood and spends most mornings trying not to vomit.

"Tabi, you're so quick to defend the Teacher, but have you forgotten what he did for you? Your own miracle?"

"What do you mean?"

"You said that the most important thing for you was experiencing the power of being forgiven and forgiving others. We need to give Sabba and Yair and Menahem time. They saw what the Teacher did. Let's pray that one day they are able to see where his power comes from."

"Humph," is all I manage as the path steepens. We're both carrying scythes, on the way up to our meadows. He's right. I've gone from experiencing the freedom of the Teacher's forgiveness to wishing for a boulder to crush three of my brother's former friends. It seems I still have a lot to learn. "Anyway, when did you get so clever?" I ask peevishly.

"There wasn't much else to do but think when I couldn't move anything below my neck."

"Have you talked with Shemayah about becoming a holy man?"

We've arrived at the lowest of our meadows, which, if we scythe it now, should still regrow enough for some autumn grazing.

"He's the one who's talked about it. He says that I've been touched by God, and that I should tell others of the wonders God has done through the Teacher."

"So, not all holy men are stupid," I mutter, avoiding looking at Phanuel, who I know will give me a gently reprimanding look. "What would Ubba say? Doesn't he want you to help him with the flock and take over from him one day?"

"I don't think I want to be a crow," says Phanuel gently. "I certainly don't want to end up like the others."

"But you're the one who's always wanting to study Shemayah's scrolls."

"That's different. I'm trying to find out what the prophets say about the chosen one who will save our people. I think the Teacher might be the one."

I don't really understand these religious matters but I still blurt out the first thing that comes to me: "Why read scrolls when you could go and find the Teacher and discover who he is for yourself? Ask him if he's the chosen one or not."

Phanuel glances at me, smiling. "And when did *you* become so clever?"

"Hah! I'm just a stupid village girl, according to our own fledgling crows."

"I've been thinking about it a lot, actually," he says slowly. "I want to wait until after your wedding, but then I'd like to go and find him."

"Oh," I reply.

He pauses to see if I'll say more, but I just pick up my scythe and get to work on the meadow. I'm not sure how I feel about my brother leaving, even if it was my suggestion. The house will feel so empty without him. Then I remind myself that I'll have gone, too. Amma and Shelamzion have decided on the wedding date. It will be after the walnut harvest and the anniversary of Sholum's death, but before the first snows. My aunt – as always – has thought through the economics of the situation. It's a time of year when apples and other fruit are in abundance, and the sheep are fat.

I always thought our one room was too cramped for a family, but that was our family with my mother antagonizing and spoiling for a fight. When I think about the new family we'll be making – just the four of us for now – I find that I'm actually looking forward to winter.

But there's not much time to think about the future when there's so much to be done in the present. By sunset we've finished scything the nearest meadow and I manage to carry some of the new hay down to the haystack myself. I'm wearing my old tunic, as I want my new ones to last. It's far too short for me, and I'll probably give it to one of the neighbour girls after the scything season is over. I'm now almost the same height as Amma. Phanuel is also broadening and putting muscle back on. He'll never be as big as Ananias, but he no longer looks sickly and skinny. We're both dark brown from the sun, our backs strong from the hard work of scything.

Once a week I climb up the mountain with the donkey to take Ubba more firewood and flour, and to bake flatbread for him. Sometimes Amma leaves Helkias with Shelamzion or a neighbour and comes with me, and then we make cheese.

For the most part, Amma seems content to work on her vegetable patch during the day, allowing a little time to gossip with neighbours. Sometimes she even has supper cooked for us when we arrive home at night. A couple of times a week I visit my aunt's. She works on buying up the best of last winter's wool from everyone and dyeing it over the summer, her roof festooned with woollen clumps of red, yellow, and blue.

"I want to try spinning with dyed wool and then try dyeing spun wool to see which method gives us stronger colours," she explains when I drop by to visit her and my uncle one summer's evening.

Yulia comes over to help with the shawls in the afternoons, but spends most of the mornings retching. As her belly swells, the morning sickness seems to lessen. She can't scythe in the fields but is determined to do something as Rohul and Azariah fuss over her too much whenever she stays at home. She's become a better spinner than I am, and is working with golden-coloured wool dyed in pomegranate rinds. Pilgrims no longer visit from other villages. Who has time for such things in summer?

Sometimes I go with Yulia down to our lake in the evenings and we wash and submerge ourselves in the waters. Over on the other side, Phanuel and Ananias swim with some of the younger boys and young men like Azariah. Thankfully, Yulia shows no inclination for spying on the boys as Sholum once did.

There's no news from the rest of the Hand. Or if there is, their families don't share it with us. It's probably a good thing the whole village is so busy over summer, with no time for divisions.

Ananias and my uncle continue to work on their wedding chests.

"What do you think of this one?" Ananias stands back, having put the finishing touches to some particularly intricately carving on a chest of mountain oak.

"It's beautiful," I whisper. "Grooms will be fighting among themselves in Blood City to buy it for their brides!"

"There's more," he says, beaming, and lifts the lid. I gasp. Ananias has used different-coloured pieces of tiny wooden squares instead of stone to produce a beautiful mosaic of swirling patterns. "Yulia told me you liked the pictures on the floor in the public baths. I thought you'd like this."

"I've never seen anything like it." I run my hands over the carved wooden exterior, which is smooth to the touch and burnished with beeswax.

"I checked with Hanan and it fits into the space they're giving us inside," he goes on.

"Wait... this is for us?" I look at him in astonishment.

"Well, the tailor must also wear trousers," he replies, quoting a village proverb. "Why should I make all these chests for other people's brides and not produce one for my own?"

"But I haven't made you anything. I can't see you wearing one of our shawls."

"You don't have to," he says.

Then he puts his arm around me. I don't stiffen or shrug him off, but lean back and enjoy the honest, hard-working smell of his sweat.

"It's big enough for all your clothes as well, and our extra bedding," I say.

Chris Aslan

"And if God blesses us with children, I can make a smaller chest for each of them."

I smile up at him. "You're really planning ahead, aren't you?"

Then I kiss him slowly and gently on the lips. I can feel him holding his breath, afraid to move, and I wonder how someone so much smaller and weaker than this man can wield so much power over him. He puts his arms around me and I feel covered by him. Then suddenly he pulls away, tripping over something in the process.

"I'm sorry, Uncle," he says and I turn to see Hanan standing beside his lathe, smirking.

I scurry over to the house. I hear my uncle chuckle but feel embarrassed nonetheless, and after that I resolve that there will be no more kissing or anything else until we're married.

I don't mention the wedding chest to my mother. She'll find out soon enough and I'll deal with her jealousy then.

This year the whole village has a good apple harvest. There were no sudden spring frosts and not much in the way of late spring hailstorms, which damage the newly forming fruits. As harvest time approaches, trains of donkeys along with their merchants arrive in the village, and after we've finished collecting huge baskets of our apples, Phanuel climbs the mountain to look after the flocks so Ubba can hire a donkey train and travel down to the lowland towns with our apples. I ask him the names of the towns he'll visit because I know them as well now.

"You should visit the public baths while you're there," I say.

"And leave all my hard-earned coins to those thieving changing-room attendants?" he asks.

I help Amma boil up all the bruised apples, which we pulp to make apple leather, setting up waxed cloths on the roof covered with the paste to dry in the autumn sun.

Ubba returns from the lowlands with sacks of lentils, beans, olives, and dried fish. He returns to his hut and Phanuel comes home.

"I visited the lake before I came back. I was starting to smell. I thought I'd walk back through the forest," he says as we sit around a common dish that evening.

"Was it your first time since –"

"Yes," Phanuel interrupts, "it was."

"Are you all right?" I ask.

He nods but looks sombre. "There were already a few walnuts on the ground. We should gather the youth together ready for the harvest."

"What?" Amma practically shouts. "You're not going anywhere near that forest, my boy."

"Amma, we've got to do our share of the harvest work," says Phanuel gently. "Trust me, I never want to climb a tree again, but I still have to go and help. And anyway, with Ananias working for Hanan and the rest of the Hand gone, who'll show the younger ones how to collect the harvest?"

I haven't thought about the others for a while and suddenly wish Sabba had returned for a few days, if only because I'd love some wild honey.

"Someone else can show them. Not you," Amma states in a tone not to be argued with.

"I'll climb the trees and Phan can collect with the other children," I state, cocking an eyebrow at him.

Much to my surprise, Phanuel, far from protesting his manhood, nods in agreement. Amma still looks unconvinced.

"Well, do you want us to have walnuts this winter or not?" I ask.

She simply snorts, which is assent enough.

We arrange to start the walnut harvest the day after next and sew burlap into sacks. Phanuel and I are now the eldest of the unmarried youth in our village, not counting Ananias, who is working on his chests. We lead the ragtag group and I notice that

I'm not the only one to have grown over this past year. Scrawny little Maryam from down our street has shot up and is beginning to develop curves, and Halafqa and Yaqim, inseparable neighbours, are almost my height, downy-lipped, and speak with uncertain voices that crack and squeak.

Returning to the place where Sholum died, I'm more affected than I care to admit, but I try not to let it show. It's easy to find *the* tree.

"Yaqim, you and Halafqa can start here," I state, pointing at the tree and holding their gaze for a moment. "Please, be careful."

They nod silently. They, too, know about this tree. Everyone does. They shimmy up it and start shaking the lower branches while others collect below.

I find one of the older, squatter trees, hitch up my tunic, and clamber up. I don't look down. I'm determined not to be mastered by the queasy feeling in my belly. We've got work to do, and without the rest of the Hand it's going to be a challenge. I hold on to branches above and step out along gnarled wood until I reach the point where my weight causes it to bend. Then, holding tight to the branches above me, I bounce and am rewarded with the patter of raining nuts. Scrawny Maryam starts collecting them below.

"My mother says girls shouldn't climb trees, and that if they do no man will marry them," she says, looking up.

"Well," I reply, shaking a branch at my shoulder vigorously, "does that mean she's not coming to my wedding?"

At midday we pause for lunch and Phanuel gathers the youth and tells them the story about unforgiveness that I heard from the Teacher. We de-husk the walnuts at the same time, and I collect a sack of husks for Shelamzion to use as brown dye. My hands are already stained from the husk juice and I resign myself to being a black-handed bride by the time the harvest is over.

No one talks about what happened last year with Sholum, but even Halafqa and Yaqim are sensible and don't take unnecessary risks, and no one makes fun of Phanuel for collecting nuts among the girls.

After a week of collection, Maryam decides to join me in the trees, and then some of the other girls do, too.

"Are you tempted to come up here as well?" I call down to Phanuel.

"I am, but I promised Amma I wouldn't," he shouts back up, and I realize Phanuel is a lot more honest than I am. He more than makes up for it by collecting far more walnuts than I ever did, and is careful about distributing the nuts he collects fairly to all the harvesters.

As with the apples, there's a good nut harvest this year, and by the time we get to the last few trees, most of the leaves have already fallen and our breath turns to fog. We probably have another two or three weeks before the first snow, and I have a wedding to think about.

Actually, most of the thinking is done for me, as Shelamzion – acting as the groom's mother – will host the wedding and has everything already planned. She has prepared a curtained-off area for me and Ananias to share. Ananias has asked one of his brothers and Phanuel to hold up his side of the wedding canopy – which Shelamzion has been embroidering – and I've asked Yulia and one of Ananias's sisters to hold up my side.

My mother sits me down and attempts to prepare me for what will happen on the wedding night. It's an embarrassing conversation for both of us. "He'll have been told not to be gentle the first time, because it's important that you bleed. They'll hang the sheets out the next day for everyone to see. But don't think it will always be like this. You'll come to enjoy those intimate moments. It will be the stitching that holds your marriage together."

Phanuel is making his own preparations. He's told our parents about his plans to leave to find the Teacher after the wedding.

"The house will be so quiet without you both," says Amma with a sob, wiping her nose with her sleeve, but she makes no move to stop Phanuel from leaving. "Of course you should go to him," she says. "He gave you your life back."

Ubba even presents Phanuel with a pouch of coins. "It's not a gift; you've earned your fair share of the apple and walnut harvest," he states, refusing to listen to any protest.

"Will you look for the others?" I ask Phanuel when we're alone.

"I don't know. I mean, I'd like to see them again. They're still like brothers to me. But religion has changed them, and I don't know if they'd even want to see me. I think it hurts Ananias even more. You know, we made a promise once that when any of us got married we'd ask someone to sew a special canopy that could be carried by all four of us on the groom's side."

"Well, I'm sure that's breaking a religious law somewhere," I state with a joyless laugh. "I don't think they'd be so willing now."

"That's what I mean. We've lost them."

On the day itself, Amma weeps so copiously that Yohannah has to take over putting the kohl around my eyes or I'd be at risk of being blinded. She also hennas my hands, which are still stained black from the walnut husks. Amma receives far more attention from the women on our street than I do, which I'm actually relieved about. I'm wearing my green tunic, which I've saved for this day, and revel in the envy it produces.

Phanuel, who has absented himself all morning to help Ananias, arrives with my betrothed and all the boys from the village, whooping and clapping as someone plays the tambour badly. They've oiled their hair with scented oils and clearly had a good long wash in the lake, despite the cold. Both Phanuel and Ananias are wearing the tunics we purchased from the Great Lake and they turn heads.

The canopy made by Shelamzion is unfurled. It's covered in embroidery and quite stunning. She's managed to keep it from me all these months. Yulia holds her growing belly with one hand and lifts her corner of the canopy with the other. People clap in time

with the tambour and the women dance and ululate as I proceed with Ananias under the canopy, up toward our new home. His mother comes up to me and ties a beautiful blue linen headscarf around my waist, then kisses me three times, as do several other wealthier villagers and close relatives. The others present me with bundles of dried fruit or whole shelled walnuts.

Halafqa and Yaqim come running over with a shallow wooden bowl and on it an impressive chunk of honeycomb, oozing honey with a couple of dead bees in it. They both have swollen marks on their face and arms but don't seem to notice the stings. I shriek with delight as it's the only honey I've seen all year, and kiss both their cheeks, which isn't allowed, but everyone laughs, and then I smear a finger in the honey and feed my husband to be, and he feeds me.

"May your marriage be sweet," the women from our street cry out.

We arrive at Shelamzion's and she's hung out the finished shawls on the walls to decorate the house and placed a new wedding felt outside for the ceremony. Several sheep Hanan purchased for the feast have been slaughtered and are now being roasted. Shemayah is there, wearing his black cloak and turban, and he prays blessings over us as the ceremony commences.

Throughout this – the feasting, the prayers of blessing from the older men and women in the village, and everything else – Ananias is by my side, and yet we barely manage more than a quick smile at each other. Finally, after most of the guests have left apart from some neighbour women who've stayed to help wash up, Shelamzion appears from inside and guides us both in with a flickering lamp in her hand. We step over the threshold and every lamp is lit, the light dancing on the walls. Shelamzion lifts the curtain and shows us to the marriage bed: a newly stuffed mattress on the floor covered in new white linen with a brazier of burning coals to keep us warm, over which she scatters some herbs that give off a fragrant smoke.

"There's still a lot of cleaning up to do, so Hanan and I won't be back for a while yet," she says. "I think it's a good evening to play the tambour. No one will hear anything else."

With that, she ducks out and we hear the door shut behind her and then the beat of the tambour playing a gentle rhythm.

"It's allowed now," I say, and cup his head in my hands, causing him to stoop, as I kiss his mouth.

We do this for a while and then he shrugs out of his bridal robe and takes off his tunic, standing before me in just his waistcloth, which is bulging.

"We should… I don't mean to rush… I'm just thinking of your honour. We'll need to display the sheets tomorrow," he says.

I nod.

"I asked Hanan the best way to start, and he said it might be easier for you if I'm undressed first, but then he thought that seeing, you know, everything, well, it might scare you." He looks at me, puzzled, hands poised to remove his waistcloth. "What do you think?"

"I think you're forgetting that I was there with Sholum when she was spying on you and the Hand and your wife-maker competition," I say with a smirk.

"And do you remember who won joint second?" he grins and drops his waistcloth.

I drink in the sight, knowing that this is permitted because he belongs to me now and I belong to him. I let him undress me and touch me and lie me down on the new mattress. And, although we're both new to this and wary of hurting each other, I feel a hunger I didn't know I had and soon he's on top of me, and any pain is so outweighed by the pleasure. While the tambour marks out a steady rhythm outside, together we match it with our own.

Chapter Twelve

"Are you sure you have everything?"

Phanuel looks around at us. We're outside our home. My old home now. I'm still not used to that. Ananias has his arm around my waist. In just two days we've become so relaxed with each other. Amma is weeping, clutching Helkias to her bosom under her shawl, and even Ubba looks close to tears. I feel a stab of guilt that I'm not more upset at my brother's departure, but the last few days have been so wonderful that I can't be anything but happy.

"You've got a glow about your cheeks as if you've been sitting too close to the fire," Phanuel told us when we arrived together this morning.

He's right. I can feel it radiating out from me. I find myself laughing for no reason.

Shelamzion and Hanan arrive and my aunt takes out a waxed traveller's cloak made of thick, woven wool with a frame of simple white stitching. It looks warm, practical, and manly. I don't know where she got it from.

"Remember us when you walk and when you wrap yourself in this at night," she says, kissing his forehead.

"And let this staff help you on your journey and protect you." Hanan hands him a beautifully carved staff similar to the one he made for the Teacher.

"This is your village, your home. You will always belong here however far your journey takes you," says Yohannah.

Then her husband comes forward, lays his hand on Phanuel's head, and prays blessing and protection over him.

Phanuel wipes away a stray tear, then embraces Shemayah, Yohannah, and each of us who've come to see him off.

"No," I say, when he comes to me. "Not yet. We'll walk down with you as far as the lake."

Then he comes to my mother and she starts to wail loudly. He holds her for a little while, rocking her as if he were the mother and she the infant. Then he turns and we leave.

"Here, let me carry it as far as the lake," says Ananias, easily swinging Phanuel's sturdy cloth bundle onto his shoulders.

"Phan, please don't forget us," I start. "Not just because, you know, this is your home and everything, but also because we need someone to show us the right way. Learn from the Teacher. He's too important to ever come all the way up here, but you can bring his teaching back with you. And make sure you get back before the others return and start bossing us around and telling us how we're doing everything wrong."

Ananias is silent as we walk down, and I glance at him and see how troubled he looks. When we get to the lake, he takes Phanuel in his arms in such a fierce but tender embrace I'm almost jealous.

"I love you so much," he whispers, and they both begin to weep. "It's always been the five of us, and then the others left and now you're leaving too, and it'll be just me here on my own," sobs my husband.

"You didn't seem very alone this morning," I state, reminding them both that I'm still here.

"I'm not sure I could have left if it wasn't for you marrying Tabita." Phanuel wipes his eyes. "Look at you, Anan. You've got a wife. You've got new parents and a craft which pays well. I'm so proud of you."

"I know," Ananias says, then he dissolves into tears again and grabs my brother in his arms, kissing his neck. "Don't forget us, and come back!" he whispers huskily.

"Tell the Teacher everything that's happened," I say as we hug. "Tell him about Yulia's pregnancy and that we follow him in our hearts even if we can't follow him with our feet like you." Then I find myself weeping as well. "Phan," I whisper into his ear as we embrace, "I came so close to losing you once. Don't let that happen again."

Ananias leans his head on mine as we stand, arms around each other's waist, weeping and waving as Phanuel disappears from view.

"He's a brave man, my brother, starting out alone like that," I say.

"He's a leader of men," says Ananias. "One day he'll lead us."

I look up at him and wonder how he knows this, but I don't doubt him. We both wipe our noses on our sleeves and I look up at the path. "Shall we head back?"

Ananias looks around. The lake is deserted but this is still the main path.

"I want you in the forest," he whispers, taking my hand and tugging me along the side of the lake to a wooded area.

"We'll get leaves everywhere," I protest, but with a smile because I like this idea.

Despite Shelamzion and Hanan loudly announcing all manner of pretexts to leave us alone in the house together, it's never enough for Ananias, who seems inexhaustible. At night, we've learned to make love almost silently, although once or twice we hear similar murmurings from the other side of the curtain. I feel an ease around Ananias that I never dreamed possible. All the awkwardness of before has gone.

It's also such a pleasure to live with Shelamzion and Hanan. I've heard cautionary tales of brides stuck with bullying mothers-in-law or jealous sisters-in-law and weeping with homesickness every night. Nothing could be further from my own experience. Every night around the common bowl there's an ease and familiarity of conversation, or a contented silence that doesn't need to be broken. Not only have I gained a husband; I feel as if I have new parents as well. Ananias tells me it's the same for him. He's not used to how much space we have behind our curtain all just for us, or how quiet the room is with no crying babies or multiple snorers.

With the harvests gathered and the sky threatening snow any day now, I can finally focus my full attention on shawl-making. Yulia is still spinning for us, but she's slowed down and is crotchety and uncomfortable with still a month or so to go before the baby is born. Most women spend the last days of autumn shelling walnuts up on the flat rooftops of their houses, but we start to visit house to house with the lighter spindles Hanan has made to enlist new spinners. We'll wait until the snow has fallen and we have a good stock of spun yarn before we progress to the hooking method and start actually making shawls. My aunt has thought through a fair system of payment, which ensures a higher profit for women than walnut shelling, and soon Hanan is producing spindles for most of the village's women. Even Menahem and Yair's mother and aunt come asking for a spindle and a lesson from Shelamzion, and for now we pretend the rift between us doesn't exist.

I sit up on the roof whenever I can and either work on a shawl or sketch out new designs. The more I think about it, the more I'm aware of the endless possibilities. I think about leaves and try a repeating pattern of them, which is so different from the straight lines I'm used to. I end up with several incomplete shawls, set aside for a while because I want to experiment with a new idea or technique. I take a simple red shawl, which was one of my first, and try threading blue yarn through it to create a contrasting, decorative frame. Shelamzion loves it and we decide to use this technique on all our shawls. Perhaps it will become the way customers identify shawls made in our village.

"Of course, other villages will soon start to copy us if we're able to build enough popularity," she explains. "That's why we've always got to think ahead."

Two days go by when I don't even cook a meal, so engrossed am I in my new creations. Shelamzion happily cooks for us, and when I apologize for my laziness she assures me that for now this is the perfect division of labour. Ananias restricts his lovemaking to the night, except once when he tells me he has a surprise for me and takes me into the woods again, which actually comes as no surprise at all.

"I wanted to make the most of this time. We won't be able to come here once the snow starts," he argues afterwards, picking dry leaves out of my hair.

"I wouldn't put it past you," I snort.

Amma comes to visit regularly, which is something she never did before. There will always be an uncomfortable rivalry between her and her sister, but for now she seems positively meek. She offers to become one of our spinners as well, although she can't keep herself from haggling over her wage.

When the first snows come, Ananias offers to help Ubba get the flock stabled and fed.

"But if you think you can just sit around all winter drinking tea while I work, then you've got another thing coming. Here," Amma says to her husband, and dumps a large sack at his feet. "I'm going to teach you to card wool. And I don't care if you think it's women's work or an affront to your honour, or that you rue the day we wed. Yes, I know what you're thinking!"

One morning I hear Ananias outside call "Amma". I wonder

if it's my mother or his who is visiting so early, but he's calling for Shelamzion. She looks pleased, but we say nothing about it. He also takes to calling Hanan "Ubba". And why shouldn't he? He still calls his actual parents "Ubba" and "Amma", and they don't mind sharing him, as they've got more than enough sons of their own.

I discuss training with Shelamzion and we decide the easiest thing would be for me to teach just three other women the hook technique to begin with. Yulia is in confinement, due to the imminent birth, so I pick two of our neighbours, both older women, and scrawny Maryam, because she's one of the best spinners and picks things up quickly.

I want them to make a shawl each under my direct supervision and then two more here in our house, where I can still keep my eye on them but focus on the next batch of shawl-makers. We start, and inevitably my mother is drawn in as well, unable to resist a whole day of gossiping with other women. She brings Helkias, whom she expects me to mind, but who ends up becoming Shelamzion's responsibility.

Once the first shawls are finished, the women try them on, rubbing the softness of them against their cheeks, and marvelling at how warm they are, despite their lightness. Shelamzion gives each woman the option of buying back her own shawl on credit and no one can resist. Despite her generosity with firewood and lamplight, it's getting really cold.

One night we're woken by banging on the door. It's a young girl who lives next door to Yulia and who's been sent to fetch me and Yohannah. Yulia's labour has started.

Azariah loiters at their gate, having been exiled after getting in his mother's and Yohannah's way. I hurry inside and, despite the cold, Yulia is bathed in sweat and moaning as Rohul smooths her hair and dabs at her brow. Yohannah is scattering dried herbs into a steaming pot over an indoor hearth and has tied the leather birthing strap over a central roof beam. Yulia clings on to it with one hand and digs her fingernails sharply into my supporting arm with the other. She follows Yohannah's instructions for when to push and when to pant, but seems more animal than human as she grunts and growls, straining until sunrise when the contractions come fast and Yohannah helps her to squat, holding on to the birthing strap with both hands and howling as the head of the baby emerges and then the rest comes slithering out after it.

Yohannah slaps the baby to make it cry, rubs it, and cuts the cord.

Rohul begins to ululate and I join in, which sends Azariah careening in through the door wanting to see his new child.

"Is it a boy? Is it a boy?" he gasps.

"Here." Yohannah wraps the baby in a warm blanket as I help Yulia onto a mattress. "Your beautiful daughter."

Yulia doesn't say anything but just weeps as she holds this baby in her arms. Soon we're all crying, but these are tears of joy as we watch a dream, held for so long, become a reality.

"What will you call her?" asks Rohul. I know she's waited long enough for her grandchild and I love her for letting Yulia choose the name despite this.

We're expecting the name of a grandmother or aunt, but Yulia whispers, "Hannah, her name is Hannah."

Yohannah nods and strokes Hannah's forehead. "Named after the woman who trusted God to open her womb. Little Hannah, may you grow up to trust in our Lord and to obey him with all your heart."

Tears roll silently down Yulia's cheeks as she whispers "Amen". Azariah lies down behind Yulia, taking them both in his arms and gently kissing his newborn child.

"Here." I have a cloth satchel with me and remove a small blue shawl I've been making specially. "To keep her warm and to remind you of our friendship."

I stay for a while to help clean up and to welcome the first women who come to visit. It will be forty days before Yulia is allowed to leave the house again, and visitors will be welcome as long as they don't come spouting nonsense about this being a devil child.

"Auntie Rohul," I say as she walks me out to their gate, "if Sabba's mother or any of that lot come here and say anything, *anything*, you come and tell me and I will silence them. Every woman in this village wants to be part of our shawl-making business and we have no space for such poison."

She nods and kisses me goodbye, her face drawn with exhaustion but her eyes alight with joy.

The reality of our new-found power dawns on me as I trudge home through the snow. I've noticed that women have become more friendly or deferential toward me since we started recruiting spinners and shawl-makers. We now have a list of spinners waiting to learn the hook technique, and one or two have even attempted bribery with offers of date syrup or winter pomegranates from the lowlands if I would just include them in the next training. What they say behind my back, well, who knows? But I intend to use this power well, and as soon as Yulia finishes her confinement I want her back and weaving with us. Let the whole village see her baby girl and what a gift from God she is.

One evening after the shawl-makers have gone home, I'm chopping onions when Shelamzion announces, "We've got thirteen or fourteen completed shawls now, and within the week that could be up to twenty. Once I've paid the women for these, that's all my coins gone. I could borrow from Hanan, but I think we should sell now, in the middle of winter when the demand for warm shawls is highest."

I nod in agreement. "Who should go?"

"I want you here, overseeing the shawl-making and continuing to train others."

"Will you go with Hanan?"

Shelamzion nods. "But I'd also like to take Ananias. The roads aren't safe in winter and there's always the possibility of robbers. Perhaps we can take one or two smaller chests to sell as well."

It's agreed. The following day is sunny and seems as good a time as any. We borrow Ubba's donkey and a neighbour's and put the shawls inside smaller wedding chests that are carried by Ubba's donkey, which is larger, while the other carries provisions, clothing, and bedding.

"Don't be alarmed if we don't return right away," says Shelamzion once the donkeys are ready. "I want to get to know Blood City better and seek useful contacts whom we can trust to give us a good price for these shawls."

It's the first time I've been apart from Ananias since our wedding, and even though I know they'll only be gone for around a week I still cling to him as they depart.

We're up to fourteen women now. During the day I'm too busy to miss Ananias, but at night my mattress feels cold and lonely without him, and the room is so empty. I try to make the most of the solitude and work on new designs in the lamplight of an evening.

Five days after they've left, as we sit working on shawls together, a son of one of the shawl-makers bursts in and shouts, "They're back, they're back!"

I drop my hook, pull on my boots, and hurry down to the entrance to our village as fast as I can. I can hear ululating and welcome, which seems a little excessive for a five-day absence, but I rush down anyway. They're not welcoming back my family, though. There, surrounded by happy relatives, and dressed in white turbans and black woollen cloaks, are two young crows: Sabba and Yair.

Yair has attempted to grow a wispy beard, which does little to make him look less pretty. Sabba, on the other hand, has filled out and the turban simply adds to his height. He cuts an imposing figure. One of his aunties, who has her head back, ululating, allows her headscarf to slip.

"Cover yourself," he hisses, and she swiftly adjusts it and falls silent.

"Where's your brother?" I call out to Yair. It's the nearest I'm willing to get to a greeting.

He turns away, as if he hasn't heard my question, but then announces to the growing throng, "Menahem had to stay behind. Our teacher said he could spare only the two of us."

Sabba's mother, my mother's cousin, runs to Sabba and flings her arms around his neck. He pats her gently but looks uncomfortable.

"Are you going to escort us to the prayer house?" he asks, looking around.

There's something about his manner, his total lack of interest in the people around him, that makes me want to break his nose, just like Azariah did. Yet this attitude, combined with his commanding presence, means that no one questions him; we simply follow.

"Where is Shemayah?" Yair demands once we're outside the prayer house. "Tell him to come out."

I look around to see if anyone else is disturbed by this. How dare this upstart speak this way? Yohannah emerges from her home to see what the noise is about and her face brightens when she sees Sabba and Yair.

"Welcome back," she says. She sees where they're heading. "We could meet outside, if you like. The prayer house is so cold and dark in winter."

Yair gives Sabba a knowing look and then announces, "We wish to meet with the village in the prayer house, the correct place for spiritual gatherings."

Amma shoots me a look. She's just arrived with Helkias in her arms, never one to miss out on anything. I'm grateful because I have a feeling that something bad is about to happen, and with Shelamzion, Ananias, and Phanuel all away, and Yulia at home, I need an ally. Even as I think this, I realize I'm already squaring up for a fight. We follow the crowd inside the prayer room as Yohannah attempts to prop the doors open to let in some light.

Yair barks rebukes at young boys who have gone to sit with their mothers on the women's benches running down one side of the room, and they wander back to the men's side, wide-eyed and close to tears. Sabba enters with Shemayah at his side. Shemayah looks small and frail beside him. I take a place on the bench beside Amma.

"I don't like this," she whispers.

Latecomers are sent to fetch other relatives or neighbours who haven't yet come. I watch faces brighten as they enter and see our boys back from their studies. But the smiles quickly fade at the severity of Sabba's expression, and they meekly take their places on one of the benches.

"It is good to be back with you all," Sabba finally announces once the prayer house is full. "We have prayed for you throughout our studies."

There are murmurs of appreciation.

"We wish we could have come sooner. When our teacher heard of the lax approach to our religion in this village, he wanted to send us immediately, to show you the correct way you must follow. He was shocked to learn how few of you observe the holy day of rest or tithe your earnings toward the Temple; how few have travelled to the Holy City with the best of their flocks to make pilgrimage and sacrifice. He wondered if our village even had a holy man to lead and guide them."

All eyes turn to Shemayah to see if he will let this insult pass. I want him to clip Sabba around the ear, but he says nothing and simply gazes sorrowfully down at the floor.

"It's time for our village to return to the true path," Yair states, mimicking the same sonorous tone Sabba used. "Our teacher has sent us back to you. We've learned much from the scrolls, the histories, and the Law."

"Shemayah," Sabba turns to him, "will you step aside and allow a new generation to lead our village back to paths of righteousness?"

I'm stunned and there's a collective intake of breath, which suggests I'm not alone. Sabba holds Shemayah in a fiery gaze, as if actively bending him to his will. I look around and no one seems willing to offer a challenge. How can we so quickly forget our own holy man and his wife, who have loved, cared for, and served our village since long before I was born?

"This is so wrong," I whisper, clutching Amma's arm.

Shemayah looks up forlornly and is about to speak.

Then a voice rings out that breaks the spell Sabba seems to hold over us.

"Where's your honey, young Sabba?" My mother clambers to her feet. "I thought you might be gathering us for something useful."

Sabba wheels on her in fury. "Silence, woman!" he spits.

"Ho! Silence, Sabba?" she mimics, working herself up quickly as only my mother can. A honey-stealer should know better than to kick the hive that is my mother's anger. "Did the tambour clatter to the ground and make you a musician? Does the donkey that's been to the Holy City think it's a pilgrim now? You put on a turban and spend a year studying scrolls – or so you tell us – and then you come here and think you can speak to your elders like this? How dare you? How *dare* you raise your voice to me after you've eaten in my house? Who cut your cord and placed you on your mother's breast? She's sitting right there." Amma points to Yohannah. "Who taught you your letters and encouraged you to study the scrolls, never once standing in your way? And this is how you treat him? You claim to speak for God? Hah! You disgust me, both of you. Go back to wherever it is you came from. You're not wanted here. You bring shame upon our village."

"A woman should not speak in here," Yair protests. "It is forbidden."

"Nor should children," I call out. "And we're not fooled by your attempt at a beard."

"She's been bewitched by her son," Sabba states in disgust. "It's that false Teacher who has led them astray."

"You dare to mention my son? You, his failed friend? Curse the day you ever entered my house!"

The prayer house fills with noise as everyone starts talking over one another.

It's Shemayah who eventually stands and calls us to order. "Perhaps we should listen to Sabba," he starts, and I can't help but groan. "It is true that I am getting on in years and have been remiss in preparing a successor. Better that the next holy men are from our village than someone coming up from the lowlands."

"I won't be told how to live by a couple of boys who think a turban makes them a teacher," shouts one of Ananias's older brothers, and there's a murmuring of agreement.

"You say that the Teacher divides, Sabba, but it's you who has come bringing division to our village," Azariah calls out, and I know Yulia would be so proud of him right now. "Why don't you both leave and never come back?"

Shemayah lifts his hands again until there is silence. "This is a matter for prayer, not argument," he says. "Let us return to our homes and seek God's wisdom. We can meet again tomorrow at sunrise."

"But this time, let it just be the men who return," Sabba calls out.

My mother turns to me with a savage smile, knowing he has just laid a trap for himself. "Are you to be a holy man for the men only, or for the whole village?" she calls out, winning the women over.

Shemayah raises his voice: "This is a matter for the whole village. We will *all* meet again at sunrise tomorrow."

I give my mother's hand a squeeze. She has used that fiery temper of hers for something good and may have just saved our village from a disaster. I pile out with the others and call the shawl-makers to join me back at my new home. I know what I must do.

"Let it be known. Tell your neighbours and anyone you meet on the street that anyone, and I mean *anyone*, who sides with Sabba, or whose husband sides with Sabba, has no place working with us. Nor will they ever. I will remember. I don't care how good a spinner or shawl-maker they are. Let it be known."

The women nod silently, and I note with satisfaction that several of the gossips head to nearby houses, eager to spread the word. How could our village simply abandon Shemayah? It's unthinkable. I know Sabba and Yair's families will side with them, but I hope most people remember all that Shemayah and Yohannah have done for our community.

For the first time since I met the Teacher I feel totally powerless. I'd forgotten what a familiar feeling it once was. So I do as Shemayah told us and I pray. I ask God to protect our village and pray that something bad would happen to Sabba. Then I remember the Teacher's story about forgiveness and I pray again, asking God to forgive me for my previous prayer and asking for his will to be done. It's a short, clumsy prayer whispered under my breath, but it's heartfelt.

I sleep badly. I eat quickly the next morning, keen to miss nothing, then put on shawl and boots and head for the prayer house. I'm shocked to find Yulia there, even though there's still a week to go before the end of her confinement. Little Hannah is bundled in the shawl I gave her and Rohul sits next to her, spinning with her drop spindle. This spindle will be a useful reminder to all the women of my threat.

"I couldn't stay at home and miss this," Yulia explains. "Not after all Yohannah has done for me."

We sit together as the room fills up. Sabba and Yair arrive with their families, and the two young crows stand at the front beside the alcove for the scrolls, as if they already own the building. Shemayah and Yohannah are among the last to enter. They both look old and defeated. I suddenly panic. What if people are swayed by Sabba and Yair? If Sabba was in control, what would be his revenge for the way we made him look yesterday? Would he find some religious ruling that means women aren't allowed to do business? I try not to shudder.

Shemayah greets the boys amicably, then turns to face us all.

"May I ask that we refrain from discussion or argument today," he says. "We've all sought the Lord and now it is time to decide as a whole community whom we would like to represent us in spiritual matters. Those who would like to appoint Sabba and Yair as our new holy men, would you please stand up now?"

All the members of Sabba and Yair's families clamber to their feet. Their immediate neighbours, who happen to be sitting near them, also stand. It feels like the beginning of a ripple that might engulf the whole prayer house. One of my best spinners stands, and I mourn for the loss of her nimble fingers. However, the ripple soon stops. Barely a third of the village are on their feet. Sabba and Yair look around expectantly and then in disgust. I don't think they considered defeat as even a remote possibility.

Disgust turns to rage. "How can ignorant villagers decide such important matters?" Sabba fumes. "Our teacher sent us here. He has authority. You should do as he commands."

"Go and fetch us some honey, Sabba," Amma taunts. She can't help herself.

Sabba strides toward her, his hand raised. Ubba leaps from his bench on the men's side and grabs Sabba's wrist.

"I've killed bears with these hands," he growls.

Sabba tugs his hand away and backs off. "Do none of you fear God?" he thunders, looking at those still seated. "Don't you fear the punishment he will send on this community of unbelievers?"

We sit in silence.

"Our teacher will hear of this. He's becoming more and more influential among the holy men of the Holy City. This is not the end," Yair spits.

They glare balefully around the room, then shake out their cloaks and storm out.

"We did it, God be praised," Yulia whispers.

But there isn't the sense of relief I was expecting. This simply feels like a temporary reprieve. People begin to whisper and then talk in small clusters, and you can almost feel the fear in the air.

Chapter Thirteen

I hear in the evening that the crows have left. It's of little comfort, though, as I don't think Sabba's were empty threats. The shawl-makers are already nervously discussing whether and how the village might experience God's wrath. True to my word, I've already told Yair's neighbour, my best spinner, that she can no longer work for us.

I'm relieved when Shelamzion, Hanan, and Ananias return. Amma joins us around the pot for our evening meal, revelling in the detail of her successful spar with Sabba and her brave husband rushing to her defence. I don't have the heart to mention the pronouncements of judgment or the threat that the crows will return. Ananias sits there, silent and brooding, and after we've finished he gets up and goes outside. At first I think he's gone to relieve himself, but when he doesn't return I put on my cloak and go looking for him. I see footprints in the snow leading up to the roof, where he stands, huddled in his cloak, staring up at the star path that is visible on clear winter nights.

I say nothing, but I open his cloak and insert myself between his arms, leaning back into him and gazing up at the night sky. I wait until he's ready to speak.

"I missed you," he says finally, kissing my headscarf.

"I missed you too," I say, "although, in a way, I'm glad you weren't here. I don't know how you'd have found seeing your best friends replaced by crows."

He says nothing but his arms tighten around me. We stay like that for a while and then I feel the contractions in his chest and realize he's silently crying.

"Come here." I turn and cradle him, even though he's so much bigger than me.

"They were my brothers," he sobs.

I just hold him and stroke his hair and kiss it as he buries his face in my shoulder.

The next day, while the shawl-makers work in our room below, I go up to the roof with Shelamzion so we can talk in private. With all the events in the village I've barely heard anything about their trip.

"I'm sorry we took so long and that you had to face our homegrown crows without us," she starts, "but it paid to take our time. At first I put all thoughts aside of selling our shawls and instead sent Ananias and Hanan off to the public baths so I could focus on selling the chests for them. There are many things I love about my husband, and about yours, but neither of them knows how to haggle. I managed to get the same price as Hanan had the trip before, despite these chests being much smaller. I also took time to explore the carpenters' quarter. There is one old carpenter named Sabbataius whose son died four years ago. He has no one to take on his business, and he wants to leave the confines of the city and return to his wife's village. Blood City is walled, so there isn't much space inside, but over his workshop they have two rooms, each a little smaller than our own, and there's also a flat roof that works as a balcony." Shelamzion pauses and takes my hands in her own. "Do you understand what I'm telling you?"

I frown. Can she mean that she and Hanan would leave us? Leave home?

"I introduced Ananias and Hanan to Sabbataius, who welcomed us to stay in their guestroom for as long as we needed. I left them there, went to the public baths, then put on a clean tunic and one of our finest shawls. Then I went to the clothing quarter of the market, posing as a potential customer. Wherever there were shawl-sellers I showed them my shawl and asked if they had anything similar but in a different colour. All their own shawls were in brown or grey wool, and soon the merchants were asking me where I'd purchased the shawl and how much it had cost. They want our merchandise, Tabi. I also enquired after prices of the shawls there, and now I know how much they sell for. Do you realize how much profit they make? Tabi, if we moved to Blood City and sold the shawls ourselves, we could easily make enough profit to live well and to pay a better wage to the shawl-makers of our village. That's why I was willing to sell all the shawls we had to three of the merchants. If we can sell the remaining chests Hanan has in the workshop, we might have enough to buy Sabbataius's workshop from him."

I say nothing, trying to take in what my aunt is saying.

"So, we would live there, in Blood City? But what about our home here?"

"We could still keep this house and the women could use it in winter as a place to work on the shawls. We'd come back during the hottest months of summer to visit family and friends."

"Do we have to go?" I ask. "Is this decided?"

Shelamzion shakes her head. "No, we'll only do this if we all agree that it's the best decision for our family. But Tabi, you've seen how people in the lowlands live. We don't have to survive winter after winter cramped together in one room."

"What do Hanan and Ananias say?"

Shelamzion pauses. "I haven't spoken to either of them about this properly yet. I wanted to talk to you first to see what you think."

My aunt wants an ally.

"I have so many questions," I reply.

"And so you should, but let's leave them for another day. For now, just think about what I've said. Why should we do all the hard work and the merchants make the profit?"

She has a point.

"One other thing, Tabi. I found out more about the miracle worker. The crows hate him, so Phan will need to be careful. They call him *the False Teacher*, and there's a group that has been commissioned to track him down. Once they've found him, they plan to wait until there are no crowds about and then arrest him. But he keeps growing in popularity. Even some of the occupiers have turned to him. One of the foreign generals living near the Great Lake had a servant who was cured by him. You can imagine what the crows thought of that. Curing the servants of idolaters!"

"When Sabba and Yair were here they were so angry about the Teacher. I just can't understand it. They saw him heal their best friend. How can they be against that?"

"Religion is power, and power is something men crave," says Shelamzion. "And it seems you've discovered your own power; taking on the crows when no one else in the village would, and threatening to cut off anyone who voted with the crows."

"Amma was the one who stood up to Sabba," I remind her. "She was the one with real courage."

Shelamzion nods slowly. "And the one who's made a dangerous enemy."

That evening around the common dish Shelamzion talks about how much money we made, making the calculations aloud and being sure to let us know how much profit the merchants are making from each shawl.

Both Ananias and Hanan shake their heads at the avarice of merchants. Shelamzion glances over at me but I say nothing. I see her tactics.

Several weeks pass, and Yulia finishes her confinement and joins us with little Hannah. She talks openly about the Teacher with the other women and passes on his teachings, including stories I'd missed in that courtyard when Yulia stayed but I'd gone to find Phanuel. I can't imagine not living near Yulia. She's become like an older sister to me. Shelamzion continues her gentle persuasion of the men.

"Did I mention that Sabbataius was talking of retiring to his wife's village and selling his workshop and the rooms above it?" she says one night, as if the thought had suddenly come to her. "He sells his own products, and has saved enough to leave the hammering and hard work of carpentry for someone else."

"He should get a good price for that workshop," Hanan muses. "The location is good for trade, and the rooms upstairs were spacious for the city."

"If we lived somewhere with two rooms, there'd still be some peace and quiet in one of them if God ever blesses us with children," I find myself saying, casting a quick glance at my aunt. It's not until I say it that I realize I'm colluding. Does this mean I'm in favour of the move?

"Well, perhaps we should consider renting a room in Blood City and trying to sell our own merchandise," says Hanan with a shrug.

My aunt tenses at this but says nothing.

We're nearing the end of winter. We now employ most of the women in the village, except those who sided with the crows. Still, in a few weeks none of them will have time for shawl-making as the ground will need tilling and seeds planting. We'll stockpile the completed new shawls ready for next autumn.

After a week of heavy snow, we have a clear sunny day and Shelamzion suggests that we drag felts up to the roof and work on our shawls in the dazzling sunlight, bundled up in our own shawls and enjoying the sun's warmth.

The evening is uneventful. However, the night is not.

I'm shaken awake, but not by human hands. The whole house is shaking. Dust and debris rain down on us from the roof beams and Ananias yelps and curls himself protectively around me. There's a deafening roar outside, like thunder but more prolonged, and the door swings open, letting in a blast of icy air.

Then the shaking and the noise stop and the only sound is of us panting and coughing and Shelamzion sobbing on the other side of the curtain. A little moonlight comes through the open door and we hurriedly dress by it.

"Avalanche," I hear Hanan state gravely. "Quick, we may have to rescue our neighbours."

Shelamzion is trying to light a lamp but her hands are shaking and the sparks from the flint don't catch the kindling.

"Here, let me," I offer, and we soon have a small fire burning in the hearth and light a lamp from it.

"We'll need to take lamps," says Hanan, "and gloves for digging."

We drag our boots on and, each shielding a lamp, make our way onto the street. Looking down at the rest of the village, nothing has changed. The moon is setting and we're an hour or so from dawn. Then I turn and look up. The setting moon reflects off the snow, and that's all I can see: snow.

"Where are the orchards?" I peer closer and realize the top cluster of houses just before the meadow isn't there either.

"Quick!" Hanan shouts, and takes Ananias around to the workshop, returning with two wooden snow shovels. "We don't have much time. If they're still alive, they're going to suffocate in their homes."

Neighbours are beginning to venture outside and Hanan calls

them to fetch shovels. There was an avalanche in the neighbouring village three years ago, but nothing like this. The older people know what to do and urge us all to hurry.

We come to the edge of the avalanche, marked with a tide of snapped and twisted branches and rubble, pushed forward by the snow. As the first men clamber over it, pulling aside branches, we can see the corner of a house. They start to dig.

"Hanan, we need someone to lead. Start organizing people," says Shelamzion. She climbs a little higher and looks around. "Yitra's house should be over there," she points, "and Yusef's around here? Come on, we need teams digging at each spot."

Hanan and Ananias split up and Hanan makes sure there are men in each digging team.

"Someone help me," a voice calls out, and I make my way toward it. It's Halafqa, one of the youth who offered me honey on my wedding day. "The snow stopped just before my house but Yaqim and his family are buried. We've got to help them."

"Do you have a spare shovel?"

Halafqa shakes his head, so I start digging with my hands.

"Wait," says Shelamzion, who joins us. "Let's take a moment to figure out exactly where their house should be. We don't want to end up digging down to the sheep pen." She paces out, looking to Halafqa as he practically lives at Yaqim's place.

"More to the left," he tells her.

Once we're satisfied, we start to dig. We stand bent over, throwing the snow out behind us like burrowing rabbits. Even with gloves on, my hands soon feel the chill, but as we work I warm up and have to discard my shawl. I think about how heavy snow is and how much is sitting on top of Yaqim's roof right now. Will it bear up under the weight? Has it already caved in? Will they still have enough air?

Someone else arrives with a shovel, and we work silently and quickly. My lamp guttered a while back but dawn is breaking now. Halafqa's shovel hits stone, and we join around him, enlarging the area. It's the flat roof of the house, which is still standing. "Thank God," Shelamzion wheezes, "but we mustn't stop now."

We continue to widen the area and then hit on the low wall that surrounds the flat roof. "Over to this side," Shelamzion commands us. "The door should be here."

We dig deeper and reach the door lintel, which just increases our speed. The door opens outwards and is still wedged tightly shut by the snow.

"Yaqim, are you all right?" Halafqa shouts as we dig down.

We can't make out words but we hear voices inside. No one needs to be told; we redouble our efforts.

Shelamzion works her fingers into the snow around the doorframe. "We need to give them fresh air," she grunts, as she has to lie on the snow to reach down to do this. "Someone get an axe!"

Soon Halafqa is battering the top of the door and splinters through a section. A hand reaches out from inside and he grabs it. "Is everyone alive?"

"Yes, thank God," we hear Yitra, Yaqim's father, call back. He gasps and gulps down the fresh air. We tunnel down until most of the snow is cleared from around the door.

"You'll have to push it from inside," Shelamzion calls out. They try but the door won't budge. We remove more snow and they push again, and this time they manage to open the door enough for each family member to squeeze out.

They look flushed and weak, and once we've dragged them out they all sit clutching their heads in pain. Then Halafqa, who is standing stretching his tired back, suddenly disappears up to his waist in snow. The roof has finally given way. We haul him up and he grabs his friend Yaqim and holds him tightly. "If you'd still been in there…" He doesn't finish the sentence. He doesn't need to.

Yitra rubs some snow on his face and shakes his head to clear it. Then he stands up to survey the snowscape that was his homestead. He laughs hollowly. "Well, at least the sheep and goats will be frozen. I can still try to sell the carcasses." We're not supposed to eat meat with blood still in it, but no one here in the mountains objects to a frozen carcass – a casualty of winter.

"We're ruined." Yitra shakes his head in despair. Their sheep and orchards are completely buried.

"We're alive," says Yitra's wife Maryam quietly, placing an arm around him. "And for now, that's all that matters."

Other families are not so fortunate.

There's a snap and a cry and then a plume of snow further along what was the street. Another roof has caved. We wade through the heavy snow over to where Hanan and others have renewed their digging with extra vigour. It doesn't take long to get down to the splintered timbers and wet mud bricks that were once the roof. Snow seems to have filled every crevice.

"Everyone stop for a moment." Hanan lifts a hand to silence us. "Can you hear us?" he shouts at the snow. We all pause, desperate to hear a muffled response, but there's nothing. He calls out again.

"Maybe they were knocked unconscious," I say, but my voice lacks conviction.

We resume our digging, but we're too late. Old Mara's is the first body we find. Her face is fixed in a silent scream, her open mouth full of snow. We drag her out unceremoniously, still hoping for survivors. Next come two of her granddaughters, then her son and his wife. It's the first time I've seen dead bodies with no one weeping or wailing over them. We don't have time. As we pull out the last body there's a faint sound, and Hanan clears away more snow to reveal one of his own cedar chests made years ago. He tries to drag it out of the snow but it's stuck. We clear the snow from around it and manage to get the lid open. Nestled in clothes and bedding is Mara's grandson, face almost purple from lack of air. Hanan picks him up and holds him aloft, and someone manages a tired cheer.

"Tabi, take him to Yulia. She'll have to feed two babies now."

I pick up the bundle and rock the child, trying to remember his name. "It's all right, everything's all right," I coo to him, trying to stop him crying, and thinking how untrue this is.

We work together for most of the day. First, we rescue the survivors. Those who are unharmed join the digging. The injured are taken to Yohannah's place to be nursed by her. She gets the older women cooking food for everyone. Then we lay out the dead. There are seventeen in total. Among them are Menahem and Yair's parents. Somehow, Yair's youngest sister, who is just four, has survived. She is taken to Yohannah, numb with shock, blue-lipped, and shivering.

Shemayah discusses with some of the older men what to do with the bodies. We could dig deep into the snow and leave them there until we have time to bury them properly, but that leaves them at risk from wild animals. If we all work together, digging through the snow and then attacking the hard, frozen earth, we might be able to bury one or two of the bodies, but seventeen?

In the end, it's decided that we will entomb all the bodies in one of the caves near the forest, and brick up the entrance with stones to prevent wild animals from entering. Burial is usually a man's job, but today we'll need everyone's help.

There isn't enough salt to put some beneath each body. Instead, Shemayah scatters the salt over the floor of the cave and then the bodies are laid next to each other, shrouded in blankets or felts or whatever we could salvage from the buried houses. We have to stack a second layer of corpses on top of the first. It feels undignified and wrong, but what else can we do?

There is less wailing and screaming at the deaths of these seventeen than there would usually be for just one fatality. No one has the energy, and we're all still too shocked. Perhaps the grief will come later. Numb and exhausted, one or two people even fall asleep as Shemayah intones prayers. Then the men heave boulders to the mouth of the cave and gradually block it, while I help the women fill in the gaps with smaller rocks and stones. It's sunset by the time we finish. I glance up at the mountain and feel hatred toward it for the way it can kill so unsparingly and still appear so immovable and unconcerned.

Chris Aslan

As I pass the prayer house I hear someone call my name. I turn to see Amma with Helkias balanced on one hip, holding hands with Menahem and Yair's little sister.

"Elisheba, this is Aunty Tabita," she says gently. Elisheba looks at me shyly, then turns her little face away, burying it against Amma's tunic.

"I'm going to look after her," says Amma.

"But we're not speaking to them," I blurt out, and even as I say it, I hate myself. What do our petty squabbles matter in the light of all this?

"What would that Teacher of yours tell you to do?" Amma arches an eyebrow.

"You're right, Amma. I'm sorry," I say. "Here, let me take Helkias. I'll come and cook for you and Ubba."

"No, you're needed at your own home," she tells me. "Yitra's family are staying with you."

I've been so concerned with burying the dead I'd forgotten about the living and where the survivors would stay. I hurry home to find Yitra, his wife Maryam, their sons Yaqim and Honi, and Grandfather Chuza seated with my husband and uncle around two large bowls as Shelamzion ladles out soup.

"You're just in time." Shelamzion attempts a smile. We sit and eat. At first we talk about who has been billeted with whom. Then little Honi asks how long they'll be staying with us.

"As long as you need to," says Shelamzion quickly. "There's no point in thinking too far ahead at this time."

"Thank you." Maryam begins to weep.

Shelamzion puts an arm around her.

I take the bowls outside to wash them in the channel. I hear movement behind me. It's Yaqim.

He says nothing, but hands me the bowls.

"It must have been terrifying being trapped in there. Was it completely dark?"

Yaqim nods. Although his shoulders are broadening and his

241

voice is deepening, he still looks like a little boy at this moment. "We couldn't light the lamps because they'd use up the air. The door opens outward, so we were trapped and I could hear the beams creaking above us and we knew we didn't have much time. We just prayed and cried. Thank you for saving us."

"You would have done the same for us," I reply.

And he nods because it's true.

After a silence he says what he's come out here to say. "Do you think your husband or uncle could make me a spindle? I want to help my mother spin. We're going to need every coin we can get."

"But it's women's work," I say in surprise. "What will people think?"

"They'll think that we need the money and that I'm willing to do whatever it takes to help."

I nod. "Would you like me to see if Hanan can take on another apprentice? Maybe you could learn wood carving."

"I already spoke to your aunt about that, but she said he can't take any more apprentices right now."

This seems odd, but I say nothing. "I'm sure Ananias can make you a spindle. Who knows? You might become one of our best spinners."

He smiles half-heartedly. We go back inside, where Shelamzion has laid down mattresses. There's just enough room for us all to fit, but we've dispensed with the dividing curtain. Grandfather Chuza is already snoring gently.

"Thank you," Maryam says again.

"Please stop thanking me; it's nothing," Shelamzion replies. "You would do the same for us."

I wonder if I should undress under the covers, but glance around and see that Grandfather Chuza is asleep fully clothed. I'm so tired that this seems the best option. My last thought before I fall asleep is that I must ask Shelamzion tomorrow why she told Yaqim that he couldn't be apprenticed.

Chapter Fourteen

The following morning there isn't a moment alone with my aunt as the whole village gathers up near the avalanche to begin the salvage. We mainly dig up frozen animal carcasses and news of the cheap meat soon reaches other villages, leading to an influx of people keen to see the damage, click their tongues in sympathy, and leave with a bargain. A fight breaks out when one of them haggles too hard, ignoring our misfortune.

We drag what clothes and bedding we can from the remains of homes before the snow melts and ruins them. We have several sunnier days and then another avalanche during the night. It wakes everyone, but it doesn't come near our village.

On the seventh day after the avalanche, Shemayah calls a meeting in the prayer house. It is time for us to properly remember the dead and there is keening and wailing as he recites the list of names. I'm seated next to Amma and Elisheba. I feel a stab of jealousy at the gentle way Amma speaks to her. She never treated me like that. Then I feel guilty when I think of all that little Elisheba has lost.

A thought occurs to me and I whisper it to Amma: "Who will tell Menahem and Yair about their parents?"

Amma shrugs. "We don't even know where they're studying or how to contact them. They'll come back to visit at some point and find out soon enough."

There's a knot of people discussing whether the avalanche was a fulfilment of Sabba's prophecy. "Remember, he told us that if we didn't follow the correct path God would bring his wrath upon the village."

"Then why was it Yair's family that died? They voted for Yair and Sabba."

"But their sister was spared. Perhaps that was God's mercy for following the true path."

"Or maybe it's just that those who lived highest up and closest to the orchards all died, because that's where the avalanche settled, however they may have voted," Amma calls out.

I wonder if this topic will come up during the prayers. In a way, it does.

"Our hearts are heavy. We will never have our lost returned to us." Shemayah looks around at us all expectantly. "It will take years to rebuild what has been destroyed, and even then there will be empty places at our meals and today there are too many empty spaces on these benches." Two women begin to wail. "But perhaps this terrible disaster can bring us some good. We have been torn apart by division but we worked together to save our neighbour, our relative. We are one village and our enemy is not each other. There are no sides. There's just us, fighting to stay alive and trusting in God to help us. You ask why there was an avalanche. We know the answer; there was a build-up of snow followed by a day of warm weather. This is how life on the mountainside is. It's dangerous and that's why we need each other, and we need God and must put our trust in him."

There are nods and tears. He's right. I see Amma hold Elisheba a little closer to her as Shemayah speaks. The prayers for the dead continue and we weep and wail together as one village.

On the way out, I pass Menahem and Yair's neighbour. Her family were relatively lucky; they lost their home but no one died. I remember how good she was at shawl-making, but how I refused to employ her after she sided with Yair during the dispute. And I think about what the Teacher would do.

"I'm so sorry about your house and your cow," I say to her.

She glances up, her eyes still red and swollen from crying.

"And I'm sorry that I stopped you making shawls with us. Shemayah was right; we should be one village and not divided. Would you like to come back?"

She nods silently and I'm about to go when she grabs my arm. "Thank your mother for me, for looking after little Elisheba." Her face crumples as if she's about to cry, but she masters her emotions. "I will come to your house tomorrow. Could I bring some of the others? Sabba's mother?"

I nod. "Anyone from the village with skill is welcome. Even the boys."

At first I'm not sure Yaqim will manage. His initial willingness to spin wanes and I realize boys find concentration harder. But his mother patiently helps him reconnect another break in his yarn, which is lumpy but slowly improving. Ananias has produced several new drop spindles in anticipation of others needing an additional source of income. After a few hours, Halafqa shows up at our door.

"I just came to watch," he explains, embarrassed. Then, lowering his voice, "Usually I'd be with Yaqim but now he's going to be here the whole time I don't know what else to do."

"There's no place for spectators," I state firmly, holding out a drop spindle for him. "If your best friend is willing to learn, why don't you join him?"

As it turns out, Halafqa is a natural and is soon helping his friend produce an even yarn. The boys take their spindles outside and we hear their laughter or the occasional squabble from up on the roof.

Hosting an additional family in our room makes Ananias frustrated with longing. Sometimes he wakes me in the middle of the night, grateful for the steady sound of Grandfather Chuza's snoring, which hopefully masks any noise we make. With the number of extra workers we have now, Yohannah has kindly opened her house and the women who live further down the mountain now meet at hers. There isn't a single family that didn't lose livestock or orchards in the avalanche and we're all going to need this additional income.

I still haven't managed to speak to Shelamzion, who seems preoccupied and closed. Finally, several days later, we shoo away Yaqim and Halafqa and several other younger boys who've joined them spinning up on the roof so we can have a proper conversation.

Shelamzion launches into her new business plan before I can ask the question that's been troubling me.

"In the short term, the avalanche might actually be good for us," Shelamzion states, hurriedly glancing up to make sure I haven't taken this the wrong way. "Although it means everyone will take longer pruning broken branches in their orchards or helping the survivors rebuild their houses, with fewer sheep to graze we might be able to get some women spinning and shawl-making into the summer instead of harvesting the summer meadows. Of course, this gives us an additional problem of potential wool shortage in the longer term, especially now that we have so many people working for us."

"What can we do?"

"Well, we could buy wool from the neighbouring villages, but I don't want to alert them to our business. Of course, people gossip and the word will get out anyway, but let's make sure we've established our markets before we attract any competition from them. Tabi?"

I'm thinking. "Most of the survivors and others who lost their livestock have managed to sell enough meat that they can afford at least a couple of lambs or kids. Why don't we call all the women together and get them to tell their husbands to buy only new lambs and goats with the best wool rather than the ones likely to get fattest quickest?"

Shelamzion grins. "If we weren't working together I'd be getting worried about you. You're the nearest thing to competition in this village." She chuckles to herself. "Oh, I forgot to tell you. I caught Maryam teaching Yitra how to spin this morning. He looked so guilty when I saw him trying, but why shouldn't the men spin or make shawls in winter? Does it have to be only women who work all the year round?"

"And now Honi wants to learn as well. If his older brother is doing it then he wants to copy him," I say. Then I pause for a moment, and decide that now is the time to ask. "Auntie, why did you tell Yaqim that Hanan and Ananias couldn't take on any more apprentices? Look how quickly you sold the wedding chests in Blood City. Surely we could afford to take on one or two more boys."

Shelamzion smooths her tunic and pauses, as if she's trying to find the right words. "As I dug through that snow, desperately praying we'd find someone alive, I asked myself why we live here when we have the financial means to make a choice. Last week it was the threat of avalanche. In a couple of weeks it'll be the spring mudslides. Then next winter we'll be crammed together in one room, huddled around a lamp. I don't want us to wait any more. I want to move to Blood City now. Let Yitra and his family live here for a year or two, as long as the women can still come and work together in winter. When they have the means they can buy the house from us.

"I told you about Sabbataius and his offer to sell his workshop. If I can persuade him to let us repay him gradually over the next few years, what are we still doing here? Hanan has the rights to several of the larger cedars. We can chop them down and have camels drag them to Blood City. There'll be enough work with just one of those trees for years to come. And as for us, we can travel between the village and the city, keeping an eye on the work here and ensuring quality. We could make Yulia our main overseer. Then we'll be the ones to see the profit from those shawls and not some greedy merchant. We can pay off Sabbataius and enjoy being one family in two bedrooms rather than three families in one. And you won't have to worry about others hearing the two of you in the middle of the night."

"You heard us, then?"

"Of course I did. No one's *that* quiet. But we don't have to live piled up together like this. Tabi, we have a chance to start again." She takes my hand in hers and looks full into my face, her eyes shining with expectation.

"When would we move?" I ask.

"As soon as possible. Before anyone else tries to buy that workshop from Sabbataius."

"Do you think he'll sell it to us even though we don't have the full amount yet?"

"Tabi, the way he looked at those wedding chests, the way he ran his finger over them... he's a master craftsman and he knows quality. And he knows that quality sells. I want to take two smaller chests, fill them with shawls, and see if I can make a deal with Sabbataius."

"But what about Uncle Hanan and Ananias? What if they don't want to move? Didn't Uncle Hanan talk about trying to rent somewhere?"

Shelamzion makes a dismissive noise. "Why throw money away like that? We need to buy a property, and we could sell shawls from the workshop rather than having to rent a shawl stall in the bazaar. Let me work on Hanan. I haven't talked to Ananias yet, though. I thought it might be better if you did."

"Ah," I say, adding a cocked eyebrow. "I can see you've really thought this through."

My aunt attempts an innocent smile but fails.

Chris Aslan

"Actually, I've been thinking about this a lot, ever since your aunt mentioned the possibility of someone buying the workshop from Sabbataius," Ananias states, chewing on a piece of flatbread.

We're sitting side by side on one of the completed chests that are waiting to be carved. The workshop is now the quietest place for us to meet, as there's always someone in our house. "Do you know what would have held me back? It's not my family. I'd miss them, but we could always visit. It's the Hand. If the Hand was still together I don't think I could ever have left, but..." He trails off.

I give his knee a squeeze. "I never thought I'd say this, but I'll really miss Ubba and Amma. Still, as long as we're together and with Hanan and Shelamzion... and we'll have our own room. Can you imagine? A whole room just for us."

"I hope it won't be just us forever," he says and pats my belly.

"We can always come back and get Yulia to pray over me if nothing's happening with babies," I say with a wink, and then turn more serious. "Also, I want to see the Teacher again, and we know he's never going to come up here. Shelamzion was saying that the crows are trying to arrest him."

Ananias nods. "I forgot about that. We haven't really had a chance to talk properly since I came back. We heard all sorts of wild rumours about him in the city. He's made some real enemies there."

"Maybe if we're in the city and he visits there'll be something we can do to help."

The next morning, before the women come to the house to resume shawl-making, the four of us meet together in the workshop to discuss the proposal. It turns out Uncle Hanan still has some reservations.

"I just want some kind of sign from God that this is the right thing for us to do," he explains. "I'm not convinced Sabbataius will agree to let us pay over the next few years. There must be other buyers who could give him the full price right now."

Shelamzion thinks for a moment. "If I return with a signed and witnessed document from him, will that be sign enough for you?"

"You can't travel alone," Hanan counters.

"Of course not," she says. "And a woman's word won't count as a witness. Ananias will come with me."

Hanan chews his lip meditatively and then nods.

"We'll need to leave tomorrow," says Shelamzion. "It'll already be the beginning of spring in the city, but perhaps there's still enough of a damp chill in the air for women to want a new shawl."

"The house will feel almost empty without you," Hanan jokes as Ananias and Shelamzion say their farewells, and Grandfather Chuza and Yaqim adjust the straps on the donkeys.

They're gone a week, although I don't have much time to miss them or to wonder how they fare, beyond saying a few simple prayers. On their return, I don't have to see the wax-sealed document Shelamzion produces to know that she's been successful. It shows in the way she holds herself.

"He wants repayment over three years, but he's willing to let us have the place now. He trusts us! It won't be easy, but I think we can do it. He's agreed to include all the tools in his workshop, which means we could hire an apprentice. He wants us to move now, as he won't leave the property unattended and wants to leave the city well before summer. I gave his wife one of our shawls as a gift. It seemed prudent."

The four of us have gathered in the workshop for this meeting. There's silence as Hanan and I digest everything.

"I didn't think it would be so soon," I state. "I thought we'd have more time to prepare the women. I'm not sure they're ready to do this alone. I'm not sure I am, either."

Shelamzion nods. "With Yulia now looking after the orphan baby as well as her own, it will be too much for her to take full responsibility for the work here. I think we should involve

Yohannah. She doesn't need to spin or weave but could help with collecting and storing the shawls and paying the salaries. Also –"

Hanan interrupts. "If we're to leave so soon, I can't sit around while you women talk. We need to consider what to take with us. How will we manage transport?"

Shelamzion nods briefly. "I've arranged for a camel trader from the city to bring his caravan here."

"How many camels is that?" I ask.

"His caravan consists of twenty beasts. He's agreed to let me pay him in shawls, which he can easily trade in other lowland cities as they're so lightweight."

Hanan's brow furrows. "We can pack most of our belongings into chests, and each camel should manage at least two large chests, possibly smaller ones if they're filled with heavy tools. We won't need twenty."

"I talked it over with Ananias. I hope you don't mind," my aunt continues smoothly. "We'll ask Zacchaeus and Levi to chop down one of the cedars we have rights to and transport the logs at the same time. You won't have time to do it with all the packing. Both their wives are working for us, so I think we can come to a satisfactory arrangement."

Hanan shrugs helplessly. Who are we to attempt to stay ahead of such a woman?

"I need to tell my parents before they hear it from someone else. Unless you've spoken to them already?" I try not to let my voice sound too testy but this is an enormous decision and I'm not sure I'm quite ready for it.

"Let them know that our new home will be their new home and that they can visit whenever they like," Shelamzion states. "We'll all be leaving something precious behind. I want to plant some spring flowers on Sholum's grave before we leave."

I've only left our village once before, and I couldn't wait then. I was so full of hope and expectation, and I didn't think about what I was leaving because I knew I was coming back. Now I've no idea what to expect, except that summer in the walled city will be unbearably hot. I'll be leaving behind Yulia and my parents. It also occurs to me that I'll be leaving behind my status. In just a short while I've gone from being a girl no one noticed to one of the most influential women in our village, known by everyone and training women three times my age. I know no one in Blood City and everything will be new.

When I break the news to them, I'm not sure how Ubba or Amma will react, but Ubba is matter-of-fact in his response.

"Ananias is your family now and you'll have children of your own one day, if God blesses you. And I expect we'll see you back here during the summers. The heat down there is unbearable."

Amma's reaction is fierier. "So my sister will live in luxury in the city from the profits of our toil here in the village?"

There is some truth to this when it comes to the shawl-making, but I point out that the women in our village need the additional income and are grateful for it.

Amma folds her arms and harrumphs. "And don't think I won't come to visit," she adds, jabbing a finger at me. "I might accustom myself to city life and find myself reluctant to return."

The idea of my mother living with us is terrifying, but I remind myself that Ubba would never leave his sheep and that she'd have to return here eventually.

The hardest person to tell is Yulia. She listens silently, the orphan baby at her breast, then quietly begins to cry.

"I don't want you to go," she sobs. "What will I do without you?"

"I know, I'm sorry." We hug and cry, trying not to squash the baby between us.

"I'm not saying you shouldn't go," she sniffs. "Just that it'll break my heart not to have you here. I waited so long for a true friend like you."

"Yes, that's what you are." I brush a strand of her hair away from her face. "A true and irreplaceable friend." I want to remind her she has her baby now – two in fact – and that she has status and acceptance in a way she didn't have before, but she knows all of that. Instead I lean my head against her shoulder and make her promise she'll come and visit me one day.

Ananias somehow senses my discomfort as I huddle next to him. He gathers himself around me and whispers, "It'll be hard, but I'll be with you. We'll have each other and our new parents. We'll make new friends."

I want to snap that it's easy for him to say this because all his friends are gone, but I remember the Teacher's words and that stops me.

There's something else I haven't told Ananias, Yulia, or anyone else. It was a clear night last night and after spending the day with Yohannah discussing her new role in our business, I ended up staying after dark and walking home through the melting snow in moonlight. It was a waxing crescent moon, which means that I'm late. I should have bled last week, but in the busyness of everything I completely forgot about it. I want to wait to be certain. I've heard the women gossiping enough times that sometimes the moon blood comes late or misses a month. It might just be that. Or I could be about to move to a new city, far from my own mother, and become a mother myself. I've never felt so unprepared.

Chapter Fifteen

"There," Shelamzion grunts as we ease the last cedar chest into position in our new home.

We're both sweating. Up in the village, there'll still be patches of snow in the shade, but for the past two days here in Blood City, a hot breeze has announced the arrival of spring, which to us feels more like summer. We've been here for four days, living all together in one room while Sabbataius and his wife lived in the other, as they packed and prepared to leave. We remained in the same room while the other was whitewashed with a fresh coat of slaked lime. Then we all moved downstairs so Hanan and Ananias could paint the second room. I kept referring to it as Sabbataius's house, until Shelamzion told me off.

"It's *our* house. This is our home, and we need to get used to calling it that."

It might take me a while. I've never moved into a stranger's house before. When I went to live with Hanan and Shelamzion it was still the house where I grew up and played with my cousin.

"Mmm, it doesn't feel right. The room still feels quite empty,"

I state, surveying the two chests, with folded mattresses and bedding atop them and the wedding felt on the floor. Shelamzion has already said this will need to be rolled up and stored in a few weeks because the weather will be too warm for it. Although this room is smaller than our one room back in the village it seems too large for just two people.

Shelamzion smiles. "It's just that we're so used to seeing all our possessions in one room, and sharing it between three families. We have the pots and plates in the kitchen downstairs now and our chests are divided between these two rooms."

A gust of wind blows the window shutter closed and she opens it, wedging a piece of wood in the lintel to keep it open. This is the thing I love most about these upper rooms. They have shutters that open out onto a flat roof, which can be kept shut for privacy or warmth in winter, but also opened to let in light and breeze. The flat roof of the workshop below makes for a balcony, and I plan to grow tubs of fresh herbs out here and sit in the spring sunshine to work on my shawls.

Although we have more living space now, I already feel the absence of a garden. I hadn't realized how often I would tear off a few sprigs of mint or coriander to flavour our food back home. Instead of the majestic views of mountains and valleys, all you can see from here are other rooftops, and then behind us the city wall. Up on the roof at home, the mountain breezes whip away the smells from the unclean place or the sheep pen. In the summer, during the scything of the summer meadows, when the breeze blows down from the mountain, the scent of wild thyme, mint, and basil hangs in the air. Here, people seem to fry with more spices, although their pungent fragrance only partially masks the smell of all the neighbourhood's unclean places. And all this is laced with a fine haze of dust that settles on furniture and felts. The comforting clang of sheep bells and the sound of wind have been replaced with the sounds of sawing and hammering, as this is where most of the carpenters and joiners live and work, along with the chatter of neighbours and crying of children, as we're all packed so tight inside these city walls.

Our house is built right into the city wall itself. I wish we were a little higher, or the walls a bit lower, so we wouldn't feel quite so trapped. There's a ladder that leads up onto the bedroom roof, and from there you can climb up onto the rampart of the city wall with great views. I climbed up once with Ananias but felt sick looking down as we were so high up, and it just reminded me of what happened to Sholum.

Shelamzion carries some bed linen into their room and I'm left alone for the first time in our own room with all our things in it. I've kept a three-legged stool that Sabbataius left behind, and placed it next to the window with my spindle on it. I've never owned a stool before. In the village we usually just drape a piece of felt over a log. For some reason, seeing my spindle and our wedding chest brings me great comfort. I crave familiarity. I hadn't realized how hard this would be, and I feel tears welling up again. This seems to happen several times a day.

I scold myself. A year ago almost to the day we set off on our journey to find the Teacher. Back then all I did was look after Phanuel. I'd never dreamed that I'd be married to a man who loved me, and that we'd have our own room and live in a city, and that I'd ride on a camel for the first time, even if it was only moments before I felt sickened by the swaying motion and had to climb down and walk. That was a sight: seeing the caravan of camels, still with their thick winter coats, ponderously climbing up the stone paths of our village. Everyone came out to stare.

We marvelled at the enormous cedar logs they were able to drag away with them, and how just one could bear the weight of two large wedding chests. Yaqim and Halafqa got too close to one of them and it bit Halafqa hard on the shoulder. I wonder how they're doing now. I had no idea I'd miss everyone so much.

Since then I thought I'd want to join Shelamzion on her trips to the bazaar to stock our kitchen, or to explore the city with

Ananias, or at least to venture out to one of the bathhouses, but all I want to do is stay here, in this place that isn't quite home yet, eating the walnuts Amma gave me as a parting gift. The furthest I've gone on my own is to the neighbourhood bakery up our street. They have a huge clay oven and bake hundreds of rounds of flatbread every morning. Shelamzion even purchased some, which seemed such an extravagance. The flour was whiter and finer, and the bread deliciously soft, but I found myself longing for our dark village bread. The only time I don't feel on edge is when I spin or work on a new shawl design, or when I'm curled up against Ananias at night. He has been waiting patiently until tonight to make love, when we'll have a whole room to ourselves. It's a luxury few could even imagine back home.

Ananias doesn't seem to be struggling at all. He's tired, but that's because they need to saw the logs into planks before the weather gets too warm, otherwise the planks won't dry and season properly. It's back-breaking work, and it's all he and my uncle do every day. At night I try to smooth out the knots in his shoulders.

Ananias gave me a tour of their workshop on the ground floor, showing me the tools Sabbataius kindly left behind for us. Much of the workshop has been taken up by the cedar logs and planks, but there's still room to work. Next to the workshop, beside the stone stairway, is a well with a bucket for drawing water and another bucket we use for hanging cheese or anything else that needs to be kept cool. Around the well are sturdy wooden shelves, built by Sabbataius, where we store our pots and pans. We eat in front of the well and then there are large doors that can be opened up to turn the front of the workshop into a shop. There's a fireplace with a chimney that draws well, and no shortage of wood shavings for kindling. I asked Shelamzion whether we'll invest in a goat or a cow, but she flatly refused on the grounds of smell as well as lack of space.

"A few chickens, perhaps, but I've endured the smell of manure all my life and have no intention of doing so any longer."

I even miss the smell of manure. I miss everything.

As for our street, people go to the main bazaar in the city square for smaller wooden items, such as chopping boards or rolling pins, but for tables, chairs, and other larger items of furniture, this is the place to come. Hanan informs me that most wedding chests here are chased with metalwork and can be found in the metalworkers' section of the city. I ask him why he doesn't find a metalworker to partner with, but he assures me that many people love our carved cedar chests, which are new and have started conversations as families display the entire dowry at weddings to impress the guests.

Sabbataius had a reputation for finely wrought stools and chairs, and he had a lathe, which he sold to one of the other stool makers further down the street. We've had several customers visit, looking for Sabbataius. Although they're disappointed to discover he has retired, Shelamzion is quick to show them the chests and has already managed to sell one after some fierce haggling. Hanan just shook his head, chuckling, and told her afterwards that she's now responsible for all sales as he'd never have got such a good price.

I've been on one outing with Shelamzion, and that was on our second day here. Although there was much to do in our new house, she was determined to show me the shawl-sellers' section of the bazaar. I would have expected shawls to sell alongside the bolts of woven wool or linen cloth for tunics. Instead, all scarves are made or sold in the same section. We passed holy men inspecting black prayer shawls and I was distracted by a stall selling women's headscarves, which at first glance seemed modest but were covered with subtle yet extravagant embroidery.

"These designs are new for this season. Modesty meets fashion," stated the woman selling the shawls.

"They're incredibly beautiful," I marvelled. "Did you make them yourself?"

"Who has time for such intricacy when I can barely keep up with the demand? They're here today, but come back tomorrow and they might all be gone."

"A risk we will have to take," Shelamzion replied, unconvinced, as she propelled me forward.

We found three stalls still selling winter shawls, and as we browsed them I stole a few details with my eyes, noting a clever drop stitch in the pattern of one woollen shawl, and observing the way another had been finished with a crenellated edge, not unlike the city walls around us.

The stallholder spoke to us in the trade language, and Shelamzion replied slowly. Then the woman, hearing the accent, switched to our language. "Most of the idolaters don't bother covering their heads in summer," she said, "but they still love wearing my shawls in winter, so I can never tell who my customers are. And I'm giving special prices for the last of my winter stock."

Shelamzion half-heartedly haggled for a scarf, but we left without buying it.

"Well, what did you think?" she asked once we were back in the centre of the city, cut through by a straight street that goes all the way from one end to the other without any of the curves and bends of the neighbourhood alleyways.

"I loved the embroidered scarves."

She waved the thought away dismissively. "We always love the new. Did you see the wool they were using? It was heavy, and clearly from lowland sheep. Our scarves are so much warmer and lighter."

"The hook techniques and designs were good, though," I pointed out. After some thought, I added, "I think you're right; we always love the new. What if our shawls are popular this coming winter but are seen as last year's fashion the year after? I want to come up with variations on one or two colours and designs for this coming winter, then we can come up with new ones again for the winter after."

Shelamzion gave my hand a squeeze. "That's the first time you've seemed like yourself since we left the village," she said.

It didn't last.

Shelamzion bustles back into the room and catches me wiping my face with my sleeve. She smiles and sighs good-naturedly, but I can tell that her patience is wearing thin. Why can't I adapt to our new situation?

"I'm sorry," I say, "I can't help it. I just miss everyone, and everything here is so new and so different. I'm sure I'll get used to it, but…" I trail off.

"Come on," she says, "we're going out. You've been cooped up here long enough. The house is looking clean, so it's about time we were, too."

She ignores my protests, gathers clean tunics for us to change into, and marches me downstairs. "You may expect us back this afternoon, perfumed and clean," she purrs at the men, mimicking the accent here. "And I know you have your planks to saw, but make sure you take yourselves to the bathhouse before the evening meal as well. We don't intend to spend the evening with men who smell of sweat."

A look of anticipation passes between the men, both savouring their first night alone with their wives.

"It's strange that we don't even know the names of the people we're living right next to," I whisper as we head down the alleyway.

"Yes, we must bake some pastries and take them round to our neighbours and introduce ourselves."

"Why haven't they done that for us? And no one offered to help us with painting the upper rooms or sawing the logs into planks. That would never have happened back home."

Shelamzion shrugs. "Here in our *new* home, people live busy lives. We could have asked for their help if we needed it."

We pass the other furniture workshops on our street. Our alleyway leads onto a broader paved street and Shelamzion stops by an open-air vendor stirring a blend of stones, spices, and parched chickpeas in a pan over hot coals.

"Do I pay extra for the stones?" Shelamzion asks playfully. Already she's losing her mountain accent and sounding more like a local.

The man smiles and hands her a cone made of a large dried leaf and then spoons the chickpeas in, removing two large stones and popping them back in the pot. He notes my puzzled expression. "The stones stop the spices sticking and burning."

"Careful, they're still really hot," Shelamzion says as we walk on toward the centre. Most people who live within the city walls seem to be traders, and the ground floor of most houses accommodates their stalls and workshops. Curiosity awakens and I wander over to a woman weaving linen in fine blues and greens on a complex loom. I'm fascinated by the mechanism and find myself staring until the weaver looks up, irritable at the interruption, and I hurry back to Shelamzion.

"There's our local prayer house," Shelamzion explains as we continue. "There are several others in the city." It never occurred to me that there would need to be more than one prayer house, but unless it was enormous, how else would everyone fit? Our neighbourhood consists mostly of our own people, but as we near the centre, there are people from all different backgrounds speaking the trade language, which I don't understand. I'm scandalized by some of the women baring their shoulders, their heads uncovered and their hair done up in hundreds of braids.

"Tabi, don't stare," says Shelamzion, pulling me onward. I peer into the gloom of one of the temples. There are fires burning inside and a fragrant smell, which Shelamzion explains is frankincense being burned to honour the gods.

"But how can there be prayer houses to the one true God, and yet all these temples to other different gods in the same place?" I ask. "Either there's one true God or there isn't."

Shelamzion doesn't bother with a reply because we're almost

at the women's bathhouse. She stops to purchase a bath kit for us to share, which includes scented oil and a scraper. While the city confuses me, it energizes her. We enter, and I'm glad I've been to one before with Yulia so it's not entirely new. We remove our clothing and Shelamzion opens a small pouch of coins and tips it out at the counter. My eyes widen, thinking this is the cost of one trip here, but the woman behind the table counts up the coins, then removes two, writing the remaining sum on a scrap of parchment with the number of our locker next to it before placing the coins in a chest behind her for safekeeping.

We enter the steam room, which takes my breath away until I get accustomed to breathing such hot, steamy air.

"This is what it'll be like in summer," says Shelamzion with a wink.

I hope she's joking.

Shelamzion turns to look at me appraisingly. "Tabi, I think you've filled out a bit more. You're beginning to look really womanly."

I blush and say nothing. We sit down and Shelamzion tries to speak to a plump middle-aged woman near us, but she doesn't understand our language. I listen as Shelamzion speaks slowly in the common tongue, straining to catch every word spoken in response. I'm going to have to learn it if we're to do business here, and I wonder how to even begin. It feels too difficult, so I just lean back against the hot marble, close my eyes, and feel the sweat trickling down me.

In the next chamber are mosaics, and I trace my fingers over the individual tesserae as we sit in a marble alcove.

"Yulia loved these," I say softly to Shelamzion. "She said that when you look too closely all you see are coloured squares with no meaning, but when you take a step back you can see that they form a bigger picture and that it means something."

Shelamzion nods. "I think she was right. And Tabi, I want you to see the bigger picture. I know everything feels too much right now, but one day you'll come here on your own or to meet up with a friend. You won't think anything of speaking to others in the trade language. It will feel like second nature, like it does when your fingers spin or hook yarn into shawls. Once these were new, complicated skills, but now it feels as if you were born with them."

I start to cry and she puts an arm around me.

"Oh, Tabi," she says and rolls her eyes.

"I can't help it," I sob.

My aunt cocks her head and frowns, then places a hand on my belly. "Tabita, are you…"

I nod. "I think so. I haven't bled for about seven weeks. And I'm just not ready for any of this."

Shelamzion throws her head back and whoops, like one of the boys in our village. Heads turn, but she ignores them. She hugs me. "I should have known. It explains all the crying. Your mother gets even more emotional during her pregnancies."

"I haven't told Ananias yet. I was going to wait until the next waxing crescent moon so I'd know for sure."

"He's worried about you; we all are. You haven't handled the transition well and now I know why. I think it would be good if you told him soon."

I nod. "I'll tell him tonight, when we're alone."

We sit back against the hot marble and I feel my hand being squeezed.

"The Lord's protection on you," she whispers.

After a while we rouse ourselves.

"Now," my aunt says, "let's figure out how these bath kits work."

We watch several women covering themselves in oil and then scraping it all off, bringing the dirt and excess skin with it.

Once we've finished in the baths and head back to the changing rooms, Shelamzion asks me what I'd like to do next. I'm feeling much better now that I've unburdened myself, and now that I understand why I've been feeling so close to tears all the time.

"Where can we find out about the Teacher?" I ask.

Shelamzion pauses in thought for a moment. "I'm not sure," she says, "but the baths have always been places of gossip. Let's see what we can find out right here."

She turns to two women who sit near us, combing the tangles from their hair. "My niece has just told me her good news," she says, patting her belly. The women smile over at me, so we know they speak our language. "Her friend was not so fortunate, but after everyone had labelled her a fruitless tree she went to see the Teacher who can work miracles. He cured her and now she has a daughter. Have you heard of this man?"

"He's never been this far north, so we haven't seen him personally," one of the women replies, "but everyone's heard of him. He's in the Holy City now for Pesakh. The crows are after him, but they fear the crowds because he's so popular."

"On what charge?" I ask.

"There are so many fanatics in that city, and between them and the idolaters it doesn't take much to stir the place up," chimes in the other. "Anyone can be accused of breaking the peace."

On our way back to Sabbataius's place, we talk about the Teacher.

"If they did arrest him, would they arrest his followers as well?" I ask. "Phan is with him."

"I don't know," says Shelamzion. "We must say prayers for him at Pesakh. They seem to take their religious festivals very seriously here. We'll have to enquire of the neighbours to make sure we do everything properly. In fact, maybe we should pay a visit to the sheep bazaar outside the city before we go home."

It's my first time leaving the city, and as soon as we're outside the walls the temperature drops and I'm almost chilly. It's wonderful to see wide-open spaces ahead of us, and when I look up I can almost make out the nearest peaks of our mountain range in the distance. The sheep bazaar is situated under a large, shady tree, and Shelamzion is appalled at the prices we're told, but is assured by the sellers that the price for a healthy male sheep will be even higher tomorrow.

"They know we have no choice with Pesakh just days away," Shelamzion mutters crossly. I'm relieved to see there are still some things about city life that don't agree with her. She counts out her coins and decides there might just be enough if she haggles hard. We move to the seller furthest away, with the least amount of custom. He doesn't speak our language but I still understand exactly what's being said as Shelamzion haggles fiercely, quite happy to stay for as long as it takes.

I inspect the sheep tethered to a stake in the ground. I've learned a thing or two about sheep from my father, and point out several defects in animals that the man has tried to disguise. This leads to theatrical displays of shock and disgust from Shelamzion as we work together to grind the seller down.

We finally leave with an underfed yearling and a burlap sack of hay, which should be enough to feed him until slaughter. He doesn't want to leave the flock, but I know how to handle sheep and give the rope around his neck a sharp yank. Shelamzion's pouch of coins is now empty, but the seller seems aggrieved enough for us to feel victorious.

As we re-enter our new street, I notice other lambs tethered outside. They're all plumper than ours and I decide to find him a place inside the workshop away from judging eyes. When we get back, Shelamzion shoos the men off to the baths, passing on the bath kit, which we can all share between us. I'm glad she hasn't become too extravagant.

I tether the sheep, feed him, and then start making bread. This will be the last time I bake bread with yeast until after Pesakh. Shelamzion heads back to the market to buy fresh bitter greens and spices. "We're going to have to learn to cook with them," she states.

I get some onions frying and beans cooking while I wait for my dough to rise. Then it occurs to me to take some butter stored in a jar in the well to make pastry dough. We should visit the neighbours with pastries, even if they haven't invited us over or offered to help. I must stop pining for home and start thinking about our new life here.

That night, we're alone in our room together. When I lie down I expect him to join me, but first he strips and then opens the shutter slightly.

"Get down – someone will see you!" I hiss.

"I want to see you by the light of the moon."

He comes over and undresses me, and I feel as if I'm being eaten by his eyes.

After the second time, we lie together.

"I'm sorry for being so tearful since we came. It was good to talk with Shelamzion about it today. I miss home so much."

"You know what the problem is with this house?" he asks, rolling onto his side and tracing his finger down me.

"There's no garden or place to grow things, and you can't see anything from the roof except more houses."

He chuckles. "And many more things besides. But the biggest problem that we can do something about is that this house doesn't have any memories. We need to create some, and the longer we're here the easier that will be."

I smile. "Well, tonight has been a good start."

He kisses me gently and I try to pull the blanket over me. "No, I don't want you covered," he says. "If you're cold, I'll keep you warm."

He wraps himself around me, and that's when I tell him the news, and let him kiss my belly, wetting it with his tears of joy.

Over the next few days the men continue sawing planks from dawn until dusk. I help Shelamzion as we prepare for Pesakh and bake pastries filled with greens to share with our neighbours, as is the custom. By good fortune our day of visitations takes place when the sky is overcast with a nip in the air. I happen to be wearing a shawl I've just completed and one of the neighbours comments on it. I ask if she would like to try it on.

"I just finished it," I explain, and she and the others look impressed.

Shelamzion is quick to offer them a neighbourly price for some of the shawls we still have for sale, making sure they realize we would make no profit on them. I'm dispatched to bring back some samples.

"I can also give you a good price because spring is almost here." Shelamzion continues shivering theatrically, and places one of the shawls I bring gratefully around her shoulders. "They make excellent gifts and additions to a dowry." My aunt could sell anything.

Younger girls are sent to invite other neighbours from up the street, and soon we have a sizeable gathering and coins change hands.

"You've just saved over a quarter on the price you would have got in the market for an inferior shawl that's not even made from pure mountain wool," Shelamzion explains, then offers a special price for any lady buying two.

Later that day we discuss what to do with the remaining shawls. Our original plan had been to carefully place them in a large wedding chest, sprinkling special herbs over each layer of shawls to keep the moths away. However, customers seeking out wedding chests will also be purchasing other dowry items, including a certain number of summer and winter tunics and robes. Our shawls have already proven popular.

"Let's show them to customers seeking wedding chests. That way we don't have to rent a stall of our own. Anyone who buys a chest can get shawls at a discount for their dowry," Shelamzion states. "Once the last planks have been sawn, I'll get Hanan to build us an awning in front of the workshop to give us some shade, and then we can display chests and hang shawls. We may not be right in the trade centre, but word travels."

Our first Pesakh is special. Hanan slaughters the sheep in the morning and we mark the lintels of every door with the blood. I haven't even begun to show yet, but still I clutch my belly as I remember the story and think of the firstborn I carry inside me.

We join the neighbourhood at the prayer house. We've been a few times. I've appreciated our new observance of rest days – even if it's more to stop the neighbours from judging us – as Hanan and Ananias are both exhausted. Shelamzion pushes me toward a young woman who is pregnant and showing, but I'm still too shy to speak to anyone. In our prayer house back home I'd know every single person there, but here I only know our family plus a few neighbours who nod to me, so I stick closely to Shelamzion.

There's one girl around my age who looks similarly shy. She's got light-coloured hair and looks too awkward for someone so pretty. She keeps one of her hands covered by a sleeve, but when she greets another woman I catch a glimpse of her hand. There's something wrong with it. The fingers haven't grown properly and it looks twisted and malformed. My first reaction is revulsion and pity. Then, in my mind's eye, I see the Teacher stretch out the hand and make it whole as everyone gasps. I blink and the vision is gone, but it feels so real I'm shaken by it. I go up and introduce myself.

"I'm from the mountains, so I apologize now if you find my accent difficult," I explain after our initial greetings. No sense pretending otherwise.

She smiles. "I like it. When did you come to the city? I'm Maryam."

"That's easy to remember," I say. "My name's Tabita."

"Is this your first Pesakh here?"

I nod. "Everything's different. I'm finding it a bit overwhelming. In our village prayer house we all know each other. Of course, it means that the women spend half the time gossiping, but I'm sure it's different here."

"Well, you're wrong on that count," Maryam chuckles. "I've been to every prayer house in the city at one time or another and there's always plenty of gossip. I'm sure it's about me half the time. In case you hadn't noticed, I have a hand that's deformed."

"I'm sure there's more to you than a deformed hand," I reply.

Maryam appraises me, a smile playing on her lips. "Would you like to sit together?"

I look back at Shelamzion, who is beaming with pleasure that I've made a friend, so off we go.

That night, after the Pesakh meal, I lie awake and talk with Ananias about the day. He asks me about the girl he saw me with and I tell him her father is an administrator for the city and that they live in one of the larger houses near the temple of Juno, just off the main straight street. "She's older than me but she's not married. I don't know if it's because of her hand. She doesn't work but she studies and speaks four different languages. And she can read scrolls. We've made a deal."

Ananias cocks an eyebrow.

"I had a look at her hand, and although it's deformed, she'd be able to hold a hook in it and could spin a spindle. I told her about our business and she said that she's always wanted to learn a craft but her father considers it unseemly for a woman of her education. I'm going to teach her to spin and she's going to teach me to speak. I need to learn the language here."

"Have you checked with Shelamzion? Will you have time?"

"I'll go over to her house one morning a week. I told Shelamzion about it and she wants me to consider going twice a week, as we can't do business if we can't talk to our customers."

For the first time since we arrived here I fall asleep with a sense of anticipation about the next day and start to think that maybe life in the city won't be completely unbearable.

Once the planks are sawn, I help Shelamzion drag chests out to our storefront, where Hanan finishes putting up an awning. He nails a reed mat over it to give us shade. Then we drape a selection of shawls from it that move gently in the spring breeze. I set up my stool in the shade and lose myself in the shawl I'm currently making. Mornings are the best time here, before the day gets too hot. Every now and then I glance back into the workshop, where Hanan and Ananias have started carving several chests they began while we were still in the village.

As the day warms, they strip to the waist and I enjoy watching the play of muscles on Ananias's arms and back as he works the saw. He catches me staring at him and smiles self-consciously before resuming his work. The air feels heavier and closer today, and after lunch clouds start to form. An hour or so later Hanan complains that he can barely see to saw and steps outside to look at the sky. It's thick with clouds but the darkness feels greater than that, and soon I'm lighting lamps. Shelamzion hurries home from the bazaar with a basket of eggs and greens.

"All the stallholders are leaving early," she says. "This isn't just a spring storm. No one's sure what's happening. People are talking of omens."

As she finishes speaking she lurches to one side. We all do. Dust rains down from the beams overhead as the ground judders beneath us. It reminds me of the avalanche.

"Quick, outside!" Ananias drags me into the street with Hanan and Shelamzion behind us.

The shaking stops and there's a profound silence everywhere: the first time I've heard real silence in the city. We remain outside, checking with the other neighbours on the street that they're all right. The quake wasn't enough to do any damage to the buildings around us, but still, it's terrifying when something as solid as the ground beneath you starts to move. Then the clouds dissipate, the sun comes out, and everything suddenly seems to be back to normal. Inside, a jar of oil has toppled over and a few woodworking tools have fallen to the ground, but that's the limit of the destruction. My aunt spits to ward off the evil eye. It's something I've never seen her do before. She catches me staring at her.

"I don't know," she says. "I've experienced earthquakes before, and this was just a tremor, but something about it feels… dark."

The following day, I take several balls of yarn, an extra hook, and the shawl I'm currently working on to Maryam's house. I've memorized how to ask, "Where is the temple of Juno?" and "Where does Maryam live?" which Shelamzion taught me.

I find Juno's temple, which is one of the largest, and go up the street that has a large workshop on the corner selling glazed ceramic effigies of the goddess, just as Maryam told me. The street is unusual for its absence of stalls. Maybe they all work as administrators. It's also completely straight, unlike any of the other roads in the city. I knock on the fourth door on the left and smile in relief when it's Maryam herself who answers the door.

"I explained to the servants that I was waiting for my friend," she says, grinning. "I'm so glad you could come."

Inside, the house is deceptively spacious and has a small courtyard in the centre with a pool, plants, and creepers. I hadn't realized how wealthy Maryam's family were and begin to feel self-conscious.

"I've prepared tea upstairs in my room," she explains. "It's lovely and light, and opens out onto the courtyard."

I smile stiffly and am suddenly aware of the broken strap as I remove my sandals, and the dusty, fraying hem of my tunic.

We enter a room of similar size to the one I share with Ananias, which has a bed in it. I've only seen them on display in the workshops on our street. It's a very foreign concept, raising a mattress off the floor on a wooden platform. There's a desk, which is another item of furniture I've only recently learned about, and a beautifully carved chair, some shelves with scrolls on them, and a mirror. I've seen handheld mirrors before and they reflect what you look like in copper or bronze, but they're usually not a fair likeness. This mirror is something else entirely. It's larger and made of highly polished silver. I catch myself in it and can't help staring. My large dark eyes stare back. I have the same eyes and nose as my mother, and a frown that makes me look like my father. I'm not sure where my mouth comes from, but the person I look most like is Phanuel.

"Yes, you do look lovely," Maryam says with a smirk.

"Sorry," I laugh, tearing myself away. "I've never seen a mirror like that before. Come over so I can see you, too."

We gaze at ourselves, Maryam keeping her deformed hand tucked out of sight, and then Maryam starts to pucker her lips and blow kisses and we both end up laughing.

"I'm glad you didn't pretend about the mirror," she says.

"What do you mean?"

Maryam hesitates, choosing her words. "You're not ashamed of who you are. You're not trying to hide anything that might be new for you, or different for someone who grew up in the mountains. I feel comfortable being around you. It helps me forget about this." She holds up her crippled hand.

I take it in mine and place my other hand over it. "I have a special friend back in my village whom I miss very much. I think you'd really like her. She taught me a lot about honesty. Our village can be a cruel place for anyone who's different, and she had weak eyes and couldn't have children."

"Had? What happened to her? Did she die?"

"No, she's very much alive, or at least she was when I left. And now she has a daughter and is looking after an orphan baby as well."

"I don't understand."

So we sit down and over tea I tell her about Yulia and the Teacher, which means I also have to explain about Phanuel and Sholum and everything else. A few times I blink away tears as I realize how much I miss my brother and my friend, and how grateful to God I am for the Teacher. There's something else I need to tell her.

"Maryam, when I first saw you at the prayer house – and please don't think I'm crazy – I had a vision of the Teacher asking you to stretch out your hand, and as you did, it became cured, just like the other one. The vision felt so real I knew I had to tell you about him. I've been told that he's never been to this city, but maybe he'll travel up here one day and you can meet him, or you could go to the Holy City. I think that's where he is now."

Maryam gives a joyless laugh. "My father won't even let me go to the bazaar on my own, much less travel to another city. I'm lucky to get to the baths and the prayer house. He thinks I'm made of clay and worries about me cracking and crumbling." She swallows and continues more quietly. "And, although I know he loves me dearly, particularly because I'm the youngest, I think there's part of him that's ashamed of me and would happily keep me at home all the time, stuck in my room, studying."

I'm not sure what to say, but squeeze her hands in mine.

"I've never spoken that aloud to anyone before today," she adds. We smile at each other, as the bond of friendship between us grows.

"I pray that the Teacher comes to our city and that my brother, Phanuel, comes with him. I'm sure he could arrange for you to meet the Teacher and I know he would cure your hand."

But that's not what happens.

As soon as I arrive back at the workshop, I know something is wrong.

"Where's Ananias?" I ask, a stab of fear suddenly clutching my heart.

"He's… he's just gone for a walk outside the city walls. He needed some time alone."

"Why? What's happened?"

"Tabi," my aunt says gently, "come and sit down." She beckons me over to the tatty, flat-weave rug in our kitchen area.

"Is it Amma? Yulia?"

"I was in the bazaar and there was so much gossip about the latest news from the Holy City. I made sure I spoke to as many different people as I could, to be sure. Tabi," she swallows, "the Teacher has been executed. He was nailed the day after Pesakh and died the same day. I asked about his closest followers and it seems that it was only the Teacher who was arrested; the others scattered. Phan should be safe. I hope that's some consolation."

I'm stunned, and it takes a moment to gather my thoughts. "But there must be some kind of mistake. Why would they execute him? I know the crows were jealous of him and wanted him locked up, but execution? What could he have done wrong?"

"Remember the earthquake on the day after Pesakh? It was much stronger in the Holy City and even damaged our Temple. They're saying it was a punishment from God for killing a righteous man. It also upset the occupiers, who are saying they had nothing to do with this and that even their governor washed his hands of it."

"No, it can't be true! Even if they tried to execute him, I saw the power he had from God. He could stop them." I get up.

"Tabi, where are you going?"

"I need to go to the bazaar or the baths. I need to find out more."

Hanan gives Shelamzion a look that says *Let her go*, and she doesn't stop me.

I hurry down our alleyway and onto the main street, and head for the bazaar. Once I'm in the food section, which is the busiest part, my ill-formed plans to simply approach traders or customers and ask them for information suddenly seem stupid. What if they don't understand me? I think a part of me knows that Shelamzion spoke the truth, even if I'm not ready to accept it. In the end I just walk through the bazaar and keep going until I reach one of the city gates on the other side of the city and walk through that.

I can see why Ananias needed to get out. Seeing open spaces and trees helps me somehow, and there are fewer people out here.

I walk past a large, shady walnut tree, where some food vendors are making the most of the new spring leaves and pleasant shade. The walnut tree reminds me of Sholum's death, and then I think of the walnut trees we somehow managed to haul Phanuel up to bring him to the Teacher.

Ignoring the vendors, I climb onto a mud-brick wall beside one of the large tree trunks, and from there I swing myself onto one of the lower branches. I want to be away from people, and the only way for that is to go up. Once I'm hidden in the foliage, I straddle a large branch and lean back against the trunk.

"God, why has this happened?" I pray silently. "He knew how dangerous the crows were. Why didn't he avoid the Holy City? Why didn't you help him?"

Everything seems to make me cry these days, but not this. I just feel a deep emptiness inside, as if I've lost my purpose before I even really knew what it was. I hadn't realized it until now, but I was so sure I'd see the Teacher again. Someone who'd affected my life so deeply couldn't just exit from it like that. I wonder where Phanuel is and if I'll ever see him again. I stay there for a while, just sitting and being, and then I remember that I'm pregnant and shouldn't be climbing trees, so I carefully make my way down.

"I wish we were in the Holy City," I whisper to Ananias that night. "Maybe we could have done something or helped the Teacher. I don't understand how this could have happened."

He's so quiet I think he might have fallen asleep. Then he says, "Maybe Sabba, Menahem, and Yair will be happy now." There's real bitterness in his voice.

"You don't think they had anything to do with this, do you? They're just boys."

Ananias shrugs and rolls away. I stroke his shoulder, even though I know it will be of no comfort to him right now. What else can I do?

On the next rest day I tell Shelamzion I'm not going to the prayer house.

"It was the crows who had the Teacher executed. Why should I listen to them boring us with their old scrolls?"

"So it was these holy men, was it? It was Yosef and his son who killed the Teacher, was it?" Shelamzion snaps, referring to the holy man at our prayer house. She doesn't often lose her temper. "You know that for a fact, do you?"

"Well, it was men like him," I counter. "And if God is so powerful, why did he let the Teacher die?"

"If God is so powerful, why did he let your brother kill my daughter, and then still cure your brother through the Teacher, while my only daughter remains under the earth?" she shoots back at me, leaving a terse silence between us. "I don't know," she shrugs. "I think of all those failed pregnancies filled with morning sickness and desperate hope, but each one ending in blood and tears. Meanwhile, my sister bore child after child, and yet she's still jealous of me. How many times did I cry out to God, Tabi; cry with wailing desperation? Then finally one of the pregnancies lasted and I had my precious Sholum. We tried for more, but I sought to content myself with one. And I was grateful to God. And then your brother killed her."

I gasp. I've never heard my aunt speak like this. Her eyes blaze, but she seems desperately fragile as well as frighteningly fierce.

"I know it was an accident and, believe me, no one was happier than I when Phan was cured by the Teacher. But still, there was no miracle for my little girl. And now she lies on the mountainside beside her grandparents and I will never see her again. She will never wed, she will never bring me grandchildren, and all I have left of her are memories, pain, and a lock of her hair."

"You took one, too?" I whisper.

She nods. "And Tabita, it is pain. Life is pain. But God is still there. I don't understand why your Teacher is gone now, or why Phan is alive and Sholum isn't. I live with the pain and the mystery, but I'm not alone. I have God in my pain, and one thing I know is this: it's better to endure pain with God than without him."

There are no words to reply, so I just get up, adjust my headscarf, and join her as we leave for the prayer house. I resolve to spend the time praying for my brother. What else can I do?

Life falls into a rhythm of sorts, marked by the sale of chests, completion of new shawl designs, which I hope to send back to the village for the women to copy, and weekly visits to Maryam's. Neither of us is a particularly good student of the other. Maryam is shocked that I can't read, as she expected me to write down new words and practise grammatical constructions. I explain that I've no interest in learning to write and that I know my numbers, which is the main thing. I get frustrated when she tries to explain tenses and adjectives and other things I don't understand, which just leave me feeling stupid. All I want is to do role-plays with her as the customer. I just need to learn how to haggle.

Teaching her to use a hook is equally maddening. She is so quick to give up and blames everything on her withered hand, even though most of the work and skill can be done with her good hand. Finally, in exasperation, I tie some of my fingers against my palm and try to mimic her disability as best I can.

"See?" I say, showing her I can still do it. "This has nothing to do with your hand. You're just not used to trying. You've got to keep practising, that's all."

"Well, the same is true for you," she states hotly. She has a point.

We decide we'd rather be friends than teachers, and I resolve to find some children near our house who only speak the trade language and offer to mind them when their mothers are at the bazaar. Necessity has always been my greatest teacher. Maryam, meanwhile, resolves to learn calligraphy, a skill her father would approve of and something she can do with her good hand.

Spring gives way to the beginning of summer. There have been wild rumours in the bazaar about the Teacher being alive after all, although there are people who were there when he was nailed and they saw someone stick a spear into him to make sure he was dead. I've stopped listening to bazaar gossip.

Sometimes Maryam meets us in the baths. Older women smile and nod at my growing belly. I didn't think I'd enjoy the baths when I'm overheated all the time anyway, but Maryam teaches me the names of body parts in the trade language as we sit and steam, and I can now say "mermaid", "sea monster", "fish", and the names of several aquatic gods, thanks to the mosaics around us. I've even managed to sell a wedding chest in the common tongue, so I am learning, but slowly.

Still, not a day goes by when I don't long to be back in the village, to get away from the heat, dust, and noise, and to see Yulia and my family again. One night as we sit together up on the balcony eating our meal in the hope of a faint breeze, it's decided that Shelamzion and Ananias will return to the village for a week or so. I beg to join them, but both Ananias and Shelamzion absolutely forbid it, as it's not good for the baby.

"Have you forgotten who we are?" I bridle. "My mother would be scything hay up in the meadows until a few days before the labour."

They won't listen to me. I think they're worried that if I go I won't come back. They might be right.

"I need to meet with the women to explain the new designs we want them to weave," I wheedle.

"I wish you could join us, Tabi, but they'll just have to manage with me," Shelamzion states firmly. "I want to teach the women how to dye their yarn, and to make sure they're storing the sheared wool properly so it doesn't get damp, dirty, or moth-eaten. Besides, you know how busy the summers are. We don't even know if the women have found time in the evenings to work on their shawls."

"The mountain air would be good for the baby. I'm going to melt if I stay here and the weather gets any hotter."

Chris Aslan

It's a nice try but it doesn't work. I buy gifts from the bazaar for Yulia and also for my parents. Shelamzion and Ananias intend to stay with them, as our house will be too crowded with Yitra's family. Ananias rolls his eyes on the morning of their departure as I check again that he's remembered my specific greetings for various loved ones. Hanan has given him permission to look for an apprentice, particularly as we're coming up to the most popular time in the city for weddings because fruit and vegetables are in season, so we'll hopefully sell our completed wedding chests.

They're away for two weeks, but it feels longer. Hanan and I are initially a little awkward with each other, as we both tend to interact more through Ananias and Shelamzion, but it's good for us, and gradually we relax. I offer to cook sweet date pastries for a young boy who lives down the street if he'll come and help me with the stall. He only speaks the trade language, and as I spin or hook shawls we talk, sometimes shouting over to Uncle Hanan for help with translation. Gradually I start to understand more of the babble around me when I go to the baths or the bazaar.

I'm asleep alone in our room when they return. I feel my way down the steps, annoyed with myself for not banking the fire, as then I'd have had an ember to light a lamp. I'm confused, because out on the street I see three silhouettes. I run up to them and have to stop myself from screaming when I recognize the third person.

I fling my arms around my brother, Phanuel.

Chapter Sixteen

We sit in the kitchen area, lamps lit and bowls of mint tea in hand. It did me good to busy myself with these mundane tasks as my mind raced with all the questions I have for him.

"Let me start," says Shelamzion. "We had to walk hard to get here tonight, and I'm quite exhausted. I'm happy to tell you more in the morning, but for now you just need to know that the women and quite a few of the men have managed to find time for shawl production, and Yulia and Yohannah have ensured the quality is generally very high. The rebuilding is going well, and I have gifts for you, and love and greetings from everyone. Your mother is furious with me for keeping you from her, and plans to make her first visit to the city to help with the baby this winter. Now," she clambers to her feet, "I'm going to bed."

Hanan gets up to join her.

"No, stay and hear about Phan," she says, smiling at him tiredly.

"Phan, I've been so worried about you and praying for you ever since we heard the terrible news about the Teacher. We didn't know what was rumour and what was true. Tell me everything."

Chris Aslan

Phanuel smiles. "I'm also pretty tired, so can I do the same as Shelamzion and just tell you briefly? I promise to answer all your questions tomorrow." I nod and he begins. "It took me a while to find the Teacher. Wherever I went he had just been. I was running out of money, but eventually I found him. He let me join his other followers, and there were around seventy of us who travelled with him. It was wealthy businesswomen who helped fund us, although some of that money was stolen by our treasurer.

"I learned so much from him; from what he taught, but also what he did. He didn't just talk to good people, but to everyone, especially if their lives were a mess. He even talked to idolaters. Watching him cure people became as normal as, I don't know, spinning wool is for you. He wasn't afraid of anyone, and kept speaking out against the crows and exposing their double standards. His closest friends kept telling him to stop antagonizing them, but you couldn't stop him if it was what God was telling him to do. Then, when we were in the Holy City for Pesakh, they came for him. We couldn't all stay in the same place, so I didn't know he'd been arrested until the next day. I was outside the governor's palace trying to find out what was going on when the crows turned the crowds against him and they called for him to be nailed. Tabi, I watched him carrying the beam. It's part of the punishment that you have to carry the very beam of wood you're going to be nailed to. I was screaming, trying to push through to help him or to do something, but soldiers kept the crowds back.

"We couldn't get up Skull Hill; they'd blocked off the road. But we could see the crosses up on the top, and when he died the sky went dark and there was an earthquake."

"We even felt it here," I add.

"Afterwards, I didn't know what to do. We'd all scattered and there was no one to lead us. I was going to come home but I didn't have enough money. One of the women who helped finance the Teacher works in the king's palace. I found her and she managed to get me a job in the kitchens, hauling sacks of grain or vegetables.

I just slept in the stables with the horses. I planned to go home once I had enough money, but then the rumours started that the Teacher wasn't dead after all."

"We heard them as well."

"I found one of his closest friends and asked him what was happening. He took me back to the place where they were staying and told me they'd gone to the tomb and it was empty. Tabi, you won't believe this, but while we were eating together, the Teacher appeared. I saw him with my own eyes. He wasn't like before; he had the marks of nailing on his body, but he looked so alive. I thought he might be a ghost or something, but we saw him eat food with us and you could touch him. I know it's hard to believe; even some of his close friends who'd been out at the market didn't believe it. But he kept showing up in different places, and then he told us to follow him out of the city. We walked out to Olive Mountain and climbed to the top, and then he left us. We saw him taken up into the sky – right up into the clouds."

Phanuel pauses for some tea and I ply him with flatbread and dates. I glance over at Ananias, who has slumped asleep against a storage pot.

"He told us to continue his work and to take his message everywhere, but to wait until he sent us a gift."

"What gift?" I ask. I'm trying not to interrupt, but I have a lot of questions.

"We didn't know either. We waited. I continued to work at the palace, and then the gift came. I wasn't there when it started, but I heard about it afterwards. The gift was him: his spirit. It could be passed on to others like a lamp's flame, and it filled them with his power and his boldness. Suddenly people everywhere were hearing about the Teacher. The crows couldn't stop it, and quite a few joined us. They're not all bad. I've prayed for people in his name and they've been cured. He told us to go out and tell everyone, so when I had enough money saved I went back home. I've been meeting with Yulia and Azariah, and then others joined us, and we've been telling the whole village about him. Then Ananias came back and I knew that I needed to come here. Look at this huge city. What an opportunity!" Phanuel yawns.

"You can stay in our room," I say, "and we can talk more tomorrow. Just answer two questions for me. First off, could your prayers cure my friend who has a deformed hand?"

"It's not me who does it. I just pray."

I nod, trying not to give way to false hope. "And secondly, did you see Sabba, Yair, or Menahem? They tried to take over the prayer house in our village, and I think they're going to go back with their teacher and try again."

A cloud passes over Phanuel's face. "They've not been back to the village yet, but Yulia told me all about it. Their teacher is one of the hardliners who's been stirring the crows up against us, as if the crows needed any help with that. I saw Sabba once on the street, but he didn't see me. I can't believe I had to hide from one of my closest friends, but they've got so much power now. They could have had me arrested..."

"God has protected you, though," I reassure him.

"I have one last question, too," says Hanan, sighing wearily. "Phanuel, are you going to be our new apprentice? Ananias was supposed to bring someone back with him."

Phanuel smiles. "I'd like to try, and I want to work hard. You don't have to pay me or anything, just let me stay here, and maybe I can take a few hours each day to go to the marketplace and tell others about Yeshua, the Teacher."

Hanan smiles, but I can tell he's unsure about this arrangement. The rest of our questions will have to wait until morning. I wake Ananias and cajole him up to our room, leaving him dressed and snoring on the mattress, and then lay out another mattress for Phanuel, who also doesn't bother to undress but falls asleep straight away. As for me, I stay awake and mull over everything I've heard.

The next morning the boys are still asleep long after sunrise. I study Phanuel's face properly in daylight. His beard is thickening and is less patchy, and he looks more grown up. I tiptoe downstairs, where Hanan is trying ineffectually to make himself breakfast.

"Let me," I say, laying a food cloth on the mat with bowls of yogurt, olives, dates, cream cheese, and apricots. "I'll go to the bazaar now and make sure we have a nice lunch ready for the others. I don't think they'll be up before noon." I pour my uncle some mint tea. "After lunch I think they all need a trip to the baths. Will you go with the boys?"

Hanan nods.

I remember the conversation I had with Shelamzion about Phanuel and Sholum. "Uncle, could I ask you something?"

He looks up.

"How do you feel about Phan? He killed Sholum, or maybe the fall would have killed her anyway, but the point is, he was part of it all, even if it was an accident. Now he's here and he'll be living with us. I know he's your nephew and you love him, but…"

Hanan swallows. "How do *you* feel? You and Sholum were inseparable."

I shrug. "I used to hate him, but that was also because I was left having to look after him. I think I wanted someone to blame, but really it was just a terrible tragedy that was no one's fault. And the Teacher taught me the importance of forgiveness. How can I expect God to forgive me if I won't forgive my brother?"

Hanan nods solemnly and clambers to his feet. He may not say much, but my uncle is full of wisdom.

Two days later I knock at Maryam's door and she's surprised when she sees that I've brought a male stranger with me.

"This is my brother, Phanuel. He's staying with us," I explain.

"Tabita tells me you've been teaching her the trade language,"

Chris Aslan

says Phanuel, or at least I think this is what he says, because he says it in the trade language. He seems pretty fluent.

Maryam raises an eyebrow and smiles. She's impressed, and welcomes us in, but is momentarily flustered because she can't take a man up to her bedroom, so we're seated in the courtyard while she calls a servant to fetch refreshments.

"Is it true what Tabi said about you?" Maryam asks.

"About me being paralysed? Yes, I was, and now I'm not. The Teacher cured me completely, and he can cure you. He's given us the power to speak in his name. That's why I came today. Would you like me to ask the spirit of Yeshua to cure your hand?"

"The spirit?" She looks uncertain. "I – I'm not sure. Let me call my mother," she says, leaving us in uncomfortable silence.

They return together with a servant bearing a tray of sweetmeats and fruit juice, which is placed on wooden legs to form a table. Phanuel tells them what happened to him in more detail and then offers to pray for Maryam.

They look at each other and then her mother shrugs. "I don't see what harm it can do, so long as we keep our expectations real."

"Maryam, stretch out your hand," says Phanuel with calm authority.

She looks to her mother, who nods, and then she stretches it out. Phanuel places his hands on hers, then tells the hand to be well in the name of Yeshua. Then he continues praying, but in a language I've never heard before.

Maryam gasps, as if in pain, and we watch, each holding our breath, as the hand grows visibly in front of us and becomes whole.

There's a loud clatter. The servant has slumped in a swoon and almost knocked the tray off its legs. Maryam's mother starts crying hysterically, which means doors open and other servants appear, along with Maryam's father, who rarely seems to leave his study.

Then Maryam yells, "It worked! God be praised, it really worked!"

285

I can't help myself; I start to ululate and then some of the other servants do as well.

Maryam and her mother cling to one another sobbing, and then their father rushes down the stairs and into the courtyard, grabbing his daughter to see the hand for himself, and soon he's weeping and hugging his wife.

"God be praised! I give him glory. I give him glory!" Maryam shouts. I've never seen her like this.

Some of the servants rush outside, desperate to tell the neighbours, and soon the courtyard is packed with people.

The father runs up to his study and then appears at the courtyard balcony. He shouts out to Phanuel, "God bless you, my son, God bless you," and throws down a large pouch of coins, which lands with a thud at our feet.

"Please, you don't have to pay me. It wasn't me who cured your daughter; it was the power of Yeshua," Phanuel calls out, and the crowded courtyard quietens down to hear him speak. "I used to be completely paralysed. You can ask my sister; she had to take care of me. But they carried me to the Teacher and he cured me. Let me tell you more about him."

Maryam's father comes back down and Phanuel motions for everyone to sit where they are. Then he begins to talk. Maryam kneels with her mother, nursing her new hand. Every now and then, when she notices someone craning their neck for a better look, she lifts it up with a grin so they can see it. I listen, hungry to know more, and Phanuel explains that the Teacher was killed at Pesakh because he was the sheep sacrifice. His blood has even more power than the blood that was smeared on the lintels of doors did to protect our ancestors when they were in slavery, because it doesn't just keep away death but brings life and hope and forgiveness. He explains that the Teacher chose death, knowing that it wasn't the end, but just as a seed has to fall to the ground and die to grow a new, more fruitful plant, now he has even more followers than he did when he was alive. Now, like a fragrant oil, he can be here with us, right now, waiting to show his power.

"Who would like to experience him?" Phanuel asks.

I scramble to my feet.

He prays for me first, touching my head, and I feel something happen which is hard to describe, but it leaves me full of joy and yet so aware of all the things I've done wrong. I find myself sobbing and praising God with all my emotions mixed up, and then, as I call out my praises to him, I realize it's in a different language. The eyes of one of the servant boys widen as he hears me. He's much darker than anyone else here, with tight, curly hair. He's clearly foreign, but he's the only one who can understand me. So I copy what Phanuel did to me and place my hands on him and continue to speak out. Then he starts weeping and praising God in that same language.

Phanuel doesn't get around to everyone, but those who have been prayed for are already praying for others. It's as if we're all taking burning sticks from a fire and lighting other people's fires with them, and everything is spreading. More people keep arriving and the crowd spills out onto the street.

I notice a crow among them. He's Yosef, the holy man from our prayer house. He looks around in confusion, and then Maryam's father comes up and prays for him and he, too, begins to weep and call out praises. A beggar on crutches turns up with someone who went to fetch him from up the street. It's not even Phanuel who prays for him, but he's cured, which causes another wave of ululation and astonished joy.

The ornate copper tray table the servant left our untouched refreshments on gets knocked over in the surge of people, and Phanuel calls out to me that we need to find somewhere bigger.

"Ask Yosef if we can go to the prayer house," I shout back.

It's Yosef and Maryam who lead the way.

I get pushed to the sides and am near the back of the crowd as it moves with purpose toward the prayer house. I'm about to elbow my way back into the fray, but I feel so overwhelmed by the experience I've just had that I want to take a moment to savour it. The courtyard rapidly empties. Even the servants have gone. I pick up the copper tray and place it back on the wooden legs it rested on. Then I sit on the floor, wrapping my arms around my swelling belly. I think about myself. I'm tough, which you have to be to survive in my village, but Yulia is tough and yet kind, and my aunt is tough and yet generous, and even Amma has surprised me with the way she took in Menahem and Yair's little sister. My heart is hard, and sometimes bitter.

"You changed my brother," I whisper in prayer, "and not just on the outside. The first thing you did was forgive him and change his heart before you cured his body. Please forgive me and change me."

Tears trickle down my face, but as I pray I feel a deep sense of peace. I stay where I am, resting in this moment. I never thought I could feel this calm sense of knowing who I am, away from the village in this unfamiliar city, but I do, and I don't want it to end.

Sometime later I'm roused by a voice. "Oh, you're still here? You're his sister, aren't you?" I look up and see a shy servant girl, a bit younger than me. "I'm just back from the prayer room. We ended up making so much commotion the idolaters turned up and ordered everyone to leave. They thought we would start a riot. Some of the other servants will be back soon, but my master's taken his daughter to visit their relatives so they can see this wonder for themselves."

"Did anyone pray for you while you were there?" I ask.

The girl grins shyly. "Yes, everyone was prayed for. Even the least important people, like me."

"There are no big people or small people to the Teacher. We're all valued."

She smiles. "Will you come back again and teach us more?"

"I don't know much myself," I explain. "But I'll see if my brother will."

Chris Aslan

As I walk home alone, the shadows lengthening, I hear people on the street talking about the marvels and wonders that have happened today. Despite Yosef being there and experiencing the Teacher's power and spirit for himself, I know what will happen next, and I start to worry about the backlash and what the crows will do.

Chapter Seventeen

"There's something so disruptive about the Teacher, isn't there? Even now, after he's gone," I state a week or so later, as I pour mint tea for Phanuel and Ananias. We're having breakfast.

"But it isn't bad," Phanuel replies.

"I'm not saying it is. But just look at what's happened since you prayed for Maryam's hand. The whole city is in uproar."

Phanuel looks puzzled, as if he doesn't quite understand what I'm saying. I raise an eyebrow at Ananias, who continues to chew meditatively.

"So, Phan, are you ready for your first day as my apprentice?" he asks. "I'll try not to be too hard on you."

Phanuel looks uncomfortable. "I know I keep delaying, but I promised I'd help Yosef at the prayer house. He wants me to tell them more about the Teacher, and he's arranged safe passage for a group of lepers who were begging outside the city gates."

"Why do they need to come into the city?" I ask, nibbling on an olive. "Why can't you go out and pray for them there?"

"Come on, Tabi. Don't you remember Malchus? Yosef wants

us to see lepers as the Teacher does," says Phanuel. "We have to stop fearing the ill and start healing them. He says that a house of prayer should be a house for everyone. And there's another group that wants to be baptized."

This public display is something new for us. The day after Maryam's hand was cured, Phanuel gathered us all in Yosef's prayer house and began to teach us. He explained that when we follow the Teacher it means we're starting a new life, and that everything we've done that's wrong can be left to die with our old way of doing things. The waters are like death and rebirth: going in to let them wash away all the old ways and coming out washed clean and ready for a new start.

Yosef led us all out of the city gates, through the suburbs, and past vineyards and fields to the river. Some people stopped on the way to invite friends or relatives, or to buy bread and fish for lunch. Once we reached the river, Phanuel waded into the water and addressed us all there. He told us this was a public celebration, like a marriage, to show everyone we were leaving our old lives behind and following Yeshua now. Many of the crows and the curious watched from the banks.

Yosef waded in first and Phanuel held him under. He came up spluttering and yelling with joy, then helped Phanuel with the next person. Shelamzion went before me and ended up helping me into the water. As I felt it cover me and held my breath with her hands on my shoulders, keeping me under, I felt a moment of panic and then let myself feel how close death was. I imagined all the things I'd done wrong being carried downstream as she helped me up, and I drew in a lungful of air and realized how good it was to be alive and to have a new start. Hair was plastered over my face, and one of the youths had to rescue my headscarf, which had come off. I needed a hand waddling out, my clothes feeling heavy against me, but it was such a special moment. Still, among the cheers and ululations came the disapproving clicking of tongues.

The crows scowled at us, arms crossed. I chose to ignore them.

Mosaic

"Abshalom, brother, come join us in the waters," Yosef called to the fattest crow, who had a particularly bushy, white-flecked beard.

"Yosef, remember all you've studied for so long. What has led you to this madness?" Abshalom called back, then lifted his voice so everyone could hear him. "This is not our way. This is not *God's* way. Turn back to the faith of your fathers!"

"Yeshua told us that he is the way," said Phanuel, holding the older man's gaze.

"Yosef, why do you follow this village boy and the teachings of a carpenter's son? Remember whose feet you've sat at. Come back to the true path."

Yosef seemed pained by this, but gestured around him. "Behold, I am doing a new thing. Can you not see it?" he replied, in a way that sounded as if he was quoting from a scroll. "Brother, open your eyes. God is doing something new here."

The crows shook their heads in dismay. "You are no brother to me," Abshalom muttered.

"You will always be my brother," Yosef called after them as they shook out their cloaks in protest and stalked off.

Since then, Abshalom and the other crows have publicly denounced Yosef and his prayer house during their sermons. If anything, though, this has led to more people coming to our prayer house just out of curiosity, and our numbers seem to grow daily. I don't think we'll all fit in at the rate we're going.

"Phan, we need to be careful," I tell him as we continue our breakfast conversation. "*You* need to be careful. Abshalom did not take kindly to being answered back by a village boy. Remember what they did to the Teacher, and don't think something like that can't happen here."

"Remember what the Teacher did to *them*, Tabi. He exposed their hypocrisy and they thought they'd killed him, but they hadn't and now no one can stop his message. We shouldn't be afraid. His love is stronger than fear."

292

"So you won't be starting your apprenticeship today, then?" Ananias says drily. "Tabi, why don't you go too and keep him out of trouble?"

"I would, dear husband," I reply, "but since Phan prayed for Shelamzion to receive the spirit of Yeshua, she's forgotten all her business sense. She left early this morning to help Maryam and Yosef at the prayer house." Phanuel looks sheepish. "She says she'll be back before noon, but yesterday she got distracted and someone needs to stay here to make lunch and sell wedding chests and shawls."

"If only I had an apprentice to help me, dear wife," says Ananias, and we grin together at Phanuel's discomfort.

"It's just that there's so much to do," he protests. "People are hungry and want to know more about the Teacher."

"So what are you sitting around here for?" I ask, shooing him to his feet as Ananias gets up, stretches, and then heads into the workshop.

In many ways it's good that Shelamzion isn't around when customers turn up, as it forces me to speak in the common tongue. I'm finding I can haggle in it quite well. I sell a chest and two shawls as part of a wedding dowry before lunch. I also redirect several people who've come looking for Phanuel. One of the men is on crutches and is accompanied by his daughter. They're not even from the city but have travelled from another town after hearing about the cures prayer can bring. I'm excited about this, but if strangers can find their way to our home, a backlash could easily happen. Surely Abshalom and the other crows know where we live, too.

At lunch it's just Hanan, Ananias, and me, and I raise my concerns.

"People know where Phan lives. What if the crows decide to make trouble?"

"We can't stay silent now," says Ananias. "People are hungry, and they want to know about the Teacher. Look at the change in Yosef."

"Well, why aren't you out there, then?" I snap. Pregnancy and the heat are making me irritable.

"I'm here, working hard, so Phan can be out there. I know he's never going to be a carpenter, and I don't have his way with words, but I want to be part of this. Phan told me if it wasn't for the businesswomen who funded the Teacher he would never have been able to travel so far and help all those people."

"I know," I hiss, "but look what happened in the village. Do you think we've seen the last of the Hand? The wounded pride of young men never forgets. One day they'll go back to the village, and when they find out that we're here, I know they'll come, and this time we can't win the women over to our side because they're all working for us."

"How much did you sell the chest for this morning?" Hanan asks.

"Uncle, I'm not worried about chests right now," I say distractedly.

"Just tell me, was it a high price?"

"Yes," I reply, eager not to be sidetracked.

"So they saw a chest, made well and from good-quality wood: a chest that will last, and should outlast the lives of the couple marrying. They recognized the craftsmanship and the detail. They lifted and shut the lid several times and saw how well the chest was joined. They saw that it was worth the price, and then they paid it."

A slow smile spreads over Ananias's face. It takes me a moment to catch up.

"You see," Hanan continues, "when something is worth it, it's worth it. However high the price, if you value it, you pay that price. All this," he gestures to the house and the workshop around us, "maybe it'll be the price we have to pay. Maybe the price will be higher." He shrugs. "Come, we should get back to work," he says.

Ananias glances at me, then joins my uncle while I clear away the remaining food and think about the wisdom I've just received.

Chris Aslan

We hear more about this price a week or so later.

"This is my friend, Epaphras," explains Phanuel, turning up at the door as I'm preparing the evening meal. "He's come all the way from the Holy City. He managed to escape."

I want to ask more, but I busy myself drawing water from the well to wash his feet and then think about sleeping arrangements, reluctantly concluding that I will have to share Shelamzion's room while all the men sleep in ours. Shelamzion has invited Yosef to join us for the meal and, once Epaphras has had a chance to enjoy bowls of fresh apricots and cherries and a bean stew, he tells us more.

The crows have struck back and executed someone for following the Teacher. This comes as a shock to all of us.

"But why? What laws had he broken?" says Shelamzion.

"It's fear," Epaphras explains. "So many people have started to follow the Way. That's what we call it. Some of the holy men – like you, Yosef – have joined us. It's breaking down the old divides. People are questioning the old teachings, comparing them with the Teacher's. Nothing like this has ever happened before and the crows want to restore order."

"And regain their power," I mutter under my breath, fanning myself, as I'm always hot and sweaty now that we're almost into summer.

"One of the hardliners is leading the fight to regain control. He's got written permissions to arrest anyone who is part of the Way. Most of us have left the Holy City to get away from him, but that doesn't mean we'll be silent. Everyone needs to hear about Yeshua."

"How long did it take you to walk here?" Hanan asks.

"It took me ten days, but that was with stops along the way. I prayed for many and told them about the Teacher. Without stopping I could have got here in a week."

"And by horse?" Hanan continues.

"With a good horse you can make the journey in three or four days," Epaphras replies. "Why?"

"We need to be prepared," Hanan says firmly. "What starts in the Holy City will make its way to the regions. Even to here. Phanuel, I think it might be safer for you to return to the village, just for a while, until this blows over. Perhaps you could take Epaphras with you."

"What? I'm not running away. I'm not afraid, Uncle, nor should any of us be. I have work here with Yosef and the prayer house." Phanuel suddenly seems very young again and a little petulant.

There's a tense silence, which is broken by Yosef. "I think your uncle is right," he says. "It doesn't have to be for long. I didn't want to worry you, but some of the other holy men came to me today, trying to win me back to the old ways. One is an old friend; we studied together. Before they left he took me aside and warned me that something has been planned. 'They're coming and they want to put an end to all this,' is what he said."

"And when were you going to tell us?" I ask.

Shelamzion motions for us all to calm down. "With the greatest affection, Phan, you aren't the apprentice we were looking for. Go back to the mountains tomorrow and take Epaphras with you. You can ask Halafqa and Yaqim to come and join us. Knowing those two, we can't ask one and not the other. This is a great opportunity for them to see the city and learn a trade. Yosef, you can tell the others at the prayer house that we all need to lie low for a while until this trouble has passed. Tabita, you can visit Maryam tomorrow and let her family know. Phan, we'll send word to you when it's safe for you to come back."

"If Halafqa and Yaqim live here, where will they sleep? You know I'm having a baby soon," I grumble, feeling self-centred even as I say it.

Shelamzion tries to keep the exasperation out of her voice. "We can figure that out nearer the time. Anyway, have you forgotten where you've come from? We can all live in one room if we need to."

"Maybe it will all come to nothing," Ananias adds, trying

to lighten the mood. "We're being cautious, which is good, but maybe they're just trying to scare us a bit."

"Well, it's working," I mutter.

I leave the men talking and retire early, but I don't sleep well. It's not just that I can never get comfortable now that my belly is so swollen, or that the night is too hot, or that I'm sleeping in an unfamiliar room with my aunt. It's the worry that I feel, like a bad meal roiling in the pit of my stomach, and it won't go away.

Phanuel and Epaphras leave early the next morning. "I wish I could come with you and see everyone and get away from this heat," I tell Phanuel as we embrace. "Pass this on to Amma."

I hand him a small bag of coins. He also has some of the shawls I've made. It seems strange sending shawls back to the village, but I've created some new designs and I think Yulia will be able to figure out how to copy them from the patterns.

"Tell her I love her and I miss her," I call out as they walk down the street, and I realize that I haven't specified whether I mean Yulia or Amma, although the same is true for both.

Ananias comes up behind me and wraps his arms around me, cradling my large belly. This small kindness unbalances me and I start to cry.

"Shh," he soothes gently, kissing my head.

I sniff and then announce that I'm going to the bazaar and the baths. "I'm constantly sweating and I can smell myself, plus I want to hear the town gossip and see if I can discover anything. I'll visit Maryam after that."

"I don't like you going alone," Shelamzion frets.

But someone needs to stay home and deal with customers, so I leave with an admonishment to be back well before noon.

The visit to the baths puts me in a better mood, but I don't learn anything new. There's religious unrest in the Holy City, which is nothing unusual, but that's all I glean. The same is true of the bazaar. This lessens my worry a little, but not much.

I constantly have to remind myself not to hold my breath, as I realize I'm preparing for something terrible to happen. The rest of the afternoon I spend at home, keeping myself busy. That night I enjoy reclaiming our bedroom. Proud as I am of our village, city life is changing me, and I don't want to have to return to sleeping in a room with six or seven people.

"I forgot to visit Maryam to tell her the news," I mumble as we're drifting off to sleep.

Ananias has an arm draped over me. He makes a muffled grunt but that's all.

The next day I leave Shelamzion at home. There are just three large wedding chests remaining, and she has decided to put up the price as a result. I head to Maryam's house. Although it's early, the sun is already beating down with a fierceness I didn't think possible. I'm wearing a light linen headscarf, which I wear low over my face to keep myself shaded. I can feel sweat dripping down the small of my back and running down the sides of my face to pool in droplets at my chin. I'm already imagining the cool, shady courtyard awaiting me at Maryam's place, and I'm hoping the servants will serve sherbet. It's a drink made from boiling fruit and honey, which is then cooled in a well or cellar. I'd never had it before I came here, but it's already a firm favourite.

I'm just wondering whether I'll ask for apricot or cherry if I'm given a choice when I almost collide with a group of crows.

"Watch where you're going, woman," one snaps.

I freeze because I recognize the voice. I glance up furtively as Sabba and a few others stride by. He's with Menahem and another young man I don't recognize. I shiver, despite the heat. They're here. Somehow I think I always knew in my bones that we would have another meeting and another confrontation; I just never thought it would be here in the city.

They didn't notice me and won't know I'm pregnant, but they're here, and if they ask anyone in the city where to find out more about the Teacher, they'll be pointed in the direction of

Yosef's prayer house, Maryam's courtyard, or our workshop. It will be so easy to find us, and then what will they do? We're in a city surrounded by walls. Suddenly I feel trapped. At least the others can run and join Phanuel heading back to the village. The best I can do is waddle.

I have to remind myself to breathe as I stand there, rooted to the spot. Then I react without thinking too much about the consequences. I follow them. I need to know what we're up against. They don't go far before ducking into an open doorway. I get as close as I dare and hear them pounding on an inner door.

"Teacher, please!" I hear Menahem call out. "We've got fresh fruit. You have to eat something. Yair can make you sherbet. It will keep your strength up."

There's a voice from inside which I can't hear, but I can tell from the three men outside that it isn't the answer they were hoping for. Then the door opens and Yair steps out, shaking his head, looking tired and irritable.

"It's no use," he says. "I've tried everything. He refuses to speak, eat, drink, or go to a doctor."

"What are we going to do?" Menahem asks.

"This is ridiculous," Sabba snaps. "Let me talk some sense into him."

He tries to push his way in but Yair and Menahem hold him back.

"Don't," Yair warns. "You'll just make things worse."

"Teacher!" Sabba shouts, gripping the doorframe. "Shaul!"

"I said, don't!" Yair hisses at Sabba, closing the door behind him. "You're not helping. He needs time, or – I don't know – but that's not helping."

"Time?" Sabba sneers. "He hasn't touched water for three days. If he carries on like that in this heat he'll be dead or unconscious by tomorrow."

The three of them stand together for a moment, and if I ignore the fourth crow, whom I don't know, it's almost as if we're back in the village. It's just hotter and dustier, and we're all that much older.

"So, what are we going to do?" Menahem asks again. "We've got the papers, so we can start the arrests anyway. We don't need him."

Yair rounds on his brother. "Really? After all he's done for you? What's got into you? Just wait another day or so. I'll try to coax some water into him this afternoon. They don't know we're here. There's no rush."

"And what then?" Sabba snaps. "Are you going to lead him, fumbling, around the city? This isn't how it was meant to be."

"Maybe we should talk to Abshalom again. He can show us where to go and then we can start the arrests," says Menahem.

"Just wait one day," Yair pleads.

He looks around and I avert my eyes, deciding it's time to make myself scarce. I try not to run — not that I could with this heavy belly — and hurry along the street toward Maryam's house.

When I arrive she embraces me and feels from the rigidity of my body that something has happened.

"What's wrong?" she asks, taking my hands in hers. "Is it the baby?"

"No," I say. "Is your father here?"

She nods.

"Call him down, quickly."

She nods again. A servant girl is hovering nearby. "Would you like some sherbet?" she asks before heading off to find him. "We have apricot or cherry."

Suddenly, flavours don't seem so important.

Maryam returns with her father and we sit together in the shade of the courtyard. I tell them what we heard from Epaphras and then add, "They're here with their leader. I saw three boys from my village who went off to become crows last year. I knew they sat at the feet of one of the hardliners, but I didn't know who

300

Chris Aslan

until just now. They're actually in our city and have warrants to make arrests, and I heard them mention Abshalom. They must mean that fat crow who watched us from the riverbank last week."

Maryam's father nods his head gravely. "This is not good. He was arguing with Yosef yesterday and threatening to call a council together to expel Yosef from the prayer house. It's the same story as Epaphras told you. They're jealous of what's happening in our prayer houses and they want to put a stop to it. Who's given them permission to make these arrests?"

"I don't know. Their leader was inside the house and wouldn't come out. I think something's wrong with him."

"Did you see him?"

I shake my head. "But I know his name is Shaul."

"Shaul? Let me go and talk to Yosef. I need to warn him. Maybe he knows who this Shaul is."

He leaves and Maryam hands me a bowl of sherbet, which I drink immediately. I can't even tell whether it's cherry or apricot. I feel short of breath and can't stop sweating.

"Are you all right?" Maryam asks, putting an arm around me.

"No. No, I'm not," I reply, shaking slightly. "Maryam, this could be really serious. I know what those boys are like. When I suddenly bumped into Sabba…" I trail off, not wanting to even think of the possible consequences.

Maryam gives my hand a squeeze. "And you know nothing about their leader, this Shaul?"

"I told you everything I know." I sigh wearily and lean back to still my heart from pounding.

"Come, let's pray for him," says Maryam, lifting her hands.

"For whom?"

"For Shaul and for these village friends of yours. Let's pray that they would discover the truth about the Teacher."

"But they're trying to get us all arrested," I protest.

"Didn't you hear what Phanuel said? The Teacher taught us to love our enemies and to pray for those who oppose us."

This is new to me: both praying with someone else and praying for people who are our enemies. I listen as Maryam prays. Then she stops. "I don't know the names of your friends from the village. Why don't you pray for them?"

"They're not my friends. They're not even friends with Ananias or Phan any more."

"Well, it sounds as if they need to discover Yeshua for themselves."

"They already have," I snap. "They were the ones who lowered Phan into the prayer house so the Teacher could cure him. They saw all that, but it's as if they're blind or something."

"Then pray that Yeshua opens their eyes," she says. "Phanuel told us how the Teacher gave many people their sight back."

I can't argue with that, so I pray.

We're still praying when Maryam's father returns with Yosef. Their expressions are grave.

"So, they've come," Yosef states calmly. "We were expecting it and here they are. They'll start with leaders. Phanuel's gone, so that's good. The next person they'll probably look for is me. We haven't got much time, and I can't return home."

I can't believe how calm he is.

"Maryam, could you take three of your servant girls to my house?" Yosef asks. "They can swap clothes with my wife and daughters, and then head to the baths. If someone is watching the house then they'll follow them. Tell my family to remain hidden until sunset and then wait near the fish market outside the South Gate. Thaddeus, could I trouble you or one of your servants for an old robe and a tunic – something a villager would wear? We can go and stay with my sister and her family out in the country for a few days."

Maryam nods, her face white, and goes to speak to the servant girls.

"What about us? What if they come looking for Phan?" I ask.

Thaddeus – Maryam's father – pauses for a moment in thought. "I'll go to the prayer house now," he says. "Someone needs to warn them quickly. I'll let them know that Phanuel left yesterday, just in case any of them are found and questioned."

"Will you be safe?" I ask.

He laughs mirthlessly. "None of us is safe, Tabita. These men have power and they won't let anyone forget it. Let me tell my wife and arrange for us to visit her relatives in the next town."

"I need to go and warn my family," I say, then add, "God be with you all. May the spirit of Yeshua protect us and hide us from our enemies."

I hurry over to the kitchen and find Maryam readying the servant girls. "God bless and protect you," I whisper as we hold each other in a quick but fierce embrace.

"Better to use the servants' entrance over here," says Maryam.

As I scuttle down the narrow side alley, it occurs to me how quickly we've adapted to being fugitives.

It takes me longer to get home because I take the back alleys and avoid anywhere too public. Every person I pass is now a potential spy looking for followers of the Way, and I almost squeal when I pass two young crows in their black robes, deep in conversation and oblivious to me.

I finally get to our street and offer hurried pleasantries to our neighbours, but when I see Shelamzion leaning against one of two remaining wedding chests, fanning herself in the heat, it's too much and I start to weep.

At first she thinks something's happened to the baby, but I call Hanan and Ananias, and we go right inside where no one can hear us. In between sobs, I explain what has happened.

"Should we leave as well?" Ananias asks.

"And go where? Back to the village? Tabita can't manage that," Hanan states.

"If they come here, it'll be Phan they're after," says Shelamzion. "And he's gone. If they ask us where, we'll just say that he's been travelling all over the country, and we don't know where he is now."

"But that's not true. We do know where he is," says Ananias quietly. "If they ask us, we can't lie. But I will run to the village myself, and warn them."

"We don't know that it'll come to that," says Hanan. "We must trust God in this. Do you think it's a coincidence that Sabba, Menahem, and Yair are with this Shaul? It's one thing arresting strangers, but would they really arrest one of their best friends? And for what? Don't Menahem and Yair realize that your mother is taking care of their little sister? That must surely count for something."

We all pause. I hadn't thought about it like that.

"Why don't we shut up the front, so it looks as if we've gone away, and then just stay back here quietly for the next day or so?" says Shelamzion. "If they turn up with arrest warrants we can escape across the rooftops."

"I can't go leaping over roofs," I protest.

Shelamzion thinks for a moment. "We could either hide you somewhere here, or we could try lowering you over the city walls."

"I think we might need thicker rope," says Hanan.

That makes us all laugh nervously.

"Phanuel will be the one they want, and I can't see what they'd gain from arresting a pregnant lady and some craftsmen," he goes on. "Let's not panic just yet. And remember, we trust God. He can cover us with his wings and protect us."

He lifts his hands and we copy him as he leads us in prayer. I keep forgetting how quietly amazing my uncle is.

When we've finished praying, Shelamzion and Ananias pack away the stall while I take an inventory of our food. I've got the basket of fresh herbs and vegetables I purchased in the bazaar, and we have plenty of flour, dried fish, olives, beans, onions, and lentils. We're not about to starve.

The men decide to work on hand carving, because it can be

done quietly without any banging, and Shelamzion keeps me busy upstairs with discussions about new shawl designs. We're soon hooking a new shawl each, and I try to lose myself in the work and not think too much. That evening we have a quiet meal together, then spend the night praying for Yosef, Thaddeus, Maryam, and the others. I don't think any of us find that sleep comes easily, but I drift off at some point because I'm startled awake just before dawn when Ananias sits bolt upright, panting and sweating.

"What's wrong?" I ask. "Did you hear something? Have they come?"

"No," he whispers, still trying to catch his breath. "I just had a dream from God; a vision. I know what I have to do. God spoke to me so clearly, I felt like I was awake, Tabi. I have to go to Shaul. I have a message from God for him. Shaul needs me and he's waiting for me to come."

"What?!" I hiss. "Do you want to get us all killed?"

"It's what God wants, Tabi. Please, don't fight me on this. I have to go."

"But what about me? And the baby?" I plead, reaching out to cling hold of him – to stop him from this madness.

"Don't," he says, pulling away from me. He splashes water on his face from a small bucket in the corner, then dresses hurriedly.

"Please, Ananias, just sit down. Let me call Shelamzion. Let's talk about this."

"Don't," he says again, this time with more aggression, as I try to reach for him. But he's already out of reach, and nothing I can say will move him.

Chapter Eighteen

My aunt slaps me hard across the face. She's never lifted a hand to me before, yet I find it strangely comforting because a good slap reminds me of Amma. I raise my hand to my cheek. The only sound in the room is my rapid breathing.

"That's it," she says, gently but firmly. "Slowly. Calm yourself down."

I try. I focus on each breath, slowing them down into something that resembles a normal rhythm.

"Now," she says, brushing down her tunic and clambering to her feet. "If my son is to go into the lion's den, he'll go with a decent meal inside him." She turns to me. "Are you going to come and help me?" I can see that she doesn't trust me near Ananias.

"I'll come in a moment," I reply shakily.

Hanan takes Ananias by the shoulders. "If you were the son of my seed, you couldn't have made me more proud of you than I am," he whispers, his voice choking with emotion. "I thank God for every day we've worked together, broken bread together, lived together. I bless the parents who raised you so well. I've never been prouder of you than I am now, my brave, righteous son."

He takes Ananias in a fierce embrace, and from the way their shoulders move I can tell they're both crying. Why can't I be like my uncle? Why can't I trust God and let my husband go?

When Ananias woke me and told me about his vision, it didn't take long for me to work myself into a state. I started shouting, and then Shelamzion and Hanan gently opened the bedroom door.

"We heard voices," said Shelamzion.

An understatement if ever there was one.

Ananias explained his dream, or tried to, but I kept interrupting.

"How do you know it was God?" I demanded. "We've all had vivid dreams. It's usually because the cover has fallen off and we're cold, or because an arm has got trapped under us or something."

"I'm telling you, Tabi, this was from God. I saw myself walking through the streets to the place where Shaul is staying. I know the way, even though I've never been there before. I know who owns the house – a man named Yahouda – and what the room looks like inside. I know that Yair will be there, and I know that Shaul was blinded by a vision of Yeshua on his way here to arrest us. How could I possibly know this if it was just a vivid dream? Don't you remember how you had a vision of the Teacher curing Maryam's withered hand?"

"There must be some mistake," I argued frantically. "Maybe I'm the one who's meant to go. They wouldn't arrest a pregnant woman, would they?" Then, struck with inspiration: "We could get a letter writer from the bazaar to write everything down, and then you could describe directions to one of the bazaar boys, promise him a few coins on his return, and dispatch him with the message for you."

Ananias took my hand gently in his. "Tabi, there's no mistake. I even asked God in my vision why he would send me to the very man who most opposes the Way and wants to arrest us all. I asked him, and he still told me to go because he has a plan for Shaul. Shaul is going to bring the message of Yeshua to the idolaters. I know it seems crazy, but you have to trust me, just as I trust God and this vision."

"Please," I began to wail. "I'm begging you. I don't want to raise this child alone. Don't do this. Think about me and the baby."

"Tabi, don't," he said.

But I did. "Please," I sobbed louder, getting down on my knees and kissing his feet. "Please, I'm begging you. Please!"

That's when I got hysterical, and then came the slap.

He avoids my gaze, and I know that I've disappointed him, so I avoid his. I pass him a bowl of olives and then refill his tea bowl. There's a tense silence. I finally break it.

"I'm sorry," I say quietly. "I know I'm being stupid, and I know that we can trust him. It's just…"

He smiles.

"I trust you, and I trust him," I finish.

He puts his bowl of tea down and gets to his feet. I scramble before him to turn his sandals at the doorway so they face the right way and are easier for him to put on, silently praying protection over his steps. I have to fight an impulse to cling to him and stop him going.

"Protect him, Lord. Cover him with your wings," I pray, rising. I touch his chest with my hand. "Be his shelter and his strong tower."

I feel the tears come, but I let go of him. Behind me, Shelamzion puts a hand on my shoulder, and my vision blurs with tears as he walks away. For a moment I think he's going to turn his head back one last time, but he doesn't.

"What if I've lost him?" I sob.

Shelamzion just turns me around and holds me to her bosom, cooing to me softly as if I were a small child.

"Now comes the hardest part," she says gently once I've cried myself out. "We have to wait."

She's right. It's awful. In no time at all I've cleared away breakfast. Now what do I do?

"I'd like some help rearranging the chests upstairs," says Shelamzion, clearly trying to keep me busy.

The chests need no rearranging, but it's a welcome distraction. We enter her room and she lifts the lid on one of the chests, an older one she doesn't tend to use much.

"I never properly emptied this out before we left the village," she says. "I'm sure I could have given half the things in here away and lightened the load of those poor camels."

She takes out dresses and an old shawl. "Why on earth did I keep this?" She flaps it out. "I should throw it out, but I think I might use it downstairs as a contrast of quality and price."

We smile together and she continues to rummage deeper. The smile fades.

"Look," she says, carefully removing a pair of small, brightly coloured, knitted socks. "These were Sholum's. I couldn't bear to give them away once she outgrew them. How selfish of me. And this," she carefully withdraws a wrapped piece of linen, "was inspired by you." She unwraps the linen to reveal a large lock of Sholum's hair, carefully braided together. "Menahem's mother tried to move you when you fell asleep next to Sholum the night before we put her on salt. Your hand was curled around her beautiful hair and she left you a lock as a keepsake. Then she thought that I might like one, too. It was much later when she gave it to me. It made me happy and broke my heart at the same time."

"I still have the lock of her hair in my wedding chest," I say, finding it hard to get the words out past the lump in my throat.

"You know, one of the hardest things about losing her was the futility of it all. What did it mean? What good did her death do anyone?" She swallows. "I trust God with Ananias, and I don't believe any harm will come to him, but if it did... If he gets arrested, or beaten, or… He would die for doing something good, something courageous that has meaning."

"I thought you were supposed to be distracting me," I reply.

We both laugh but with tears in our eyes.

"This isn't a time for distraction. We aren't powerless. It's a time to pray," she says.

So that's what we do. When I run out of words in our language, I pray in the language I was given when I received the spirit of Yeshua. I don't know what it is I'm praying, but as I pray I gain a sense of how big God is and how small this Shaul and all the other enemies of the Teacher are. I'm not sure how long we pray for, but when we stop I turn to my aunt.

"I'm going. I'm going to join them. I need to take some food for them. I have to tell Menahem and Yair that their sister lives and is well taken care of."

Shelamzion looks confused.

"I didn't hear his voice. I didn't have a vision like Ananias did, but I just know deep inside myself that this is what I'm called to do. And I'm not afraid any more. Look." I hold out my hand and it doesn't tremble.

Shelamzion looks into my eyes searchingly and then gives my hand a squeeze. "Let me help you prepare the food. We still have olives and dried fish, and you can take the leftover lentils from last night for them."

We place the lentils and olives in a bowl with high sides, and the rest of the food is put into a simple cloth bag, which I wear over my shoulder. My aunt doesn't question me again or seem worried, and I admire her faith and maturity.

"There's one more thing," she says. "Let me see if I can find it. I think I know which one it's in." She opens one of the three remaining wedding chests, where shawls are layered carefully between dried herbs to keep the moths away. "Here." She hands me a stack of shawls and digs deeper. "Found it." She hands me a shawl, much like the others, and I stare at her blankly.

"Tabi, I may not be as good a designer as you, but I do remember each shawl and who made it. This was made by Yair and Menahem's mother. It was the last shawl she made before she stopped working for us. I want you to give it to them. We all need something to remember our loved ones by."

She stuffs it gently into the bag and I silently thank God for giving me such a wonderful example of what it means to be a woman.

"Hanan!" she calls.

My uncle emerges from the workshop, dusting wood shavings from his hands. "The Lord has called Tabi to take food to Shaul and his followers," she says matter-of-factly.

Hanan nods as if this is the most sensible idea in the world.

"We'll come back, when... when it's all over," I say.

"The Lord go with you, Tabi," says Hanan.

"He's right beside you," Shelamzion adds.

I swallow, then turn and head for the street. They don't need to see me shed any more tears. It feels good to be outside, even though it's almost midday and the sun is pounding down on my headscarf.

I don't think about what's going to happen; I just put one foot in front of the next and head toward Maryam's house. When I get to Juno's temple and the one street in the whole city that isn't crooked, I turn and head for the house where I saw Sabba and the others. It's only when I stand before it that, just for a moment, my calm deserts me. I don't mind taking a beating, but I don't know what I'd do if I lost the baby, or if I saw that they'd hurt my husband.

I calm myself and commit everything to the Lord. I breathe out and then, before I breathe in again, I rap on the door three times. After a moment or two it opens.

"What do you want?" Menahem asks, distracted. "We don't need any hawkers here."

"Menahem, it's me," I say, staring up and pushing my headscarf back.

"Tabita? You as well?" he says.

I still don't know what the situation is, so I decide to move quickly. "I've come with something for you and Yair. There's food for you all, but also a gift from my aunt. You must have heard about the avalanche by now. This was the last shawl your mother made before she died. It's for you both to remember her by. And don't worry about your sister. My mother is taking good care of her."

Menahem takes the shawl and holds it up to his face, breathing in the smell of wool. He looks exhausted and close to tears. "You'd better come in," he says dully, standing aside for me to enter. The room is empty and dark, and it smells of rancid sweat and sickness.

"Where are they?" I ask, holding the hem of my headscarf over my nose to blunt the smell. He says nothing but leads me through this room to another, then out to a courtyard where a small vine and a creeping plant with bright flowers provide shade. Under it, sitting cross-legged on a woven rug, are Yair, Ananias, the young man I recognize from the other day, and an older man whom I take to be Shaul.

"I brought food," I say and then, seeing the bread and jugs on the rug, I add, "More food."

Ananias stands up, grinning, and comes over to embrace me and take the bag. "Shaul, this is my wife, Tabita," he says.

"Thank you for coming, and for your kind gift. Please join us; you're most welcome," says Shaul with a shy smile.

He's not what I was expecting. He's short, and seems to squint like Yulia used to. His long, thinning hair is wet and has left damp patches where it touches his tunic. The same is true of Ananias and Yair.

"What happened? Did you go to the baths?" I ask.

"I just baptized them," Ananias explains. "There's a purification pool fed by a natural spring in the cellar."

"What?" I turn to Menahem, who looks dry.

He just shakes his head. "I'm not ready."

I feel my mouth open and close a few times. Shaul pours some mint tea into a bowl and hands it to me.

"I'm sorry, I d-don't understand," I stammer.

"You'll be the first person I tell this to," Shaul says, "but I hope you won't be the last."

So he tells me how he was one of the hardliners, trained abroad but returned to our holy land. He first heard about Yeshua from Sabba, Menahem, and Yair, and thought things had finally been dealt with when Yeshua was executed. But the disunity among the people and the religious dissension just grew worse as rumours abounded that the Teacher was alive, and as the Way began to publicly cure the sick in the Teacher's name.

The Way kept growing in strength and numbers, and had to be stopped. Shaul was there when the first follower of the Way was stoned to death. The man being stoned almost seemed to welcome it. Shaul felt the only way to deal with this fanaticism was to be even more fanatical than they were, and to show no mercy. He started with public arrests and floggings, and soon the Way had either fled or hidden. That's when he obtained the warrants to come here and work with the prayer houses to stamp out this heresy. He'd even demanded public executions, but the other crows hadn't been ready for that.

"I chose five of my most trusted followers, plus some Temple guards, and we set off north. On the seventh day we were nearing the hill to the south of here, where you can see the whole city laid out before you. I walked ahead and wanted to run the final distance, full of bloodlust. And that's when it happened.

"There was a sudden flash of brightness. I thought we'd been hit by lightning but there were no clouds. Then I saw him before me, glowing like the sun. I heard his voice and he called me by name. He asked me why I was against him and oppressing him. I asked who he was and he told me, 'I am Yeshua, the one you're persecuting.' It was Yeshua himself. Then he told me to get up, enter the city, and wait here until I was told what to do.

"The light was so bright that I'd fallen to my knees. After hearing that voice I felt cut to the heart and held my head in my hands. What had I done? All my life I've sought to serve God faithfully, and I thought I was doing just that. How could I have been so wrong? I felt a hand on my shoulder and heard Sabba's voice. I looked up at him but could see only darkness. My eyes were open but I was blind. I couldn't stop weeping. I'd failed God and this was my punishment. My eyesight wasn't particularly good before, but at least I could see something. Just moments before, I'd been ready to enter this city and strike terror into the hearts of any who opposed me. Now my followers had to guide me by the hand. I heard people clicking their tongues in pity as we entered through the southern gates. What was to become of me? We'd arranged to stay here with my friend Yahouda, who leads one of the central prayer houses. All I knew was that I would never disobey God's voice again, and that I would do as Yeshua had commanded and wait, in prayer, until I received further instruction."

"We didn't see anything on the road," Yair adds. "But we heard the voice. All of us did, didn't we, Men?"

He looks over at Menahem, who nods dully, his eyes vacant.

"I tried to look after our teacher, but he wouldn't eat or drink a thing, and was just getting weaker by the hour. All he did was pray. We didn't know what to do. Sabba wanted us to start with the arrests anyway, but I said we should wait until our teacher was better. Then this morning I heard a knock at the door. It was Ananias, the last person I expected to see."

Ananias takes over. "I knew what I had to do. It just felt like I was reliving each step of the vision I'd already had. I came in and told Shaul who I was, and that the same Yeshua he'd met on the road wanted to open his eyes to his good news because it wasn't only for our people but for everyone. I placed my hands on him and prayed for the spirit of Yeshua to come, and then something fell from his eyes. It looked like fish scales."

"And I could see again," says Shaul. "I knew I'd been given a second chance, and that there was a reason for my sight. The world is so much bigger than this city or province or country. Yeshua is for everyone."

"I've learned many things from our teacher," says Yair quietly, "but maybe the most important lesson is to admit when you're wrong. I, *we*, made a mistake about Yeshua. I also want to follow him. That's why I asked Ananias to baptize me as well. Yeshua was willing to give my teacher a second chance. I want that, too." He pauses. "I'm sorry for the way I treated you and Phan and the others. You were right and I was wrong. Can you forgive me?"

I'm silent, but only because this is all happening so quickly.

Luckily, Ananias is quicker to respond than I am, and just puts an arm around Yair. "I never stopped loving you as my brother and I never will," he says quietly, ruffling Yair's hair.

"And you?" I look at Menahem and the other crow.

"I haven't been baptized yet," says the other one, "but how can I deny what I heard on the road here and what I saw happen with my own eyes this morning? I've never seen the power of God like that. I need to know more, but I think I believe. Oh, and my name's Eutolmus."

"I'm glad to hear your story," I say, realizing that I mean it. "How about you, Men?"

Menahem sighs and rubs his face with his hands. "Yair, Tabi brought us this. It's the last shawl Amma made before she died. It's so we have something to remember her by." He passes the shawl to his brother.

There's silence and then he looks up when he sees us all waiting.

"I don't know. I don't know what I think. Nothing has turned out the way I thought it would. I need some time."

"What about Sabba?" I ask.

"He left early this morning with Yahouda before Ananias got here. He's not back yet," says Yair.

"Do you know when they'll be back?" I ask.

Yair shrugs. "I don't know. I've had my hands full looking after Shaul."

Ananias sees my concern. "Menahem, do you know where Sabba went?"

Menahem is silent for a moment. "He didn't say, but it was pretty obvious last night that he wasn't going to wait any longer."

"Sabba wouldn't act without my permission," Shaul bristles, and I see something of what the old Shaul must have been like. "He can't. Those warrants were made out in my name – not his or anyone else's."

Menahem shrugs. "We didn't know what was happening with you, and I think he got tired of waiting."

"We have to do something." I turn to Ananias.

"They have no jurisdiction, like I said. I have all the warrants with their seals here with me. They're written for me. Yair, fetch my leather bag."

Yair comes back shortly. "It's gone," he says.

"We have to go!" I grab Ananias, then fumble with my sandals. I don't even bother retrieving the cloth bag or the empty bowl for the lentils.

"I won't be able to keep up with you," I pant as we hurry down the street. "Don't wait for me. Just go. If Shelamzion and Hanan are still at the house, take them and go. I'll meet you at the north gate."

"Keep them safe, keep them safe," I whisper under my breath as I waddle home as quickly as I can.

When I finally get to our street the other women stare at me, shaking their heads and clicking their tongues. One of the mothers takes her daughter in her arms, as if to shield her from me. It feels as if a trapdoor has opened beneath where my heart is supposed to be, because now I know that we're too late and the arrests have already happened.

Chapter Nineteen

I rush inside to find shawls strewn everywhere. The remaining wedding chests have been knocked over. The kitchen area around the well is strewn with shards of broken plates and bowls, and some enterprising mice have already discovered the hanging grain sack, which has been slashed open, creating a mound of grain they dart over. In the midst of all this stands Ananias.

"We're too late," he says, then begins to cry.

He's always so strong and dependable that whenever I see him weep it moves me deeply.

"Is it my fault, Tabi? What if they've beaten them or done something worse?"

"We weren't away for long," I reply. "I don't think they'll have done anything with them yet."

"Except question them. They know that we know where Phan is. And when they don't get the answers they want… well, we all know what happens next."

I feel unnaturally calm in this odd reversal of our usual roles. "They'll take them to one of the prayer houses for questioning.

It'll probably be Abshalom's, because that's the largest one and it's right in the centre. Let's start there."

We hurry out, ignoring the neighbours. Ananias slows down so I can keep up. It's unspoken, but we want to face whatever's in store for us together.

As we get near the central prayer house there's a crowd outside and we know we've come to the right place. I curse under my breath. "I should have checked behind the brick upstairs where Shelamzion keeps the coins. Maybe we could have bribed someone."

We try to elbow our way through the crowd to get inside the prayer house, but I'm in no fit state to squeeze through anything, much less a tightly jostling crowd. "Do you want to climb up on the roof, make a hole, and lower me down?" I ask.

He smiles briefly. "Not the roof but the servants' entrance."

We head down a side street and find a door, which Ananias pounds on.

A woman opens it a crack, scowling.

"Is Sabba here? Or Yahouda? We must see them at once," I state with as much authority as I can muster. She looks back inside and then at us, then shrugs.

"You won't get anywhere near them. They're having a huge debate or something, but a woman in your condition can't be getting squashed in that crowd."

She leads us along a corridor and through a courtyard, then to the back doors into the prayer house. We open them and are hit by a blast of heat from all the people and the commotion going on inside.

Shaul is there and he's arguing loudly with Abshalom, Sabba, and a man I assume from his large black cloak to be Yahouda. Behind them, hands tied with rope, I see Shelamzion, Hanan, some of the servant girls from Maryam's house, and a handful of other followers of the Way who were baptized in the river at the same time as I was. They look tense, but not frightened. I scan their faces and arms for signs of bruising. Then I realize they're engrossed in the debate.

"And remind me, Sabba, you who called me Teacher until today, what is the eighth commandment given us by the Lord?" asks Shaul.

Sabba glowers and says nothing.

"Or would you like me to remind you?" Shaul states loudly. "You must not steal. Does anyone here disagree with this commandment from the Lord himself? And yet I find today that documents, each signed and sealed and written to me – not to you or anyone else – giving me – and not you or anyone else – the right to make arrests, are missing, along with my leather bag, and here you are with them. Should it not be you on trial right now? And what is your complaint against these people? People who have not stolen, as far as I know. They simply believe something we've all been told to wait for – the coming of the chosen one: the Messiah."

The man has a way with words and I can see why the boys ended up following him. Heads nod and people whisper to each other. It's hard to believe he's on our side. He speaks with all the pomp and authority of a crow, yet he's one of us now.

"I know that many of you call us crows. Not to our faces, of course. You still fear us. But when our backs are turned you complain about the power we wield and the control we hold over you. So, let me ask you: when was the last time you heard a crow admit he was wrong? And not just wrong concerning some trivial matter, but wrong about the most important thing of all: how to serve the Lord our God with all our heart, mind, and spirit. I have been proved wrong, and if you'll permit me I'd like to tell you about it."

The crowd is completely silent, spellbound by Shaul's words as he retells the story of the journey here and seeing Yeshua, then becoming blind. He paces the room, looking at everyone, including those behind him who are still tied up with ropes. When he gets to the bit about Ananias, he beckons him over.

Finally he concludes, "So I'm not here to arrest anyone. Why are these brothers and sisters of ours still bound with ropes? Why are we oppressing them instead of thanking them for showing us the right way?"

He comes before them and kneels down, causing a flurry of excited whispers among the crowd.

"Please, forgive me. I ask that you would welcome me as a brother; not because I deserve it, but because of the grace and mercy of Yeshua." He turns. "And what of all of you? Don't you want to follow our Messiah as well?"

"But what of the Law?" someone cries out.

"Excellent, excellent," Shaul replies, then begins to answer.

Meanwhile, I go over to Hanan and Shelamzion and the others and begin to untie the ropes that bind them. I don't even check behind me to see if someone will try to stop me. Ananias is soon by my side.

"We were never afraid," Shelamzion whispers. "We felt the Lord's presence so powerfully, even when they were rampaging through the house breaking things."

"All I could think of was that if we were put in prison or beaten, I would still have no regrets about following Yeshua," adds Hanan.

There's no time for more talk or embraces. Once they're freed they help untie the others. Soon there is no one left bound. We turn our attention back to the debate. Voices are raised and Sabba spits with fury.

"How has he bewitched you, too? Is no one safe? Do you know the sacrifices I made to sit at your feet? You have betrayed us and everything we know to be true. You are no teacher of mine. We should arrest him as well!" He looks around wildly for support.

"Sabba, do you want to arrest me because you think I'm wrong or because you know I'm right?" Shaul asks with quiet authority.

"Abshalom, are you going to stand for this, in your own prayer house?" Sabba demands.

Chris Aslan

Abshalom shrugs. "You have no jurisdiction here. You told me Shaul supported the arrests. He's right; the warrants are all in his name."

"Will no one do what is right?" Sabba pleads.

He looks around. Yair and Menahem both avoid eye contact. Seeing no ally, Sabba storms out, elbowing the crowd savagely as he cuts a path to the door. Yahouda follows. Menahem looks to Yair and then to Sabba, then remains where he's seated with his head in his hands.

Once they're gone, Shaul asks the crowd, "Who here would like to follow their Messiah, Yeshua?"

Men and women begin to clamber to their feet. The last thing I see before I'm called to pray for people is the lone figure of Menahem wandering slowly toward the prayer house door.

Chapter Twenty

It's dark by the time we finally return to our street. Shelamzion had invited Yair, Eutolmus, and Shaul to join us for supper. They declined but asked if they could stay with us from tomorrow as it's unlikely that Yahouda will let them stay in his house beyond tonight. We return to our street and the neighbours pretend not to stare.

"Should we say something to them?" I ask under my breath.

Shelamzion gives an almost imperceptible shake of the head. "No, let the one with most curiosity or compassion come to visit us, and we can tell her what happened. She'll soon spread the word. They'll hear it tomorrow, anyway, whether in the bazaar or the baths."

"Speaking of which, is it safe for us to be outside now? Can we go to the baths tomorrow?"

I smell disgusting. Growing up in my village you soon get accustomed to the different kinds of sweat. Sometimes it depends on the person or what they've recently eaten, but there's also a particularly sour smell that has nothing to do with hard labour; it's a simple result of prolonged anxiety, and that's what I smell of.

"The sun's set but it's still baking hot," I complain. "I wish we were back in the village."

"And miss out on all that our Lord is doing here in the city?" Hanan asks ironically as he picks up a shard of Shelamzion's favourite bowl just outside our house. Shelamzion lights several lamps, which illuminate the destruction around us, although, credit to our neighbours, the shawls are still strewn where they were earlier, and it seems nothing has been stolen.

"We should have insisted that Yair and Shaul come for supper. Then they could have helped us clean up this mess," I mutter as I start sweeping up spilled grains and broken pottery.

"Let's see what we can use to make a meal from first and finish cleaning afterwards. We haven't eaten since this morning," says Shelamzion.

I suddenly realize how hungry and thirsty I am.

Most of the destruction is on the ground floor. Upstairs, the chests have all been opened and the stuff taken out and strewn around, but nothing is broken or missing.

"They must have thought Phan was hiding in one of them," I say as Ananias and Hanan lift a chest that has been knocked over.

I wander downstairs to draw water from the well and to help Shelamzion with supper.

We don't say much during the meal. We're all spent. After supper we start to clean up. We make an inventory of loss, which amounts largely to broken bowls and plates, and to wasted grains and lentils.

"The chests weren't damaged when they overturned them, thankfully," Shelamzion says.

"Of course not," Hanan responds, affronted. "It'd take more than a few knocks to damage one of my pieces. As I said before, if it's valuable it's worth paying for."

His words aren't lost on me.

Mosaic

The next morning, Ananias comes with me and Shelamzion to the bazaar. We need new bowls and plates, as well as sacks of grain, beans, and lentils. While we're at it, we might as well buy fresh fruit and vegetables and a nice big melon seeing as the season has started. One of the melon sellers comes from the village where Yosef and his family are hiding. We send word that it's now safe to return. Once we've made our purchases and Ananias has left with a donkey cart, Shelamzion and I head for the baths. The day is already stiflingly hot and I didn't think I'd want to sit somewhere even hotter, but stepping out of my sweaty tunic and feeling warm water lap away the tension of yesterday is wonderful.

At first I slump in a daze, sweat dripping from my nose, but then Shelamzion nudges me. She's listening to the gossip.

"My sister lives on the street where they made the arrests, so I'm in full possession of all the facts," boasts one lady, while three others eagerly press her for more. "This Shaul character from the Holy City was the very man who had come to put a stop to all this religious nonsense, and then he turns out to be one of them all along, standing in the main prayer house and arguing that this Yeshua is the Chosen One. He even called him 'the Son of God'. Can you imagine?"

I glance at Shelamzion, and by silent agreement we decide not to engage in the conversation but to simply enjoy a respite from everything.

"I wonder how Yulia is," I say quietly, tracing my hand along the mosaic-tiled wall. "She said that mosaics reveal life as it is: all a mess when you look too closely, but a clearer picture when you step back." I look up at Shelamzion. "I hope she's all right and that Phan got there safely. What if Sabba goes to the village? He won't rest until he's enacted some sort of revenge for the betrayal he feels from Shaul."

Shelamzion shrugs. "Look at what happened yesterday. None of it made sense... Ananias going to the very home of our greatest threat and yet..." she gestures sweepingly at the complicated mosaic of some kind of ocean man with a trident in his hand, "we can't always see the big picture."

That evening, Shaul, Yair, and Eutolmus arrive, bringing their travel bags with them. "As I thought, Yahouda encouraged us to find lodgings elsewhere."

While Shelamzion finishes preparing the meal, and Ananias and Yair sit together awkwardly re-establishing their friendship, Hanan and I arrange mattresses and bedding upstairs for the three guests.

Ananias and Yair look morose. I give my husband a questioning look.

"It's Menahem," he says. "He decided to stay with Sabba. I was so sure he would side with us."

"He looked exhausted," I state. "Maybe it's better that he doesn't rush a decision."

"Well, Eutolmus wasn't totally sure either, but at least he decided to stay with us," says Yair.

"I have hope for all who've sat at my feet," says Shaul. "If the Lord can change me, he can change them."

"I haven't given up on them either," says Ananias. "I want to visit them tomorrow, just me and them. Let me see if I can reason with them and remind them of our friendship."

The next day I go with Ananias to Yahouda's house. I want to make sure no harm comes to him, plus it's near Maryam's and I plan to see if she's returned yet. We go first to Maryam's, where a servant boy tells me they should be coming back in a few days.

No one answers when we knock at the door where the Hand were staying. After a while I realize that this is guest accommodation, so we knock at the next courtyard along.

A middle-aged woman answers and scowls when I ask about the visitors.

"Don't tell me you're from the Way, too?"

She softens when Ananias tells her he's looking for Sabba and Menahem.

"Gone, they are. Back to the Holy City. What's there to hang around here for?"

We begin our return journey in silence. The day is already unpleasantly hot.

"Do you remember Sabba's honey?" I ask. "He was the only one who ever managed to collect it. No matter how hard or how painful, he could do it. He never gives up. I'm worried for us. I still don't think we've seen the last of him. Next time those arrest warrants will be made out in his name."

Ananias chews his lip in thought. "Maybe it's a good thing Menahem is with him. Who knows? He might talk Sabba round."

"Has anyone ever talked Sabba round to anything?" I ask, and the conversation ends there.

Yosef returns a few days later and can hardly believe what has happened in his absence. We introduce him to Shaul, and Yosef invites Shaul, Yair, and Eutolmus to stay in his guest courtyard.

The house is quieter and I'm relieved to be back in our bedroom alone. The weather gets hotter by the day, just as my baby grows, making each day a little sweatier and less comfortable than the one before. The Way continues to expand and Shelamzion is becoming more involved in helping Yosef with the women at the prayer house. Shaul continues to confound the crows with his arguments, and another holy man has decided to follow the Way. I mainly hear about these things at mealtimes, as I don't leave the house much. It's too hot to be outside for long.

All I can think about is the heat, and how much I just want the baby out of me. I wake at dawn and try to cook, clean, or work on a shawl before the sun rises too high. When it does, I collapse in a sweaty stupor as the heat shimmers off the flat roof outside my shutters. Closing the shutters keeps some of the heat out but also any breezes, which means the air inside becomes stifling. When she's around and has the time and patience, Shelamzion draws cool water from the well and flicks it around my bedroom, makes me a cool compress to wear over my eyes and forehead, and then fans us both. We long for cool mountain breezes and vow that next year we'll return to the village during the hottest summer months.

"You can still go. Save yourself. You don't have to stay here for me," I protest dramatically.

"What would my sister say?" she asks.

We both smile, too hot to laugh properly.

Yair often visits in the evenings, and it's good to see Ananias reconnect with him. He's not the only one who is keen for Yair's company. Maryam tells me how much she enjoys the songs Yair is composing about Yeshua on the lyre. She's right. They're beautiful, and we start singing them at the prayer house. She asks me if it would be improper to have some lessons. Her blushes give away her true intent.

"Would your father approve of you marrying a village boy?" I ask.

"He's my brother in Yeshua," she replies, before hurriedly adding, "except, of course, you can't marry brothers. Not that I'm thinking about that," she glances at me, "much."

"Well, Yosef speaks highly of him, and particularly of the care he takes in looking after others," I state. "And those beautiful eyelashes! I think you should start lessons straight away."

Everyday life, the heat, and the pregnancy all preoccupy me, so I push any worries about Sabba and Menahem to the back of my mind. The city is now cloaked in a permanent haze of dust that hangs in the air, as it hasn't rained for months. I don't know how or why people bear it.

Maryam takes pity on me, or tires of my complaining. She arranges for us to visit the family of one of their servants, who lives in a village next to a small lake. Shelamzion doesn't want me walking, so we hitch a bumpy ride on the back of a donkey cart. In the village itself I discover how ignorant Maryam is about things I thought everyone knew and teach her to recognize trees from their leaves and not just from their fruit, how to make fruit leather from bruised fruit, and even how to stay afloat in water. There's a reedy section of the lake, which provides plenty of cover and is reserved for women to wash in. We wade up to our necks in the water and I delight in feeling cool for the first time since spring. I show her how to relax in the water, lying back and gently moving her arms and legs to stay afloat. She gets the hang of it but not before swallowing a fair bit of lake water first.

Afterwards we watch women collecting reeds to weave into simple baskets. There are larger, sturdier baskets made from willow. Both Maryam and I purchase one as they're cheaper than in the city, and our generous hosts have already insisted that we're not to return home without filling our baskets with peaches and plums from their trees.

When Thaddeus heard about the request for music lessons with Yair, he purchased an ornate lyre for Maryam, which she's brought with her. We teach the village children songs Yair has written, then tell them some of the Teacher's stories. I feel alive being back in a village, even if it isn't mine. I miss walking barefoot through tilled earth, pulling up onions, and weeding. I'm reluctant to return to the city, and manage to persuade Maryam to stay one extra day.

We return with our host's son and his donkey cart, our baskets full of fruit. There are more sentries than usual at the city gate as we enter, and everyone leaving is thoroughly searched. A donkey cart carrying sacks of firewood is stopped and each sack is opened and shaken.

"You're lucky you're not trying to leave with those baskets or you'd have to empty each one," says a sentry waving us through.

We wonder what's going on.

We arrive at the kitchen entrance to Maryam's courtyard, ready to unload her basket of fruit, but Maryam's mother hurries out and grabs hold of her daughter, fear written all over her face. "Thank God, you're both safe."

She looks up at me, trembling. I'm still seated on the donkey cart.

"What's happened?" Maryam asks.

"Haven't you heard?" she asks, then corrects herself. "Of course not, you've been in the countryside."

"Heard what?" I ask.

"Your friends are back," she says, turning to me grimly. "And this time they have papers to arrest Shaul and return him to the Holy City in chains."

"Sabba?" I ask.

"I don't know their names," she snaps impatiently. "One of the servants saw them entering Yosef's courtyard."

"And was it just Shaul they wanted?" Maryam asks.

"Who knows? They might decide to arrest the rest of us while they're at it."

"Did they arrest him at Yosef's?" I ask.

"No!" she hisses. "He's down in the cellar with Yair. I've already had to tell them once to pray silently. If the house is searched they'll find him eventually, and we can't move him out of the city because the gates are all being guarded and people searched."

"Could we move him to Yosef's place after they've searched it?" I say. "He could stay in a different house each night."

Maryam's mother shakes her head dismissively. "They'll have people watching the streets. This is Shaul we're talking about. All he's done for the past few weeks is preach in the public squares. Everyone knows what he looks like."

"Then what do we do?" says Maryam.

"I think you should head straight back the way you came to the village," says Maryam's mother. "I want you out of harm's way. Levi's returning anyway. Couldn't he take you?"

Maryam argues with her but I've stopped listening.

"Wait, I think I have an idea," I state. "Do you have a wedding felt?"

Both mother and daughter look perplexed, and then I remember that felts are only popular in the mountains. "Or a rug or carpet? It needs to be big enough that we can roll Shaul up in it."

"Tabi, you saw how thoroughly they searched everyone leaving the city. They'll unroll the carpet and discover Shaul in no time."

"Yes, I know we can't smuggle him out in a carpet, but we can just get him to my house."

"And what happens when they search your house?" says Maryam's mother. "They know your family is part of the Way."

"Let me worry about that. We just need to get him there. Do you have a carpet: yes or no?"

"Come on," says Maryam, helping me off the donkey cart. "Levi, you too. We'll need help bringing the rug down."

"I'll fetch Shaul and Yair," says the mother, heading toward the cellar.

Maryam shows us a beautiful pile carpet in her parents' bedroom.

"Don't you have anything less... expensive?" I ask. "Just a stripy flat-weave like they sell near the vegetable bazaar."

"Well, why didn't you say so?" says Maryam, leading us into a room where the servant girls all sleep.

It's a thick flat-weave that should keep Shaul nicely hidden. We roll it up and Levi drags it downstairs to the donkey cart. Shaul and Yair are there with a travel bag each.

"We need to do this quickly. Shaul, you lie down on the edge of the rug and we'll roll you up in it."

Shaul is almost meek, and Maryam has to help Levi and Yair haul the rug up onto the donkey cart.

"Yair, you're going to need to come, too. We can both sit against the rug and position the baskets of fruit around it so it just looks like we've come back from a few days in the village. Levi, I'll give you directions. Let's make sure that we talk and laugh and look relaxed."

"He'll hide us under the shelter of his wings," says a muffled voice from inside the carpet.

Chris Aslan

"No talking from you." I prod the rug.

There isn't time for goodbyes, and when I wave farewell to Maryam she doesn't notice, staring longingly at Yair.

"Where will you hide me when we get to your house?" asks a voice from the carpet.

"This won't work if you speak," I hiss.

Then I start to tell Yair in a loud voice what we did in the village, pausing my narrative to give Levi directions. Once I run out of things to say, I just start from the beginning again. We barely attract a glance, as most people are grateful to be getting home from the bazaar or their places of work after a long, hot summer's day. We reach my street and I begin to feel cautiously hopeful about my plan. I direct Levi to steer the donkey to our workshop entrance, but then Menahem steps out from the shadows. The brothers stare at each other as the donkey cart pulls up beside Menahem. He glances inside the cart and sees the rug.

"He's in there." Menahem doesn't say it as if it's a question.

Yair simply nods. There's no point in pretending otherwise.

"Give me a hand," Menahem states flatly.

Again, Yair simply nods.

It's funny. None of us thinks about trying to make a run for it. We've been caught out, and now there will be consequences, particularly for Shaul. But who knows if Sabba will be merciful even to me given the many times I've slighted him in the past?

Levi doesn't realize who Menahem is, and grins at him as they start to carry the rug inside. Menahem is toying with us, but he doesn't seem to be relishing the experience. He unrolls the rug, and Shaul gets up and pats the dust off his clothes.

"Do what you came for, brother," he says to Menahem quietly.

I wonder if Menahem will bind his hands with rope or if he's brought manacles and chains with him.

I look up as Shelamzion, Hanan, and Ananias join us.

"He's doing what he came for," Ananias states, moving to stand beside Menahem.

331

"I came to warn you," says Menahem, "but I'm too late. All the gates are being watched and everyone is being searched. There's no way out, and soon all the gates will be closed for the night. I persuaded Sabba to start with Yosef's house. They'll search Thaddeus's place next, and then come here at dawn tomorrow. That gives you one last meal together. I'm sorry. That's all the help I can give."

"How have you been, Menahem? You seem weary." Shaul seems oblivious to the danger he's in, but now that he mentions it, Menahem is not looking great.

"Men?" Yair steps toward him. "Come here."

I see tears in their eyes as they embrace.

Menahem deflates in Yair's arms. "I've missed you so much, brother. I don't know who I am any more. I'm so tired. I don't sleep any more. I have no peace. I'm just so tired of being angry all the time. At first it helped. It felt good to be angry about the Teacher, and that anger saved me when we heard about the avalanche and our family. I didn't have to feel the pain of losing everyone or feel any guilt that we weren't there and didn't save them. The anger kept me going. It was fuel for a fire. I couldn't wait to end the Way, here in the city: to see everyone weeping and in chains. Instead, our leader got blinded and wouldn't eat, and then Ananias came to help the very man sent to torment him. And then Tabi turned up with Amma's shawl, and I didn't know what to do. Without my anger, what was left?"

"This is left," says Shelamzion. "It took courage to come here to warn us. It took kindness. That's who you are when you turn away from your anger."

"But it's all been for nothing," Menahem says, eyes to the ground.

"No it hasn't," I state. "I have a plan to get Shaul out of the city tonight." The others wait in anticipation. "You see these baskets? They're made from willow and they're really strong. Why can't we lower Shaul over the city wall in one of them? It's almost dark already."

I wait for someone to find fault with the plan.

"Come with me," says Ananias to the others. "I'll show you. You can see the rampart on the city wall from our roof."

"Shaul, it's best if you stay inside for now, until it gets dark," says Shelamzion. "Why don't you make Levi feel at home? Levi, will you stay the night with us?"

Levi nods and Shaul sits down next to him.

"What have you heard about Yeshua?" he asks, then begins to tell him more.

I join the others on the roof. "What do you think?" I ask.

"I think it'll work." Ananias flashes me a smile. "We won't be able to use a lamp and we'll have to be quiet, as people will be sleeping outside on their roofs to escape the heat. Let's see whether Hanan has found a strong enough rope."

Back in the workshop, Hanan shows us his handiwork. He's emptied one of the baskets of fruit and has attached two ropes to it. He is now measuring coils of rope to make sure there's enough to get Shaul all the way to the ground.

Shaul is reluctantly dragged away from Levi and tries to crouch in the basket as Ananias, Menahem, and Hanan practise lifting it. It's heavy, but they're strong. The basket might spin a bit, but otherwise we think it'll work.

"Why don't you boys catch up on the balcony?" I say. "You can plan the escape there."

Despite the circumstances, Ananias's eyes shine. I can see that he's just happy to be with his closest friends again, and I want them to enjoy this brief moment of friendship together. I make mint tea for Hanan, Shaul, and Levi, then prepare supper with Shelamzion.

By the time we sit down to eat, Levi is introduced to us all as our new brother of the Way. He smiles modestly and we all congratulate him. I'm still not sure if Menahem has also decided to follow Yeshua yet, but he's with us and he's helping Shaul escape, so that's a start.

"What will Sabba say when you don't show up this evening?" I ask.

Menahem frowns. "I know what you think, but there's still good in him. I've seen it. He'll be worried when I don't turn up tonight, and then tomorrow, when he discovers I'm gone, he'll feel betrayed and will be furious."

"Maybe you and Yair should leave tonight, too."

Yair looks at his brother. "We need to go back to start rebuilding and look after our sister. And I want to see Phan. What do you think?"

Menahem nods. "I've thought about going back, but I couldn't face it on my own. If we go together…"

"Phan will be thrilled to see you," I add.

"I remember how furious Sabba was when he arrested us," says Shelamzion. "I think it's a good idea that you're both long gone before they come here tomorrow."

The brothers nod. It makes sense.

Then she glances at me. "I have another suggestion," she says evenly. "Tabi, while you were away I sold another wedding chest. Phan hasn't sent us a new apprentice and we really need someone else to work with us. Ananias, I think we should also send you. You can go back to the village and bring Halafqa and Yaqim here."

Ananias immediately protests. "I can't leave Tabi, not in her condition. And what if Sabba tries to arrest you all tomorrow?"

"For what? There's no proof that Shaul was here. We're just entertaining a guest who brought back our daughter from the countryside. What have we done?"

"But you said yourself that Sabba was violent before and broke things," says Ananias.

"I'll put away the new plates and bowls, and there are a few old pots I'd quite happily have an excuse to replace. I'll make sure we use them for breakfast."

"What if he wants to break more than plates?" asks Ananias.

Shelamzion shrugs. "We trust our Lord. We treat Sabba with

dignity and respect, and we trust that God will protect us. And if something happens, well, we still trust him."

Ananias looks at me. "I agree," I state. "I think you should go. It will almost be the whole Hand together again, and I think Menahem and Yair will need your support and a reminder that they still have family."

"Just don't antagonize Sabba," says Menahem, looking pointedly at me.

Shelamzion and Ananias can't help smiling. I'm about to protest but I know they're right.

After supper I prepare bags of food for Shaul and the boys to take with them. They'll travel together for the first few hours until their paths diverge. We have a big discussion about timing. We decide that the escape must happen soon, partly because Shaul will need to put as much distance between him and the city as possible, but also because it'll be darkest before the moon rises and there will still be noise from the roofs as people prepare to sleep, which should mask any sound we make.

The meal finishes with prayer. Then we take the basket and rope and head up to our bedroom, through the shutters, and onto the flat roof. There's a faint gleam from the rising moon behind the city wall. We take it in turns to climb up the ladder that leads onto the bedroom roof.

"Goodbye, and remember us. We'll be praying for you," says Hanan, clasping Shaul's hand. Shaul embraces him.

There isn't time for any more farewells.

From there, Ananias and Hanan climb onto the rampart first and secure ropes around their waists. We can't see much but we hear the sound of Ananias and Hanan grunting as Shaul climbs over the wall to lower himself into the basket and they bear his weight. The ropes creak as they're stretched taut. Then there's the sound of the rope being let out. It's slow and steady, and Hanan and Ananias manage to do it without breathing too loudly.

"Done," Hanan whispers down to us as they begin to tug the basket back up.

I jump as something brushes my shoulder, but it's just rope spooling as the basket arrives at the top. I squeeze Yair's shoulder goodbye, and he goes down next, followed by Menahem. Once they've reached the ground, Ananias comes down from the rampart so Levi can take his place. He's sweating from the hard work, and when he takes me in his arms he sticks to me everywhere, but I don't mind.

I suddenly think of so much I want to say to him, but we agreed to do this in silence.

"He is with you," I whisper as quietly as I can in his ear, and I feel a brief kiss on my lips in return.

I wait until he's up the ladder, and I hear the creak of the ropes as he eases himself into the basket. Then I fumble my way up the ladder. Once I'm on the rampart I look over, and in the rising moonlight that still hasn't crested the city walls I watch as Levi and Hanan begin to let the rope out and the huddled figure of my husband jerkily descends. I'm glad the walls are so reassuringly thick because my stomach lurches when I look down.

I remember when I was lowered down by a rope into that crowded prayer house. I was so full of hope and fear and love and hate, and then I met the Teacher and he started to change my life, and the lives of everyone I know.

There's a muffled thud as Ananias reaches the bottom, and I can just make out the four silhouettes as they set off at a gentle jog. Shaul is such an unlikely addition: the very man who fed the division of the Hand and was so against us. Now, in the dim light and as they get further away, it's impossible to distinguish individual people. They're just one.

Hanan and Levi have pulled up the empty basket. I linger for one more moment, enjoying the breeze that never makes it down inside the city. Then Hanan helps me back down the ladder.

Tomorrow will bring Sabba in all his fury. I don't know how

Chris Aslan

the day will end, but I trust God with tomorrow, and with my baby and with my family, and I know that, right now, here in the dark, he is beside me.

Chapter Twenty-One

Once we're back on the ground floor, Shelamzion has me help her fill the basket with onions, and the ropes are tidied away by Hanan. After all traces of what we've done have gone we sit together, at a loss for what to do.

"I'll probably try to leave at dawn tomorrow," says Levi. He looks uncomfortable knowing he's deserting us, but then we barely know one another, and what benefit would there be in his being here when Sabba comes?

"Tell your village about the Teacher," says Shelamzion.

We arrange for Levi to sleep in my room, and I move my mattress in with Hanan and Shelamzion. Despite the heat we all sleep clothed, not knowing when we might hear pounding at the door.

I lie awake, thinking about the fury and rage we'll encounter tomorrow, and wonder how Sabba can be so blind to the truth. Does he even remember the boy he was, not so long ago, when he carried his friend to the Teacher?

"Are you asleep?" I say quietly.

Chris Aslan

"I'm not sure any of us will be sleeping much tonight," Shelamzion whispers back.

"Uncle?"

"No, I'm not asleep either."

"Why lie here and worry? Let's pray for Sabba."

"I'll light a lamp," says Shelamzion.

"No need," I say quietly.

I hear the rustle of clothing and we each sit up.

"Do you remember how Phan told us what the Teacher said about enemies? We should love them. I haven't been very good at that. I've always tried to outwit Sabba or outdo him, and that's how he'll feel tomorrow when he realizes Shaul and Menahem are gone. He must be feeling lonely and angry. It can't be easy for him. Let's pray that the Lord will bless him."

So, that's what we do. I can't remember when or how we stop, but at some point I must have fallen asleep. When I wake, I know what I must do. The shutters are open to let in the night air, and the sky is a dark purple, which means dawn is coming.

I shake Shelamzion awake. "I need some money. I know where the pouches are – can I help myself? It won't be much."

She looks sleepy and confused.

"Just trust me. I know what I need to do."

I rise quickly, splash some water on my face from a bucket beside the well, then take the coins and leave. The streets are empty, but the first to rise will be the merchants selling fruit and vegetables. They're already setting up their stalls by the time I arrive. I have to be quick and get past them to the honey-sellers. Only one man is up. Bees buzz lazily around the various large clay pots he begins to roll out diagonally on their rims.

"Your finest honey, with comb. I have no time to haggle, and I know when it's been diluted with date syrup," I state.

"All my honey is of the finest quality," he begins, warming up his sales pitch.

"I told you, I don't have time." I spot the pot with the finest glaze and lift the lid, spooning a finger up and licking it. "Is there comb with it?" I've brought my own dish. "How much?"

I'm aghast at the price, but plant the coins in his palm, tutting at the extortion. I have no need for muslin to cover it, and once the honeycomb and extra dollops of honey have filled my dish I rush over to a man who has just finished unloading bundles of fresh herbs from his donkey, their stems wrapped in wet burlap.

"I'm in desperate need of transport. I must be somewhere quickly, and I can't run in my condition."

"You want to take my donkey? How do I know you'll return it?"

"I can't run, but you can. Come on, let's go. I'll pay you well. It's not far."

I sit sideways on the donkey. The man makes a hissing sound the donkey knows well and we set off at a fast trot. I'm trying to stay on the donkey and give directions without spilling the honey. We manage, and I arrive outside Yahouda's house with just one line of honey soaking through my tunic where I haven't caught it in time.

I pay the donkey's owner twice the going rate, then pound on the door. A servant girl answers it.

"I'm here to see Sabba. It's urgent. I have news for him."

She looks at me uncertainly for a moment. I wonder if I'm too late and he's already on his way to our house. Then she nods and lets me in. I'm led through to the guest courtyard where I first met Shaul. Sabba is eating a simple breakfast alone and looks up at my arrival.

"I brought this," I say, holding out my offering to him. "I asked for the best, but I know it won't be anywhere near as good as the honey you used to find."

"What are you doing here? If you've come to beg – "

"No, no, I haven't. I've just come to talk. Can I?" I place the dish of honey on the floor cloth and kneel beside it.

The servant girl is hovering, but Sabba waves her away.

"So, what do you want?" He tears off some flatbread, dips it into the honey, and samples it, wrinkling his nose in disappointment.

"No one can rival you when it comes to honey. You're one of the bravest and most persistent people I know. Who else would dare climb such tall trees and risk the wrath of the swarm?"

A smile flits across his face. "Are you here to stall me while they try to escape?"

"No, that happened last night. We lowered Shaul and the rest of the Hand over the wall in a basket on a rope."

I see his jaws and fist clench.

"So you come here with honey to gloat? Do you think you're protected because you're with child?" he says with the quiet growl of a dog before it bites.

"Sabba, I didn't have to tell you. I came to confess. I came to tell you how sorry I am. Not about the basket and the escape, but about you. Do you remember when Phan was stuck on that filthy mattress for all those months? Did he tell you that I almost poisoned him? He asked me to, as a mercy, but I refused out of spite. I was so cruel to him, but you and the Hand were... you were better than his own family." I hadn't expected to cry, but I do. "Do you remember how you and Phan memorized those scrolls? You didn't have to come, but you did, and you chose to ignore the stench. And you made sure Phan never felt pity. You were more of a brother to him than I ever was a sister. Remember how it was when you led us down the mountainside with Phan on that pallet? Doesn't it seem insane that we were willing to travel all that way just for a rumour? You did it because of love.

"You've always loved my brother. You've been a true friend to him. Soon Phan and Ananias and Menahem and Yair will all be together, and it will be such a wonderful reunion, but I know they won't really be happy, because you're not there. You should be there with them. They are your brothers, your family. Even now I sometimes feel jealous at how much my husband loves you and the Hand." I laugh amid the tears. "I know he would do anything for you and loves you more than his own brothers.

"But I haven't. I've treated you with dishonour. I mocked and poured scorn on you rather than trying to listen and understand. I used my position in the village to coerce the women to vote against you. I've treated you as my enemy."

"I am your enemy," he says quietly. "We both know it."

"But you can't be," I sob. "You're my relative. You're from my village. You're Sabba. You're the one I travelled three days with because your love for Phan and my duty toward him were enough. What is the Hand without you? I haven't just failed you; I've failed the Teacher. He said we should love our enemies. If you are my enemy, well, I haven't loved you. I haven't forgiven you." I pause because I'm sobbing. "I'm... I'm so very sorry."

"I will spare you," he says, his voice shaking. I'm not sure if it's anger or some other emotion. "And your uncle and aunt."

"Thank you, but that's not what I'm asking for. I'm asking that you forgive me because I've wronged you. But also, I'm digging. When the avalanche happened we had to try to work out the exact location of each buried house. We had to be quick, but we couldn't rush or we'd miscalculate. We didn't know what we'd find as we dug down: whether there was still life hidden and waiting under the snow, or whether there was death. We found both. I was there, Sabba. And I'm here now, to dig. I think there's still life there. I remember you, Sabba. You know, I was even there with Sholum when she was spying on you at the lake."

He clenches his jaw, and then, perhaps to our mutual surprise, he laughs. "So you know who the winner was, then," he says.

I glimpse the old, confident Sabba I once knew. "Well, I didn't look, I was too embarrassed. But I heard you all."

We smile for a moment, remembering happier times.

"Menahem didn't want to leave you," I add. "I saw him last night. He was worried about you, but he had to go. He's tired. He said anger had helped him at first, particularly when he lost so much in the avalanche, but now he's tired of being angry. I remember feeling that way. I was so angry and bitter about what happened to Sholum. He's not saying that he's ready to follow the Teacher yet, but he's not opposed to him any more."

"That's nice for him, but I'm alone now."

"But you don't have to be. Please, Sabba, come and have breakfast with us. Let's talk about the village. Let's remember who we were, but also look at who we've become. I was so bitter, so – I don't know – I shut down. Life just didn't have any meaning to it, and I just lived because I didn't really have much of a choice. And Phan... well, you remember what he was like. I wonder if I'd still be caring for him now, or if I'd have eventually given him those berries if the Teacher hadn't cured him. And Yulia, and Yair – you should hear the songs he's been writing – and Shaul. I can see why you sat at his feet. He's completely dedicated his life to serving God. We're all still the same, but we're all different."

I've run out of words to say, and too many words aren't helpful either. I sense a battle within him.

Then I clamber to my feet in an ungainly fashion. "If it's a boy, I want to call him Sabba," I state, cradling my belly. "I'd even let you teach him to hunt for honey." I stretch out a hand to him. "Come."

He looks up at me.

"You were coming to our house this morning anyway. Come, and we'll eat together and I'll show you where we let the basket down if you want, and then you can arrest us or do whatever it is you want."

He still sits, looking up at me, and I wish I knew what was going on inside his head right now.

"Please?" I add, my hand outstretched.

Then he puts his hand in mine, even though he can effortlessly rise out of a cross-legged position without my help.

"Do you remember that time you and the Hand went hunting for eagle chicks?" I ask with a smile.

Mosaic

We leave the house together, walking down the winding alleyways of a city that will never truly be home. On our way we pass the local public baths, and I glance up at the wall outside. There's a mosaic of a sea monster frolicking in the waves. From this distance you can't tell that it's actually made up of lots of tiny pieces.

Chris Aslan

Acknowledgments

For those unfamiliar with the original source material of this story, you can find accounts in the Gospel of Mark, chapter 2 (there are plenty of free online Bibles in every language) and in the Book of Acts, chapter 9.

Along with these two accounts, which provided the narrative push for the story, was a quote from Yeshua in the Gospel of Luke, chapter 12, verse 52 (NIV): "From now on there will be five in one family divided against each other, three against two and two against three."

If you'd like to find out more about Yeshua, the New Testament is the best place to start. You may also enjoy a TV series currently available on YouTube called *The Chosen*.

This might sound strange, but I want to thank Tabita and her world for the way they have helped me. This book has taken longer to write and fit around work, and has been a much-needed place to escape and immerse myself during some really tough times. One of those moments happened in the summer of 2018, when I heard that my good friend Ryan had been tragically murdered in eastern Georgia, along with his wife and four-year-old son. I'd like to honour and remember this fellow adventurer, carpet geek, sharer of Jesus, and lover of the Caucasus and Central Asia, and its peoples. My life feels so much poorer without him in it.

Tabita's world may not seem like much of a "happy place", given how tough mountain life was, but for me, writing the village was a real highlight and a point of nostalgia, blending memory with imagination. I remembered childhood trips out of the noise and pollution of Beirut up to the mountains; part of the same range as Tabita's own mountains. I also drew on my experiences of living in tough mountain communities in Kyrgyzstan and Tajikistan, where winters are still an ordeal to get through. A family I lived with in the mountains of Badakhshan kept a bear cub before I arrived, which would wrestle with the children – until it became a little too good at winning and had to go.

Once more, I'm grateful to Richard Bauckham's Jesus and the Eyewitnesses, from which I usually pillage names for my characters. Gratitude and apologies to Doctor Iain Pickett – an expert in the Levant region and a good friend – for not implementing all the suggested changes regarding nomadic patterns of sheep grazing and other details, which I decided I could probably get away with!

Thanks to the readers who really helped polish the first draft, and particularly the ending: the Revd David Lewis, Erin Crider, Shahnaz Farahi, Cathy Priest, Emma Goode, Pat Alexander, Coco Mbassi, Tim Stevenson, Rachael and Chris Warrington, Gilly Hall, Steve Holloway, Tom Stubbings, and Michelle Varley. You've all been a real help and support. Thanks for your encouragement! Special thanks to Jessica Gladwell, who first commissioned *Alabaster* and has edited these first three books, and to Joy Tibbs, who managed this title. I'm grateful, as ever, to have the wonderful Sarah Coleman produce another fabulous cover.

Thanks, too, to my wonderful parents for their love, stability, and support, and for letting me monopolize their dining-room table whenever I stay. Like Tabita, I also feel like a work in progress as I try to follow the Teacher, often forgetting lessons once learned or failing to put them into practice. I hope this story will encourage you to keep following, even when the cost is high.

If you haven't already read the previous books in this series, check out

Alabaster and *Manacle*

...available now!